PENGUIN BOOKS

THE NEVERENDING STORY

Michael Ende was born in Garmisch-Partenkirchen, Germany, in 1929. After attending drama school from 1948 to 1950, he worked variously as an actor, a writer of sketches and plays, a director of the Volkstheater in Munich, and a film critic for the Bavarian broadcasting company. His first novel for children, *Jim Knopf and Lukas the Engine Driver,* was published in Germany in 1960 to great popular and critical acclaim, and both radio and television series based on the *Jim Knopf* books were soon produced. In 1973 he published another award-winning children's novel, *Momo.* When *The Neverending Story* was first published in Germany, in 1979, it immediately became the number-one bestseller and remained in that position for three years. It has since been published in many different languages all over the world, including Japanese, and has enchanted readers in each country in which it has appeared.

MICHAEL ENDE

THE NEVERENDING STORY

Translated from the German by Ralph Manheim
Illustrated by Roswitha Quadflieg

PENGUIN BOOKS

PENGUIN BOOKS
Published by the Penguin Group
Penguin Books USA Inc.,
375 Hudson Street, New York, New York 10014, U.S.A.
Penguin Books Ltd, 27 Wrights Lane, London W8 5TZ, England
Penguin Books Australia Ltd, Ringwood, Victoria, Australia
Penguin Books Canada Ltd, 10 Alcorn Avenue,
Toronto, Ontario, Canada M4V 3B2
Penguin Books (N.Z.) Ltd, 182–190 Wairau Road, Auckland 10, New Zealand

Penguin Books Ltd, Registered Offices:
Harmondsworth, Middlesex, England

First published in Germany as *Die unendliche Geschichte* by
K. Thienemanns Verlag 1979
This translation first published in the United States of America by
Doubleday & Company, Inc., 1983
Published simultaneously in Great Britain by Allen Lane
Published in Great Britain in Penguin Books 1984
Reprinted in this edition 1984
Published in the United States of America in Penguin Books 1984

15 17 19 21 23 22 20 18 16

Copyright © K. Thienemanns Verlag, Stuttgart, 1979
Translation copyright © Doubleday & Company, Inc., 1983
All rights reserved

Library of Congress Catalog Card Number: 84-60935

ISBN 0 14 00.7431 7

Printed in the United States of America
Set in Baskerville

This inscription could be seen on the glass door of a small shop, but naturally this was only the way it looked if you were inside the dimly lit shop, looking out at the street through the plate-glass door.

Outside, it was a gray, cold, rainy November morning. The rain ran down the glass and over the ornate letters. Through the glass there was nothing to be seen but the rain-splotched wall across the street.

Suddenly the door was opened so violently that a little cluster of brass bells tinkled wildly, taking quite some time to calm down. The cause of this hubbub was a fat little boy of ten or twelve. His wet, dark-brown hair hung down over his face, his coat was soaked and dripping, and he was carrying a school satchel slung over his shoulder. He was rather pale and out of breath, but, despite the hurry he had been in a moment before, he was standing in the open doorway as though rooted to the spot.

Before him lay a long, narrow room, the back of which was lost in the half-light. The walls were lined with shelves filled with books of all shapes and sizes. Large folios were piled high on the floor, and on several tables lay heaps of smaller, leather-bound books, whose spines glittered with gold. The far end of the room was blocked off by a shoulder-high wall of books, behind which the light of a lamp could be seen. From time to time a ring of smoke rose up in the lamplight, expanded, and vanished in darkness. One was reminded of the smoke signals that Indians used for sending news from hilltop to hilltop. Apparently someone was sitting there, and, sure enough, the little boy heard a cross voice from behind the wall of books: 'Do your wondering inside or outside, but shut the door. There's a draft.'

The boy obeyed and quietly shut the door. Then he approached the wall of books and looked cautiously around the corner. There, in a high worn leather wing chair sat a short, stout man in a rumpled black suit that looked frayed and somehow dusty. His paunch was held in by a vest with a flower design. He was bald except for outcroppings of white hair over his ears. His red face suggested a vicious bulldog. A gold-rimmed pince-nez was perched on his bulbous nose. He was smoking a curved pipe, which dangled from one corner of his mouth and pulled his whole cheek out of shape. On his lap he held a book, which he had evidently been reading, for in closing it he had left the thick forefinger of his left hand between the leaves as a kind of bookmark.

With his right hand he now removed his spectacles and examined the fat little boy, who stood there dripping. After a while, the man narrowed his eyes, which made him look more vicious than ever, and muttered: 'Goodness gracious.' Then he opened his book and went on reading.

The little boy didn't know quite what to do, so he just stood there, gaping. Finally the man closed his book — as before, with his finger between the pages — and growled: 'Listen, my boy, I can't abide children. I know it's the style nowadays to make a terrible fuss over you — but I don't go for it. I simply have no use for children. As far as I'm concerned, they're no good for anything but screaming, torturing people, breaking things, smearing books with jam and tearing the pages. It never dawns on them that grown-ups may also have their troubles and cares. I'm only telling you this so you'll know where you're at. Anyway, I have no children's books and I wouldn't sell you the other kind. So now we understand each other, I hope!'

After saying all this without taking his pipe out of his mouth, he opened his book again and went on reading.

The boy nodded silently and turned to go, but somehow he felt that he couldn't take this last remark lying down. He turned around and said softly: 'All children aren't like that.'

Slowly the man looked up and again removed his spectacles. 'You still here? What must one do to be rid of you? And what was this terribly important thing you had to tell me?'

'It wasn't terribly important,' said the boy still more softly. 'I only wanted . . . to say that all children aren't the way you said.'

'Really?' The man raised his eyebrows in affected surprise. 'Then you must be the big exception. I presume?'

The fat boy didn't know what to say. He only shrugged his shoulders a little, and turned to go.

'And anyway,' he heard the gruff voice behind him, 'where are your manners? If you had any, you'd have introduced yourself.'

'My name is Bastian,' said the boy. 'Bastian Balthazar Bux.'

'That's a rather odd name,' the man grumbled. 'All those Bs. Oh well, you can't help it. You didn't choose it. My name is Carl Conrad Coreander.'

'That makes three Cs.'

'Hmm,' the man grumbled. 'Quite right.'

He puffed a few clouds. 'Oh well, our names don't really matter, as we'll never see each other again. But before you leave, there's just one thing I'd like to know: What made you come bursting into my shop like that? It looked to me as if you were running away from something. Am I right?'

Bastian nodded. Suddenly his round face was a little paler than before and his eyes a little larger.

'I suppose you made off with somebody's cashbox,' Mr Coreander conjectured, 'or knocked an old woman down, or whatever little scamps like you do nowadays. Are the police after you, boy?'

Bastian shook his head.

'Speak up,' said Mr Coreander. 'Whom were you running away from?'

'The others.'

'What others?'

'The children in my class.'

'Why?'

'They won't leave me alone.'

'What do they do to you?'

'They wait for me outside the schoolhouse.'

'And then what?'

'Then they shout all sorts of things. And push me around and laugh at me.'

'And you just put up with it?'

Mr Coreander looked at the boy for a while disapprovingly. Then he asked: 'Why don't you just give them a punch on the nose?'

Bastian gaped. 'No, I wouldn't want to do that. And besides, I can't box.'

'How about wrestling?' Mr Coreander asked. 'Or running, swimming, football, gymnastics? Are you no good at any of them?'

The boy shook his head.

'In other words,' said Mr Coreander, 'you're a weakling.'

Bastian shrugged his shoulders.

'But you can still talk,' said Mr Coreander. 'Why don't you talk back at them when they make fun of you?'

'I tried . . .'

'Well . . . ?'

'They threw me into a garbage can and tied the lid on. I yelled for two hours before somebody heard me.'

'Hmm,' Mr Coreander grumbled. 'And now you don't dare?'

Bastian nodded.

'In that case,' Mr Coreander concluded, 'you're a scaredy-cat too.'

Bastian hung his head.

'And probably a hopeless grind? Best in the class, teacher's pet? Is that it?'

'No,' said Bastian, still looking down. 'I was put back last year.'

'Good Lord!' cried Mr Coreander. 'A failure all along the line.'

Bastian said nothing, he just stood there in his dripping coat. His arms hung limp at his sides.

'What kind of things do they yell when they make fun of you?' Mr Coreander wanted to know.

'Oh, all kinds.'

'For instance?'

'Namby Pamby sits on the pot. The pot cracks up, says Namby Pamby: I guess it's 'cause I weigh a lot!'

'Not very clever,' said Mr Coreander. 'What else?'

Bastian hesitated before listing: 'Screwball, nitwit, braggart, liar . . .'

'Screwball? Why do they call you that?'

'I talk to myself sometimes.'

'What kind of things do you say?'

'I think up stories. I invent names and words that don't exist. That kind of thing.'

'And you say these things to yourself? Why?'

'Well, nobody else would be interested.'

Mr Coreander fell into a thoughtful silence.

'What do your parents say about this?'

Bastian didn't answer right away. After a while he mumbled: 'Father doesn't say anything. He never says anything. It's all the same to him.'

'And your mother?'

'She – she's gone.'

'*Your parents are divorced?*'

'*No,*' said Bastian. '*She's dead.*'

At that moment the telephone rang. With some difficulty Mr Coreander pulled himself out of his armchair and shuffled into a small room behind the shop. He picked up the receiver and indistinctly Bastian heard him saying his name. After that there was nothing to be heard but a low mumbling.

Bastian stood there. He didn't quite know why he had said all he had and admitted so much. He hated being questioned like that. He broke into a sweat as it occurred to him that he was already late for school. He'd have to hurry, oh yes, he'd have to run — but he just stood there, unable to move. Something held him fast, he didn't know what.

He could still hear the muffled voice from the back room. It was a long telephone conversation.

It came to Bastian that he had been staring the whole time at the book that Mr Coreander had been holding and that was now lying on the armchair. He couldn't take his eyes off it. It seemed to have a kind of magnetic power that attracted him irresistibly.

He went over to the chair, slowly held out his hand, and touched the book. In that moment something inside him went click!, *as though a trap had shut. Bastian had a vague feeling that touching the book had started something irrevocable, which would now take its course.*

He picked up the book and examined it from all sides. It was bound in copper-colored silk that shimmered when he moved it about. Leafing through the pages, he saw the book was printed in two colors. There seemed to be no pictures, but there were large, beautiful capital letters at the beginning of the chapters. Examining the binding more closely, he discovered two snakes on it, one light and one dark. They were biting each other's tail, so forming an oval. And inside the oval, in strangely intricate letters, he saw the title:

The Neverending Story

Human passions have mysterious ways, in children as well as grown-ups. Those affected by them can't explain them, and those who haven't known them have no understanding of them at all. Some people risk their lives to conquer a mountain peak. No one, not even they themselves, can really explain why. Others ruin themselves trying to win the heart of a certain person who wants nothing to do with them. Still others are destroyed by their devotion to the pleasures of the table. Some are so bent on winning a game of chance that they lose everything they own, and some sacrifice everything for a dream that can never come true. Some think their only hope of happiness lies in being somewhere else, and spend their whole lives traveling from place to place. And some find no rest until they have become powerful. In short, there are as many different passions as there are people.

Bastian Balthazar Bux's passion was books.

If you have never spent whole afternoons with burning ears and rumpled hair, forgetting the world around you over a book, forgetting cold and hunger –

If you have never read secretly under the bedclothes with a flashlight, because your father or mother or some other well-meaning person has switched off the lamp on the plausible ground that it was time to sleep because you had to get up so early –

If you have never wept bitter tears because a wonderful story has come to an end and you must take your leave of the characters with whom you have shared so many adventures, whom you have loved and admired, for whom you have hoped and feared, and without whose company life seems empty and meaningless –

If such things have not been part of your own experience, you probably won't understand what Bastian did next.

Staring at the title of the book, he turned hot and cold, cold and hot. Here was just what he had dreamed of, what he had longed for ever since the passion for books had taken hold of him: A story that never ended! The book of books!

He had to have this book – at any price.

At any price? That was easily said. Even if he had had more to offer than the bit of pocket money he had on him – this cranky Mr Coreander had given him clearly to understand that he would never sell him a single book. And he certainly wouldn't give it away. The situation was hopeless.

Yet Bastian knew he couldn't leave without the book. It was clear to him that he had only come to the shop because of this book. It had called him in some mysterious way, because it wanted to be his, because it had somehow always belonged to him.

Bastian listened to the mumbling from the little back room. In a twinkling, before he knew it, he had the book under his coat and was hugging it with both arms. Without a sound he backed up to the street door, keeping an anxious eye on the other door, the one leading to the back room. Cautiously he turned the door handle. To keep the brass bells from ringing, he opened

*the glass door just wide enough for him to slip through. He quietly closed
the door behind him.*

Only then did he start running.

*The books, copybooks, pens and pencils in his satchel jiggled and rattled
to the rhythm of his steps. He had a stitch in his side. But he kept on running.*

*The rain ran down his face and into his collar. The wet cold passed
through his coat, but Bastian didn't feel it. He felt hot all over, but not from
running.*

*His conscience, which hadn't let out a peep in the bookshop, had suddenly
woken up. All the arguments that had seemed so convincing melted away like
snowmen under the fiery breath of a dragon.*

He had stolen. He was a thief!

*What he had done was worse than common theft. That book was certainly
the only one of its kind and impossible to replace. It was surely Mr Coreander's
greatest treasure. Stealing a violinist's precious violin or a king's crown wasn't
at all the same as filching money from a cash drawer.*

*As he ran, he hugged the book tight under his coat. Regardless of what
this book might cost him, he couldn't bear to lose it. It was all he had left
in the world.*

Because naturally he couldn't go home anymore.

*He tried to imagine his father at work in the big room he had furnished
as a laboratory. Around him lay dozens of plaster casts of human teeth, for
his father was a dental technician. Bastian had never stopped to ask himself
whether his father enjoyed his work. It occurred to him now for the first time,
but now he would never be able to ask him.*

*If he went home now, his father would come out of his lab in a white
smock, possibly holding a plaster cast, and he would ask: 'Home so soon?'
'Yes,' Bastian would answer. 'No school today?' – He saw his father's quiet,
sad face, and he knew he couldn't possibly lie to him. Much less could he
tell him the truth. No, the only thing left for him was to go away somewhere.
Far, far away. His father must never find out that his son was a thief. And
maybe he wouldn't even notice that Bastian wasn't there anymore. Bastian
found this thought almost comforting.*

*He had stopped running. Walking slowly, he saw the schoolhouse at the
end of the street. Without thinking, he was taking his usual route to school.
He passed a few people here and there, yet the street seemed deserted. But to
a schoolboy arriving very, very late, the world around the schoolhouse always*

seems to have gone dead. At every step he felt the fear rising within him. Under the best of circumstances he was afraid of school, the place of his daily defeats, afraid of his teachers, who gently appealed to his conscience or made him the butt of their rages, afraid of the other children, who made fun of him and never missed a chance to show him how clumsy and defenseless he was. He had always thought of his school years as a prison term with no end in sight, a misery that would continue until he grew up, something he would just have to live through.

But when he now passed through the echoing corridors with their smell of floor wax and wet overcoats, when the lurking stillness suddenly stopped his ears like cotton, and when at last he reached the door of his classroom, which was painted the same old-spinach color as the walls around it, he realized that this, too, was no place for him. He would have to go away. So he might as well go at once.

But where to?

Bastian had read stories about boys who ran away to sea and sailed out into the world to make their fortune. Some became pirates or heroes, others grew rich and when they returned home years later no one could guess who they were.

But Bastian didn't feel up to that kind of thing. He couldn't conceive of anyone taking him on as a cabin boy. Besides, he had no idea how to reach a seaport with suitable ships for such an undertaking.

So where could *he go?*

Suddenly he thought of the right place, the only place where – at least for the time being – no one would find him or even look for him.

The attic of the school was large and dark. It smelled of dust and mothballs. Not a sound to be heard, except for the muffled drumming of the rain on the enormous tin roof. Great beams blackened with age rose at regular intervals from the plank floor, joined with other beams at head height, and lost themselves in the darkness. Here and there spider webs as big as hammocks swayed gently in the air currents. A milky light fell from a skylight in the roof.

The one living thing in this place where time seemed to stand still was a little mouse that came hobbling across the floor, leaving tiny footprints in the dust – and between them a fine line, a tailprint. Suddenly it stopped and pricked up its ears. And then it vanished – whoosh! – into a hole in the floor.

The mouse had heard the sound of a key in a big lock. The attic door opened slowly, with a loud squeak. For a moment a long strip of light crossed the room. Bastian slipped in. Then, again with a squeak, the door closed. Bastian put the big key in the lock from inside and turned it. Then he pushed the bolt and heaved a sigh of relief. Now no one could possibly find him. No one would look for him here. The place was seldom used – he was pretty sure of that – and even if by chance someone had something to do in the attic today or tomorrow, he would simply find the door locked. And the key would be gone. And even if they somehow got the door open, Bastian would have time to hide behind the junk that was stored here.

Little by little, his eyes got used to the dim light. He knew the place. Some months before, he had helped the janitor to carry a laundry basket full of old copybooks up here. And then he had seen where the key to the attic door was kept – in a wall cupboard next to the topmost flight of stairs. He hadn't thought of it since. But today he had remembered.

Bastian began to shiver, his coat was soaked through and it was cold in the attic. The first thing to do was find a place where he could make himself more or less comfortable, because he took it for granted that he'd have to stay here a long time. How long? The question didn't enter his head, nor did it occur to him that he would soon be hungry and thirsty.

He looked around for a while. The place was crammed with junk of all kinds; there were shelves full of old files and records, benches and ink-stained desks were heaped up every which way, a dozen old maps were hanging on an iron frame, there were blackboards that had lost a good deal of their black, and cast-iron stoves, broken-down pieces of gymnasium equipment – including a horse with the stuffing coming out through the cracks in its hide – and a number of soiled mats. There were also quite a few stuffed animals – at least what the moths had left of them – a big owl, a golden eagle, a fox, and so on, cracked retorts and other chemical equipment, a galvanometer, a human skeleton hanging on a clothes rack, and a large number of cartons full of old books and papers. Bastian finally decided to make his home on the pile of old gym mats. When he stretched out on them, it was almost like lying on a sofa. He dragged them to the place under the skylight where the light was best. Not far away he found a pile of gray army blankets; they were dusty and ragged but that didn't matter now. He carried them over to his nest. He took off his wet coat and hung it on the clothes rack beside the skeleton. The skeleton jiggled and swayed, but Bastian had no fear of it, maybe because he was used to such things at home. He also removed his wet shoes. In his stocking feet he squatted down on the mats and wrapped himself *in the gray blankets like an Indian. Beside him lay his school satchel — and the copper-colored book.*

It passed through his mind that the rest of them down in the classroom would be having history just then. Maybe they'd be writing a composition on some deadly dull subject.

Bastian looked at the book.

'I wonder,' he said to himself, 'what's in a book while it's closed. Oh, I know it's full of letters printed on paper, but all the same, something must be happening, because as soon as I open it, there's a whole story with people I don't know yet and all kinds of adventures and deeds and battles. And sometimes there are storms at sea, or it takes you to strange cities and countries. All those things are somehow shut up in a book. Of course you have to read it to find out. But it's already there, that's the funny thing. I just wish I knew how it could be.'

Suddenly an almost festive mood came over him.

He settled himself, picked up the book, opened it to the first page, and began to read

The Neverending Story.

I

Fantastica in Danger

L L the beasts in Howling Forest were safe in their caves, nests, and burrows.

It was midnight, the storm wind was whistling through the tops of the great ancient trees. The towering trunks creaked and groaned.

Suddenly a faint light came zigzagging through the woods, stopped here and there, trembling fitfully, flew up into the air, rested on a branch, and a moment later hurried on. It was a glittering sphere about the size of a child's ball; it moved in long leaps, touched the ground now and then, then bounded up again. But it wasn't a ball.

It was a will-o'-the-wisp. It had lost its way. And that's something quite unusual even in Fantastica, because ordinarily will-o'-the-wisps make others lose their way.

Inside this ball of light there was a small, exceedingly active figure, which ran and jumped with all its might. It was neither male nor female, for such distinctions don't exist among will-o'-the-wisps. In its right hand it carried a tiny white flag, which glittered behind it. That meant it was either a messenger or a flag-of-truce bearer.

You'd think it would have bumped into a tree, leaping like that in the darkness, but there was no danger of that, for will-o'-the-wisps are incredibly nimble and can change directions in the middle of a leap. That explains the zigzagging, but in a general sort of way it moved in a definite direction.

Up to the moment when it came to a jutting crag and started back in a fright. Whimpering like a puppy, it sat down on the fork of a tree and pondered awhile before venturing out and cautiously looking around the crag.

Up ahead it saw a clearing in the woods, and there in the light of a campfire sat three figures of different sizes and shapes. A giant, who looked as if the whole of him were made of gray stone, lay stretched out on his belly. He was almost ten feet long. Propped up on one elbow, he was looking into the fire. In his weather-beaten stone face, which seemed strangely small in comparison with his powerful shoulders, his teeth stood out like a row of steel chisels. The will-o'-the-wisp recognized him as belonging to the family of rock chewers. These were creatures who lived in a mountain range inconceivably far from Howling Forest – but they not only lived *in* the mountain range, they also lived *on* it, for little by little they were eating it up. Rocks were their only food. Luckily a little went a long way. They could live for weeks and months on a single bite of this – for them – extremely nutritious fare. There weren't very many rock chewers, and besides it was a large mountain range. But since these giants had been there a long time – they lived to a greater age than most of the inhabitants of Fantastica – those mountains had come, over the years, to look very strange – like an enormous Swiss cheese, full of holes and grottoes. And that is why they were known as the Cheesiewheezies.

But the rock chewers not only fed on stone, they made everything they needed out of it: furniture, hats, shoes, tools, even cuckoo clocks. So it was not surprising that the vehicle of this particular giant, which was now leaning against a tree behind him, was a sort of bicycle made entirely of this material, with two wheels that looked like enormous millstones. On the whole, it suggested a steamroller with pedals.

The second figure, who was sitting to the right of the first, was a little night-hob. No more than twice the size of the will-o'-the-wisp, he looked like a pitch-black, furry caterpillar sitting up. He had little pink hands, with which he gestured violently as he spoke, and below his tousled black hair two big round eyes glowed like moons in what was presumably his face.

Since there were night-hobs of all shapes and sizes in every part of Fantastica, it was hard to tell by the sight of him whether this one had come from far or near. But one could guess that he was traveling, because the usual mount of the night-hobs, a large bat, wrapped in its wings like a closed umbrella, was hanging head-down from a nearby branch.

It took the will-o'-the-wisp some time to discover the third person on the left side of the fire, for he was so small as to be scarcely discernible from that distance. He was one of the tinies, a delicately built little fellow in a bright-colored suit and a top hat.

The will-o'-the-wisp knew next to nothing about tinies. But it had once heard that these people built whole cities in the branches of trees and that the houses were connected by stairways, rope ladders, and ramps. But the tinies lived in an entirely different part of the boundless Fantastican Empire, even farther away than the rock chewers. Which made it all the more amazing that the mount which had evidently carried the tiny all this way was, of all things, a snail. Its pink shell was surmounted by a gleaming silver saddle, and its bridle, as well as the reins fastened to its feelers, glittered like silver threads.

The will-o'-the-wisp couldn't get over it that three such different creatures should be sitting there so peacefully, for harmony between different species was by no means the rule in Fantastica. Battles and wars were frequent, and certain of the species had been known to feud for hundreds of years. Moreover, not all the inhabitants of Fantastica were good and honorable, there were also thieving, wicked, and cruel ones. The will-o'-the-wisp itself belonged to a family that was hardly reputed for truthfulness or reliability.

After observing the scene in the firelight for some time, the will-o'-the-wisp noticed that each of the three had something white, either a flag or a white scarf worn across his chest. Which meant that they were messengers or flag-of-truce bearers, and that of course accounted for the peaceful atmosphere.

Could they be traveling on the same business as the will-o'-the-wisp?

What they were saying couldn't be heard from a distance because of the howling wind in the treetops. But since they respected one another as messengers, mightn't they recognize the will-o'-the-wisp in the same capacity and refrain from harming him? It had to ask someone the way, and there seemed little likelihood of finding a better opportunity at this hour in the middle of the woods. So plucking up courage, it ventured out of its hiding place and hovered trembling in mid-air, waving its white flag.

The rock chewer, whose face was turned in that direction, was first to notice the will-o'-the-wisp.

'Lots of traffic around here tonight,' he crackled. 'Here comes another one.'

'Hoo, it's a will-o'-the-wisp,' whispered the night-hob, and his moon eyes glowed. 'Pleased to meet you!'

The tiny stood up, took a few steps toward the newcomer, and chirped: 'If my eyes don't deceive me, you are here as a messenger.'

'Yes indeed,' said the will-o'-the-wisp.

The tiny removed his red top hat, made a slight bow, and twittered: 'Oh, do join us. We, too, are messengers. Won't you be seated?'

And with his hat he motioned toward an empty place by the fire.

'Many thanks,' said the will-o'-the-wisp, coming timidly closer.

'Allow me to introduce myself. My name is Blubb.'

'Delighted,' said the tiny. 'Mine is Gluckuk.'

The night-hob bowed without getting up. 'My name is Vooshvazool.'

'And mine,' the rock chewer crackled, 'is Pyornkrachzark.'

All three looked at the will-o'-the-wisp, who was wriggling with embarrassment. Will-o'-the-wisps find it most unpleasant to be looked full in the face.

'Won't you sit down, dear Blubb?' said the tiny.

'To tell the truth,' said the will-o'-the-wisp, 'I'm in a terrible hurry. I only wanted to ask if by any chance you knew the way to the Ivory Tower.'

'Hoo,' said the night-hob. 'Could you be going to see the Childlike Empress?'

'Exactly,' said the will-o'-the-wisp. 'I have an important message for her.'

'What does it say?' the rock chewer crackled.

'But you see,' said the will-o'-the-wisp, shifting its weight from foot to foot, 'it's a secret message.'

'All three of us – hoo – have the same mission as you,' replied Vooshvazool, the night-hob. 'That makes us partners.'

'Maybe we even have the same message,' said Gluckuk, the tiny.

'Sit down and tell us,' Pyornkrachzark crackled.

The will-o'-the-wisp sat down in the empty place.

'My home,' it began after a moment's hesitation, 'is a long way from here. I don't know if any of those present has heard of it. It's called Moldymoor.'

'Hoo!' cried the night-hob delightedly. 'A lovely country!'

The will-o'-the-wisp smiled faintly.

'Yes, isn't it?'

'Is that all you have to say, Blubb?' Pyornkrachzark crackled. 'What is the purpose of your trip?'

'Something has happened in Moldymoor,' said the will-o'-the-wisp haltingly, 'something impossible to understand. Actually, it's still happening. It's hard to describe – the way it began was – well, in the east of our country there's a lake – that is, there *was* a lake – Lake Foamingbroth we called it. Well, the way it began was like this. One day Lake Foamingbroth wasn't there anymore – it was gone. See?'

'You mean it dried up?' Gluckuk inquired.

'No,' said the will-o'-the-wisp. 'Then there'd be a dried-up lake. But there isn't. Where the lake used to be there's nothing – absolutely nothing. Now do you see?'

'A hole?' the rock chewer grunted.

'No, not a hole,' said the will-o'-the-wisp despairingly. 'A hole, after all, is something. This is nothing at all.'

The three other messengers exchanged glances.

'What – hoo – does this nothing look like?' asked the night-hob.

'That's just what's so hard to describe,' said the will-o'-the-wisp unhappily. 'It doesn't look like anything. It's – it's like – oh, there's no word for it.'

'Maybe,' the tiny suggested, 'when you look at the place, it's as if you were blind.'

The will-o'-the-wisp stared openmouthed.

'Exactly!' it cried. 'But where – I mean how – I mean, have you had the same . . . ?'

'Wait a minute,' the rock chewer crackled. 'Was it only this one place?'

'At first, yes,' the will-o'-the-wisp explained. 'That is, the place got bigger little by little. And then all of a sudden Foggle, the father of the frogs, who lived in Lake Foamingbroth with his family, was gone too. Some of the inhabitants started running away. But little by little the same thing happened to other parts of Moldymoor. It usually started with just a little chunk, no bigger than a partridge egg. But then these chunks got bigger and bigger. If somebody put his foot into one of them by mistake, the foot – or hand – or whatever else he put in – would be gone too. It didn't hurt – it

was just that a part of whoever it was would be missing. Some
would even fall in on purpose if they got too close to the Nothing.
It has an irresistible attraction – the bigger the place, the stronger
the pull. None of us could imagine what this terrible thing might
be, what caused it, and what we could do about it. And seeing
that it didn't go away by itself but kept spreading, we finally decided
to send a messenger to the Childlike Empress to ask her for advice
and help. Well, I'm the messenger.'

The three others gazed silently into space.

After a while, the night-hob sighed: 'Hoo! It's the same where
I come from. And I'm traveling on the exact same errand – hoo hoo!'

The tiny turned to the will-o'-the-wisp. 'Each one of us,' he
chirped, 'comes from a different province of Fantastica. We've met
here entirely by chance. But each one of us is going to the Childlike
Empress with the same message.'

'And the message,' grated the rock chewer, 'is that all Fantastica
is in danger.'

The will-o'-the-wisp cast a terrified look at each one in turn.

'If that's the case,' it cried, jumping up, 'we haven't a moment
to lose.'

'We were just going to start,' said the tiny. 'We only stopped to
rest because it's so awfully dark here in Howling Forest. But now
that you've joined us, Blubb, you can light the way.'

'Impossible,' said the will-o'-the-wisp. 'Would you expect me to
wait for someone who rides a snail? Sorry.'

'But it's a racing snail,' said the tiny, somewhat miffed.

'Otherwise – hoo hoo –' the night-hob sighed, 'we won't tell you
which way to go.'

'Who are you people talking to?' the rock chewer crackled.

And sure enough, the will-o'-the-wisp hadn't even heard the
other messengers' last words, for it was already flitting through the
forest in long leaps.

'Oh well,' said the tiny, pushing his top hat onto the back of his
head, 'maybe it wouldn't have been such a good idea to follow a
will-o'-the-wisp.'

'To tell the truth,' said the night-hob, 'I prefer to travel on my
own. Because I, for one, fly.'

With a quick 'hoo hoo' he ordered his bat to make ready. And *whish!* Away he flew.

The rock chewer put out the campfire with the palm of his hand. 'I, too, prefer to go by myself,' he crackled in the darkness. 'Then I don't need to worry about squashing some wee creature.'

Rattling and grinding, he rode his stone bicycle straight into the woods, now and then thudding into a tree giant. Slowly the clatter receded in the distance.

Gluckuk, the tiny, was last to set out. He seized the silvery reins and said: 'All right, we'll see who gets there first. Geeyap, old-timer, geeyap.' And he clicked his tongue.

And then there was nothing to be heard but the storm wind howling in the treetops.

The clock in the belfry struck nine. Reluctantly Bastian's thought turned back to reality. He was glad the Neverending Story had nothing to do with that.

He didn't like books in which dull, cranky writers describe humdrum events in the very humdrum lives of humdrum people. Reality gave him enough of that kind of thing, why should he read about it? Besides, he couldn't stand it when a writer tried to convince him of something. And these humdrum books, it seemed to him, were always trying to do just that.

Bastian liked books that were exciting or funny, or that made him dream. Books where made-up characters had marvelous adventures, books that made him imagine all sorts of things.

Because one thing he was good at, possibly the only thing, was imagining things so clearly that he almost saw and heard them. When he told himself stories, he sometimes forgot everything around. him and awoke — as though from a dream — only when the story was finished. And this book was just like his own stories! In reading it, he had heard not only the creaking of the big trees and the howling of the wind in the treetops, but also the different voices of the four comical messengers. And he almost seemed to catch the smell of moss and forest earth.

Down in the classroom they were starting in on nature study. That consisted almost entirely in counting pistils and stamens. Bastian was glad to be up here in his hiding place, where he could read. This, he thought, was just the right book for him!

A week later Vooshvazool, the little night-hob, arrived at his destination. He was the first. Or rather, he thought he was first, because he was riding through the air.

Just as the setting sun turned the clouds to liquid gold, he noticed that his bat was circling over the Labyrinth. That was the name of an enormous garden, extending from horizon to horizon and filled with the most bewitching scents and dreamlike colors. Broad avenues and narrow paths twined their way among copses, lawns, and beds of the rarest, strangest flowers in a design so artful and intricate that the whole plain resembled an enormous maze. Of course, it had been designed only for pleasure and amusement, with no intention of endangering anyone, much less of warding off an enemy. It would have been useless for such purposes, and the Childlike Empress required no such protection, because in all the unbounded reaches of Fantastica there was no one who would have thought of attacking her. For that there was a reason, as we shall soon see.

While gliding soundlessly over the flowery maze, the night-hob sighted all sorts of animals. In a small clearing between lilacs and laburnum, a group of young unicorns was playing in the evening sun, and once, glancing under a giant bluebell, he even thought he saw the famous phoenix in its nest, but he wasn't quite certain, and such was his haste that he didn't want to turn back to make sure. For at the center of the Labyrinth there now appeared, shimmering in fairy whiteness, the Ivory Tower, the heart of Fantastica and the residence of the Childlike Empress.

The word 'tower' might give someone who has never seen it the wrong idea. It had nothing of the church or castle about it. The Ivory Tower was as big as a whole city. From a distance it looked like a pointed mountain peak twisted like a snail shell. Its highest point was deep in the clouds. Only on coming closer could you notice that this great sugarloaf consisted of innumerable towers, turrets, domes, roofs, oriels, terraces, arches, stairways, and balustrades, all marvelously fitted together. The whole was made of the whitest Fantastican ivory, so delicately carved in every detail that it might have been taken for the latticework of the finest lace.

These buildings housed the Childlike Empress's court, her

chamberlains and maidservants, wise women and astrologers, magicians and jesters, messengers, cooks and acrobats, her tightrope walkers and storytellers, heralds, gardeners, watchmen, tailors, shoemakers and alchemists. And at the very summit of the great tower lived the Childlike Empress in a pavilion shaped like a magnolia blossom. On certain nights, when the full moon shone most gloriously in the starry sky, the ivory petals opened wide, and the Childlike Empress would be sitting in the middle of the glorious flower.

Riding on his bat, the little night-hob landed on one of the lower terraces, where the stables were located. Someone must have announced his arrival, for five imperial grooms were there waiting for him. They helped him out of his saddle, bowed to him, and held out the ceremonial welcome cup. As etiquette demanded, Vooshvazool took only a sip and then returned the cup. Each of the grooms took a sip, then they bowed again and led the bat to the stables. All this was done in silence. On reaching its appointed place, the bat touched neither food nor drink, but immediately rolled up, hung itself head-down on a hook, and fell into a deep sleep. The little night-hob had demanded a bit too much of his mount. The grooms left it alone and crept away from the stable on tiptoes.

In this stable there were many other mounts: two elephants, one pink and one blue, a gigantic griffon with the forequarters of an eagle and the hindquarters of a lion, a winged horse, whose name was once known even outside of Fantastica but is now forgotten, several flying dogs, a few other bats, and several dragonflies and butterflies for especially small riders. In other stables there were still other mounts, which didn't fly but ran, crawled, hopped, or swam. And each had a groom of its own to feed and take care of it.

Ordinarily one would have expected to hear quite a cacophony of different voices: roaring, screeching, piping, chirping, croaking, and chattering. But that day there was utter silence.

The little night-hob was still standing where the grooms had left him. Suddenly, without knowing why, he felt dejected and discouraged. He too was exhausted after the long trip. And not even the knowledge that he had arrived first could cheer him up.

Suddenly he heard a chirping voice. 'Hello, hello! If it isn't my good friend Vooshvazool! So glad you've finally made it!'

The night-hob looked around, and his moon eyes flared with amazement, for on a balustrade, leaning negligently against a flower pot, stood Gluckuk, the tiny, tipping his red top hat.

'Hoo hoo!' went the bewildered night-hob. And again: 'Hoo hoo!' He just couldn't think of anything better to say.

'The other two haven't arrived yet. I've been here since yesterday morning.'

'How – hoo hoo – how did you do it?'

'Simple,' said the tiny with a rather condescending smile. 'Didn't I tell you I had a racing snail?'

The night-hob scratched his tangled black head fur with his little pink hand.

'I must go to the Childlike Empress at once,' he said mournfully.

The tiny gave him a pensive look.

'Hmm,' he said. 'I put in for an appointment yesterday.'

'Put in for an appointment?' asked the night-hob. 'Can't we just go in and see her?'

'I'm afraid not,' chirped the tiny. 'We'll have a long wait. You can't imagine how many messengers have turned up.'

'Hoo hoo,' the night-hob sighed. 'How come?'

'You'd better take a look for yourself,' the tiny twittered. 'Come with me, my dear Vooshvazool. Come with me!'

The two of them started out.

The High Street, which wound around the Ivory Tower in a narrowing spiral, was clogged with a dense crowd of the strangest creatures. Enormous beturbaned djinns, tiny kobolds, three-headed trolls, bearded dwarfs, glittering fairies, goat-legged fauns, nixies with wavy golden hair, sparkling snow sprites, and countless others were milling about, standing in groups, or sitting silently on the ground, discussing the situation or gazing glumly into the distance.

Vooshvazool stopped still when he saw them.

'Hoo hoo,' he said. 'What's going on? What are they all doing here?'

'They're all messengers,' Gluckuk explained. 'Messengers from all over Fantastica. All with the same message as ours. I've spoken with several of them. The same menace seems to have broken out everywhere.'

The night-hob gave vent to a long wheezing sigh.

'Do they know,' he asked, 'what it is and where it comes from?'

'I'm afraid not. Nobody knows.'

'What about the Childlike Empress?'

'The Childlike Empress,' said the tiny in an undertone, 'is ill, very ill. Maybe that's the cause of this mysterious calamity that's threatening all Fantastica. But so far none of the many doctors who've been conferring in the Magnolia Pavilion has discovered the nature of her illness or found a cure for it.'

'That,' said the night-hob breathlessly, 'is – hoo hoo – terrible.'

'So it is,' said the tiny.

In view of the circumstances, Vooshvazool decided not to put in for an appointment.

Two days later Blubb, the will-o'-the-wisp, arrived. Of course, he had hopped in the wrong direction and made an enormous detour.

And finally – three days after that – Pyornkrachzark, the rock chewer, appeared. He came plodding along on foot, for in a sudden frenzy of hunger he had eaten his stone bicycle.

During the long waiting period, the four so unalike messengers became good friends. From then on they stayed together.

But that's another story and shall be told another time.

II

Atreyu's Mission

ECAUSE of their special importance, deliberations concerning the welfare of all Fantastica were held in the great throne room of the palace, which was situated only a few floors below the Magnolia Pavilion.

The large circular room was filled with muffled voices. The four hundred and ninety-nine best doctors in Fantastica had assembled there and were whispering or mumbling with one another in groups of varying sizes. Each one had examined the Childlike Empress – some more recently than others – and each had tried to help her with his skill. But none had succeeded, none knew the nature or cause of her illness, and none could think of a cure for it. Just then the five hundredth doctor, the most famous in all Fantastica, whose knowledge was said to embrace every existing medicinal herb, every magic philtre and secret of nature, was examining the patient. He had been with her for several hours, and all his assembled colleagues were eagerly awaiting the result of his examination.

Of course, this assembly was nothing like a human medical congress. To be sure, a good many of the inhabitants of Fantastica were more or less human in appearance, but at least as many resembled animals or were even farther from the human. The doctors inside the hall were just as varied as the crowd of messengers milling about outside. There were dwarf doctors with white beards and humps, there were fairy doctoresses in shimmering silvery-blue robes and with glittering stars in their hair, there were water sprites with big round bellies and webbed hands and feet (sitz baths had been installed for them). There were white snakes, who had coiled up on the long table at the center of the room; there were witches, vampires, and ghosts, none of whom are generally reputed to be especially benevolent or conducive to good health.

If you are to understand why these last were present, there is one thing you have to know:

The Childlike Empress – as her title indicates – was looked upon as the ruler over all the innumerable provinces of the Fantastican Empire, but in reality she was far more than a ruler; she was something entirely different.

She didn't rule, she had never used force or made use of her power. She never issued commands and she never judged anyone.

She never interfered with anyone and never had to defend herself against any assailant; for no one would have thought of rebelling against her or of harming her in any way. In her eyes all her subjects were equal.

She was simply there in a special way. She was the center of all life in Fantastica.

And every creature, whether good or bad, beautiful or ugly, merry or solemn, foolish or wise – all owed their existence to her existence. Without her, nothing could have lived, any more than a human body can live if it has lost its heart.

All knew this to be so, though no one fully understood her secret. Thus she was respected by all the creatures of the Empire, and her health was of equal concern to them all. For her death would have meant the end of them all, the end of the boundless Fantastican realm.

Bastian's thoughts wandered.

Suddenly he remembered the long corridor in the hospital where his mother had been operated on. He and his father had sat waiting for hours outside the operating room. Doctors and nurses hurried this way and that. When his father asked about his wife, the answer was always evasive. No one really seemed to know how she was doing. Finally a bald-headed man in a white smock had come out to them. He looked tired and sad. Much as he regretted it, he said, his efforts had been in vain. He had pressed their hands and mumbled something about 'heartfelt sympathy.'

After that, everything had changed between Bastian and his father.

Not outwardly. Bastian had everything he could have wished for. He had a three-speed bicycle, an electric train, plenty of vitamin pills, fifty-three books, a golden hamster, an aquarium with tropical fish in it, a small camera, six pocketknives, and so forth and so on. But none of all this really meant anything to him.

Bastian remembered that his father had often played with him in the past. He had even told him stories. No longer. He couldn't talk to his father anymore. There was an invisible wall around his father, and no one could get through to him. He never found fault and he never praised. Even when Bastian was put back in school, his father hadn't said anything. He had only looked at him in his sad, absent way, and Bastian felt that as far as his father was concerned he wasn't there at all. That was how his father usually made him feel. When they sat in front of the television screen in the evening, Bastian saw that his father wasn't even looking at it, that his thoughts were far away. Or when they both sat there with books, Bastian saw that his father wasn't reading at all. He'd been looking at the same page for hours and had forgotten to turn it.

Bastian knew his father was sad. He himself had cried for many nights— sometimes he had been so shaken by sobs that he had to vomit – but little by little it had passed. And after all he was still there. Why didn't his father ever speak to him, not about his mother, not about important things, but just for the feel of talking together?

'If only we knew,' said a tall, thin fire sprite, with a beard of red flames, 'if only we knew what her illness is. There's no fever, no swelling, no rash, no inflammation. She just seems to be fading away – no one knows why.'

As he spoke, little clouds of smoke came out of his mouth and formed figures. This time they were question marks.

A bedraggled old raven, who looked like a potato with feathers stuck onto it every which way, answered in a croaking voice (he was a head cold and sore throat specialist): 'She doesn't cough, she hasn't got a cold. Medically speaking, it's no disease at all.' He adjusted the big spectacles on his beak and a cast a challenging look around.

'One thing seems obvious,' buzzed a scarab (a beetle, sometimes known as a pill roller): 'There is some mysterious connection between her illness and the terrible happenings these messengers from all Fantastica have been reporting.'

'Oh yes!' scoffed an ink goblin. 'You see mysterious connections everywhere.'

'My dear colleague!' pleaded a hollow-cheeked ghost in a long white gown. 'Let's not get personal. Such remarks are quite irrelevant. And please – lower your voices.'

Conversations of this kind were going on in every part of the throne room. It may seem strange that creatures of so many different kinds were able to communicate with one another. But nearly all the inhabitants of Fantastica, even the animals, knew at least two languages: their own, which they spoke only with members of their own species and which no outsider understood, and the universal language known as High Fantastican. All Fantasticans used it, though some in a rather peculiar way.

Suddenly all fell silent, for the great double door had opened. In stepped Cairon, the far-famed master of the healer's art.

He was what in older times had been called a centaur. He had the body of a man from the waist up, and that of a horse from the waist down. And Cairon was furthermore a black centaur. He hailed from a remote region far to the south, and his human half was the color of ebony. Only his curly hair and beard were white, while the horselike half of him was striped like a zebra. He was wearing a strange hat plaited of reeds. A large golden amulet hung from a chain around his neck, and on this amulet one could make out two snakes, one light and one dark, which were biting each other's tail and so forming an oval.

Everyone in Fantastica knew what the medallion meant. It was the badge of one acting on orders from the Childlike Empress, acting in her name as though she herself were present.

It was said to give the bearer mysterious powers, though no one knew exactly what these powers were. Everyone knew its name: AURYN.

But many, who feared to pronounce the name, called it the 'Gem' or the 'Glory'.

In other words, the book bore the mark of the Childlike Empress!

A whispering passed through the throne room, and some of the doctors were heard to cry out. The Gem had not been entrusted to anyone for a long, long time.

Cairon stamped his hooves two or three times. When the disorder subsided, he said in a deep voice: 'Friends, don't be too upset. I shall only be wearing AURYN for a short time. I am merely a go-between. Soon I shall pass the Gem on to one worthier.'

A breathless silence filled the room.

'I won't try to misrepresent our defeat with high-sounding words.

The Childlike Empress's illness has baffled us all. The one thing we know is that the destruction of Fantastica began at the same time as this illness. We can't even be sure that medical science can save her. But it is possible – and I hope none of you will be offended at what I am going to say – it is possible that we, we who are gathered here, do not possess *all* knowledge, *all* wisdom. Indeed it is my last and only hope that somewhere in this unbounded realm there is a being wiser than we are, who can give us help and advice. Of course, this is no more than a possibility. But one thing is certain: The search for this savior calls for a pathfinder, someone who is capable of finding paths in the pathless wilderness and who will shrink from no danger or hardship. In other words: a hero. And the Childlike Empress has given me the name of this hero, to whom she entrusts her salvation and ours. His name is Atreyu, and he lives in the Grassy Ocean beyond the Silver Mountains. I shall transmit AURYN to him and send him on the Great Quest. Now you know all there is to know.'

With that, the old centaur thumped out of the room.

Those who remained behind exchanged looks of bewilderment.

'What was this hero's name?' one of them asked.

'Atreyu or something of the kind,' said another.

'Never heard of him,' said the third. And all four hundred and ninety-nine doctors shook their heads in dismay.

The clock in the belfry struck ten. Bastian was amazed at how quickly the time had passed. In class, every hour seemed to drag on for an eternity. Down below, they would be having history with Mr Drone, a gangling, ordinarily ill-tempered man, who delighted in holding Bastian up to ridicule because he couldn't remember the dates when certain battles had been fought or when someone or other had reigned.

The Grassy Ocean behind the Silver Mountains was many days' journey from the Ivory Tower. It was actually a prairie, as long and wide and flat as an ocean. Its whole expanse was covered with tall, juicy grass, and when the wind blew, great waves passed over it with a sound like troubled water.

The people who lived there were known as 'Grass People' or 'Greenskins'. They had blue-black hair, which the men as well as the women wore long and often in pigtails, and their skin was olive green. They led a hard, frugal life, and their children, girls as well as boys, were brought up to be brave, proud, and generous. They learned to bear heat, cold, and great hardship and were tested for courage at an early age. This was necessary because the Greenskins were a nation of hunters. They obtained everything they needed either from the hard, fibrous prairie grass or from the purple buffaloes, great herds of which roamed the Grassy Ocean.

These purple buffaloes were about twice the size of common bulls or cows; they had long, purplish-red hair with a silky sheen and enormous horns with tips as hard and sharp as daggers. They were peaceful as a rule, but when they scented danger or thought they were being attacked, they could be as terrible as a natural cataclysm. Only a Greenskin would have dared to hunt these beasts, and moreover they used no other weapons than bows and arrows. The Greenskins were believers in chivalrous combat, and often it was not the hunted but the hunter who lost his life. The Greenskins loved and honored the purple buffaloes and held that only those willing to be killed by them had the right to kill them.

News of the Childlike Empress's illness and the danger threatening all Fantastica had not yet reached the Grassy Ocean. It was a long, long time since any traveler had visited the tent colonies of the Greenskins. The grass was juicier than ever, the days were bright, and the nights full of stars. All seemed to be well.

But one day a white-haired black centaur appeared. His hide was dripping with sweat, he seemed totally exhausted, and his bearded face was haggard. On his head he wore a strange hat plaited of reeds, and around his neck a chain with a large golden amulet hanging from it. It was Cairon.

He stood in the open space at the center of the successive rings of tents. It was there that the elders held their councils and that the people danced and sang old songs on feast days. He waited for the Greenskins to assemble, but it was only very old men and women and small children wide-eyed with curiosity who crowded around him. He stamped his hooves impatiently.

'Where are the hunters and huntresses?' he panted, removing his hat and wiping his forehead.

A white-haired woman with a baby in her arms replied: 'They are still hunting. They won't be back for three or four days.'

'Is Atreyu with them?' the centaur asked.

'Yes, stranger, but how can it be that you know him?'

'I don't know him. Go and get him.'

'Stranger,' said an old man on crutches, 'he will come unwillingly, because this is *his* hunt. It starts at sunset. Do you know what that means?'

Cairon shook his mane and stamped his hooves.

'I don't know, and it doesn't matter. He has something more important to do now. You know this sign I am wearing. Go and get him.'

'We see the Gem,' said a little girl. 'And we know you have come from the Childlike Empress. But who are you?'

'My name is Cairon,' the centaur growled. 'Cairon the physician, if that means anything to you.'

A bent old woman pushed forward and cried out: 'Yes, it's true. I recognize him. I saw him once when I was young. He is the greatest and most famous doctor in all Fantastica.'

The centaur nodded. 'Thank you, my good woman,' he said. 'And now perhaps one of you will at last be kind enough to bring this Atreyu here. It's urgent. The life of the Childlike Empress is at stake.'

'I'll go,' cried a little girl of five or six.

She ran away and a few seconds later she could be seen between the tents galloping away on a saddleless horse.

'At last!' Cairon grumbled. Then he fell into a dead faint. When he revived, he didn't know where he was, for all was dark around him. It came to him only little by little that he was in a large tent, lying on a bed of soft furs. It seemed to be night, for through a cleft in the door curtain he saw flickering firelight.

'Holy horseshoes!' he muttered, and tried to sit up. 'How long have I been lying here?'

A head looked in through the door opening and pulled back again. Someone said: 'Yes, he seems to be awake.'

Then the curtain was drawn aside and a boy of about ten stepped in. His long trousers and shoes were of soft buffalo leather. His body was bare from the waist up, but a long purple-red cloak, evidently woven from buffalo hair, hung from his shoulders. His long blue-black hair was gathered together and held back by leather thongs. A few simple white designs were painted on the olive-green skin of his cheeks and forehead. His dark eyes flashed angrily at the intruder; otherwise his features betrayed no emotion of any kind.

'What do you want of me, stranger?' he asked. 'Why have you come to my tent? And why have you robbed me of my hunt? If I had killed the big buffalo today – and my arrow was already fitted to my bowstring – I'd have been a hunter tomorrow. Now I'll have to wait a whole year. Why?'

The old centaur stared at him in consternation.

'Am I to take it,' he asked, 'that you are Atreyu?'

'That's right, stranger.'

'Isn't there someone else of the same name? A grown man, an experienced hunter?'

'No. I and no one else am Atreyu.'

Sinking back on his bed of furs, old Cairon gasped: 'A child! A little boy! Really, the decisions of the Childlike Empress are hard to fathom.'

Atreyu waited in impassive silence.

'Forgive me, Atreyu,' said Cairon, controlling his agitation with the greatest difficulty. 'I didn't mean to hurt your feelings, but the surprise has been just too great. Frankly, I'm horrified. I don't know what to think. I can't help wondering: Did the Childlike Empress really know what she was doing when she chose a youngster like you? It's sheer madness! And if she did it intentionally, then ... then ...'

With a violent shake of his head, he blurted out: 'No! No! If I had known whom she was sending me to, I'd have refused to entrust you with the mission. I'd have refused!'

'What mission?' Atreyu asked.

'It's monstrous!' cried Cairon indignantly. 'It's doubtful whether even the greatest, most experienced of heroes could carry out this mission ... and you! ... She's sending you into the unfathomable to look for the unknown ... No one can help you, no one can advise you, no one can foresee what will befall you. And yet you must decide at once, immediately, whether or not you accept the mission. There's not a moment to be lost. For ten days and nights I have galloped almost without rest to reach you. But now – I almost wish I hadn't got here. I'm very old, I'm at the end of my strength. Give me a drink of water, please.'

Atreyu brought a pitcher of fresh spring water. The centaur drank deeply, then he wiped his beard and said somewhat more calmly: 'Thank you. That was good. I feel better already. Listen to me, Atreyu. You don't have to accept this mission. The Childlike Empress leaves it entirely up to you. She never gives orders. I'll tell her how it is and she'll find someone else. She can't have known you were a little boy. She must have got you mixed up with someone else. That's the only possible explanation.'

'What is this mission?' Atreyu asked.

'To find a cure for the Childlike Empress,' the centaur answered, 'and save Fantastica.'

'Is she sick?' Atreyu asked in amazement.

Cairon told him how it was with the Childlike Empress and what the messengers had reported from all parts of Fantastica. Atreyu asked many questions and the centaur answered them to the best of his ability. They talked far into the night. And the more Atreyu learned of the menace facing Fantastica, the more his face, which at first had been so impassive, expressed unveiled horror.

'To think,' he murmured finally with pale lips, 'that I knew nothing about it!'

Cairon cast a grave, anxious look at the boy from under his bushy white eyebrows.

'Now you know the lie of the land,' he said. 'And now perhaps you understand why I was so upset when I first laid eyes on you. Still, it was you the Childlike Empress named. "Go and find Atreyu," she said to me. "I put all my trust in him," she said. "Ask him if he's willing to attempt the Great Quest for me and for Fantastica." I don't know why she chose you. Maybe only a little boy like you can do whatever has to be done. I don't know, and I can't advise you.'

Atreyu sat there with bowed head, and made no reply. He realized that this was a far greater task than his hunt. It was doubtful whether the greatest hunter and pathfinder could succeed; how then could he hope . . . ?

'Well?' the centaur asked. 'Will you?'

Atreyu raised his head and looked at him.

'I will,' he said firmly.

Cairon nodded gravely. Then he took the chain with the golden amulet from his neck and put it around Atreyu's.

'AURYN gives you great power,' he said solemnly, 'but you must not make use of it. For the Childlike Empress herself never makes use of her power. AURYN will protect you and guide you, but whatever comes your way you must never interfere, because from this moment on your own opinion ceases to count. For that same reason you must go unarmed. You must let what happens happen. Everything must be equal in your eyes, good and evil, beautiful and ugly, foolish and wise, just as it is in the eyes of the Childlike Empress. You may only search and inquire, never judge. Always remember that, Atreyu!'

'AURYN!' Atreyu repeated with awe. 'I will be worthy of the Glory. When should I start?'

'Immediately,' said Cairon. 'No one knows how long your Great Quest will be. Every hour may count, even now. Say goodbye to your parents and your brothers and sisters.'

'I have none,' said Atreyu. 'My parents were both killed by a buffalo, soon after I was born.'

'Who brought you up?'

'All the men and women together. That's why they called me Atreyu, which in our language means "Son of All"!'

No one knew better than Bastian what that meant. Even though his father was still alive and Atreyu had neither father nor mother. To make up for it, Atreyu had been brought up by all the men and women together and was the 'son of all', while Bastian had no one – and was really 'nobody's son'. All the same, Bastian was glad to have this much in common with Atreyu, because otherwise he resembled him hardly at all, neither physically nor in

*courage and determination. Yet Bastian, too, was engaged in a Great Quest
and didn't know where it would lead him or how it would end.*

'In that case,' said the old centaur, 'you'd better go without
saying goodbye. I'll stay here and explain.'

Atreyu's face became leaner and harder than ever.

'Where should I begin?' he asked.

'Everywhere and nowhere,' said Cairon. 'From now on you will
be on your own, with no one to advise you. And that's how it will
be until the end of the Great Quest – however it may end.'

Atreyu nodded.

'Farewell, Cairon.'

'Farewell, Atreyu. And – much luck!'

The boy turned away and was leaving the tent when the centaur
called him back. As they stood face to face, the old centaur put
both hands on Atreyu's shoulders, looked him in the eye with a
respectful smile, and said slowly: 'I think I'm beginning to see why
the Childlike Empress chose you, Atreyu.'

The boy lowered his head just a while. Then he went out quickly.

His horse, Artax, was standing outside the tent. He was small
and spotted like a wild horse. His legs were short and stocky, but
he was the fastest, most tireless runner far and wide. He was still
saddled as Atreyu had ridden him back from the hunt.

'Artax,' Atreyu whispered, patting his neck. 'We're going away,
far, far away. No one knows if we shall ever come back!'

The horse nodded his head and gave a brief snort.

'Yes, master,' he said. 'But what about your hunt?'

'We're going on a much greater hunt,' said Atreyu, swinging
himself into the saddle.

'Wait, master,' said the horse. 'You've forgotten your weapons.
Are you going without your bow and arrow?'

'Yes, Artax,' said Atreyu. 'I have to go unarmed because I am
bearing the Gem.'

'Humph!' snorted the horse. 'And where are we going?'

'Wherever you like, Artax,' said Atreyu. 'From this moment on
we shall be on the Great Quest.'

With that they galloped away and were swallowed up by the darkness.

At the same time, in a different part of Fantastica, something happened which went completely unnoticed. Neither Atreyu nor Artax had the slightest inkling of it.

On a remote night-black heath the darkness condensed into a great shadowy form. It became so dense that even in that moonless, starless night it came to look like a big black body. Its outlines were still unclear, but it stood on four legs and green fire glowed in the eyes of its huge shaggy head. It lifted up its great snout and stood for a long while, sniffing the air. Then suddenly it seemed to find the scent it was looking for, and a deep, triumphant growl issued from its throat.

And off it ran through the starless night, in long, soundless leaps.

The clock in the belfry struck eleven. From the downstairs corridors arose the shouts of children running out to the playground.

Bastian was still squatting cross-legged on the mats. His legs had fallen asleep. He wasn't an Indian after all. He stood up, took his sandwich and an apple out of his satchel, and paced the floor. He had pins and needles in his feet, which took some time to wake up.

Then he climbed onto the horse and straddled it. He imagined he was Atreyu galloping through the night on Artax's back. He leaned forward and rested his head on his horse's neck.

'Gee!' he cried. 'Run, Artax! Gee! Gee!'

Then he became frightened. It had been foolish of him to shout so loud. What if someone had heard him? He waited awhile and listened. But all he heard was the intermingled shouts from the yard.

Feeling rather foolish, he climbed down off the horse. Really, he was behaving like a small child!

He unwrapped his sandwich and shined the apple on his trousers. But just as he was biting into it, he stopped himself.

'No,' he said to himself aloud. 'I must carefully apportion my provisions. Who knows how long they will have to last me.'

With a heavy heart he rewrapped his sandwich and returned it to his satchel along with the apple. Then with a sigh he settled down on the mats and reached for the book.

III

Morla the Aged One

AIRON, the old black centaur, sank back on his bed of furs as Artax's hoofbeats were dying away. After so much exertion he was at the end of his strength. The women who found him next day in Atreyu's tent feared for his life. And when the hunters came home a few days later, he was hardly any better, but he managed nevertheless to tell them why Atreyu had ridden away and would not be back soon. As they were all fond of the boy, their concern for him made them grave. Still, they were proud that the Childlike Empress had chosen him for the Great Quest – though none claimed to understand her choice.

Old Cairon never went back to the Ivory Tower. But he didn't die and he didn't stay with the Greenskins in the Grassy Ocean. His destiny was to lead him over very different and unexpected pathways. But that is another story and shall be told another time.

That same night Atreyu rode to the foot of the Silver Mountains. It was almost morning when he finally stopped to rest. Artax grazed a while and drank water from a small mountain stream. Atreyu wrapped himself in his red cloak and slept a few hours. But when the sun rose, they were already on their way.

On the first day they crossed the Silver Mountains, where every road and trail was known to them, and they made quick progress. When he felt hungry, the boy ate a chunk of dried buffalo meat and two little grass-seed cakes that he had been carrying in his saddlebag – originally they had been intended for his hunt.

'Exactly!' said Bastian. 'A man has to eat now and then.'

He took his sandwich out of his satchel, unwrapped it, broke it carefully in two pieces, wrapped one of them up again and put it away. Then he ate the other.

Recess was over. Bastian wondered what his class would be doing next. Oh yes, geography, with Mrs Flint. You had to reel off rivers and their tributaries, cities, population figures, natural resources, and industries. Bastian shrugged his shoulders and went on reading.

By sunset the Silver Mountains lay behind them, and again they stopped to rest. That night Atreyu dreamed of purple buffaloes. He saw them in the distance, roaming over the Grassy Ocean, and he tried to get near them on his horse. In vain. He galloped, he spurred his horse, but they were always the same distance away.

The second day they passed through the Singing Tree Country. Each tree had a different shape, different leaves, different bark, but all of them in growing – and this was what gave the country its name – made soft music that sounded from far and near and joined in a mighty harmony that hadn't its like for beauty in all Fantastica. Riding through this country wasn't entirely devoid of danger, for many a traveler had stopped still as though spellbound and forgotten everything else. Atreyu felt the power of these marvelous sounds, but didn't let himself be tempted to stop.

The following night he dreamed again of purple buffaloes. This time he was on foot, and a great herd of them was passing. But they were beyond the range of his bow, and when he tried to come closer, his feet clung to the ground and he couldn't move them. His frantic efforts to tear them loose woke him up. He started out at once, though the sun had not yet risen.

The third day, he saw the Glass Tower of Eribo, where the inhabitants of the region caught and stored starlight. Out of the starlight they made wonderfully decorative objects, the purpose of which, however, was known to no one in all Fantastica but their makers.

He met some of these folk; little creatures they were, who seemed to have been blown from glass. They were extremely friendly and provided him with food and drink, but when he asked them who might know something about the Childlike Empress's illness, they sank into a gloomy, perplexed silence.

The next night Atreyu dreamed again that the herd of purple buffaloes was passing. One of the beasts, a particularly large, imposing bull, broke away from his fellows and slowly, with no sign of either fear or anger, approached Atreyu. Like all true hunters, Atreyu knew every creature's vulnerable spot, where an arrow wound would be fatal. The purple buffalo put himself in such a position as to offer a perfect target. Atreyu fitted an arrow to his bow and pulled with all his might. But he couldn't shoot. His fingers seemed to have grown into the bowstring, and he couldn't release it.

Each of the following nights he dreamed something of the sort. He got closer and closer to the same purple buffalo – he recognized him by a white spot on his forehead – but for some reason he was never able to shoot the deadly arrow.

During the days he rode farther and farther, without knowing where he was going or finding anyone to advise him. The golden amulet he wore was respected by all who met him, but none had an answer to his question.

One day he saw from afar the flaming streets of Salamander, the city whose inhabitants' bodies are of fire, but he preferred to keep away from it. He crossed the broad plateau of the Sassafranians, who are born old and die when they become babies. He came to the jungle temple of Muwamath, where a great moonstone pillar hovers in midair, and he spoke to the monks who lived there. And again no one could tell him anything.

He had been traveling aimlessly for almost a week, when on the seventh day and the following night two very different encounters changed his situation and state of mind.

Cairon's story of the terrible happenings in all parts of Fantastica had made an impression on him, but thus far the disaster was something he had only heard about. On the seventh day he was to see it with his own eyes.

Toward noon, he was riding through a dense dark forest of enormous gnarled trees. This was the same Howling Forest where the four messengers had met some time before. That region, as Atreyu knew, was the home of bark trolls. These, as he had been told, were giants and giantesses, who themselves looked like gnarled tree trunks. As long as they stood motionless, as they usually did, you could easily mistake them for trees and ride on unsuspecting. Only when they moved could you see that they had branchlike arms and crooked, rootlike legs. Though exceedingly powerful, they were not dangerous – at most they liked to play tricks on travelers who had lost their way.

Atreyu had just discovered a woodland meadow with a brook twining through it, and had dismounted to let Artax drink and graze. Suddenly he heard a loud crackling and thudding in the woods behind him.

Three bark trolls emerged from the woods and came toward him. A cold shiver ran down his spine at the sight of them. The first, having no legs or haunches, was obliged to walk on his hands. The second had a hole in his chest, so big you could see through it. The third hopped on his right foot, because the whole left half of him was missing, as if he had been cut through the middle.

When they saw the amulet hanging from Atreyu's neck, they nodded to one another and came slowly closer.

'Don't be afraid,' said the one who was walking on his hands, and his voice sounded like the groaning of a tree. 'We're not exactly pretty to look at, but in this part of Howling Forest there's no one else left who might warn you. That's why we've come.'

'Warn?' Atreyu asked. 'Against what?'

'We've heard about you,' moaned the one with the hole in his chest. 'And we've been told about your Quest. Don't go any further in this direction, or you'll be lost.'

'The same thing will happen to you as happened to us,' sighed the halved one. 'Would you like that?'

'What *has* happened to you?' Atreyu asked.

'The Nothing is spreading,' groaned the first. 'It's growing and growing, there's more of it every day, if it's possible to speak of more *nothing*. All the others fled from Howling Forest in time, but we didn't want to leave our home. The Nothing caught us in our sleep and this is what it did to us.'

'Is it very painful?' Atreyu asked.

'No,' said the second bark troll, the one with the hole in his chest. 'You don't feel a thing. There's just something missing. And once it gets hold of you, something more is missing every day. Soon there won't be anything left of us.'

'In what part of the woods did it begin?' Atreyu asked.

'Would you like to see it?' The third troll, who was only half a troll, turned to his fellow sufferers with a questioning look. When they nodded, he said: 'We'll take you to a place where there's a good view of it. But you must promise not to go any closer. If you do, it will pull you in.'

'All right,' said Atreyu. 'I promise.'

The three turned about and made for the edge of the forest. Leading Artax by the bridle, Atreyu followed them. For a while they went this way and that way between enormous trees, then finally they stopped at the foot of a giant tree so big that five grown men holding hands could scarcely have girdled it.

'Climb as high as you can,' said the legless troll, 'and look in the direction of the sunrise. Then you'll see – or rather *not* see it.'

Atreyu pulled himself up by the knots and bumps on the tree. He reached the lower branches, hoisted himself to the next, climbed and climbed until he lost sight of the ground below him. Higher and higher he went; the trunk grew thinner and the more closely spaced side branches made it easier to climb. When at last he reached the crown, he turned toward the sunrise. And then he saw it:

The tops of the trees nearest him were still green, but the leaves of those farther away seemed to have lost all color; they were gray. A little farther on, the foliage seemed to become strangely transparent, misty, or, better still, unreal. And farther still there was nothing, absolutely nothing. Not a bare stretch, not darkness, not some lighter color; no, it was something the eyes could not bear, something that made you feel you had gone blind. For no eye can bear the sight of utter nothingness. Atreyu held his hand before his face and nearly fell off his branch. He clung tight for a moment, then climbed down as fast as he could. He had seen enough. At last he really understood the horror that was spreading through Fantastica.

When he reached the foot of the great tree, the three bark trolls had vanished. Atreyu swung himself into the saddle and galloped as fast as Artax would carry him in the direction that would take him away from this slowly but irresistibly spreading Nothing. By nightfall he had left Howling Forest far behind him; only then did he stop to rest.

That night a second encounter, which was to give his Great Quest a new direction, awaited him.

He dreamed – much more distinctly than before – of the purple buffalo he had wanted to kill. This time Atreyu was without his bow and arrow. He felt very, very small and the buffalo's face filled the whole sky. And the face spoke to him. He couldn't understand every word, but this is the gist of what it said:

'If you had killed me, you would be a hunter now. But because you let me live, I can help you, Atreyu. Listen to me! There is, in Fantastica, a being older than all other beings. In the north, far, far from here, lie the Swamps of Sadness. In the middle of those swamps there is a mountain, Tortoise Shell Mountain it's called. There lives Morla the Aged One. Go and see Morla the Aged One.'

Then Atreyu woke up.

The clock in the belfry struck twelve. Soon Bastian's classmates would be going down to the gym for their last class. Today they'd probably be playing with the big, heavy medicine ball which Bastian handled so awkwardly that neither of the two teams ever wanted him. And sometimes they played with a small hard-rubber ball that hurt terribly when it hit you. Bastian was an easy mark and was always getting hit full force. Or perhaps they'd be climbing rope – an exercise that Bastian especially detested. Most of the others would be all the way to the top while he, with his face as red as a beet, would be dangling like a sack of flour at the very bottom of the rope, unable to climb as much as a foot. They'd all be laughing their heads off. And Mr Menge, the gym teacher, had a special stock of gibes just for Bastian.

Bastian would have given a good deal to be like Atreyu. He'd have shown them.

He heaved a deep sigh.

Atreyu rode northward, ever northward. He allowed himself and his little horse only the most necessary stops for sleep and food. He rode by day and he rode by night, in the scorching sun and the pelting rain. He looked neither to the left nor the right and asked no more questions.

The farther northward he went, the darker it grew. An unchanging, leaden-gray twilight filled the days. At night the northern lights played across the sky.

One morning, when time seemed to be standing still in the murky light, he looked out from a hilltop and finally glimpsed the Swamps of Sadness. Clouds of mist drifted over them. Here and there he distinguished little clumps of trees. Their trunks divided at the bottom into four, five, or more crooked stilts, which made the trees look like great many-legged crabs standing in the black water. From the brown foliage hung aerial roots resembling motionless tentacles. It was next to impossible to make out where there was solid ground between the pools of water and where there was only a covering of water plants.

Artax whinnied with horror.

'Are we going in there, master?'

'Yes,' said Atreyu. 'We must find Tortoise Shell Mountain. It's at the center of those swamps.'

He urged Artax on and Artax obeyed. Step by step, he tested the firmness of the ground, but that made progress very slow. At length Atreyu dismounted and led Artax by the bridle. Several times the horse sank in, but managed to pull himself loose. But the farther they went into the Swamps of Sadness, the more sluggish became his movements. He let his head droop and barely dragged himself forward.

'Artax,' said Atreyu. 'What's the matter?'

'I don't know, master. I think we should turn back. There's no sense in all this. We're chasing after something you only dreamed about. We won't find anything. Maybe it's too late even now. Maybe the Childlike Empress is already dead, and everything we're doing is useless. Let us turn back, master.'

Atreyu was astonished. 'Artax,' he said. 'You've never spoken like this. What's the matter? Are you sick?'

'Maybe I am,' said Artax. 'With every step we take, the sadness grows in my heart. I've lost hope, master. And I feel so heavy, so heavy. I can't go on!'

'But we must go on!' cried Atreyu. 'Come along, Artax!'

He tugged at the bridle, but Artax stood still. He had sunk in up to his belly. And he made no further effort to extricate himself.

'Artax!' cried Atreyu. 'You mustn't let yourself go. Come. Pull yourself out or you'll sink.'

'Leave me, master,' said the little horse. 'I can't make it. Go on alone. Don't bother about me. I can't stand the sadness anymore. I want to die!'

Desperately Atreyu pulled at the bridle, but the horse sank deeper and deeper. When only his head emerged from the black water, Atreyu took it in his arms.

'I'll hold you, Artax,' he whispered. 'I won't let you go under.'

The little horse uttered one last soft neigh.

'You can't help me, master. It's all over for me. Neither of us knew what we were getting into. Now we know why they are called the Swamps of Sadness. It's the sadness that has made me so heavy. That's why I'm sinking. There's no help.'

'But I'm here, too,' said Atreyu, 'and I don't feel anything.'

'You're wearing the Gem, master,' said Artax. 'It protects you.'

'Then I'll hang it around your neck!' Atreyu cried. 'Maybe it will protect you too.'

He started taking the chain off his neck.

'No,' the little horse whinnied. 'You mustn't do that, master. The Glory was entrusted to you, you weren't given permission to pass it on as you see fit. You must carry on the Quest without me.'

Atreyu pressed his face into the horse's cheek.

'Artax,' he whispered. 'Oh, my Artax!'

'Will you grant my last wish?' the little horse asked.

Atreyu nodded in silence.

'Then I beg you to go away. I don't want you to see my end. Will you do me that favor?'

Slowly Atreyu arose. Half the horse's head was already in the black water.

'Farewell, Atreyu, my master!' he said. 'And thank you.'

Atreyu pressed his lips together. He couldn't speak. Once again he nodded to Artax, then he turned away.

Bastian was sobbing. He couldn't help it. His eyes filled with tears and he couldn't go on reading. He had to take out his handkerchief and blow his nose before he could go on.

Atreyu waded and waded. For how long he didn't know. The mist grew thicker and he felt as if he were blind and deaf. It seemed to him that he had been wandering around in circles for hours. He stopped worrying about where to set his foot down, and yet he never sank in above his knees. By some mysterious means, the Childlike Empress's amulet led him the right way.

Then suddenly he saw a high, steep mountain ahead of him. Pulling himself up from crag to crag, he climbed to the rounded top. At first he didn't notice what this mountain was made of. But from the top he overlooked the whole mountain, and then he saw that it consisted of great slabs of tortoise shell, with moss growing in the crevices between them.

He had found Tortoise Shell Mountain.

But the discovery gave him no pleasure. Now that his faithful little horse was gone, it left him almost indifferent. Still, he would have to find out who this Morla the Aged One was, and where she actually lived.

While he was mulling it over, he felt a slight tremor shaking the mountain. Then he heard a hideous wheezing and lip-smacking, and a voice that seemed to issue from the innermost bowels of the earth: 'Sakes alive, old woman, somebody's crawling around on us.'

In hurrying to the end of the ridge, where the sounds had come from, Atreyu had slipped on a bed of moss. Since there was nothing for him to hold on to, he slid faster and faster and finally fell off the mountain. Luckily he landed on a tree, which caught him in its branches.

Looking back at the mountain, he saw an enormous cave. Water was splashing and gushing inside, and something was moving. Slowly the something came out. It looked like a boulder as big as a house. When it came into full sight, Atreyu saw that it was a head attached to a long wrinkled neck, the head of a turtle. Its eyes were black and as big as ponds. The mouth was dripping with muck and water weeds. This whole Tortoise Shell Mountain – it suddenly dawned on Atreyu – was one enormous beast, a giant swamp turtle; Morla the Aged One.

The wheezing, gurgling voice spoke again: 'What are you doing here, son?'

Atreyu reached for the amulet on his chest and held it in such a way that the great eyes couldn't help seeing it.

'Do you recognize this, Morla?'

She took a while to answer: 'Sakes alive! A U R Y N. We haven't seen that in a long time, have we, old woman? The emblem of the Childlike Empress – not in a long time.'

'The Childlike Empress is sick,' said Atreyu. 'Did you know that?'

'It's all the same to us. Isn't it, old woman?' Morla replied. She seemed to be talking to herself, perhaps because she had had no one else to talk to for heaven knows how long.

'If we don't save her, she'll die,' Atreyu cried out. 'The Nothing is spreading everywhere. I've seen it myself.'

Morla stared at him out of her great empty eyes.

'We don't mind, do we, old woman?'

'But then we shall all die!' Atreyu screamed. 'Every last one of us!'

'Sakes alive!' said Morla. 'But what do we care? Nothing matters to us anymore. It's all the same to us.'

'But you'll be destroyed too, Morla!' cried Atreyu angrily. 'Or do you expect, because you're so old, to outlive Fantastica?'

'Sakes alive!' Morla gurgled. 'We're old, son, much too old. Lived long enough. Seen too much. When you know as much as we do, nothing matters. Things just repeat. Day and night, summer and winter. The world is empty and aimless. Everything circles around. Whatever starts up must pass away, whatever is born must die. It all cancels out, good and bad, beautiful and ugly. Everything's empty. Nothing is real. Nothing matters.'

Atreyu didn't know what to answer. The Aged One's dark, empty, pond-sized eyes paralyzed his thoughts. After a while, he heard her speak again:

'You're young, son. If you were as old as we are, you'd know there's nothing but sadness. Why shouldn't we die, you and I, the Childlike Empress, the whole lot of us? Anyway, it's all flim-flam, meaningless games. Nothing matters. Leave us in peace, son. Go away.'

Atreyu tensed his will to fight off the paralysis that flowed from her eyes.

'If you know so much,' he said, 'you must know what the Childlike Empress's illness is and whether there's a cure for it.'

'We do, we do! Don't we, old woman?' Morla wheezed. 'But it's all the same to us whether she's saved or not. So why should we tell you?'

'If it's really all the same to you,' Atreyu argued, 'you might just as well tell me.'

'We could, we could! Couldn't we, old woman?' Morla grunted. 'But we don't feel like it.'

'Then it's *not* all the same to you. Then you yourself don't believe what you're saying.'

After a long silence he heard a deep gurgling and belching. That must have been some kind of laughter, if Morla the Aged One was still capable of laughing. In any case, she said: 'You're a sly one, son. Really sly. We haven't had so much fun in a long time. Have we, old woman? Sakes alive, it's true. We might just as well tell you. Makes no difference. Should we tell him, old woman?'

A long silence followed. Atreyu waited anxiously for Morla's answer, taking care not to interrupt the slow, cheerless flow of her thoughts. At last she spoke:

'Your life is short, son. Ours is long. Much too long. But we both live in time. You a short time. We a long time. The Childlike Empress has always been there. But she's not old. She has always been young. She still is. Her life isn't measured by time, but by names. She needs a new name. She keeps needing new names. Do you know her name, son?'

'No,' Atreyu admitted. 'I never heard it.'

'You couldn't have,' said Morla. 'Not even we can remember it. Yet she has had many names. But they're all forgotten. Over and done with. But without a name she can't live. All the Childlike Empress needs is a new name, then she'll get well. But it makes no difference whether she gets well or not.'

She closed her pond-sized eyes and began slowly to pull in her head.

'Wait!' cried Atreyu. 'Where can she get a name? Who can give her one? Where can I find the name?'

'None of us,' Morla gurgled. 'No inhabitant of Fantastica can give her a new name. So it's hopeless. Sakes alive! It doesn't matter. Nothing matters.'

'Who then?' cried Atreyu in despair. 'Who can give her the name that will save her and save us all?'

'Don't make so much noise!' said Morla. 'Leave us in peace

and go away. Even we don't know who can give her a name.'

'If you don't know,' Atreyu screamed even louder, 'who does?'

She opened her eyes a last time.

'If you weren't wearing the Gem,' she wheezed, 'we'd eat you up, just to have peace and quiet. Sakes alive!'

'Who?' Atreyu insisted. 'Tell me who knows, and I'll leave you in peace forever.'

'It doesn't matter,' she replied. 'But maybe Uyulala in the Southern Oracle knows. She may know. It's all the same to us.'

'How can I get there?'

'You can't get there at all, son. Not in ten thousand days' journey. Your life is too short. You'd die first. It's too far. In the south. Much too far. So it's all hopeless. We told you so in the first place, didn't we, old woman? Sakes alive, son. Give it up. And most important, leave us in peace.'

With that she closed her empty-gazing eyes and pulled her head back into the cave for good. Atreyu knew he would learn no more from her.

At that same time the shadowy being which had condensed out of the darkness of the heath picked up Atreyu's trail and headed for the Swamps of Sadness. Nothing and no one in all Fantastica would deflect it from that trail.

Bastian had propped his head on his hand and was looking thoughtfully into space.

'Strange,' he said aloud, 'that no one in all Fantastica can give the Childlike Empress a new name.' If it had been just a matter of giving her a name, Bastian could easily have helped her. He was tops at that. But unfortunately he was not in Fantastica, where his talents were needed and would even have won him friends and admirers. On the other hand, he was glad not to be there. Not for anything in the world would he have ventured into such a place as the Swamps of Sadness. And then this spooky creature of darkness that was chasing Atreyu without his knowing it. Bastian would have liked to warn him, but that was impossible. All he could do was hope, and go on reading.

IV

Ygramul the Many

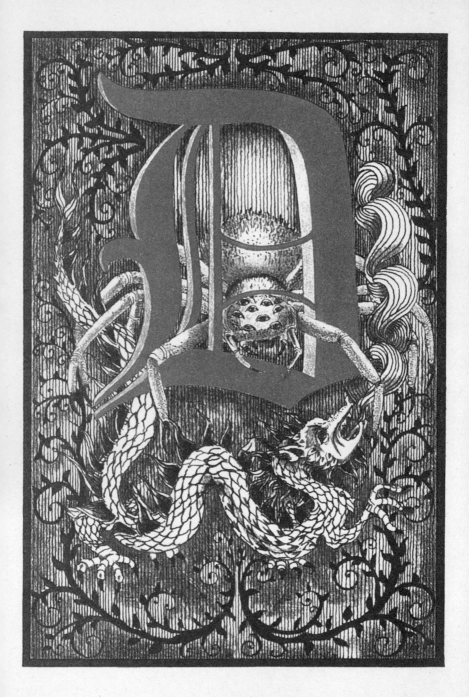

IRE hunger and thirst pursued Atreyu. It was two days since he had
left the Swamps of Sadness, and since then he had been wandering
through an empty rocky wilderness. What little provisions he had
taken with him had sunk beneath the black waters with Artax. In
vain, Atreyu dug his fingers into the clefts between stones in the
hope of finding some little root, but nothing grew there, not even
moss or lichen.

At first he was glad to feel solid ground beneath his feet, but
little by little it came to him that he was worse off than ever. He
was lost. He didn't even know what direction he was going in, for
the dusky grayness was the same all around him. A cold wind blew
over the needlelike rocks that rose up on all sides, blew and blew.

Uphill and downhill he plodded, but all he saw was distant
mountains with still more distant ranges behind them, and so on
to the horizon on all sides. And nothing living, not a beetle, not
an ant, not even the vultures which ordinarily follow the weary
traveler until he falls by the wayside.

Doubt was no longer possible. This was the Land of the Dead
Mountains. Few had seen them, and fewer still escaped from them
alive. But they figured in the legends of Atreyu's people. He
remembered an old song:

> Better the huntsman
> Should perish in the swamps,
> For in the Dead Mountains
> There is a deep, deep chasm,
> Where dwelleth Ygramul the Many,
> The horror of horrors.

Even if Atreyu had wanted to turn back and had known what
direction to take, it would not have been possible. He had gone
too far and could only keep on going. If only he himself had been
involved, he might have sat down in a cave and quietly waited for
death, as the Greenskin hunters did. But he was engaged in the
Great Quest: the life of the Childlike Empress and of all Fantastica
was at stake. He had no right to give up.

And so he kept at it. Uphill and down. From time to time he
realized that he had long been walking as though in his sleep, that

his mind had been in other realms, from which they had returned none too willingly.

Bastian gave a start. The clock in the belfry struck one. School was over for the day.

He heard the shouts and screams of the children running into the corridors from the classrooms and the clatter of many feet on the stairs. For a while there were isolated shouts from the street. And then the schoolhouse was engulfed in silence.

The silence descended on Bastian like a great heavy blanket and threatened to smother him. From then on he would be all alone in the big schoolhouse – all that day, all that night, there was no knowing how long. This adventure of his was getting serious.

The other children were going home for lunch. Bastian was hungry too, and he was cold in spite of the army blankets he was wrapped in. Suddenly he lost heart, his whole plan seemed crazy, senseless. He wanted to go home, that very minute. He could just be in time. His father wouldn't have noticed anything yet. Bastian wouldn't even have to tell him he had played hooky. Of course, it would come out sooner or later, but there was time to worry about that. But the stolen book? Yes, he'd have to own up to that too. In the end, his father would resign himself as he did to all the disappointments Bastian had given him. Anyway, there was nothing to be afraid of. Most likely his father wouldn't say anything, but just go and see Mr Coreander and straighten things out.

Bastian was about to put the copper-colored book into his satchel. But then he stopped.

'No,' he said aloud in the stillness of the attic. 'Atreyu wouldn't give up just because things were getting a little rough. What I've started I must finish. I've gone too far to turn back. Regardless of what may happen, I have to go forward.'

He felt very lonely, yet there was a kind of pride in his loneliness. He was proud of standing firm in the face of temptation.

He was a little like Atreyu after all.

A time came when Atreyu really could not go forward. Before him lay the Deep Chasm.

The grandiose horror of the sight cannot be described in words. A yawning cleft, perhaps half a mile wide, twined its way through the Land of the Dead Mountains. How deep it might be there was no way of knowing.

Atreyu lay on a spur at the edge of the chasm and stared down into darkness which seemed to extend to the innermost heart of the earth. He picked up a stone the size of a tennis ball and hurled it as far as he could. The stone fell and fell, until it was swallowed up in the darkness. Though Atreyu listened a long while, he heard no sound of impact.

There was only one thing Atreyu could do, and he did it. He skirted the Deep Chasm. Every second he expected to meet the 'horrors of horrors', known to him from the old song. He had no idea what sort of creature this might be. All he knew was that its name was Ygramul.

The Deep Chasm twisted and turned through the mountain waste, and of course there was no path at its edge. Here too there were abrupt rises and falls, and sometimes the ground swayed alarmingly under Atreyu's feet. Sometimes his path was barred by gigantic rock formations and he would have to feel his way, painfully, step by step, around them. Or there would be slopes covered with smooth stones that would start rolling toward the Chasm as soon as he set foot on them. More than once he was within a hairbreadth of the edge.

If he had known that a pursuer was close behind him and coming closer by the hour, he might have hurried and taken dangerous risks. It was that creature of darkness which had been after him since the start of his journey. Since then its body had taken on recognizable outlines. It was a pitch-black wolf, the size of an ox. Nose to the ground, it trotted along, following Atreyu's trail through the stony desert of the Dead Mountains. Its tongue hung far out of its mouth and its terrifying fangs were bared. The freshness of the scent told the wolf that its prey was only a few miles ahead.

But suspecting nothing of his pursuer, Atreyu picked his way slowly and cautiously.

As he was groping through the darkness of a tunnel under a mountain, he suddenly heard a noise that he couldn't identify because it bore no resemblance to any sound he had ever heard. It was a kind of jangling roar. At the same time Atreyu felt that the whole mountain about him was trembling, and he heard blocks of stone crashing down its outer walls. For a time he waited to see whether the earthquake, or whatever it might be, would abate. Then, since it did not, he crawled to the end of the tunnel and cautiously stuck his head out.

And then he saw: An enormous spider web was stretched from edge to edge of the Deep Chasm. And in the sticky threads of the web, which were as thick as ropes, a great white luckdragon was struggling, becoming more and more entangled as he thrashed about with his tail and claws.

Luckdragons are among the strangest animals in Fantastica. They bear no resemblance to ordinary dragons, which look like loathsome snakes and live in deep caves, diffusing a noxious stench and guarding some real or imaginary treasure. Such spawn of chaos are usually wicked or ill-tempered, they have batlike wings with which they can rise clumsily and noisily into the air, and they spew fire and smoke. Luckdragons are creatures of air, warmth, and pure joy. Despite their great size, they are as light as a summer cloud, and consequently need no wings for flying. They swim in the air of heaven as fish swim in water. Seen from the earth, they look like slow lightning flashes. The most amazing thing about them is their song. Their voice sounds like the golden note of a large bell, and when they speak softly the bell seems to be ringing in the distance. Anyone who has heard this sound will remember it as long as he lives and tell his grandchildren about it.

But the luckdragon Atreyu saw could hardly have been in a mood for singing. His long, graceful body with its pearly, pink-and-white scales hung tangled and twisted in the great spider web. His bristling fangs, his thick, luxuriant mane, and the fringes on his tail and limbs were all caught in the sticky ropes. He could hardly move. The eyeballs in his lionlike head glistened ruby-red.

The splendid beast bled from many wounds, for there was something else, something very big, that descended like a dark cloud on the dragon's white body. It rose and fell, rose and fell, all the while changing its shape. Sometimes it resembled a gigantic long-legged spider with many fiery eyes and a fat body encased in shaggy black hair; then it became a great hand with long claws that tried to crush the luckdragon, and in the next moment it changed to a giant scorpion, piercing its unfortunate victim with its venomous sting.

The battle between the two giants was fearsome. The luckdragon was still defending himself, spewing blue fire that singed the cloud-monster's bristles. Smoke came whirling through the crevices in the rock, so foul-smelling that Atreyu could hardly breathe. Once the luckdragon managed to bite off one of the monster's long legs. But instead of falling into the chasm, the severed leg hovered for a time in mid-air, then returned to its old place in the black cloud-body. And several times the dragon seemed to seize one of the monster's limbs between its teeth, but bit into the void.

Only then did Atreyu notice that the monster was not a single, solid body, but was made up of innumerable small steel-blue insects which buzzed like angry hornets. It was their compact swarm that kept taking different shapes.

This was Ygramul, and now Atreyu knew why she was called 'the Many'.

He sprang from his hiding place, reached for the Gem, and shouted at the top of his lungs: 'Stop! In the name of the Childlike Empress, stop!'

But the hissing and roaring of the combatants drowned out his voice. He himself could barely hear it.

Without stopping to think, he set foot on the sticky ropes of the web, which swayed beneath him as he ran. He lost his balance, fell, clung by his hands to keep from falling into the dark chasm, pulled himself up again, caught himself in the ropes, fought free and hurried on.

At last Ygramul sensed that something was coming toward her. With the speed of lightning, she turned about, confronting Atreyu with an enormous steel-blue face. Her single eye had a vertical pupil, which stared at Atreyu with inconceivable malignancy.

A cry of fear escaped Bastian.

A cry of terror passed through the ravine and echoed from side to side. Ygramul turned her eye to left and right, to see if someone else had arrived, for that sound could not have been made by the boy who stood there as though paralyzed with horror.

Could she have heard my cry? Bastian wondered in alarm. But that's not possible.

And then Atreyu heard Ygramul's voice. It was very high and slightly hoarse, not at all the right kind of voice for that enormous face. Her lips did not move as she spoke. It was the buzzing of a great swarm of hornets that shaped itself into words.

'A Twolegs,' Atreyu heard. 'Years upon years of hunger, and now two tasty morsels at once! A lucky day for Ygramul!'

Atreyu needed all his strength to keep his composure. He held the Gem up to the monster's one eye and asked: 'Do you know this emblem?'

'Come closer, Twolegs!' buzzed the many voices. 'Ygramul doesn't see well.'

Atreyu took one step closer to the face. The mouth opened, showing innumerable glittering feelers, hooks, and claws in place of a tongue.

'Still closer,' the swarm buzzed.

He took one more step, which brought him near enough to distinguish the innumerable steel-blue insects which whirled around in seeming confusion. Yet the face as a whole remained motionless.

'I am Atreyu,' he said. 'I have come on a mission from the Childlike Empress.'

'Most inopportune!' said the angry buzzing after a time. 'What do you want of Ygramul? As you can see, she is very busy.'

'I want this luckdragon,' said Atreyu. 'Let me have him.'

'What do you want him for, Atreyu Twolegs?'

'I lost my horse in the Swamps of Sadness. I must go to the Southern Oracle, because only Uyulala can tell me who can give the Childlike Empress a new name. If she doesn't get one, she will die and all Fantastica with her – you too, Ygramul.'

'Ah!' the face drawled. 'Is that the reason for all the places where there is nothing?'

'Yes,' said Atreyu. 'So you too know of them. But the Southern

Oracle is too long a journey for a lifetime. That's why I'm asking you for this luckdragon. If he carries me through the air, I may get there before it's too late.'

Out of the whirling swarm that made up the face came a sound suggesting the giggling of many voices.

'You're all wrong, Atreyu Twolegs. We know nothing of the Southern Oracle and nothing of Uyulala, but we do know that this dragon cannot carry you. And even if he were in the best of health, the trip would take so long that the Childlike Empress would die of her illness in the meantime. You must measure your Quest, Atreyu, in terms not of your own life but of hers.'

The gaze of the eye with the vertical pupil was almost unbearable.

'That's true,' he said in a small voice.

'Besides,' the motionless face went on, 'the luckdragon has Ygramul's poison in his body. He has less than an hour to live.'

'Then there's no hope,' Atreyu murmured. 'Not for him, not for me, and not for you either, Ygramul.'

'Oh well,' the voice buzzed. 'Ygramul would at least have had one good meal. But who says it's Ygramul's last meal? She knows a way of getting you to the Southern Oracle in a twinkling. But the question is: Will you like it?'

'What is that way?'

'That is Ygramul's secret. The creatures of darkness have their secrets too, Atreyu Twolegs. Ygramul has never revealed hers. And you too must swear you'll never tell a soul. For it would be greatly to Ygramul's disadvantage if it were known, yes, greatly to her disadvantage.'

'I swear! Speak!'

The great steel-blue face leaned forward just a little and buzzed almost inaudibly.

'You must let Ygramul bite you.'

Atreyu shrank back in horror.

'Ygramul's poison,' the voice went on, 'kills within an hour. But to one who has it inside him it gives the power to wish himself in any part of Fantastica he chooses. Imagine if that were known! All Ygramul's victims would escape her.'

'An hour?' cried Atreyu. 'What can I do in an hour?'

'Well,' buzzed the swarm, 'at least it's more than all the hours remaining to you here.'

Atreyu struggled with himself.

'Will you set the luckdragon free if I ask it in the name of the Childlike Empress?' he finally asked.

'No!' said the face. 'You have no right to ask that of Ygramul even if you are wearing AURYN, the Gem. The Childlike Empress takes us all as we are. That's why Ygramul respects her emblem.'

Atreyu was still standing with bowed head. Ygramul had spoken the truth. He couldn't save the white luckdragon. His own wishes didn't count.

He looked up and said: 'Do what you suggested.'

Instantly the steel-blue cloud descended on him and enveloped him on all sides. He felt a numbing pain in the left shoulder. His last thought was: 'To the Southern Oracle!'

Then the world went black before his eyes.

When the wolf reached the spot a short time later, he saw the giant spider web – but there was no one in sight. There the trail he had been following broke off, and try as he might, he could not find it again.

Bastian stopped reading. He felt miserable, as though he himself had Ygramul's poison inside him.

'Thank God I'm not in Fantastica,' he muttered. 'Luckily, such monsters don't exist in reality. Anyway, it's only a story.'

But was it only a story? How did it happen that Ygramul, and probably Atreyu as well, had heard Bastian's cry of terror?

Little by little, this book was beginning to give him a spooky feeling.

V

The Gnomics

VER so slowly Atreyu awoke to the world. He saw that he was still in the mountains, and for a terrible moment he suspected that Ygramul had deceived him.

But these, he soon realized, were entirely different mountains. They seemed to consist of great rust-red blocks of stone, piled in such a way as to form strange towers and pyramids. In between these structures the ground was covered with bushes and shrubbery. The air was blazing hot. The country was bathed in glaring sunlight.

Shading his eyes with his hand, Atreyu looked around him and discovered, about a mile away, an irregularly shaped arch, perhaps a hundred feet high. It too appeared to consist of piled stone blocks.

Could that be the entrance to the Southern Oracle? As far as he could see, there was nothing behind the arch, only an endless empty plain, no building, no temple, no grove, nothing suggesting an oracle.

Suddenly, while he was wondering what to do, he heard a deep, bronzelike voice: 'Atreyu!' And then again: 'Atreyu!'

Turning around, he saw the white luckdragon emerging from one of the rust-red towers. Blood was pouring from his wounds, and he was so weak he could barely drag himself along.

'Here I am, Atreyu,' he said, merrily winking one of his ruby-red eyes. 'And you needn't be so surprised. I was pretty well paralyzed when I was caught in that spider web, but I heard everything Ygramul said to you. So I thought to myself: She has bitten me too, after all, so why shouldn't I take advantage of the secret as well? That's how I got away from her.'

Atreyu was overjoyed.

'I hated leaving you to Ygramul,' he said. 'But what could I do?'

'Nothing,' said the luckdragon. 'You've saved my life all the same – even if I had something to do with it.'

And again he winked, this time with the other eye.

'Saved your life,' Atreyu repeated, 'for an hour. That's all we have left. I can feel Ygramul's poison burning my heart away.'

'Every poison has its antidote,' said the white dragon. 'Everything will turn out all right. You'll see.'

'I can't imagine how,' said Atreyu.

'Neither can I,' said the luckdragon. 'But that's the wonderful part of it. From now on you'll succeed in everything you attempt. Because I'm a luckdragon. Even when I was caught in the web, I didn't give up hope. And as you see, I was right.'

Atreyu smiled.

'Tell me, why did you wish yourself here and not in some other place where you might have been cured?'

'My life belongs to you,' said the dragon, 'if you'll accept it. I thought you'd need a mount for this Great Quest of yours. And you'll soon see that crawling around the country on two legs, or even galloping on a good horse, can't hold a candle to whizzing through the air on the back of a luckdragon. Are we partners?'

'We're partners,' said Atreyu.

'By the way,' said the dragon. 'My name is Falkor.'

'Glad to meet you,' said Atreyu, 'but while we're talking, what little time we have left is seeping away. I've got to do something. But what?'

'Have luck,' said Falkor. 'What else?'

But Atreyu heard no more. He had fallen down and lay motionless in the soft folds of the dragon's body.

Ygramul's poison was taking effect.

When Atreyu – no one knows how much later – opened his eyes again, he saw nothing but a very strange face bent over him. It was the wrinkliest, shriveledest face he had ever seen, and only about the size of a fist. It was as brown as a baked apple, and the eyes in it glittered like stars. The head was covered with a bonnet made of withered leaves.

Atreyu felt a little drinking cup held to his lips.

'Nice medicine! Good medicine!' mumbled the wrinkled little lips in the shriveled face. 'Just drink, child. Do you good.'

Atreyu sipped. It tasted strange. Kind of sweet and sour.

Atreyu found it painful to speak. 'What about the white dragon?' he asked.

'Doing fine!' the voice whispered. 'Don't worry, my boy. You'll get well. You'll both get well. The worst is over. Just drink. Drink.'

Atreyu took another swallow and again sleep overcame him, but this time it was the deep, refreshing sleep of recovery.

The clock in the belfry struck two.

Bastian couldn't hold it in any longer. He simply had to go. He had felt the need for quite some time, but he hadn't been able to stop reading. Besides, he had been afraid to go downstairs. He told himself that there was nothing to worry about, that the building was deserted, that no one would see him. But still he was afraid, as if the school were a person watching him.

But in the end there was no help for it; he just had to go!

He set the open book down on the mat, went to the door and listened with pounding heart. Nothing. He slid the bolt and slowly turned the big key in the lock. When he pressed the handle, the door opened, creaking loudly.

He padded out in his stocking feet, leaving the door behind him open to avoid unnecessary noise. He crept down the stairs to the second floor. The students' toilet was at the other end of the long corridor with the spinach-green classroom doors. Racing against time, Bastian ran as fast as he could and just made it.

As he sat there, he wondered why heroes in stories like the one he was reading never had to worry about such problems. Once – when he was much younger – he had asked his religion teacher if Jesus Christ had had to go like an ordinary person. After all, he had taken food and drink like everyone else. The class had howled with laughter, and the teacher, instead of an answer, had given him several demerits for 'insolence'. He hadn't meant to be insolent.

'Probably,' Bastian now said to himself, 'these things are just too unimportant to be mentioned in stories.'

Yet for him they could be of the most pressing and embarrassing importance.

He was finished. He pulled the chain and was about to leave when he heard steps in the corridor outside. One classroom door after another was opened and closed, and the steps came closer and closer.

Bastian's heart pounded in his throat. Where could he hide? He stood glued to the spot as though paralyzed.

The washroom door opened, luckily in such a way as to shield Bastian. The janitor came in. One by one, he looked into the stalls. When he came to the one where the water was still running and the chain swaying a little, he hesitated for a moment and mumbled something to himself. But when the water stopped running he shrugged his shoulders and went out. His steps died away on the stairs.

Bastian hadn't dared breathe the whole time, and now he gasped for air. He noticed that his knees were trembling.

As fast as possible he padded down the corridor with the spinach-green doors, up the stairs, and back into the attic. Only when the door was locked and bolted behind him did he relax.

With a deep sigh he settled back on his pile of mats, wrapped himself in his army blankets, and reached for the book.

When Atreyu awoke for the second time, he felt perfectly rested and well. He sat up.

It was night. The moon was shining bright, and Atreyu saw he was in the same place where he and the white dragon had collapsed. Falkor was still lying there. His breathing came deep and easy and he seemed to be fast asleep. His wounds had been dressed.

Atreyu noticed that his own shoulder had been dressed in the same way, not with cloth but with herbs and plant fibers.

Only a few steps away there was a small cave, from which issued a faint beam of light.

Taking care not to move his left arm, Atreyu stood up cautiously and approached the cave. Bending down – for the entrance was very low – he saw a room that looked like an alchemist's workshop in miniature. At the back an open fire was crackling merrily. Crucibles, retorts, and strangely shaped flasks were scattered all about. Bundles of dried plants were piled on shelves. The little table in the middle of the room and the other furniture seemed to be made of root wood, crudely nailed together.

Atreyu heard a cough, and then he saw a little man sitting in an armchair by the fire. The little man's hat had been carved from a root and looked like an inverted pipe bowl. The face was as brown and shriveled as the face Atreyu had seen leaning over him when he first woke up. But this one was wearing big eyeglasses, and the features seemed sharper and more anxious. The little man was reading a big book that was lying in his lap.

Then a second little figure, which Atreyu recognized as the one that had bent over him, came waddling out of another room. Now Atreyu saw that this little person was a woman. Apart from her bonnet of leaves, she – like the man in the armchair – was wearing a kind of monk's robe, which also seemed to be made of withered leaves. Humming merrily, she rubbed her hands and busied herself with a kettle that was hanging over the fire. Neither of the little people would have reached up to Atreyu's knee. Obviously they belonged to the widely ramified family of the gnomes, though to a rather obscure branch.

'Woman!' said the little man testily. 'Get out of my light. You are interfering with my research!'

'You and your research!' said the woman. 'Who cares about that? The important thing is my health elixir. Those two outside are in urgent need of it.'

'Those two,' said the man irritably, 'will be far more in need of my help and advice.'

'Maybe so,' said the little woman. 'But not until they are well. Move over, old man!'

Grumbling, the little man moved his chair a short distance from the fire.

Atreyu cleared his throat to call attention to his presence. The two gnomes looked around.

'He's already well,' said the little man. 'Now it's my turn.'

'Certainly not!' the little woman hissed. 'He'll be well when I say so. It'll be your turn when I say it's your turn.'

She turned to Atreyu.

'We would invite you in, but it's not quite big enough, is it? Just a moment. We shall come out to you.'

Taking a small mortar, she ground something or other into a powder, which she tossed in the kettle. Then she washed her hands, dried them on her robe, and said to the little man: 'Stay here until I call you, Engywook. Understand?'

'Yes, Urgl, I understand,' the little man grumbled. 'I understand only too well.'

The female gnome came out of the cave and looked up at Atreyu from under knitted brows.

'Well, well. We seem to be getting better, don't we?'

Atreyu nodded.

The gnome climbed up on a rocky ledge, level with Atreyu's face, and sat down.

'No pain?' she asked.

'None worth mentioning,' Atreyu answered.

'Nonsense!' the old woman snapped. 'Does it hurt or doesn't it?'

'It still hurts,' said Atreyu, 'but it doesn't matter.'

'Not to you, perhaps, but it does to me! Since when does the patient tell the doctor what matters? What do you know about it? If it's to get well, it *has to* hurt. If it stopped hurting, your arm would be dead.'

'I'm sorry,' said Atreyu, who felt like a scolded child. 'I only wanted to say ... that is, I wanted to thank you.'

'What for?' said Urgl impatiently. 'I'm a healer, after all. I've only done my professional duty. Besides, Engywook, that's my old man, saw the Glory hanging on your neck. So what would you expect?'

'What about Falkor?' Atreyu asked. 'How's he getting along?'

'Falkor? Who's that?'

'The white luckdragon.'

'Oh. I don't know yet. Took a little more punishment than you. But then he's bigger and stronger, so he ought to make it. Why not? Needs a little more rest. Where did you ever pick up that poison? And where have you come from all of a sudden? And where are you going? And who are you in the first place?'

Engywook was standing in the mouth of the cave. He listened as Atreyu answered Urgl's questions. When Urgl opened her mouth to speak again, he shouted: 'Hold your tongue, woman! Now it's my turn.'

Removing his pipe-bowl hat, he scratched his bald head, and said: 'Don't let her tone bother you, Atreyu. Old Urgl is a little crude, but she means no harm. My name is Engywook. We are the well-known Gnomics. Ever hear of us?'

'No,' Atreyu confessed.

Engywook seemed rather offended.

'Oh well,' he said. 'Apparently you don't move in scientific circles, or someone would undoubtedly have told you that you couldn't find a better adviser than yours truly if you're looking for Uyulala in the Southern Oracle. You've come to the right address, my boy.'

'Don't give yourself airs,' Urgl broke in. Then she climbed down from her ledge and, grumbling to herself, vanished into the cave.

Engywook ignored her comment.

'I can explain everything,' he went on. 'I've studied the question all my life. Inside and out. I set up my observatory just for that. I'm in the last stage of a great scientific work on the Oracle. "The Riddle of Uyulala, solved by Professor Engywook." That's the title. Sounds all right, doesn't it? To be published in the very near future. Unfortunately a few details are still lacking. You can help me, my boy.'

'An observatory?' asked Atreyu, who had never heard the word.

Engywook nodded and, beaming with pride, motioned Atreyu to follow him.

A narrow path twined its way upward between great stone blocks. In some places where the grade was especially steep, tiny steps had been cut out of the stone. Of course, they were much too small for Atreyu's feet and he simply stepped over them. Even so, he had a hard time keeping up with the gnome.

'Bright moonlight tonight,' said Engywook. 'You'll see them all right.'

'See who?' Atreyu asked. 'Uyulala?'

Engywook only frowned and shook his head.

At last they came to the top of the hill. The ground was flat, but on one side there was a natural stone parapet. In the middle of this wall there was a hole, obviously the work of gnomian hands. And behind the hole, on a stand made of root wood, stood a small telescope.

Engywook looked through the telescope and made a slight adjustment by turning some screws. Then he nodded with satisfaction and invited Atreyu to look. To put himself on a level with it, Atreyu had to lie down on the ground and prop himself on his elbows.

The telescope was aimed at the great stone arch, or more specifically at the lower part of the left pillar. And beside this pillar, as Atreyu now saw, an enormous sphinx was sitting motionless in the moonlight. The forepaws, on which she was propped, were those of a lion, the hindquarters were those of a bull; on her back she bore the wings of an eagle, and her face was that of a human woman – in form at any rate, for the expression was far from human. It was hard to tell whether this face was smiling or whether it expressed deep grief or utter indifference. After looking at it for some time, Atreyu seemed to see abysmal wickedness and cruelty, but a moment later he had to correct his impression, for he found only unruffled calm.

'Don't bother!' he heard the gnome's deep voice in his ear. 'You won't solve it. It's the same with everyone. I've observed it all my life and I haven't found the answer. Now for the other one.'

He turned one of the screws. The image passed the opening of the arch, through which one saw only the empty plain. Then the right-hand pillar came into Atreyu's view. And there, in the same posture, sat a second sphinx. The enormous body shimmered like liquid silver in the moonlight. She seemed to be staring fixedly at the first, just as the first was gazing fixedly at her.

'Are they statues?' asked Atreyu, unable to avert his eyes.

'Oh no!' said Engywook with a giggle. 'They are real live sphinxes – very much alive! You've seen enough for now. Come, we'll go down. I'll explain everything.'

And he held his hand in front of the telescope, so that Atreyu could see no more. Neither spoke on the way back.

VI

The Three Magic Gates

ALKOR was still sound asleep when Engywook brought Atreyu back
to the gnomes' cave. In the meantime Urgl had moved the little
table into the open and put on all sorts of sweets and fruit and
herb jellies.

There were also little drinking cups and a pitcher of fragrant
herb tea. The table was lit by two tiny oil lamps.

'Sit down!' Urgl commanded. 'Atreyu must eat and drink something to give him strength. Medicine alone is not enough.'

'Thank you,' said Atreyu. 'I'm feeling fine already.'

'No back talk!' Urgl snapped. 'As long as you're here, you'll do
as you're told. The poison in your body has been neutralized. So
there's no reason to hurry, my boy. You've all the time you need.
Just take it easy.'

'It's not on my account,' said Atreyu. 'But the Childlike Empress
is dying. Even now, every hour may count.'

'Rubbish!' the old woman grumbled. 'Haste makes waste. Sit
down! Eat! Drink!'

'Better give in,' Engywook whispered. 'I know the woman from
A to Z. When she wants something, she gets it. Besides, you and
I have a lot to talk about.'

Atreyu squatted cross-legged at the tiny table and fell to. Every
bite and every swallow made him feel as if warm, golden life were
flowing into his veins. Only then did he notice how weak he had
been.

*Bastian's mouth watered. It seemed to him that he could smell the aroma
of the gnomes' meal. He sniffed the air, but of course it was only imagination.*

*His stomach growled audibly. In the end he couldn't stand it any longer.
He took his apple and the rest of his sandwich out of his satchel and ate
them both. After that, though far from full, he felt a little better.*

*Then he realized that this was his last meal. The word 'last' terrified
him. He tried not to think of it.*

'Where do you get all these good things?' Atreyu asked Urgl.

'Ah, sonny,' she said. 'It takes lots of running around to find
the right plants. But he – this knuckleheaded Engywook of mine
– insists on living here because of his all-important studies. Where
the food is to come from is the least of his worries.'

'Woman,' said Engywook with dignity, 'how would you know what's important and what isn't? Be off with you now, and let us talk.'

Mumbling and grumbling, Urgl withdrew into the little cave and a moment later Atreyu heard a great clatter of pots and pans.

'Don't mind her,' said Engywook under his breath. 'She's a good old soul, she just needs something to grumble about now and then. Listen to me, Atreyu. I'm going to let you in on a few things you need to know about the Southern Oracle. It's not easy to get to Uyulala. In fact, it's rather difficult. But I don't want to give you a scientific lecture. Maybe it will be better if you ask questions. I tend to lose myself in details. Just fire away.'

'All right,' said Atreyu. 'Who or what is Uyulala?'

Engywook gave him an angry look. 'Botheration!' he spluttered. 'You're so blunt, so direct. Just like my old woman. Couldn't you start with something else?'

Atreyu thought a while. Then he asked: 'That big stone gate with the sphinxes. Is that the entrance?'

'That's better,' said Engywook. 'Now we'll get somewhere. Yes, that gate is the entrance, but then come two more gates. And Uyulala's home is behind the third – if one can speak of her having a home.'

'Have you yourself ever been with her?'

'Don't be absurd!' replied Engywook, again somewhat nettled. 'I am a scientist. I have collected and collated the statements of all the individuals who have been there. The ones who have come back, that is. Very important work. I can't afford to take personal risks. It could interfere with my work.'

'I see,' said Atreyu. 'Now what about these three gates?'

Engywook stood up, folded his hands behind his back, and paced.

'The first,' he lectured, 'is known as the Great Riddle Gate; the second is the Magic Mirror Gate; and the third is the No-Key Gate ...'

'Strange,' Atreyu broke in. 'As far as I could see, there was nothing behind that stone gate but an empty plain. Where are the other gates?'

'Be still!' Engywook scolded. 'How can I make myself clear if you keep interrupting? It's very complicated: The second gate isn't there until a person has gone through the first. And the third isn't there until the person has the second behind him. And Uyulala isn't there until he has passed through the third. Simply not there. Do you understand?'

Atreyu nodded, but preferred to say nothing for fear of irritating the gnome.

'Through my telescope you have seen the first, the Great Riddle Gate. And the two sphinxes. That gate is always open. Obviously. There's nothing to close. But even so, no one can get through' – here Engywook raised a tiny forefinger – 'unless the sphinxes close their eyes. And do you know why? The gaze of a sphinx is different from the gaze of any other creature. You and I and everyone else – our eyes take something in. We see the world. A sphinx sees nothing. In a sense she is blind. But her eyes send something out. And what do her eyes send out? All the riddles of the universe. That's why these sphinxes are always looking at each other. Because only another sphinx can stand a sphinx's gaze. So try to imagine what happens to one who ventures into the area where those two gazes meet. He freezes to the spot, unable to move until he has solved all the riddles of the world. If you go there, you'll find the remains of those poor devils.'

'But,' said Atreyu, 'didn't you say that their eyes sometimes close? Don't they have to sleep now and then?'

'Sleep?' Engywook was shaken with giggles. 'Goodness gracious! A sphinx sleep? I should say not. You really are an innocent. Still, there's some point to your question. All my research, in fact, hinges on that particular point. The sphinxes shut their eyes for some travelers and let them through. The question that no one has answered up until now is this: Why one traveler and not another? Because you mustn't suppose they let wise, brave, or good people through, and keep the stupid, cowardly, and wicked out. Not a bit of it! With my own eyes I've seen them admit stupid fools and treacherous knaves, while decent, sensible people have given up after being kept waiting for months. And it seems to make no difference whether a person has some serious reason for consulting the Oracle, or whether he's just come for the fun of it.'

'Haven't your investigations suggested some explanation?' Atreyu asked.

Angry flashes darted from Engywook's eyes.

'Have you been listening or haven't you? Didn't I just say that so far no one has answered that question? Of course, I've worked up a few theories over the years. At first I thought the sphinxes' judgment might be guided by certain physical characteristics – size, beauty, strength, and so on. But I soon had to drop that idea. Then I toyed with numerical patterns. The idea, for instance, that three out of five were regularly excluded, or that only prime-numbered candidates were admitted. That worked pretty well for the past, but for forecasting it was no use at all. Since then I've come to the conclusion that the sphinxes' decision is based on pure chance and that no principle whatever is involved. But my wife calls my conclusion scandalous, un-Fantastican, and absolutely unscientific.'

'Are you starting your old nonsense again?' came Urgl's angry voice from the cave. 'Shame on you! Such skepticism only shows that the bit of brain you once had has dried up on you.'

'Hear that?' said Engywook with a sigh. 'And the worst of it is that she's right.'

'What about the Childlike Empress's amulet?' Atreyu asked. 'Do you think they'll respect it? They too are natives of Fantastica, after all.'

'Yes, I suppose they are,' said Engywook, shaking his apple-sized head. 'But to respect it they'd have to *see* it. And they don't see anything. But their gaze would strike you. And I'm not so sure the sphinxes would obey the Childlike Empress. Maybe they are greater than she is. I don't know, I don't know. Anyway, it's most worrisome.'

'Then what do you advise?' Atreyu asked.

'You will have to do what all the others have done. Wait and see what the sphinxes decide – without hoping to know why.'

Atreyu nodded thoughtfully.

Urgl came out of the cave. In one hand she held a bucket with some steaming liquid in it, and under her other arm she was carrying a bundle of dried plants. Muttering to herself, she went to the luckdragon, who was still lying motionless, fast asleep. She started climbing around on him and changing the dressings on his wounds. Her enormous patient heaved one contented sigh and stretched; otherwise he seemed unaware of her ministrations.

'Couldn't you make yourself a little useful?' she said to Engywook as she was hurrying back to the kitchen, 'instead of sitting around like this, talking rubbish?'

'I am making myself *extremely* useful,' her husband called after her. 'Possibly more useful than you, but that's more than a simple-minded woman like you will ever understand!'

Turning to Atreyu, he went on: 'She can only think of practical matters. She has no feeling for the great overarching ideas.'

The clock in the belfry struck three.

By now Bastian's father must have noticed – if he was ever going to – that Bastian hadn't come home. Would he worry? Maybe he'd go looking for him. Maybe he had already notified the police. Maybe calls had gone out over the radio. Bastian felt a sick pain in the pit of his stomach.

But if the police had been notified, where would they look for him? Could they possibly come to this attic?

Had he locked the door when he came back from the toilet? He couldn't remember. He got up and checked. Yes, the door was locked and bolted.

Outside, the November afternoon was drawing to a close. Ever so slowly the light was failing.

To steady his nerves, Bastian paced the floor for a while. Looking about him, he discovered quite a few things one wouldn't have expected to find in a school. For instance, a battered old Victrola with a big horn attached – God only knew when and by whom it had been brought here. In one corner there were some paintings in ornate gilt frames. They were so faded that hardly anything could be made out – only here and there a pale, solemn-looking face that shimmered against a dark background. And then there was a rusty, seven-armed candelabrum, still holding the stumps of thick wax candles, bearded with drippings.

Bastian gave a sudden start, for looking into a dark corner he saw some-one moving. But when he looked again, it dawned on him that he had only seen himself, reflected in a large mirror that had lost half its silvering. He

*went closer and looked at himself for a while. He was really nothing much
to look at, with his pudgy build and his bowlegs and pasty face. He shook
his head and said aloud: 'No!'*

*Then he went back to his mats. By then it was so dark that he had to
hold the book up to his eyes.*

'Where were we?' Engywook asked.

'At the Great Riddle Gate,' Atreyu reminded him.

'Right. Now suppose you've managed to get through. Then –
and only then – the second gate will be there for you. The Magic
Mirror Gate. As I've said, I myself have not been able to observe
it, what I tell you has been gleaned from travelers' accounts. This
second gate is both open and closed. Sounds crazy, doesn't it? It
might be better to say: neither closed nor open. Though that doesn't
make it any less crazy. The point is that this gate seems to be a
big mirror or something of the kind, though it's made neither of
glass nor of metal. What it is made of, no one has ever been able
to tell me. Anyway, when you stand before it, you see yourself.
But not as you would in an ordinary mirror. You don't see your
outward appearance; what you see is your real innermost nature.
If you want to go through, you have to – in a manner of speaking
– go into yourself.'

'Well,' said Atreyu. 'It seems to me that this Magic Mirror Gate
is easier to get through than the first.'

'Wrong!' cried Engywook. Once again he began to trot back and
forth in agitation. 'Dead wrong, my friend! I've known travelers
who considered themselves absolutely blameless to yelp with horror
and run away at the sight of the monster grinning out of the mirror
at them. We had to care for some of them for weeks before they
were even able to start home.'

'We!' growled Urgl, who was passing with another bucket. 'I
keep hearing "we". When did *you* ever take care of anybody?'

Engywook waved her away.

'Others,' he went on lecturing, 'appear to have seen something
even more horrible, but had the courage to go through. What some
saw was not so frightening, but it still cost every one of them an
inner struggle. Nothing I can say would apply to all. It's a different
experience each time.'

'Good,' said Atreyu. 'Then at least it's *possible* to go through this Magic Mirror Gate?'

'Oh yes, of course it's possible, or it wouldn't be a gate. Where's your logic, my boy?'

'But it's also possible to go around it,' said Atreyu. 'Or isn't it?'

'Yes indeed,' said Engywook. 'Of course it is. But if you do that, there's nothing more behind it. The third gate isn't there until you've gone through the second. How often do I have to tell you that?'

'I understand. But what about this third gate?'

'That's where things get really difficult! Because, you see, the No-Key Gate is closed. Simply closed. And that's that! There's no handle and no doorknob and no keyhole. Nothing. My theory is that this single, hermetically closed door is made of Fantastican selenium. You may know that there's no way of destroying, bending or dissolving Fantastican selenium. It's absolutely indestructible.'

'Then there's no way of getting through?'

'Not so fast. Not so fast, my boy. Certain individuals have got through and spoken with Uyulala. So the door can be opened.'

'But how?'

'Just listen. Fantastican selenium reacts to our will. It's our will that makes it unyielding. But if someone succeeds in forgetting all purpose, in wanting nothing at all – to him the gate will open of its own accord.'

Atreyu looked down and said in an undertone: 'If that's the case – how can I possibly get through? How can I manage not to *want* to get through?'

Engywook sighed and nodded, nodded and sighed.

'Just what I've been saying. The No-Key Gate is the hardest.'

'But if I succeed after all,' Atreyu asked, 'will I then be in the Southern Oracle?'

'Yes,' said the gnome.

'But who or what is Uyulala?'

'No idea,' said the gnome, and his eyes sparkled with fury. 'None of those who have reached her has been willing to tell me. How can I be expected to complete my scientific work if everyone cloaks himself in mysterious silence? I could tear my hair out – if I had any left. If you reach her, Atreyu, will you tell me? Will you? One of these days my thirst for knowledge will be the death of me, and no one, no one is willing to help. I beg you, promise you'll tell me.'

Atreyu stood up and looked at the Great Riddle Gate, which lay bathed in moonlight.

'I can't promise that, Engywook,' he said softly, 'though I'd be glad to show my gratitude. But if no one has told you who or what Uyulala is, there must be a reason. And before I know what that reason is, I can't decide whether someone who hasn't seen her with his own eyes has a right to know.'

'In that case, get away from me!' screamed the gnome, his eyes literally spewing sparks. 'All I get is ingratitude! All my life I wear myself out trying to reveal a secret of universal interest. And no one helps me. I should never have bothered with you.'

With that he ran into the little cave, and a door could be heard slamming within.

Urgl passed Atreyu and said with a titter: 'The old fool means no harm. But he's always running into such disappointments with this ridiculous investigation of his. He wants to go down in history as the one who has solved the great riddle. The world-famous gnome Engywook. You mustn't mind him.'

'Of course not,' said Atreyu. 'Just tell him I thank him with all my heart for what he has done for me. And I thank you too. If it's allowed, I will tell him the secret – if I come back.'

'Then you're leaving us?' Urgl asked.

'I have to,' said Atreyu. 'There's no time to be lost. Now I shall go to the Oracle. Farewell! And in the meantime take good care of Falkor, the luckdragon.'

With that he turned away and strode toward the Great Riddle Gate.

Urgl watched the erect figure with the blowing cloak vanish among the rocks and ran after him, crying: 'Lots of luck, Atreyu!'

But she didn't know whether he had heard or not. As she waddled back to her little cave, she muttered to herself: 'He'll need it all right – he'll need lots of luck.'

Atreyu was now within fifty feet of the great stone gate. It was

much larger than he had judged from a distance. Behind it lay a
deserted plain. There was nothing to stop the eye, and Atreyu's
gaze seemed to plunge into an abyss of emptiness. In front of the
gate and between the two pillars Atreyu saw only innumerable
skulls and skeletons – all that was left of the varied species of
Fantasticans who had tried to pass through the gate but had been
frozen forever by the gaze of the sphinxes.

But it wasn't these gruesome reminders that stopped Atreyu. What
stopped him was the sight of the sphinxes.

He had been through a good deal in the course of the Great
Quest – he had seen beautiful things and horrible things – but up
until now he had not known that one and the same creature can
be both, that beauty can be terrifying.

The two monsters were bathed in moonlight, and as Atreyu
approached them, they seemed to grow beyond measure. Their
heads seemed to touch the moon, and their expression as they looked
at each other seemed to change with every step he took. Currents
of a terrible, unknown force flashed through the upraised bodies
and still more through the almost human faces. It was as though
these beings did not merely exist, in the way marble for instance
exists, but as if they were on the verge of vanishing, but would re-
create themselves at the same time. For that very reason they seemed
far more real than anything made of stone.

Fear gripped Atreyu.

Fear not so much of the danger that threatened him as of something above and beyond his own self. It hardly grazed his mind
that if the sphinxes' gaze should strike him he would freeze to the
spot forever. No, what made his steps heavier and heavier, until
he felt as though he were made of cold gray lead, was fear of the
unfathomable, of something intolerably vast.

Yet he went on. He stopped looking up. He kept his head bowed
and walked very slowly, foot by foot, towards the stone gate. Heavier
and heavier grew his burden of fear. He thought it would crush
him, but still he went on. He didn't know whether the sphinxes
had closed their eyes or not. Would he be admitted? Or would this
be the end of his Great Quest? He had no time to lose in worrying.
He just had to take his chances.

At a certain point he felt sure that he had not enough will power left to carry him a single step forward. And just then he heard the echo of his footfalls within the great vaulted gate. Instantly every last shred of fear fell from him, and he knew that whatever might happen he would never again be afraid.

Looking up, he saw that the Great Riddle Gate lay behind him. The sphinxes had let him through.

Up ahead, no more than twenty paces away, where previously there had been nothing but the great empty plain, he saw the Magic Mirror Gate. This gate was large and round like a second moon (for the real moon was still shining high in the sky) and it glittered like polished silver. It was hard to imagine how anyone could pass through a metal surface, but Atreyu didn't hesitate for a moment. After what Engywook had said, he expected a terrifying image of himself to come toward him out of the mirror, but now that he had left all fear behind him, he hardly gave the matter a thought.

What he saw was something quite unexpected, which wasn't the least bit terrifying, but which baffled him completely. He saw a fat little boy with a pale face – a boy his own age – and this little boy was sitting on a pile of mats, reading a book. The little boy had large, sad-looking eyes, and he was wrapped in frayed gray blankets. Behind him a few motionless animals could be distinguished in the half-light – an eagle, an owl, and a fox – and farther off there was something that looked like a white skeleton. He couldn't make out exactly what it was.

Bastian gave a start when he realized what he had just read. Why, that was him! The description was right in every detail. The book trembled in his hands. This was going too far. How could there be something in a book that applied only to this particular moment and only to him? It could only be a crazy accident. But a very remarkable accident.

'Bastian,' he said aloud, 'you really are a screwball. Pull yourself together.'

He had meant to say this very sternly, but his voice quavered a little, for he was not quite sure that what had happened was an accident.

Just imagine, he thought. What if they've really heard of me in Fantastica! Wouldn't that be wonderful?

But he didn't dare say it aloud.

A faint smile of astonishment played over Atreyu's lips as he passed into the mirror image – he was rather surprised that he was succeeding so easily in something that others had found insuperably difficult. But on the way through he felt a strange, prickly shudder. He had no suspicion of what had really happened to him.

For when he emerged on the far side of the Magic Mirror Gate, he had lost all memory of himself, of his past life, aims, and purposes. He had forgotten the Great Quest that had brought him there, and he didn't even know his own name. He was like a newborn child.

Up ahead of him, only a few steps away, he saw the No-Key Gate, but he had forgotten its name and forgotten that his purpose in passing through it was to reach the Southern Oracle. He had no idea why he was there or what he was supposed to do. He felt light and cheerful and he laughed for no reason, for the sheer pleasure of it.

The gate he saw before him was as small and low as a common door and stood all by itself – with no walls around it – on the empty plain. And this door was closed.

Atreyu looked at it for a while. It seemed to be made of some material with a coppery sheen. It was nice to look at, but Atreyu soon lost interest. He went around the gate and examined it from behind, but the back looked no different than the front. And there was neither handle nor knob nor keyhole. Obviously this door could not be opened, and anyway why would anyone want to open it, since it led nowhere and was just standing there. For behind the gate there was only the wide, flat, empty plain.

Atreyu felt like leaving. He turned back, went around the Magic Mirror Gate, and looked at it for some time without realizing what it was. He decided to go away,

'No, no, don't go away,' said Bastian aloud. 'Turn around. You have to go through the No-Key Gate!'

but then turned back to the No-Key Gate. He wanted to look at its coppery sheen again. Once more, he stood in front of the gate, bending his head to the left, bending it to the right, enjoying himself. Tenderly he stroked the strange material. It felt warm and almost alive. And the door opened by a crack.

Atreyu stuck his head through, and then he saw something he hadn't seen on the other side when he had walked around the gate. He pulled his head back, looked past the gate, and saw only the empty plain. He looked again through the crack in the door and saw a long corridor formed by innumerable huge columns. And farther off there were stairs and more pillars and terraces and more stairs and a whole forest of columns. But none of these columns supported a roof. For above them Atreyu could see the night sky.

He passed through the gate and looked around him with wonderment. The door closed behind him.

The clock in the belfry struck four.

Little by little, the murky light was failing. It was getting too dark to read by. Bastian put the book down.

What was he to do now?

There was bound to be electric light in this attic. He groped his way to the door and ran his hand along the wall, but couldn't find a switch. He looked on the opposite side, and again there was none.

He took a box of matches from his trouser pocket (he always had matches on him, for he had a weakness for making little fires), but they were damp and the first three wouldn't light. In the faint glow of the fourth he tried to locate a light switch, but there wasn't any. The thought of having to spend the whole evening and night here in total darkness gave him the cold shivers. He was no baby, and at home or in any other familiar place he had no fear of the dark, but this enormous attic with all these weird things in it was something else again.

The match burned his fingers and he threw it away.

For a while he just stood there and listened. The rain had let up and now he could barely hear the drumming on the big tin roof.

Then he remembered the rusty, seven-armed candelabrum he had seen. He groped his way across the room, found the candelabrum, and dragged it to his pile of mats.

He lit the wicks in the thick stubs – all seven – and a golden light spread. The flames crackled faintly and wavered now and then in the draft.

With a sigh of relief, Bastian picked up the book.

VII

The Voice of Silence

LADNESS buoyed Atreyu's heart as he strode into the forest of columns which cast black shadows in the bright moonlight. In the deep silence that surrounded him he barely heard his own footfalls. He no longer knew who he was or what his name was, how he had got there or what he was looking for. He was full of wonder, but quite undismayed.

The floor was made of mosaic tiles, showing strange ornamental designs or mysterious scenes and images. Atreyu passed over it, climbed broad steps, came to a vast terrace, descended another set of steps, and passed down a long avenue of stone columns. He examined them, one after another, and it gave him pleasure to see that each was decorated with different signs and symbols. Farther and farther he went from the No-Key Gate.

At last, when he had gone heaven knows how far, he heard a hovering sound in the distance and stopped to listen. The sound came closer, it was a singing voice, but it seemed very, very sad, almost like a sob at times. This lament passed over the columns like a breeze, then stopped in one place, rose and fell, came and went, and seemed to move in a wide circle around Atreyu.

He stood still and waited.

Little by little, the circle became smaller, and after a while he was able to understand the words the voice was singing:

> 'Oh, nothing can happen more than once,
> But all things must happen one day.
> Over hill and dale, over wood and stream,
> My dying voice will blow away ...'

Atreyu turned in the direction of the voice, which darted fitfully among the columns, but he could see no one.

'Who are you?' he cried.

The voice came back to him like an echo: 'Who are you?'

Atreyu pondered.

'Who am I?' he murmured. 'I don't know. I have a feeling that I once knew. But does it matter?'

The singing voice answered:

> 'If questions you would ask of me,
> You must speak in poetry,

> For rhymeless talk that strikes my ear
> I cannot hear, I cannot hear ...'

Atreyu hadn't much practice in rhyming. This would be a difficult conversation, he thought, if the voice only understood poetry. He racked his brains for a while, then he came out with:

> 'I hope it isn't going too far,
> But could you tell me who you are?'

This time the voice answered at once:

> 'I hear you now, your words are clear,
> I understand as well as hear.'

And then, coming from a different direction, it sang:

> 'I thank you, friend, for your good will.
> I'm glad that you have come to me.
> I am Uyulala, the voice of silence.
> In the Palace of Deep Mystery.'

Atreyu noticed that the voice rose and fell, but was never wholly silent. Even when it sang no words or when he was speaking, a sound hovered in the air.

For a time it seemed to stand still; then it moved slowly away from him. He ran after it and asked:

> 'Oh, Uyulala, tell me where you're hid.
> I cannot see you and so wish I did.'

Passing him by, the voice breathed into his ear:

> 'Never has anyone seen me,
> Never do I appear.
> You will never see me,
> And yet I am here.'

'Then you're invisible?' he asked. But when no answer came, he remembered that he had to speak in rhyme, and asked:

> 'Have you no body, is that what you mean?
> Or is it only that you can't be seen?'

He heard a soft, bell-like sound, which might have been a laugh or a sob. And the voice sang:

> 'Yes and no and neither one.
> I do not appear
> In the brightness of the sun
> As you appear,
> For my body is but sound
> That one can hear but never see,
> And this voice you're hearing now
> Is all there is of me.'

In amazement, Atreyu followed the sound this way and that way through the forest of columns. It took him some time to get a new question ready:

> 'Do I understand you right?
> Your body is this melody?
> But what if you should cease to sing?
> Would you cease to be?'

The answer came to him from very near:

> 'Once my song is ended,
> What comes to others soon or late,
> When their bodies pass away,
> Will also be my fate.
> My life will last the time of my song,
> But that will not be long.'

Now it seemed certain that the voice was sobbing, and Atreyu, who could not understand why, hastened to ask:

> 'Why are you so sad? Why are you crying?
> You sound so young. Why speak of dying?'

And the voice came back like an echo:

> 'I am only a song of lament,
> The wind will blow me away.
> But tell me now why your were sent.
> What have you come to say?'

The voice died away among the columns, and Atreyu turned in all directions, trying to pick it up again. For a little while he heard nothing, then, starting in the distance, the voice came quickly closer. It sounded almost impatient:

> 'Uyulala is answer. Answers on questions feed.
> So ask me what you've come to ask,
> For questions are her need.'

Atreyu cried out:

> 'Then help me, Uyulala, tell me why
> You sing a plaint as if you soon must die.'

And the voice sang:

> 'The Childlike Empress is sick,
> And with her Fantastica will die.
> The Nothing will swallow this place,
> It will perish and so will I.
> We shall vanish into the Nowhere and Never,
> As though we had never been.
> The Empress needs a new name
> To make her well again.'

Atreyu pleaded:

> 'Oh, tell me, Uyulala, oh, tell me who can give
> The Childlike Empress the name, which alone
> will let her live.'

The voice replied:

> 'Listen and listen well
> To the truth I have to tell.
> Though your spirit may be blind
> To the sense of what I say,
> Print my words upon your mind
> Before you go away.
> Later you may dredge them up
> From the depths of memory,
> Raise them to the light of day
> Exactly as they flow from me.
> Everything depends on whether
> You remember faithfully.'

For a time he heard only a plaintive sound without words. Then suddenly the voice came from right next to him, as though someone were whispering into his ear:

'Who can give the Childlike Empress
The new name that will make her well?
Not you, not I, no elf, no djinn,
Can save us from the evil spell.
For we are figures in a book —
We do what we were invented for,
But we can fashion nothing new
And cannot change from what we are.
But there's a realm outside Fantastica,
The Outer World is its name,
The people who live there are rich indeed
And not at all the same.
Born of the Word, the children of man,
Or humans, as they're sometimes called,
Have had the gift of giving names
Ever since our worlds began,
In every age it's they who gave
The Childlike Empress life,
For wondrous new names have the power to save.
But now for many and many a day,
No human has visited Fantastica,
For they no longer know the way.
They have forgotten how real we are,
They don't believe in us anymore.
Oh, if only one child of man would come,
Oh, then at last the thing would be done.
If only one would hear our plea.
For them it is near, but for us too far,
Never can we go out to them,
For theirs is the world of reality.
But tell me, my hero, you so young,
Will you remember what I have sung?'

'Oh yes!' cried Atreyu in his bewilderment. He was determined to imprint every word on his memory, though he had forgotten what for. He merely had a feeling that it was very, very important.

But the singsong voice and the effort of hearing and speaking in rhymes made him sleepy. He murmured:

'I will remember. I will remember every word.
But tell me, what shall I do with what I've heard?'

And the voice answered:

'That is for you alone to decide.
I've told you what was in my heart.
So this is when our ways divide,
When you and I must part.'

Almost half asleep, Atreyu asked:

'But if you go away,
Where will you stay?'

Again he heard the sobbing in the voice, which receded more and more as it sang:

'The Nothing has come near,
The Oracle is dying.
No one again will hear
Uyulala laughing, sighing.
You are the last to hear
My voice among the columns,
Sounding far and near.
Perhaps you will accomplish
What no one else has done,
But to succeed, young hero,
Remember what I have sung.'

And then, farther and farther in the distance, Atreyu heard the words:

'Oh, nothing can happen more than once,
But all things must happen one day.
Over hill and dale, over wood and stream,
My dying voice will blow away.'

That was the last Atreyu heard.

He sat down, propped his back against a column, looked up at the night sky, and tried to understand what he had heard. Silence settled around him like a soft, warm cloak, and he fell asleep.

When he awoke in the cold dawn, he was lying on his back, looking up at the sky. The last stars paled. Uyulala's voice still sounded in his thoughts. And then suddenly he remembered everything that had gone before and the purpose of his Great Quest.

At last he knew what was to be done. Only a human, a child of man, someone from the world beyond the borders of Fantastica, could give the Childlike Empress a new name. He would just have to find a human and bring him to her.

Briskly he sat up.

Ah, thought Bastian. How gladly I would help her! Her and Atreyu too. What a beautiful name I would think up! If I only knew how to reach Atreyu. I'd go this minute. Wouldn't he be amazed if I were suddenly standing before him! But it's impossible. Or is it?

And then he said under his breath: 'If there's any way of my getting to you in Fantastica, tell me, Atreyu. I'll come without fail. You'll see.'

When Atreyu looked around, he saw that the forest of columns with its stairways and terraces had vanished. Whichever way he looked there was only the empty plain that he had seen behind each of the three gates before going through. But now the gates were gone, all three of them.

He stood up and again looked in all directions. It was then that he discovered, in the middle of the plain, a patch of Nothing like those he had seen in Howling Forest. But this time it was much nearer. He turned around and ran the other way as fast as he could.

He had been running for some time when he saw, far in the distance, a rise in the ground and thought it might be the stony rust-red mountains where the Great Riddle Gate was.

He started toward it, but he had a long way to go before he was close enough to make out any details. Then he began to have doubts. The landscape looked about right, but there was no gate to be seen. And the stones were not red, but dull gray.

Then, when he had gone much farther, he saw two great stone pillars with a space between them. The lower part of a gate, he thought. But there was no arch above it. What had happened?

Hours later, he reached the spot and discovered the answer. The great stone arch had collapsed and the sphinxes were gone.

Atreyu threaded his way through the ruins, then climbed to the top of a stone pyramid and looked out, trying to locate the place where he had left the Gnomics and the luckdragon. Or had they fled from the Nothing in the meantime?

At last he saw a tiny flag moving this way and that behind the balustrade of Engywook's observatory. Atreyu waved both arms, cupped his hands around his mouth, and shouted: 'Ho! Are you still there?'

The sound of his voice had hardly died away when a pearly-white luckdragon rose from the hollow where the gnomes had their cave and flew through the air with lazy, sinuous movements. He must have been feeling playful, for now and then he turned over on his back and looped-the-loop so fast that he looked like a burst of white flame. And then he landed not far from the pyramid where Atreyu was standing. When he propped himself on his forepaws, he was so high above Atreyu that to bring his head close to him, he had to bend his long, supple neck sharply downward. Rolling his ruby-red eyeballs for joy, stretching his tongue far out of his wide-open gullet, he boomed in his bronze-bell voice: 'Atreyu, my friend and master! So you've finally come back! I'm so glad! We had almost given up hope – the gnomes, that is, not I.'

'I'm glad too!' said Atreyu. 'But what has happened in this one night?'

'One night?' cried Falkor. 'Do you think it's been only one night? You're in for a surprise. Climb on, I'll carry you.'

Atreyu swung himself up on the enormous animal's back. It was his first time aboard a luckdragon. And though he had ridden wild horses and was anything but timid, this first short ride through the air took his breath away. He clung fast to Falkor's flowing mane, and Falkor called back with a resounding laugh: 'You'll just have to get used to it.'

'At least,' Atreyu called back, gasping for air, 'you seem to be well again.'

'Pretty near,' said the dragon. 'Not quite.'

Then they landed outside the gnomes' cave, and there in the entrance were Engywook and Urgl waiting for them.

Engywook's tongue went right to work: 'What have you seen and done? Tell us all about it! Those gates, for instance? Do they bear out my theories? And who or what is Uyulala?'

But Urgl cut him off. 'That'll do! Let the boy eat and drink. What do you think I've cooked and baked for? Plenty of time later for your idle curiosity.'

Atreyu climbed down off the dragon's back and exchanged greetings with the gnomes. Again the little table was set with all sorts of delicacies and a steaming pot of herb tea.

The clock in the belfry struck five. Bastian thought sadly of the two chocolate nut bars that he kept in his bedside table at home in case he should be hungry at night. If he had suspected that he would never go back there, he could have brought them along as an iron ration. But it was too late to think of that now.

Falkor stretched out in the little gully in such a way that his huge head was near Atreyu and he could hear everything.

'Just imagine,' he said. 'My friend and master thinks he was gone for only one night.'

'Was it longer?' Atreyu asked.

'Seven days and seven nights,' said Falkor. 'Look, my wounds are almost healed.'

Then for the first time Atreyu noticed that his own wound too was healed. The herb dressing had fallen off. He was amazed. 'How can it be? I passed through three magic gates. I talked with Uyulala, then I fell asleep. But I can't possibly have slept that long.'

'Space and time,' said Engywook, 'must be different in there. Anyway, no one had ever stayed in the Oracle as long as you. What happened? Are you finally going to speak?'

'First,' said Atreyu, 'I'd like to know what has happened here.'

'You can see for yourself,' said Engywook. 'The colors are all fading. Everything is getting more and more unreal. The Great Riddle Gate isn't there anymore. It looks as if the Nothing were taking over.'

'What about the sphinxes? Where have they gone? Did they fly away? Did you see them go?'

'We saw nothing,' Engywook lamented. 'We hoped you could tell us something. Suddenly the stone gate was in ruins, but none of us saw or heard a thing. I even went over and examined the wreckage. And do you know what I found? The fragments are as old as the hills and overgrown with gray moss, as if they had been lying there for hundreds of years, as if the Great Riddle Gate had never existed.'

'It was there, though,' said Atreyu under his breath, 'because I went through it. And then I went through the Magic Mirror Gate and the No-Key Gate.'

And then Atreyu reported everything that had happened to him. Now he remembered every last detail.

As Atreyu told them his story, Engywook, who at first had impatiently demanded further information, became more and more subdued. And when Atreyu repeated almost word for word what Uyulala had told him, the gnome said nothing at all. His shriveled little face had taken on a look of deepest gloom.

'Well,' said Atreyu in conclusion. 'Now you know the secret. Uyulala is just a voice. She can only be heard. She *is* where she sings.'

For a time Engywook was silent. When he spoke, his voice was husky: 'You mean she *was*.'

'Yes,' said Atreyu. 'She herself said no one else would ever hear her speak. I was the last.'

Two little tears flowed down Engywook's wrinkled cheeks.

'All for nothing!' he croaked. 'My whole life work, all my research, my year-long observations. At last someone brings me the last stone for my scientific edifice, finally I'm in a position to complete my work, to write the last chapter – and it's absolutely futile and superfluous. It's no longer of the slightest interest to anyone, because the object under investigation has ceased to exist. There go my hopes. All shattered.'

He seemed to break into a fit of coughing, but actually he was shaken with sobs.

Moved to sympathy, Urgl stroked his bald little head and mumbled: 'Poor old Engywook! Poor old Engywook! Don't let it get you down. You'll find something else to occupy you.'

'Woman!' Engywook fumed at her. 'What you see before you is not a poor old Engywook, but a tragic figure.'

Once again he ran into the cave, and again a door was heard slamming within. Urgl shook her head and sighed. 'He means no harm,' she muttered. 'He's a good old sort. If only he weren't plumb crazy!'

When they had finished eating, Urgl stood up and said: 'I've got to pack now. We can't take much with us, but we will need a few things. I'd better hurry.'

'You're going away?' Atreyu asked.

Urgl nodded. 'We have no choice,' she said sadly. 'Where the Nothing takes hold, nothing grows. And now, my poor old man has no reason to stay. We'll just have to see how we make out. We'll find a place somewhere. But what about you? What are your plans?'

'I have to do as Uyulala told me,' said Atreyu. 'Try and find a human and take him to the Childlike Empress to give her a new name.'

'Where will you look for this human?' Urgl asked.

'I don't know,' said Atreyu. 'Somewhere beyond the borders of Fantastica.'

'We'll get there!' came Falkor's bell-like voice. 'I'll carry you. You'll see, we'll be lucky.'

'In that case,' Urgl grunted, 'you'd better get started.'

'Maybe we could give you a lift,' Atreyu suggested. 'For part of the way.'

'That's all I need,' said Urgl. 'You won't catch me gallivanting around in the air. A self-respecting gnome keeps his feet on the ground. Besides, you mustn't let us delay you. You have more important things to do – for us all.'

'But I want to show my gratitude,' said Atreyu.

'The best way of doing that is to get started and stop frittering the time away with useless jibber-jabber.'

'She's got something there,' said Falkor. 'Let's go, Atreyu.'

Atreyu swung himself up on the luckdragon's back. One last time he turned back and shouted: 'Goodbye!'

But Urgl was already inside the cave, packing.

When some hours later she and Engywook stepped out into the open, each was carrying an overloaded back-basket, and again they were busily quarreling. Off they waddled on their tiny, crooked legs, and never once looked back.

Later on, Engywook became very famous, in fact, he became the most famous gnome in the world, but not because of his scientific investigations. That, however, is another story and shall be told another time.

At the moment when the two gnomes were starting out, Atreyu was far away, whizzing through the skies of Fantastica on the back of Falkor, the white luckdragon.

Involuntarily Bastian looked up at the skylight, trying to imagine how it would be if Falkor came cutting through the darkening sky like a dancing white flame, if he and Atreyu were coming to get him.

'Oh my,' he sighed. 'Wouldn't that be something!'

He could help them, and they could help him. He would be saved and so would Fantastica.

VIII

The Wind Giants

IGH in the air rode Atreyu, his red cloak flowing behind him. His blue-black hair fluttered in the wind. With steady, wavelike movements Falkor, the white luckdragon, glided through the mists and tatters of clouds . . .

Up and down and up and down and up and down . . .

How long had they been flying? For days and nights and more days – Atreyu had lost track. The dragon had the gift of flying in his sleep. Farther and farther they flew. Sometimes Atreyu dozed off, clinging fast to the dragon's white mane. But it was only a light, restless sleep. And more and more his waking became a dream, all hazy and blurred.

Shadowy mountains passed below him, lands and seas, islands and rivers . . . Atreyu had lost interest in them, and gave up trying to hurry Falkor as he had done on first leaving the Southern Oracle. For then he had been impatient, thinking it a simple matter, for one with a dragon to ride, to reach the border of Fantastica and cross it to the Outer World.

He hadn't known how very large Fantastica was.

Now he had to fight the leaden weariness that was trying to overpower him. His eyes, once as keen as a young eagle's, had lost their distant vision. From time to time he would pull himself upright and try to look around, but then he would sink back and stare straight ahead at the dragon's long, supple body with its pearly pink-and-white scales. Falkor was tired too. His strength, which had seemed inexhaustible, was running out.

More than once in the course of their long flight they had seen below them spots which the Nothing had invaded and which gave them the feeling that they were going blind. Seen from that height, many of these spots seemed relatively small, but others were as big as whole countries. Fear gripped the luckdragon and his rider, and at first they changed direction to avoid looking at the horror. But, strange as it may seem, horror loses its power to frighten when repeated too often. And since the patches of Nothing became more and more frequent, the travelers were gradually getting used to them.

They had been flying in silence for quite some time when suddenly Falkor's bronze-bell tone rang out: 'Atreyu, my little master. Are you asleep?'

'No,' said Atreyu, though actually he had been caught up in a terrifying dream. 'What is it, Falkor?'

'I've been wondering if it wouldn't be wiser to turn back.'

'Turn back? Where to?'

'To the Ivory Tower. To the Childlike Empress.'

'You want us to go to her empty-handed?'

'I wouldn't call it that, Atreyu. What *was* your mission?'

'To discover the cause of her illness and find out what would cure it.'

'But,' said Falkor, 'nothing was said about your bringing her the cure.'

'What do you mean?'

'Maybe it's a mistake, trying to cross the border of Fantastica in search of a human.'

'I don't see what you're driving at, Falkor. Explain yourself.'

'The Childlike Empress is deathly sick,' said the dragon, 'because she needs a new name. Morla the Aged One told you that. But only a human, only a child of man from the Outer World can give her this name. Uyulala told you that. So you've actually completed your mission. It seems to me you should let the Childlike Empress know it as soon as possible.'

'But it won't do her a bit of good,' Atreyu protested, 'unless I bring her the human who can save her.'

'Don't be so sure,' said Falkor. 'She has much greater power than you or I. Maybe she would have no difficulty in bringing a human to Fantastica. Maybe she has ways that are unknown to you and me and everyone else in Fantastica. But to do so she needs to know what you have found out. If that's the way it is, there's no point in our trying to find a human on our own. She might even die while we're looking. But maybe if we turn back in time, we can save her.'

Atreyu made no answer. The dragon could be right, he reflected. But then he could be wrong. If he went back now with his message, the Childlike Empress might very well say: What good does that do me? And now it's too late to send you out again.

He didn't know what to do. And he was tired, much too tired to decide anything.

'You know, Falkor,' he said, hardly above a whisper, 'you may be right. Or you may be wrong. Let's fly on a little further. Then if we haven't come to a border, we'll turn back.'

'What do you mean by a little further?' the dragon asked.

'A few hours,' Atreyu murmured. 'Oh well, just *one* hour.'

'All right,' said Falkor, 'just *one* hour.'

But that one hour was one hour too many.

They hadn't noticed that the sky in the north was black with clouds. In the west the sky was aflame, and ugly-looking clouds hung down over the horizon like seaweed. In the east a storm was rising like a blanket of gray lead, and all around it there were tatters of cloud that looked like blue ink blots. And from the south came a sulfur-yellow mist, streaked with lightning.

'We seem to be getting into bad weather,' said Falkor.

Atreyu looked in all directions.

'Yes,' he said. 'It looks bad. But what can we do but fly on?'

'It would be more sensible,' said Falkor, 'to look for shelter. If this is what I think, it's no joke.'

'What *do* you think?' Atreyu asked.

'I think it's the four Wind Giants, starting one of their battles. They're almost always fighting to see which is the strongest and should rule over the others. To them it's a sort of game, because they have nothing to fear. But God help anyone who gets caught in their little tiffs.'

'Can't you fly higher?' Atreyu asked.

'Beyond their reach, you mean? No, I can't fly that high. And as far as I can see, there's nothing but water below us. Some enormous ocean. I don't see any place to hide in.'

'Then,' said Atreyu, 'we'll just have to wait till they get here. Anyway, there's something I want to ask them.'

'What?!' cried the dragon, so terrified that he jumped, in a manner of speaking, sky-high.

'If they are the four Wind Giants,' Atreyu explained, 'they must know all four corners of Fantastica. If anyone can tell us where the borders are, it's them.'

'Good Lord!' cried the dragon. 'You think you can just stop and chat with Wind Giants?'

'What are their names?' Atreyu asked.

'The one from the north,' said Falkor, 'is called Lirr, the one from the east is Baureo, the one from the south is Sheerek, and the one from the west is Mayestril. But tell me, Atreyu. What are you? Are you a little boy or a bar of iron? How come you're not afraid?'

'When I passed through the sphinxes' gate,' Atreyu replied, 'I lost all my fear. And besides, I'm wearing the emblem of the Childlike Empress. Everyone in Fantastica respects it. Why shouldn't the Wind Giants?'

'Oh, they will,' cried Falkor, 'they will. But they're stupid, and nothing can make them stop fighting one another. You'll see.'

Meanwhile the storm clouds from all four directions had converged. It seemed to Atreyu that he was at the center of a huge funnel, which was revolving faster and faster, mixing the sulfur-yellow, the leaden gray, the blood-red, and the deep black all together. He and his white dragon were spun about in a circle like a matchstick in a great whirlpool. And then he saw the Wind Giants.

Actually all he saw was faces, because their limbs kept changing in every possible way – from long to short, from clear-cut to misty – and they were so knotted together in a monstrous free-for-all that it was impossible to make out their real shapes, or even how many of them there were. The faces too were constantly changing; now they were round and puffed, now stretched from top to bottom or from side to side. But at all times they could be told apart. They opened their mouths and bellowed and roared and howled and laughed at one another. They didn't even seem to notice the dragon and his rider, who were gnats in comparison to the Wind Giants.

Atreyu raised himself as high as he could. With his right hand he reached for the golden amulet on his chest and shouted at the top of his lungs: 'In the name of the Childlike Empress, be still and listen.'

And the unbelievable happened!

As though suddenly stricken dumb, they fell silent. Their mouths closed, and eight gigantic goggle-eyes were directed at AURYN. The tempest stopped and the air was deathly still.

'Answer me!' cried Atreyu. 'Where are the borders of Fantastica? Do you know, Lirr?'

'Not in the north,' said the black cloud face.

'And you, Baureo?'

'Not in the east,' said the leaden-gray cloud face.

'You tell me, Sheerek!'

'There is no border in the south,' said the sulfur-yellow cloud face.

'Mayestril, do you know?'

'No border in the west,' said the fiery-red cloud face.

And then they all spoke as with one mouth: 'Who are you, who bear the emblem of the Childlike Empress and don't know that Fantastica has no borders?'

Atreyu made no reply. He was stunned. It had never occurred to him that Fantastica might have no borders whatsoever. Then his whole Quest had been for nothing.

He hardly noticed it when the Wind Giants resumed their war game. He had given up caring what would happen to him. He clung fast to the dragon's mane when they were hurled upward by a whirlwind. The lightning played around them, they were spun in a circle and almost drowned in a downpour of rain. They were sucked into a fiery wind that nearly burned them up, but a moment later a hailstorm, consisting not of stones but of icicles as long as spears, flung them downward. So it went: up and down, down and up, this way and that. The Wind Giants were fighting for power.

A gust of wind turned Falkor over on his back. 'Hold tight!' he shouted.

But it was too late. Atreyu had lost his hold and fell. He fell and fell, and then he lost consciousness.

When he came to, Atreyu was lying on white sand. He heard the sound of waves, and when he looked around he saw that he had been washed up on a beach. It was a gray, foggy day, but there was no wind. The sea was calm and there was no sign that the Wind Giants had been fighting a battle only a short time before. The beach was flat and there were no hills or rocks in sight, only a few gnarled and crooked trees which, seen through the mist, looked like great clawed hands.

Atreyu sat up. Seeing his red buffalo-hair cloak a few steps away,

he crawled over to it and threw it over his shoulders. To his surprise, it was almost dry. So he must have been lying there for quite
a while.

How had he got there? Why hadn't he drowned?

Dimly he remembered arms that had carried him, and strange
singing voices. Poor child, beautiful child! Hold him! Don't let him
go under!

Perhaps it had only been the sound of the waves.

Or could it have been sea nymphs and water sprites? Probably
they had seen the Glory and that was why they had saved him.

Involuntarily, he reached for the amulet – it was gone. There
was no chain around his neck. He had lost the Gem.

'Falkor!' he shouted as loud as he could. He jumped up and ran
back and forth, shouting in all directions: 'Falkor! Falkor! Where
are you?'

No answer came – only the slow, steady sound of the waves breaking against the beach.

Heaven only knew where the Wind Giants had driven the white
dragon. Maybe Falkor was looking for his little master in an entirely
different place, miles and miles away. Maybe he wasn't even alive.

No longer was Atreyu a dragon rider, and no longer was he the
Childlike Empress's messenger. He was only a little boy. And all
alone.

The clock in the belfry struck six.

*By then it was dark outside. The rain had stopped. Not a sound to be
heard. Bastian stared into the candle flames.*

Then he gave a start. The floor had creaked.

*He thought he heard someone breathing. He held his breath and listened.
Except for the small circle of light shed by the candles, it was dark in the
big attic.*

*Didn't he hear soft steps on the stairs? Hadn't the handle of the attic
door moved ever so slowly?*

Again the floor creaked.

What if there were ghosts in this attic!

*'Nonsense!' said Bastian none too loudly. 'There's no such thing! Every-
one knows that.'*

Then why were there so many stories about them?

Maybe all the people who say ghosts don't exist are just afraid to admit that they do.

Atreyu wrapped himself up tight in his red cloak, for he was cold, and started inland. The country, as far as he could see through the fog, was flat and monotonous. The only change he noticed as he strode along was the appearance among the stunted trees of bushes which looked as if they were made of rusty sheet metal and were almost as hard. You could easily hurt yourself brushing against them if you weren't careful.

About an hour later, Atreyu came to a road paved with bumpy, irregularly shaped stones. Thinking it was bound to lead somewhere, he decided to follow it but preferred to walk on the soft ground beside the bumpy paving stones. The road kept twisting and turning, though it was hard to see why, for there was no sign of any hill, pond, or stream. In that part of the country everything seemed to be crooked.

Atreyu hadn't been skirting the road for very long when he heard a strange thumping sound. It was far away but coming closer. It sounded like the muffled beat of a big drum. In between beats he heard a tinkling of bells and a shrill piping that could have been made by fifes. He hid behind a bush by the side of the road and waited to see what would happen.

Slowly the strange music came closer, and then the first shapes emerged from the fog. They seemed to be dancing, but it was a dance without charm or gaiety. The dancers jumped grotesquely, rolled on the ground, crawled on all fours, leapt into the air, and carried on like crazy people. But all Atreyu could hear was the slow, muffled drumbeats, the shrill fifes, and a whimpering and panting from many throats.

More and more figures appeared, the procession seemed endless. Atreyu looked at the dancers' faces; they were ashen gray and bathed in sweat, and the eyes had a wild feverish glow. Some of the dancers lashed themselves with whips.

They're mad, Atreyu thought, and a cold shiver ran down his spine.

The procession consisted mostly of night-hobs, kobolds, and ghosts. There were vampires as well, and quite a few witches, old ones with great humps and beards, but also young ones who looked beautiful and wicked. If he had had AURYN, he would have approached them and asked what was going on. As it was, he preferred to stay in his hiding place until the mad procession had passed and the last straggler vanished hopping and limping in the fog.

Only then did he venture out on the road and look after the ghostly procession. Should he follow them? He couldn't make up his mind. By that time, to tell the truth, he didn't know if there was anything that he should or should not do.

For the first time he was fully aware of how much he needed the Childlike Empress's amulet and how helpless he was without it. And not only or even mainly because of the protection it had given him – it was thanks to his own strength, after all, that he had stood up to all the hardships and terrors and the loneliness of his Quest – but as long as he had carried the emblem, he had never been at a loss for what to do. Like a mysterious compass, it had guided his thoughts in the right direction. And now that was changed, now he had no secret power to lead him.

He had no idea what to do, but he couldn't bear to stand there as though paralyzed. So he made himself follow the muffled drumming, which could still be heard in the distance.

While making his way through the fog – always careful to keep a suitable distance between himself and the last stragglers – he tried to put his thoughts in order.

Why, oh, why hadn't he listened when Falkor advised him to fly straight to the Childlike Empress? He would have brought her Uyulala's message and returned the Gem. Without AURYN and without Falkor, he would never be able to reach her. She would wait for him till her last moment, hoping he would come, trusting him to save her and Fantastica – but in vain.

That in itself was bad enough, but still worse was what he had learned from the Wind Giants, that Fantastica had no borders. If there was no way of leaving Fantastica, then it would be impossible to call in a human form across the border. Because Fantastica was endless, its end was inevitable.

But while he was stumbling over the bumpy paving stones in

the fog, Uyulala's gentle voice resounded in his memory, and a spark of hope was kindled in his heart.

Lots of humans had come to Fantastica in the past and given the Childlike Empress glorious new names. That's what she had sung. So there was a way from the one world to the other!

> 'For them it is near, but for us too far,
> Never can we go out to them.'

Yes, those were Uyulala's words. Humans, the children of man, had forgotten the way. But mightn't just one of them, a single one, remember?

His own hopeless situation mattered little to Atreyu. What mattered was that a human should hear Fantastica's cry of distress and come to the rescue, as had happened many times before. Perhaps, perhaps one had already started out and was on his way.

'Yes! Yes!' Bastian shouted. Then, terrified of his own voice, he added more softly: 'I'd go and help you if I knew how. I don't know the way, Atreyu. I honestly don't.'

The muffled drumbeats and the shrill piping had stopped. Without noticing it, Atreyu had come so close to the procession that he almost ran into the last stragglers. Since he was barefoot, his steps were soundless – but that wasn't why those creatures took no notice of him. He could have been stomping with hobnailed boots and shouting at the top of his lungs without attracting their attention.

By that time the procession had broken up and the spooks were scattered over a large muddy field interspersed with gray grass. Some swayed from side to side, others stood or sat motionless, but in all their eyes there was a feverish glow, and they were all looking in the same direction.

Then Atreyu saw what they were staring at in fascinated horror. On the far side of the field lay the Nothing.

It was the selfsame Nothing that he had seen from the bark trolls' treetop, or on the plain where the Magic Gates of the Southern Oracle had stood, or looking down from Falkor's back – but up until then he had always seen it from a distance. This time it was close by. It cut across the entire landscape and was coming slowly but irresistibly closer.

Atreyu saw that the spooks in the field ahead of him were twitching and quivering. Their limbs were convulsed and their mouths were wide open, as though they had wanted to scream or laugh, though not a sound came out of them. And then all at once – like leaves driven by a gust of wind – they rushed toward the Nothing. They leapt, they rolled, they flung themselves into it.

The last of the ghostly crowd had just vanished when Atreyu felt to his horror that his own body was beginning to take short, convulsive steps in the direction of the Nothing. He felt drawn to it by an unreasoning desire, and braced his will against it. He commanded himself to stand still. Slowly, very slowly, he managed to turn around and step by step, as though bucking a powerful current, to struggle forward. The force of attraction weakened and he ran, ran with all his might over the bumpy paving stones. He slipped, fell, picked himself up, and ran on. He had no time to wonder where this foggy road would lead him.

He followed the senseless twists and turns of the road until high pitch-black ramparts appeared in the fog ahead of him. Behind them several crooked towers jutted into the gray sky. The heavy wooden wings of the town gate were rotting away and hung loose on rusty hinges.

Atreyu went in.

It was growing colder and colder in the attic. Bastian's teeth were chattering.

What if he should get sick – what would become of him then? He might come down with pneumonia, like Willy, a boy in his class. Then he would die all alone in this attic. There'd be no one to help him.

He'd have been very glad just then to have his father come and save him.

But go home? No, he couldn't. He'd rather die.

He took the rest of the army blankets and wrapped them around him.

After a while he felt warmer.

IX

Spook City

N the endless sky, somewhere above the roaring waves, Falkor's voice rang out like a great bronze bell:

'Atreyu! Where are you, Atreyu?' The Wind Giants had long finished their war game and had stormed apart. They would meet again in this or some other place, to continue their battle as they had done since time immemorial. They had already forgotten the white dragon and his little rider, for they remembered nothing and knew nothing except their own enormous power.

When Atreyu fell, Falkor tried to reach him and catch him. But a sudden whirlwind had driven the dragon upward and far away. When he returned, the Wind Giants were raging over another part of the sea. Falkor tried desperately to find the place where Atreyu had fallen, but even a white luckdragon can't possibly find anything as tiny as a little boy in the seething foam of an angry ocean.

But Falkor wouldn't give up. He flew high into the air to get a better view, then he skimmed the waves or flew in larger and larger circles, all the while calling Atreyu by name.

Being a luckdragon, he never doubted for a moment that everything would come out all right in the end. And his mighty voice resounded amid the roaring of the waves: 'Atreyu! Atreyu, where are you?'

Atreyu wandered through the deathly stillness of a deserted city. The place seemed to be under a curse, a city of haunted castles and houses, inhabited only by ghosts. Like everything else in this country, the streets were crooked. Enormous spider webs were suspended over them, and a foul smell rose from the cellars and well shafts.

At first Atreyu darted from wall to wall for fear that someone would see him, but after a while he didn't even bother to hide. The streets and squares were deserted, and nothing stirred in the houses. He went into some of them, but found only overturned furniture, tattered curtains, broken china and glassware – signs of devastation but no inhabitants. On one table there was still a half-eaten meal, dishes with black soup in them, and some sticky chunks of something that may have been bread. He ate some of both. The taste was disgusting, but he was very hungry. It struck him as almost fitting that he should end up in this town. Just the place, he thought, for someone who had given up hope.

Bastian was weak with hunger.

For some strange reason his thoughts turned to Anna's apple strudel — the best apple strudel in the whole world.

Anna came three times a week. She would do a bit of typing for Bastian's father and put the house in order. And usually she would cook or bake something. She was a strapping, bouncy woman with an unrestrained, cheery laugh. Bastian's father was polite to her but seemed hardly aware of her presence. She was seldom able to bring a smile to his worried face. But when she was there, the place was a little more cheerful.

Though unmarried, Anna had a little daughter. Her name was Christa, she was three years younger than Bastian, and she had beautiful blond hair. At first Anna had brought Christa with her almost every time. Christa was very shy. Bastian spent hours telling her his stories, and she would sit there still as a mouse, watching him wide-eyed. She looked up to Bastian, and he was very fond of her.

But a year ago Anna had sent her daughter to a boarding school in the country. Since then she and Bastian had seldom seen each other.

Bastian had been rather cross with Anna. She had tried to explain why it was better for Christa, but he wasn't convinced.

Even so, he could never resist her apple strudel.

He wondered in his distress how long a person could go without eating. Three days? Two? Maybe you'd get hallucinations after twenty-four hours. On his fingers Bastian counted the hours he had been there. At least ten. Maybe more. If only he had saved his sandwich, or at least his apple.

In the flickering candlelight the glass eyes of the fox, the owl, and the huge eagle looked almost alive. Their moving shadows loomed large on the attic wall.

Atreyu went out into the street again and wandered aimlessly about. He passed through neighborhoods where all the houses were small and so low that he could reach up to the eaves, and others lined with mansions many stories high, the fronts of which were adorned with statues. But all these statues were of skeletons or demons, which grimaced down at the forlorn wanderer.

Then suddenly he stopped stock-still.

From not far away he heard a raucous wailing that sounded so plaintive, so hopeless that it cut him to the heart. All the despair, all the desolation of the creatures of darkness was in that lament, which echoed back from the walls of distant buildings, until in the end it sounded like the howling of a scattered wolf pack.

Atreyu followed the sound, which gradually grew weaker and ended in a hoarse sob. He had to search for some time. He passed a gateway, entered a narrow, lightless court, passed through an arch, and finally came to a damp, grimy backyard. And there, chained, lay a gigantic, half-starved werewolf. Each rib stood out separately under its mangy fur, the vertebrae looked like the teeth of a saw, and its tongue dangled from its half-open mouth.

Slowly Atreyu approached him. When the werewolf noticed him, it raised its great head with a jerk. A greenish light flared up in its eyes.

For a time the two looked at each other without a word, without a sound. Finally the wolf let out a soft, dangerous-sounding growl: 'Go away. Let me die in peace.'

Atreyu didn't stir. Just as softly he answered: 'I heard your call. That's why I came.'

The werewolf's head sank back. 'I didn't call anyone,' he growled. 'I was singing my own dirge.'

'Who are you?' Atreyu asked, taking a step closer.

'I am Gmork, the werewolf.'

'Why are you lying here chained?'

'They forgot me when they went away.'

'Who are they?'

'The ones who chained me.'

'Where did they go?'

Gmork made no answer. He watched Atreyu from under half-closed lids. After a long silence, he said: 'You don't belong here, little stranger. Neither in this city, nor in this country. What have you come here for?'

Atreyu bowed his head.

'I don't know how I got here. What is the name of this city?'

'It is the capital of the most famous country in all Fantastica,' said

Gmork. 'More stories are told about this country and this city than about any other. Surely you've heard of Spook City and the Land of Ghosts?'

Atreyu noded slowly.

Gmork hadn't taken his eyes off the boy. He was amazed that this green-skinned boy should look at him so quietly out of his black eyes and show no sign of fear.

'And who are you?' he asked.

Atreyu thought awhile before answering.

'I'm Nobody.'

'What do you mean by that?'

'I mean that I once had a name. It can't be named anymore. That makes me Nobody.'

The werewolf bared his hideous fangs for a moment in what was no doubt intended as a smile. He was familiar with mental anguish of every kind and sensed a certain kinship in the boy.

'If that's the case,' he said, 'then Nobody has heard me and Nobody has come to me, and Nobody is speaking to me in my last hour.'

Atreyu nodded again. Then he asked: 'Can Nobody free you from your chain?'

The greenish light in the werewolf's eyes flickered. He began to growl and to lick his chops.

'You'd really do that?' he blurted out. 'You'd really set a hungry werewolf free? Do you know what that means? Nobody would be safe from me.'

'I know,' said Atreyu. 'But I'm Nobody. Why should I be afraid of you?'

He wanted to approach Gmork. But again the wolf uttered his deep, terrifying growl. The boy shrank back.

'Don't you *want* me to set you free?' he asked.

All at once the werewolf seemed very tired.

'You can't do that. But if you come within my reach, I'll have to tear you to pieces, my boy. That would delay my end a little, an hour or two. So keep away from me and let me die in peace.'

Atreyu thought it over.

'Maybe,' he said finally. 'Maybe I can find you something to eat. I'll look around.'

Slowly Gmork opened his eyes. The greenish fire had gone out of them.

'Go to hell, you little fool! Do you want to keep me alive until the Nothing gets here?'

'I thought,' Atreyu stammered, 'that maybe if I brought you food and you were full, I could get close enough to take off your chain . . .'

Gmork gnashed his teeth.

'Do you think I wouldn't have bitten through it myself if this were an ordinary chain?'

As though to prove his point, he clamped his jaws on the chain. The chain jangled as he tugged and pulled at it. After a while he let it go.

'It's a magic chain. Only the person who put it on can take it off. But she will never come back.'

'Who is that?'

Gmork whimpered like a whipped dog. It was some time before he was calm enough to answer.

'It was Gaya, the Dark Princess.'

'Where has she gone?'

'She has leapt into the Nothing – like everyone else around here.'

Atreyu remembered the mad dancers he had seen outside the city in the foggy countryside.

'Why didn't they run away?' he murmured.

'Because they had given up hope. That makes you beings weak. The Nothing pulls at you, and none of you has the strength to resist it for long.'

Gmork gave a deep, malignant laugh.

'What about yourself?' Atreyu asked. 'You speak as if you weren't one of us?'

Gmork watched him out of the corner of his eye.

'I am not one of you.'

'Then where are you from?'

'Don't you know what a werewolf is?'

Atreyu shook his head.

'You know only Fantastica,' said Gmork. 'There are other worlds. The world of humans, for instance. But there are creatures who have no world of their own, but are able to go in and out of many worlds. I am one of those. In the human world, I appear in human form, but I'm not human. And in Fantastica, I take on a Fantastican form – but I'm not one of you.'

Atreyu sat down on the ground and gazed at the dying werewolf out of great dark eyes.

'You've been in the world of humans?'

'I've often gone back and forth between their world and yours.'

'Gmork,' Atreyu stammered, and he couldn't keep his lips from trembling, 'can you tell me the way to the world of humans?'

A green spark shone in Gmork's eyes. He seemed to be laughing deep inside.

'For you and your kind it's easy to get there. There's only one hitch: You can never come back. You'll have to stay forever. Do you want to?'

'What must I do?' Atreyu asked. His mind was made up.

'What everyone else around here has done before you. You must leap into the Nothing. But there's no hurry. Because you'll do it sooner or later in any case, when the last parts of Fantastica go.'

Atreyu stood up.

Gmork saw that the boy was trembling all over. Not knowing why, he spoke reassuringly: 'Don't be afraid. It doesn't hurt.'

'I'm not afraid,' said Atreyu. 'But I never expected to get my hope back in a place like this. And thanks to you!'

Gmork's eyes glowed like two thin green moons.

'You have nothing to hope for, sonny – whatever your plans may be. When you turn up in the world of humans, you won't be what you are here. That's the secret that no one in Fantastica can know.'

Atreyu stood there with his arms dangling.

'What will I be? Tell me the secret.'

For a long time Gmork neither spoke nor moved. Atreyu was beginning to fear that the answer would never come, but at length the werewolf breathed heavily and spoke:

'What do you think I am, sonny? Your friend? Take care. I'm only passing the time with you. At the moment you can't even leave here. I hold you fast with your hope. But as I speak, the Nothing is creeping in from all sides and closing around Spook City. Soon there will be no way out. Then you will be lost. If you stay and listen, your decision is already made. But you can still escape if you choose.'

The cruel line around Gmork's mouth deepened. Atreyu hesitated for just a moment. Then he whispered: 'Tell me the secret. What will I be in the world of humans?'

Again Gmork sank into a long silence. His breath came in convulsive gasps. Then suddenly he raised himself on his forepaws. Atreyu had to look up at him. And then for the first time he saw how big and terrifying the werewolf was. When Gmork spoke, his voice was like the jangling of chains.

'Have you seen the Nothing, sonny?'

'Yes, many times.'

'What does it look like?'

'As if one were blind.'

'That's right – and when you get to the human world, the Nothing will cling to you. You'll be like a contagious disease that makes humans blind, so they can no longer distinguish between reality and illusion. Do you know what you and your kind are called there?'

'No,' Atreyu whispered.

'Lies!' Gmork barked.

Atreyu shook his head. All the blood had gone out of his lips.

'How can that be?'

Gmork was enjoying Atreyu's consternation. This little talk was cheering him up. After a while, he went on:

'You ask me what you will be there. But what are you here? What are you creatures of Fantastica? Dreams, poetic inventions, characters in a neverending story. Do you think you're real? Well yes, here in your world you are. But when you've been through the Nothing, you won't be real anymore. You'll be unrecognizable. And you will be in another world. In that world, you Fantasticans won't be anything like yourselves. You will bring delusion and madness into the human world. Tell me, sonny, what do you suppose will become of all the Spook City folk who have jumped into the Nothing?'

'I don't know,' Atreyu stammered.

'They will become delusions in the minds of human beings, fears where there is nothing to fear, desires for vain, hurtful things, despairing thoughts where there is no reason to despair.'

'All of us?' asked Atreyu in horror.

'No,' said Gmork, 'there are many kinds of delusion. According to what you are here, ugly or beautiful, stupid or clever, you will become ugly or beautiful, stupid or clever lies.'

'What about me?' Atreyu asked. 'What will I be?'

Gmork grinned.

'I won't tell you that. You'll see. Or rather, you won't see, because you won't be yourself anymore.'

Atreyu stared at the werewolf with wide-open eyes.

Gmork went on:

'That's why humans hate Fantastica and everything that comes from here. They want to destroy it. And they don't realize that by trying to destroy it they multiply the lies that keep flooding the human world. For these lies are nothing other than creatures of Fantastica who have ceased to be themselves and survive only as living corpses, poisoning the souls of men with their fetid smell. But humans don't know it. Isn't that a good joke?'

'And there's no one left in the human world,' Atreyu asked in a whisper, 'who doesn't hate and fear us?'

'I know of none,' said Gmork. 'And it's not surprising, because you yourselves, once you're there, can't help working to make humans believe that Fantastica doesn't exist.'

'Doesn't exist?' the bewildered Atreyu repeated.

'That's right, sonny,' said Gmork. 'In fact, that's the heart of the matter. Don't you see? If humans believe Fantastica doesn't exist, they won't get the idea of visiting your country. And as long as they don't know you creatures of Fantastica as you really are, the Manipulators do what they like with them.'

'What can they do?'

'Whatever they please. When it comes to controlling human

beings there is no better instrument than lies. Because, you see, humans live by beliefs. And beliefs can be manipulated. The power to manipulate beliefs is the only thing that counts. That's why I sided with the powerful and served them – because I wanted to share their power.'

'I want no part in it!' Atreyu cried out.

'Take it easy, you little fool,' the werewolf growled. 'When your turn comes to jump into the Nothing, you too will be a nameless servant of power, with no will of your own. Who knows what use they will make of you? Maybe you'll help them persuade people to buy things they don't need, or hate things they know nothing about, or hold beliefs that make them easy to handle, or doubt the truths that might save them. Yes, you little Fantastican, big things will be done in the human world with your help, wars started, empires founded . . .'

For a time Gmork peered at the boy out of half-closed eyes. Then he added: 'The human world is full of weak-minded people, who think they're as clever as can be and are convinced that it's terribly important to persuade even the children that Fantastica doesn't exist. Maybe they will be able to make good use of you.'

Atreyu stood there with bowed head.

Now he knew why humans had stopped coming to Fantastica and why none would come to give the Childlike Empress new names. The more of Fantastica that was destroyed, the more lies flooded the human world, and the more unlikely it became that a child of man should come to Fantastica. It was a vicious circle from which there was no escape. Now Atreyu knew it.

And so did someone else: Bastian Balthazar Bux.

He now realized that not only was Fantastica sick, but the human world as well. The two were connected. He had always felt this, though he could not have explained why it was so. He had never been willing to believe that life had to be as gray and dull as people claimed. He heard them saying: 'Life is like that,' but he couldn't agree. He never stopped believing in mysteries and miracles.

And now he knew that someone would have to go to Fantastica to make both worlds well again.

If no human knew the way, it was precisely because of the lies and delusions that came into the world because Fantastica was being destroyed. It was these lies and delusions that made people blind.

With horror and shame Bastian thought of his own lies. He didn't count the stories he made up. That was something entirely different. But now and then he had told deliberate lies – sometimes out of fear, sometimes as a way of getting something he wanted, sometimes just to puff himself up. What inhabitants of Fantastica might he have maimed and destroyed with his lies?

One thing was plain: He too had contributed to the sad state of Fantastica. And he was determined to do something to make it well again. He owed it to Atreyu, who was prepared to make any sacrifice to bring Bastian to Fantastica. He had to find the way.

The clock in the belfry struck eight.

The werewolf had been watching Atreyu closely.

'Now you know how you can get to the human world,' he said. 'Do you still want to go, sonny?'

Atreyu shook his head.

'I don't want to turn into a lie,' he said.

'You'll do that whether you like it or not,' said Gmork almost cheerfully.

'But what about you? Why are you here?'

'I had a mission,' Gmork said reluctantly.

'You too?'

Atreyu looked at the werewolf with interest, almost with sympathy.

'Were you successful?'

'No. If I had been, I wouldn't be lying here chained. Everything went pretty well until I came to this city. The Dark Princess, who ruled here, received me with every honor. She invited me to her palace, fed me royally, and did everything to make me think she was on my side. And naturally the inhabitants of this Land of Ghosts rather appealed to me, they made me feel at home, so to speak. The Dark Princess was very beautiful in her way – to my taste at least. She stroked me and ran her fingers through my coat. No one had ever caressed me like that. In short, I lost my head and let

my tongue get out of hand. She pretended to admire me; I lapped
it up, and in the end I told her about my mission. She must have
cast a spell on me, because I am ordinarily a light sleeper. When
I woke up, I had this chain on me. And the Dark Princess was
standing there. "Gmork," she said. "You forgot that I too am one
of the creatures of Fantastica. And that to fight against Fantastica
is to fight against me. That makes you my enemy, and I've out-
smarted you. This chain can never be undone by anyone but me.
But I am going into the Nothing with all my menservants and maidservants, and I shall never come back." Then she turned on her
heel and left me. But all the spooks didn't follow her example. It
was only when the Nothing came closer that more and more of
them were unable to resist its attraction. If I'm not mistaken, the
last of them have just gone. Yes, sonny, I fell into a trap, I listened
too long to that woman. But you have fallen into the same trap,
you've listened too long to me. For in these moments the Nothing
has closed around the city like a ring. You're caught and there's
no escape.'

'Then we'll die together,' said Atreyu.

'So we will,' said Gmork, 'but in very different ways, you little
fool. For I shall die before the Nothing gets here, but you will be
swallowed up by it. There's a big difference. Because I die first,
my story is at an end. But yours will go on forever, in the form
of a lie.'

'Why are you so wicked?' Atreyu asked.

'Because you creatures had a world,' Gmork replied darkly, 'and
I didn't.'

'What was your mission?'

Up until then Gmork had been sitting up. Now he slumped to
the ground. He was plainly at the end of his strength, and he spoke
in raucous gasps.

'Those whom I serve decided that Fantastica must be destroyed.
But then they saw that their plan was endangered. They had learned
that the Childlike Empress had sent out a messenger, a great hero
– and it looked as if he might succeed in bringing a human to
Fantastica. They wanted to have him killed before it was too late.
That was why they sent me, because I had been in Fantastica and

knew my way around. I picked up his trail right away, I tracked him day and night – gradually coming closer – through the Land of the Sassafranians – the jungle temple of Muwamath – Howling Forest – the Swamps of Sadness – the Dead Mountains – but then in the Deep Chasm by Ygramul's net, I lost the track, he seemed to have dissolved into thin air. I went on searching, he had to be somewhere. But I never found his trail again, and this is were I ended up. I've failed. But so has he, for Fantastica is going under! I forgot to tell you, his name was Atreyu.'

Gmork raised his head. The boy had taken a step back.

'I am Atreyu,' he said.

A tremor ran through the werewolf's shrunken body. It came again and again and grew stronger and stronger. Then from his throat came a panting cough. It grew louder and more rasping; it swelled to a roar that echoed back from the city's walls. The werewolf was laughing.

It was the most horrible sound Atreyu had ever heard. Never again was he to hear anything like it.

And then suddenly it stopped.

Gmork was dead.

For a long time Atreyu stood motionless. At length he approached the dead werewolf – he himself didn't know why – bent over the head and touched the shaggy black fur. And in that moment, quicker than thought, Gmork's teeth snapped on Atreyu's leg. Even in death, the evil in him had lost none of its power.

Desperately Atreyu tried to break open the jaws. In vain. The gigantic teeth, as though held in place by steel clamps, dug into his flesh. Atreyu sank to the grimy pavement beside the werewolf's corpse.

And step by step, soundless and irresistible, the Nothing advanced from all sides, through the high black wall surrounding the city.

X

The Flight to the Ivory Tower

ust as Atreyu passed through the somber gateway of Spook City and started on the exploration that was to end so dismally in a squalid backyard, Falkor, the luckdragon, was making an astonishing discovery.

While searching tirelessly for his little friend and master, he had flown high into the clouds. On every side lay the sea, which was gradually growing calmer after the great storm that had churned it from top to bottom. Suddenly, far in the distance, Falkor caught sight of something that puzzled and intrigued him. It was as though a beam of golden light were going on and off, on and off, at regular intervals. And that beam of light seemed to point directly at him, Falkor.

He flew toward it as fast as he could, and when he was directly over it he saw that the light signal came from deep down in the water, perhaps from the bottom of the sea.

Luckdragons, as we know, are creatures of air and fire. Not only is the liquid element alien to them; it is also their enemy. Water can extinguish them like a flame, or it can asphyxiate them, for they never stop breathing in air through their thousands of pearly scales. They feed on air and heat and require no other nourishment, but without air and heat they can only live a short time.

Falkor didn't know what to do. He didn't even know what the strange blinking under the sea was, or whether it had anything to do with Atreyu.

But he didn't hesitate for long. He flew high into the sky, turned around, and head down, pressing his legs close to his body, which he held stiff and straight as a telegraph pole, he plummeted. The water spouted like a fountain as he hit the sea at top speed. The shock was so great that he almost lost consciousness, but he forced himself to open his ruby-red eyes. By then the blinking beam was close, only a few body lengths ahead of him. Air bubbles were forming around his body, as in a saucepan full of water just before it boils. He felt that he was cooling and weakening. With his last strength he dived still deeper – and then the source of light was within reach. It was AURYN, the Gem. Luckily the chain of the amulet had got caught on a coral branch growing out of the wall of an under-sea chasm. Otherwise the Gem would have fallen into the bottomless depths.

Falkor seized it and put the chain around his neck for fear of losing it – for he felt that he was about to faint.

When he came to, he didn't know where he was, for to his amazement he was flying through the air, and when he looked down, there was the sea again. He was flying in a very definite direction and very fast, faster than would have seemed possible in his weakened condition. He tried to slow down, but soon found that his body would not obey him. An outside will far stronger than his own had taken possession of his body and was guiding it. That will came from AURYN, the amulet suspended from a chain around his neck.

The day was drawing to a close when at last Falkor sighted a beach in the distance. He couldn't see much of the country beyond, it seemed to be hidden by fog. But when he came closer, he saw that most of the land had been swallowed up by the Nothing, which hurt his eyes and gave him the feeling of being blind.

At that point Falkor would probably have turned back if he had been able to do as he wanted. But the mysterious power of the gem forced him to fly straight ahead. And soon he knew why, for in the midst of the endless Nothing he discovered a small island that was still holding out, an island covered with high-gabled houses and crooked towers. Falkor had a strong suspicion whom he would find there, and from then on it was not only the powerful will of the amulet that spurred him on but his own as well. It was almost dark in the somber backyard where Atreyu lay beside the dead werewolf. The luckdragon was barely able to distinguish the boy's light-colored body from the monster's black coat. And the darker it grew, the more they looked like one body.

Atreyu had long given up trying to break loose from the steel vise of the werewolf's jaws. Dazed with fear and weakness, he was back in the Grass Ocean. Before him stood the purple buffalo he had not killed. He called to the other children, his companions of the hunt, who by then had no doubt become real hunters. But no one answered. Only the giant buffalo stood there motionless, looking at him. Atreyu called Artax, his horse, but he didn't come, and his cheery neigh was nowhere to be heard. He called the Child-like Empress, but in vain. He wouldn't be able to tell her anything. He hadn't become a hunter, and he was no longer a messenger. He was Nobody.

Atreyu had given up.

But then he felt something else: the Nothing. It must be very near, he thought. Again he felt its terrible force of attraction. It made him dizzy. He sat up and, groaning, tugged at his leg. But the fangs held fast.

And in that he was lucky. For if Gmork's jaws had not held him, Falkor would have come too late.

As it was, Atreyu suddenly heard the luckdragon's bronze voice in the sky above him: 'Atreyu! Are you there, Atreyu?'

'Falkor!' Atreyu shouted. And then he cupped his hands around his mouth and shouted: 'Falkor! Falkor! I'm here. Help me! I'm here!'

And then he saw Falkor's white body darting like a living streak of lightning through the square of darkening sky, far away at first, then closer. Atreyu kept shouting and Falkor answered in his bell-like voice. Then at last the dragon in the sky caught sight of the boy down below, no bigger than a bright speck in a dark hole.

Falkor prepared for a landing, but the backyard was small, there was hardly any light left, and the dragon brushed against one of the high-gabled houses. The roof collapsed with a roar. Falkor felt an agonizing pain; the sharp edge of the roof had cut deep into his body. This wasn't one of his usual graceful landings. He came tumbling down on the grimy wet pavement next to Atreyu and the dead Gmork.

He shook himself, sneezed like a dog coming out of the water, and said: 'At last! So this is where you are! Oh well, I seem to have got here on time!'

Atreyu said nothing. He threw his arms around Falkor's neck and buried his face in the dragon's silvery-white mane.

'Come!' said Falkor. 'Climb on my back. We have no time to lose.'

Atreyu only shook his head. And then Falkor saw that Atreyu's leg was imprisoned in the werewolf's jaws.

'Don't worry,' he said, rolling his ruby-red eyeballs. 'We'll fix that in a jiffy.'

He set to with both paws, trying to pry Gmork's teeth apart. They didn't budge by a hairbreadth.

Falkor heaved and panted. It was no use. Most likely he would never have set his young friend free if luck hadn't come to his help. But luckdragons, as we know, are lucky, and so are those they are fond of.

When Falkor stopped to rest, he bent over Gmork's head to get a better look at it in the dark, and it so happened that the Child-like Empress's amulet, which was hanging from the chain on the dragon's neck, touched the werewolf's forehead. Instantly the jaws opened, releasing Atreyu's leg.

'Hey!' cried Falkor. 'What do you think of that?'

There was no answer from Atreyu.

'What's wrong?' cried Falkor. 'Atreyu, where are you?'

He groped in the darkness for his friend, but Atreyu wasn't there. And while the dragon was trying to pierce the darkness with his glowing red eyes, he himself felt the pull that had snatched Atreyu away from him. The Nothing was coming too close for comfort. But AURYN protected the luckdragon from the pull.

Atreyu was free from the werewolf's jaws, but not from the pull of the Nothing. He tried to fight it, to kick, to push, but his limbs no longer obeyed him. A few feet more, and he would have been lost forever.

In that moment, quick as lightning, Falkor grabbed him by his long blue-black hair, and carried him up into the night-black sky.

The clock in the belfry struck nine.

Neither Atreyu nor Falkor could say later how long they had flown through the impenetrable darkness. Had it been only one night? Perhaps time had stopped for them and they were hovering motionless in the limitless blackness. It was the longest night Atreyu had ever known; and the same was true for Falkor, who was much older.

But even the longest and darkest of nights passes sooner or later. And when the pale dawn came, they glimpsed the Ivory Tower on the horizon.

Here it seems necessary to pause for a moment and explain a special feature of Fantastican geography. Continents and oceans, mountains and watercourses, have no fixed locations as in the real world. Thus it would be quite impossible to draw a map of Fantastica. In Fantastica you can never be sure in advance what will be next to what. Even the directions – north, south, east, and west – change from one part of the country to another. And the same goes for summer and winter, day and night. You can step out of a blazing hot desert straight into snowfields. In Fantastica there are no measurable distances, so that 'near' and 'far' don't at all mean what they do in the real world. They vary with the traveler's wishes and state of mind. Since Fantastica has no boundaries, its center can be anywhere – or to put it another way, it is equally near to, or far from, anywhere. It all depends on who is trying to reach the center. And the innermost center of Fantastica is the Ivory Tower.

To his surprise Atreyu found himself sitting on the luckdragon's back. He couldn't remember how he had got there. All he remembered was that Falkor had pulled him up by the hair. Feeling cold, he gathered in his cloak, which was fluttering behind him. And then he saw that it was gray. It had lost its color, and so had his skin and hair. And Falkor, as Atreyu discovered in the rising light, was no better off. The dragon looked unreal, more like a swath of gray mist than anything else. They had both come too close to the Nothing.

'Atreyu, my little master,' the dragon said softly. 'Does your wound hurt very badly?' About his own wound he said nothing.

'No,' said Atreyu. 'I don't feel anything anymore.'

'Have you a fever?'

'No, Falkor. I don't think so. Why do you ask?'

'I can feel you trembling,' said the dragon. 'What in the world can make Atreyu tremble now?'

After a short silence Atreyu said: 'We'll be there soon! And then I'll have to tell the Childlike Empress that nothing can save her. That's harder than anything else I've had to do.'

'Yes,' said Falkor even more softly. 'That's true.'

They flew in silence, drawing steadily nearer to the Ivory Tower. After a while the dragon spoke again.

'Have you seen her, Atreyu?'

'Who?'

'The Childlike Empress. Or rather, the Golden-eyed Commander of Wishes. Because that's how you must address her when you come into her presence.'

·'No, I've never seen her.'

'I have. That was long ago. Your great-grandfather must have been a little boy at the time. And I was a young cloud-snapper with a head full of foolishness. One night I saw the moon, shining so big and round, and I tried to grab it out of the sky. When I finally gave up, I dropped with exhaustion and landed near the Ivory Tower. That night the Magnolia Pavilion had opened its petals wide, and the Childlike Empress was sitting right in the middle of it. She cast a glance at me, just one short glance, but − I hardly know how to put it − that glance made a new dragon of me.'

'What does she look like?'

'Like a little girl. But she's much older than the oldest inhabitants of Fantastica. Or rather, she's ageless.'

'Yes,' said Atreyu. 'But now she's deathly sick. How can I tell her that there's no hope?'

'Don't try to mislead her. She can't be fooled. Tell her the truth.'

'But suppose it kills her?'

'I don't think it will work out that way,' said Falkor.

'You wouldn't,' said Atreyu, 'because you're a luckdragon.'

For a long while nothing was said.

When at last they spoke together for the third time, it was Atreyu who broke the silence.

'Falkor,' he said, 'I'd like to ask you one more thing.'

'Fire away.'

'*Who* is she?'

'What do you mean?'

'AURYN has power over all the inhabitants of Fantastica, the creatures of both light and darkness. It also has power over you and me. And yet the Childlike Empress never exerts power. It's as if she weren't there. And yet she is in everything. Is she like us?'

'No,' said Falkor, 'she's not like us. She's not a creature of Fantastica. We all exist because she exists. But she's of a different kind.'

'Then is she . . .' Atreyu hesitated. 'Is she human?'

'No,' said Falkor, 'she's not human.'

'Well then . . .' And Atreyu repeated his question. 'Who *is* she?'

After a long silence Falkor answered: 'No one in Fantastica knows, no one can know. That's the deepest secret of our world. I once heard a wise man say that if anyone were to know the whole answer, he would cease to exist. I don't know what he meant. That's all I can tell you.'

'And now,' said Atreyu, 'she'll die and we'll die with her, and we'll never know her secret.'

This time Falkor made no answer, but a smile played around the corners of his leonine mouth, as though to say: Nothing of the kind will happen.

After that they spoke no more.

A little later they flew over the outer edge of the 'Labyrinth,' the maze of flower beds, hedges, and winding paths that surrounded the Ivory Tower on all sides. To their horror, they saw that there too the Nothing had been at work. True, it had touched only small spots in the Labyrinth, but those spots were all about. The once bright-colored flower beds and shrubbery in between were now gray and withered. The branches of once graceful little trees were gnarled and bare. The green had gone out of the meadows, and a faint smell of rot and mold rose up to the newcomers. The only colors left were those of swollen giant mushrooms and of garish, poisonous-looking blooms that suggested nothing so much as the figments of a maddened brain. Enfeebled and trembling, the innermost heart of Fantastica was still resisting the inexorable encroachment of the Nothing.

But the Ivory Tower at the center still shimmered pure, immaculately white.

Ordinarily flying messengers landed on one of the lower terraces. But Falkor reasoned that since neither he nor Atreyu had the strength to climb the long spiraling street leading to the top of the Tower, and since time was of the essence, the regulations and rules of etiquette could reasonably be ignored. He therefore decided on an emergency landing. Swooping down over the ivory buttresses, bridges, and balustrades, he located, just in time, the uppermost end of the spiraling High Street, which lay just outside the palace grounds. Plummeting to the roadway, he went into a skid, made several complete turns, and finally came to a stop tail-first.

Atreyu, who had been clinging with both arms to Falkor's neck, sat up and looked around. He had expected some sort of reception, or at least a detachment of palace guards to challenge them – but far and wide there was no one to be seen. All the life seemed to have gone out of the gleaming white buildings roundabout.

'They've all fled!' he thought. 'They've left the Childlike Empress alone. Or she's already . . .'

'Atreyu,' Falkor whispered. 'You must give the Gem back to her.'

Falkor removed the golden chain from his neck. It fell to the ground.

Atreyu jumped down off Falkor's back – and fell. He had forgotten his wound. He reached for the Glory and put the chain around his neck. Then, leaning on the dragon, he rose painfully to his feet.

'Falkor,' he said. 'Where must I go?'

But the luckdragon made no answer. He lay as though dead.

The street ended in front of an enormous, intricately carved gate which led through a high white wall. The gate was open.

Atreyu hobbled through it and came to a broad, gleaming-white stairway that seemed to end in the sky. He began to climb. Now and then he stopped to rest. Drops of his blood left a trail behind him.

At length the stairway ended. Ahead of him lay a long gallery. He staggered ahead, clinging to the balustrade for support. Next he came to a courtyard that seemed to be full of waterfalls and fountains, but by then he couldn't be sure of what he was seeing.

He struggled forward as in a dream. He came to a second, smaller gate; then there was a long, narrow stairway, which took him to a garden where everything – trees, flowers, and animals – was carved from ivory. Crawling on all fours, he crossed several arched bridges without railings which led to a third gate, the smallest of all. He dragged himself through it on his belly and, slowly raising his eyes, saw a dome-shaped hall of gleaming-white ivory, and on top of it the Magnolia Pavilion. There was no path or stairway leading up to it.

Atreyu buried his head in his hands.

No one who reaches or has reached that pavilion can say how he got there. The last stretch of the way must come to him as a gift.

Suddenly Atreyu was in the doorway. He went in – and found himself face to face with the Golden-eyed Commander of Wishes.

She was sitting, propped on many cushions, on a soft round couch at the center of the great round blossom. She was looking straight at him. She seemed infinitely frail and delicate. Atreyu could see how ill she was by the pallor of her face, which seemed almost transparent. Her almond-shaped eyes, the color of dark gold, were serene and untroubled. She smiled. Her small, slight body was wrapped in an ample silken gown which gleamed so white that the magnolia petals seemed dark beside it. She looked like an indescribably beautiful little girl of no more than ten, but her long, smoothly combed hair, which hung down over her shoulders, was as white as snow.

Bastian gave a start.

Something incredible had happened.

Thus far he had been able to visualize every incident of the Neverending Story. Some of them, it couldn't be denied, were very strange, but they could somehow be explained. He had formed a clear picture of Atreyu riding on the luckdragon, of the Labyrinth and the Ivory Tower.

These pictures, however, existed only in his imagination. But when he came to the Magnolia Pavilion, he saw the face of the Childlike Empress – if only for a fraction of a second, for the space of a lightning flash. And not only in his thoughts, but with his eyes! It wasn't his imagination, of that Bastian was sure. He had even seen details that were not mentioned in the description, such as her eyebrows, two fine lines that might have been drawn with India ink, arching over her golden eyes, or her strangely elongated earlobes, or the way her head tilted on her slender neck. Bastian knew that he had never in all his life seen anything so beautiful as this face. And in that same moment he knew her name: Moon Child. Yes, beyond a doubt, that was her name.

And Moon Child had looked at him – at him, Bastian Balthazar Bux.

She had looked at him with an expression that he could not interpret. Had she too been taken by surprise? Had there been a plea in that look? Or longing? Or . . . what could it be?

He tried to remember Moon Child's eyes, but was no longer able to.

He was sure of only one thing: that her glance had passed through his eyes and down into his heart. He could still feel the burning trail it had left behind. That glance, he felt, was embedded in his heart, and there it glittered like a mysterious jewel. And in a strange and wonderful way it hurt.

Even if Bastian had wanted to, he couldn't have defended himself against this thing that had happened to him. However, he didn't want to. Oh no, not for anything in the world would he have parted with that jewel. All he wanted was to go on reading, to see Moon Child again, to be with her.

It never occurred to him that he was getting into the most unusual and perhaps the most dangerous of adventures. But even if he had known this, he wouldn't have dreamed of shutting the book.

With a trembling forefinger he found his place and went on reading.

The clock in the belfry struck ten.

XI

The Childlike Empress

NITTING his brow, powerless to utter a single word, Atreyu stood gazing at the Childlike Empress. He had no idea how to begin or what to do. He had often tried to imagine this moment, he had prepared words and phrases, but they had all gone out of his head.

At length she smiled at him. Her voice when she spoke was as soft as the voice of a bird singing in its sleep.

'You have returned from the Great Quest, Atreyu.'

Atreyu hung his head.

'Yes,' he managed to say.

After a short silence she went on: 'Your lovely cloak has turned gray. Your hair is gray and your skin is like stone. But all that will be as it was, or better. You'll see.'

Atreyu felt as if a band had tightened around his throat. All he could do was nod his head. Then he heard the sweet soft voice saying: 'You have carried out your mission . . .'

Were these words meant as a question? Atreyu didn't know. He didn't dare look up to read the answer in her face. Slowly he reached for the golden amulet and removed the chain from his neck. Without raising his eyes, he held it out to the Childlike Empress. He tried to kneel as messengers did in the stories and songs he had heard at home, but his wounded leg refused to do his bidding. He fell at the Childlike Empress's feet, and there he lay with his face to the floor.

She bent forward, picked up AURYN, and let the chain glide through her fingers.

'You have done well,' she said, 'and I am pleased with you.'

'No!' cried Atreyu almost savagely. 'It was all in vain. There's no hope.'

A long silence followed. Atreyu buried his face in the crook of his elbow, and his whole body trembled. How would she react? With a cry of despair, a moan, words of bitter reproach or even anger? Atreyu couldn't have said what he expected. Certainly not what he heard. Laughter. A soft, contented laugh. Atreyu's thoughts were in a whirl, for a moment he thought she had gone mad. But that was not the laughter of madness. Then he heard her say: 'But you've brought him with you.'

Atreyu looked up.

'Who?'

'Our savior.'

He looked into her eyes and found only serenity. She smiled again.

'Golden-eyed Commander of Wishes,' he stammered, now for the first time using the official words of address that Falkor had recommended. 'I . . . no, really . . . I don't understand.'

'I can see that by the look on your face,' she said. 'But whether you understand or not, you've done it. And that's what counts, isn't it?'

Atreyu said nothing. He couldn't even think of a question to ask. He stood there openmouthed, staring at the Childlike Empress.

'I saw him,' she went on, 'and he saw me.'

'When?' Atreyu asked.

'Just as you came in. You brought him with you.'

Involuntarily Atreyu looked around.

'Then where is he? I don't see anyone but you and me.'

'Oh, the world is full of things you don't see. You can believe me. He isn't in our world yet. But our worlds have come close enough together for us to see each other. For a twinkling the thin wall between us became transparent. He will be with us soon and then he will call me by the new name that he alone can give me. Then I shall be well, and so will Fantastica.'

As the Childlike Empress was speaking, Atreyu raised himself with difficulty. He looked up to her as she lay on her bed of cushions. His voice was husky when he asked: 'Then you've known my message all along? What Morla the Aged One told me in the Swamps of Sadness, what the mysterious voice of Uyulala in the Southern Oracle revealed to me – you knew it all?'

'Yes,' she said. 'I knew it before I sent you on the Great Quest.'

Atreyu gulped.

'Why,' he finally managed to ask, 'why did you send me then? What did you expect me to do?'

'Exactly what you did,' she replied.

'What I did . . .' Atreyu repeated slowly. His forehead clouded over. 'In that case,' he said angrily, 'it was all unnecessary. There was no need of sending me on the Great Quest. I've heard that your decisions are often mysterious. That may be. But after all I've been through I hate to think that you were just having a joke at my expense.'

The Childlike Empress's eyes grew grave.

'I was not having a joke at your expense, Atreyu,' she said. 'I am well aware of what I owe you. All your sufferings were necessary. I sent you on the Great Quest – not for the sake of the message you would bring me, but because that was the only way of calling our savior. He took part in everything you did, and he has come all that long way with you. You heard his cry of fear when you were talking with Ygramul beside the Deep Chasm, and you saw him when you stood facing the Magic Mirror Gate. You entered into his image and took it with you, and he followed you, because he saw himself through your eyes. And now, too, he can hear every word we are saying. He knows we are talking about him, he knows we have set our hope in him and are expecting him. Perhaps he even understands that all the hardship you, Atreyu, took upon yourself was for his sake and that all Fantastica is calling him.'

Little by little the darkness cleared from Atreyu's face.

After a while he asked: 'How can you know all that? The cry by the Deep Chasm and the image in the magic mirror? Did you arrange it all in advance?'

The Childlike Empress picked up AURYN, and said, while putting the chain around her neck: 'Didn't you wear the Gem the whole time? Didn't you know that through it I was always with you?'

'Not always,' said Atreyu. 'I lost it.'

'Yes. Then you were really alone. Tell me what happened to you then.'

Atreyu told her the story.

'Now I know why you turned gray,' said the Childlike Empress. 'You were too close to the Nothing.'

'Gmork, the werewolf, told me,' said Atreyu, 'that when a Fantastican is swallowed up by the Nothing, he becomes a lie. Is that true?'

'Yes, it is true,' said the Childlike Empress, and her golden eyes darkened. 'All lies were once creatures of Fantastica. They are made of the same stuff – but they have lost their true nature and become unrecognizable. But, as you might expect from a half-and-half creature like Gmork, he told you only half the truth. There are two ways of crossing the dividing line between Fantastica and the human world, a right one and a wrong one. When Fantasticans are cruelly dragged across it, that's the wrong way. When humans, children of man, come to our world of their own free will, that's the right way. Every human who has been here has learned something that could be learned only here, and returned to his own world a changed person. Because he had seen you creatures in your true form, he was able to see his own world and his fellow humans with new eyes. Where he had seen only dull, everyday reality, he now discovered wonders and mysteries. That is why humans were glad to come to Fantastica. And the more these visits enriched our world, the fewer lies there were in theirs, the better it became. Just as our two worlds can injure each other, they can also make each other whole again.'

For a time both were silent. Then she went on: 'Humans are our hope. One of them must come and give me a new name. And he will come.'

Atreyu made no answer.

'Do you understand now, Atreyu,' she asked, 'why I had to ask so much of you? Only a long story full of adventures, marvels, and dangers could bring our savior to me. And that was your story.'

Atreyu sat deep in thought. At length he nodded.

'Yes, Golden-eyed Commander of Wishes, now I understand. I thank you for choosing me. Forgive my anger.'

'You had no way of knowing these things,' she answered. 'And that too was necessary.'

Again Atreyu nodded. After a short silence he said: 'But I'm very tired.'

'You have done enough, Atreyu. Would you like to rest?'

'Not yet. First I would like to see the happy outcome of my story. If, as you say, I've carried out my mission, why isn't the savior here yet? What's he waiting for?'

'Yes,' said the Childlike Empress softly. 'What is he waiting for?'

Bastian felt his hands growing moist with excitement.

'I can't do it,' he said. 'I don't even know what I'm supposed to do. Maybe the name I've thought of isn't the right one.'

'May I ask you another question?' said Atreyu.

'Of course,' she answered with a smile.

'Why do you need a new name to get well?'

'Only the right name gives beings and things their reality,' she said. 'A wrong name makes everything unreal. That's what lies do.'

'Maybe the savior doesn't yet know the right name to give you.'

'Oh yes he does,' she assured him.

Again they sat silent.

'I know it all right,' said Bastian. 'I knew it the moment I laid eyes on her. But I don't know what I have to do.'

Atreyu looked up.

'Maybe he wants to come and just doesn't know how to go about it.'

'All he has to do,' said the Childlike Empress, 'is to call me by my new name, which he alone knows. Nothing more.'

Bastian's heart pounded. Should he try? What if he didn't succeed? What if he was wrong? What if they weren't talking about him but about some entirely different savior? How could he be sure they really meant him?

'Could it be,' said Atreyu after a while, 'that he doesn't know it's him and not somebody else we're talking about?'

'No,' said the Childlike Empress. 'Not after all the signs he has had. He can't be that stupid.'

'I'll give it a try,' said Bastian. But he couldn't get a word out of his mouth.

What if it actually worked? Then he would somehow be transported to Fantastica. But how? Maybe he would have to go through some sort of change. And what would that be like? Would it hurt? Would he lose consciousness? And did he really want to go to Fantastica? He wanted to go to Atreyu and the Childlike Empress, but he wasn't at all keen on all those monsters the place was swarming with.

'Maybe he hasn't got the courage,' Atreyu suggested.

'Courage?' said the Childlike Empress. 'Does it take courage to say my name?'

'Then,' said Atreyu, 'I can think of only one thing that may be holding him back.'

'And what would that be?'

After some hesitation Atreyu blurted out: 'He just doesn't want to come here. He just doesn't care about you or Fantastica. We don't mean a thing to him.'

The Childlike Empress stared wide-eyed at Atreyu.

'No! No!' Bastian cried out. 'You mustn't think that! It's not that at all. Oh, please, please, don't think that! Can you hear me? It's not like that, Atreyu.'

'He promised me he would come,' said the Childlike Empress. 'I saw it in his eyes.'

'Yes, that's true. And I will come soon. I just need time to think. It's not so simple.'

Atreyu hung his head and the two of them waited a long while in silence. But the savior did not appear, and there wasn't the slightest sign to suggest that he was trying to attract their attention.

Bastian was thinking of how it would be if he suddenly stood before them in all his fatness, with his bowlegs and his pasty face. He could literally see the disappointment in the Childlike Empress's face when she said to him: 'What brings you here?'

And Atreyu might even laugh.

The thought brought a blush to Bastian's cheeks.

Obviously they were expecting a prince, or at any rate some sort of hero. He just couldn't appear before them. It was out of the question. He would do anything for them. Anything but that!

When at last the Childlike Empress looked up, the expression of her face had changed. Atreyu was almost frightened at its grandeur and severity. He knew where he had once seen that expression: in the sphinxes.

'There is one more thing I can do,' she said. 'But I don't like it, and I wish he wouldn't make me.'

'What is that?' Atreyu asked in a whisper.

'Whether he knows it or not, he is already part of the Never-ending Story. He can no longer back out of it. He made me a promise and he has to keep it. But by myself I can't make him.'

'Who in all Fantastica,' Atreyu asked, 'can do what you cannot?'

'Only one person,' she replied. 'If he wants to. The Old Man of Wandering Mountain.'

Atreyu looked at the Childlike Empress in amazement.

'The Old Man of Wandering Mountain?' he repeated, stressing every word. 'You mean he exists?'

'Did you doubt it?'

'The old folk in our tent camps tell the children about him when they're naughty. They say he writes everything down in a book, whatever you do or fail to do, and there it stays in the form of a beautiful or an ugly story. When I was little, I believed it, but then I decided it was only an old wives' tale to frighten children.'

'You never can tell about old wives' tales,' she said with a smile.

'Then you know him?' Atreyu asked. 'You've seen him?'

She shook her head.

'If I find him,' she said, 'it will be our first meeting.'

'Our old folk also say,' Atreyu went on, 'that you never can know where the Old Man's mountain will be at any particular time. They say that when he appears it's always unexpectedly, now here, now there, and that you can only run across him by accident, or because the meeting was fated.'

'That's true,' said the Childlike Empress. 'You can't look for the Old Man of Wandering Mountain. You can only find him.'

'Does that go for you too?'

'Yes,' she said, 'for me too.'

'But what if you don't find him?'

'If he exists I'll find him,' she said with a mysterious smile.

Her answer puzzled Atreyu. Hesitantly he asked: 'Is he – is he like you?'

'He is like me,' she replied, 'because he is my opposite in every way.'

Atreyu saw that with such questions he would get nothing out of her. And another thought weighed on him.

'You are deathly sick, Golden-eyed Commander of Wishes,' he said almost sternly. 'You won't go far by yourself. All your servants and courtiers seem to have abandoned you. Falkor and I would be glad to take you wherever you wish, but, frankly, I don't know if Falkor has the strength. And my foot – well, you've seen that it won't carry me.'

'Thank you, Atreyu,' she said. 'Thank you for your brave and loyal offer. But I'm not planning to take you with me. To find the Old Man of Wandering Mountain, one must be alone. And even now Falkor is not where you left him. He has been moved to a place where his wounds will be healed and his strength renewed. And you too, Atreyu, will soon be in that same place.'

Her fingers played with AURYN.

'What place is that?'

'There's no need for you to know that now. You will be moved in your sleep. And one day you will know where you were.'

'But how can I sleep?' cried Atreyu, so shaken that he lost his sense of tact. 'How can I sleep when I know you may die any minute?'

The Childlike Empress laughed softly.

'I'm not quite as forsaken as you think. I've already told you that there are some things you can't hope to understand. I have my seven Powers, which belong to me as your memory or courage or thoughts belong to you. They cannot be seen or heard, and yet they are with me at this moment. I shall leave three of them with you and Falkor to look after you, and I shall take the other four with me as my escort. You needn't worry, Atreyu. You can sleep easy.'

At these words, all the accumulated weariness of the Great Quest descended on Atreyu like a dark veil. Yet it was not the leaden weariness of exhaustion, but a gentle longing for sleep. He still had many questions to ask the Golden-eyed Commander of Wishes, but he felt that her last words had vanquished all his wishes but one, the wish for sleep. His eyes closed and, still in a sitting position, he glided into the darkness.

The clock in the steeple struck eleven.

As though far in the distance, Atreyu heard the Childlike Empress give an order in a soft voice. Then he felt powerful arms lifting him gently and carrying him away.

For a long time, all was dark and warm around him. Much later he half awoke when a soothing liquid touched his parched lips and ran down his throat. He had a vague impression that he was in a great cave with walls of gold. He saw the white luckdragon lying beside him. And then he saw, or thought he saw, a gushing fountain in the middle of the cave, encircled by two snakes, a light one and a dark one, which were biting each other's tail.

But then an invisible hand brushed over his eyes. The feel of it was infinitely soothing, and again he fell into a deep and dreamless sleep.

At that moment, the Childlike Empress left the Ivory Tower. She lay bedded on soft silken cushions in a glass litter, which seemed to be moving under its own power, but was actually being carried by four of the Empress's invisible servants.

They crossed the Labyrinth garden, or rather, what was left of it, making frequent detours, since many of the paths ended in the Nothing.

When at length they left the Labyrinth, the invisible carriers stopped. They seemed to be waiting for a command.

The Childlike Empress sat up on her cushions and cast a glance back at the Ivory Tower.

Then, sinking back, she said: 'Keep going! Just keep going – no matter where.'

Blown by the wind, her snow-white hair trailed behind the glass litter like a flag.

XII

The Old Man
of Wandering Mountain

ONG-THUNDERING avalanches descended from the heights, snow-
storms raged between towering ice-coated summits, dipped into
hollows and ravines, and swept howling onward over the great white
expanse of the glaciers. Such weather was not at all unusual for
this part of the country, for the Mountain of Destiny – that was
its name – was the highest in all Fantastica, and its peaks literally
jutted into the heights of heaven.

Not even the most intrepid mountain climbers ventured into these
fields of everlasting ice. It had been so very, very long since anyone
had succeeded in climbing this mountain that the feat had been
forgotten. For one of Fantastica's many strange laws decreed that
no one could climb the Mountain of Destiny until the last successful
climber had been utterly forgotten. Thus anyone who managed to
climb it would always be the first.

No living creature could survive in that icy waste – except for
a handful of gigantic ice-glumps – who could barely be called living
creatures, for they moved so slowly that they needed years for a
single step and whole centuries for a short walk. Which meant, of
course, that they could only associate with their own kind and knew
nothing at all about the rest of Fantastica. They thought of themselves as the only living creatures in the universe.

Consequently, they were puzzled to the point of consternation
when they saw a tiny speck twining its way upward over perilous
crags and razor-sharp ridges, then vanishing into deep chasms and
crevasses, only to reappear higher up.

That speck was the Childlike Empress's glass litter, still carried
by four of her invisible Powers. It was barely visible, for the glass
it was made of looked very much like ice, and the Childlike
Empress's white gown and white hair could hardly be distinguished
from the snow roundabout.

She had traveled many days and nights. The four Powers had
carried her through blinding rain and scorching sun, through
darkness and moonlight, onward and onward, just as she had
ordered, 'no matter where.' She was prepared for a long journey
and all manner of hardship, since she knew that the Old Man of
Wandering Mountain could be everywhere or nowhere.

Still, the four invisible Powers were not guided entirely by chance in their choice of an itinerary. As often as not, the Nothing, which had already swallowed up whole regions, left only a single path open. Sometimes the possibilities narrowed down to a bridge, a tunnel, or a gateway, and sometimes they were forced to carry the litter with the deathly ill Empress over the waves of the sea. These carriers saw no difference between liquid and solid.

Tireless and persevering, they had finally reached the frozen heights of the Mountain of Destiny. And they would go on climbing until the Childlike Empress gave them another order. But she lay still on her cushions. Her eyes were closed and she said nothing. The last words she had spoken were the 'no matter where' she had said on leaving the Ivory Tower.

The litter was moving through a deep ravine, so narrow that there was barely room for it to pass. The snow was several feet deep, but the invisible carriers did not sink in or even leave footprints. It was very dark at the bottom of this ravine, which admitted only a narrow strip of daylight. The path was on a steady incline and the higher the litter climbed, the nearer the daylight seemed. And then suddenly the walls leveled off, opening up a view of a vast white expanse. This was the summit, for the Mountain of Destiny culminated not, like most other mountains, in a single peak, but in this high plateau, which was as large as a whole country.

But then, surprisingly enough, a smaller, odd-looking mountain arose in the midst of the plateau. It was rather tall and narrow, something like the Ivory Tower, but glittering blue. It consisted of innumerable strangely shaped stone teeth, which jutted into the sky like great inverted icicles. And about halfway up the mountain three such teeth supported an egg the size of a house.

Behind the egg large blue columns resembling the pipes of an enormous organ rose in a semicircle. The great egg had a circular opening, which might have been a door or a window. And in that opening a face appeared. The face was looking straight at the litter.

The Childlike Empress opened her eyes.

'Stop!' she said softly.

The invisible Powers stopped.

The Childlike Empress sat up.

'It's the Old Man of Wandering Mountain,' she said. 'I must

go the last stretch of the way alone. Whatever may happen, wait here for me.'

The face in the circular opening vanished.

The Childlike Empress stepped out of the litter and started across the great snowfield. It was hard going, for she was bare-footed, and there was an icy crust on the snow. At every step she broke through, and the ice cut her tender feet. The wind tugged at her white hair and her gown.

At last she came to the blue mountain and stood facing the smooth stone teeth.

The dark circular opening disgorged a long ladder, much longer than there could possibly have been room for in the egg. It soon extended to the foot of the blue mountain, and when the Childlike Empress took hold of it she saw that it consisted of letters, which were fastened together. Each rung of the ladder was a line. The Childlike Empress started climbing, and as she climbed from rung to rung, she read the words:

TURN BACK! TURN BACK AND GO AWAY!
FOR COME WHAT WILL AND COME WHAT MAY,
NEVER IN ANY TIME OR PLACE
MUST YOU AND I MEET FACE TO FACE.
TO YOU ALONE, O CHILDLIKE ONE,
THE WAY IS BARRED, TO YOU ALONE.
TURN BACK, TURN BACK, FOR NEVER SHALL
BEGINNING SEEK THE END OF ALL.
THE CONSEQUENCE OF YOUR INTRUSION
CAN ONLY BE EXTREME CONFUSION.

She stopped to rest and looked up. She still had a long way to go. So far she hadn't even gone halfway.

'Old Man of Wandering Mountain,' she said aloud. 'If you don't want us to meet, you needn't have written me this ladder. It's your disinvitation that brings me.'

And she went on climbing.

WHAT YOU ACHIEVE AND WHAT YOU ARE
IS RECORDED BY ME, THE CHRONICLER.
LETTERS UNCHANGEABLE AND DEAD

FREEZE WHAT THE LIVING DID AND SAID.
THEREFORE BY COMING HERE TO ME
YOU INVITE CATASTROPHE.
THUS IS THE END OF WHAT YOU ONCE BEGAN.
YOU WILL NEVER BE OLD, AND I, OLD MAN,
WAS NEVER YOUNG. WHAT YOU AWAKEN
I LAY TO REST. BE NOT MISTAKEN:
IT IS FORBIDDEN THAT LIFE SHOULD SEE
ITSELF IN DEAD ETERNITY.

Again she had to stop to catch her breath.

By then the Childlike Empress was high up and the ladder was swaying like a branch in the snowstorm. Clinging to the icy letters that formed the rungs of the ladder, she climbed the rest of the way.

BUT IF YOU STILL REFUSE TO HEED
THE WARNING OF THE LADDER'S SCREED,
IF YOU ARE STILL PREPARED TO DO
WHAT IN TIME AND SPACE IS FORBIDDEN YOU,
I WON'T ATTEMPT TO HOLD YOU BACK,
THEN WELCOME TO THE OLD MAN'S SHACK.

When the Childlike Empress had those last rungs behind her, she sighed and looked down. Her wide white gown was in tatters, for it had caught on every bend and crossbar of the message-ladder. Oh well, she had known all along that letters were hostile to her. She felt the same way about them.

From the ladder she stepped through the circular opening in the egg. Instantly it closed behind her, and she stood motionless in the darkness, waiting to see what would happen next.

Nothing at all happened for quite some time.

At length she said softly: 'Here I am.' Her voice echoed as in a large empty room – or was it another, much deeper voice that had answered her in the same words?

Little by little, she made out a faint reddish glow in the darkness. It came from an open book, which hovered in midair at the center of the egg-shaped room. It was tilted in such a way that she could see the binding, which was of copper-colored silk, and on the binding, as on the Gem, which the Childlike Empress wore around her neck, she saw an oval formed by two snakes biting each other's tail. Inside this oval was printed the title:

The Neverending Story

Bastian's thoughts were in a whirl. This was the very same book that he was reading! He looked again. Yes, no doubt about it, it was the book he had in his hand. How could this book exist inside itself?

The Childlike Empress had come closer. On the other side of the hovering book she now saw a man's face. It was bathed in a bluish light. The light came from the print of the book, which was bluish green.

The man's face was as deeply furrowed as if it had been carved in the bark of an ancient tree. His beard was long and white, and his eyes were so deep in their sockets that she could not see them. He was wearing a dark monk's robe with a hood, and in his hand he was holding a stylus, with which he was writing in the book. He did not look up.

The Childlike Empress stood watching him in silence. He was not really writing. His stylus glided slowly over the empty page and the letters and words appeared as though of their own accord.

The Childlike Empress read what was being written, and it was exactly what was happening at that same moment: 'The Childlike Empress read what was being written . . .'

'You write down everything that happens,' she said.

'Everything that I write down happens,' was the answer, spoken in the deep, dark voice that had come to her like an echo of her own voice.

Strange to say, the Old Man of Wandering Mountain had not opened his mouth. He had written her words and his, and she had heard them as though merely remembering that he had just spoken. 'Are you and I and all Fantastica,' she asked, 'are we all recorded in this book?'

He wrote, and at the same time she heard his answer: 'No, you've got it wrong. This book *is* all Fantastica – and you and I.'

'But where is this book?'

And he wrote the answer: 'In the book.'

'Then it's all a reflection of a reflection?' she asked.

He wrote, and she heard him say: 'What does one see in a mirror reflected in a mirror? Do you know that, Golden-eyed Commander of Wishes?'

The Childlike Empress said nothing for a while, and the Old Man wrote that she said nothing.

Then she said softly: 'I need your help.'

'I knew it,' he said and wrote.

'Yes,' she said. 'I supposed you would. You are Fantastica's memory, you know everything that has happened up to this moment. But couldn't you leaf ahead in your book and see what's going to happen?'

'Empty pages' was the answer. 'I can only look back at what *has* happened. I was able to read it while I was writing it. And I know it because I have read it. And I wrote it because it happened. The Neverending Story writes itself by my hand.'

'Then you don't know why I've come to you?'

'No.' And as he was writing, she heard the dark voice: 'And I wish you hadn't. By my hand everything becomes fixed and final – you too, Golden-eyed Commander of Wishes. This egg is your grave and your coffin. You have entered into the memory of Fantastica. How do you expect to leave here?'

'Every egg,' she said, 'is the beginning of new life.'

'True,' the Old Man wrote and said, 'but only if its shell bursts open.'

'You can open it,' cried the Childlike Empress. 'You let me in.'

'Your power let you in. But now that you're here, your power is gone. We are shut up here for all time. Truly, you shouldn't have come. This is the end of the Neverending Story.'

The Childlike Empress smiled. She didn't seem troubled in the least.

'You and I,' she said, 'can't prolong it. But there is someone who can.'

'Only a human,' wrote the Old Man, 'can make a fresh start.'

'Yes,' she replied, 'a human.'

Slowly the Old Man of Wandering Mountain raised his eyes and saw the Childlike Empress for the first time. His gaze seemed to come from the darkest distance, from the end of the universe. She stood up to it, answered it with her golden eyes. A silent, immobile battle was fought between them. At length the Old Man bent over his book and wrote: 'For you too there is a borderline. Respect it.'

'I will,' she said, 'but the one of whom I speak, the one for whom I am waiting, crossed it long ago. He is reading this book while you are writing it. He hears every word we are saying. He is with us.'

'That is true!' she heard the Old Man's voice as he was writing. 'He too is part and parcel of the Neverending Story, for it is his own story.'

'Tell me the story!' the Childlike Empress commanded. 'You, who are the memory of Fantastica – tell me the story from the beginning, word for word as you have written it.'

The Old Man's writing hand began to tremble.

'If I do that, I shall have to write everything all over again. And what I write will happen again.'

'So be it!' said the Childlike Empress.

Bastian was beginning to feel uncomfortable.

What was she going to do? It had something to do with him. But if even the Old Man of Wandering Mountain was trembling ...

The Old Man wrote and said: 'If the Neverending Story contains itself, then the world will end with this book.'

And the Childlike Empress answered: 'But if the hero comes to us, new life can be born. Now the decision is up to him.'

'You are ruthless indeed,' the Old Man said and wrote. 'We shall enter the Circle of Eternal Return, from which there is no escape.'

'Not for us,' she replies, and her voice was no longer gentle, but as hard and clear as a diamond. 'Nor for him – unless he saves us all.'

'Do you really want to entrust everything to a human?'

'I do.'

But then she added more softly: 'Or have you a better idea?'

After a long silence the Old Man's dark voice said: 'No.'

He bent low over the book in which he was writing. His face was hidden by his hood.

'Then do what I ask.'

Submitting to her will, the Old Man of Wandering Mountain began telling the Neverending Story from the beginning.

At that moment the light cast by the pages of the book changed color. It became reddish like the letters that now formed under the Old Man's stylus. His monk's habit and the hood also took on the color of copper. And as he wrote, his deep, dark voice resounded.

Bastian too heard it quite clearly.

Yet he did not understand the first words the Old Man said. They sounded like: 'Skoob dlo rednaeroc darnoc Irac.'

Strange, Bastian thought. Why is the Old Man suddenly talking a foreign language? Or was it some sort of magic spell?

The Old Man's voice went on and Bastian couldn't help listening.

'This inscription could be seen on the glass door of a small shop, but naturally this was only the way it looked if you were inside the dimly lit shop, looking out at the street through the plate-glass door.

'Outside, it was a gray, cold, rainy November morning. The rain ran down the glass and over the ornate letters. Through the glass there was nothing to be seen but the rain-splotched wall across the street.'

Bastian was rather disappointed. I don't know that story, he thought. That's not in the book I've been reading. Oh well, it only goes to show that I've been mistaken the whole time. I really thought the Old Man would start telling the Neverending Story from the beginning.

'Suddenly the door was opened so violently that a little cluster of brass bells tinkled wildly, taking quite some time to calm down. The cause of this hubbub was a fat little boy of ten or twelve. His wet, dark-brown hair hung down over his face, his coat was soaked and dripping, and he was carrying a school satchel slung over his shoulder. He was rather pale and out of breath, but, despite the hurry he had been in a moment before, he was standing in the open doorway as though rooted to the spot.'

As Bastian read this and listened to the deep, dark voice of the Old Man of Wandering Mountain, a roaring started up in his ears and he saw spots before his eyes.

Why, this was all about him! And it was the Neverending Story. He, Bastian, was a character in the book which until now he had thought he was reading. And heaven only knew who else might be reading it at the exact same time, also supposing himself to be just a reader.

And now Bastian was afraid. He felt unable to breathe, as though shut up in an invisible prison. He didn't want to read anymore, he wanted to stop.

But the deep, dark voice of the Old Man of Wandering Mountain went on,

and there was nothing Bastian could do about it. He held his hands over his ears, but it was no use, because the voice came from inside him. He tried desperately to tell himself – though he knew it wasn't true – that the resemblance to his own story was some crazy accident,

but the deep, dark voice went on,

and ever so clearly he heard it saying:

' "Where are your manners? If you had any, you'd have introduced yourself." '

' "My name is Bastian," said the boy. "Bastian Balthazar Bux." '

In that moment Bastian made a profound discovery. You wish for something, you've wanted it for years, and you're sure you want it, as long as you know you can't have it. But if all at once it looks as though your wish might come true, you suddenly find yourself wishing you had never wished for any such thing.

That is exactly how it was with Bastian.

Now that he was in danger of getting his wish, he would have liked best to run away. But since you can't run 'away' unless you have some idea where you're at, Bastian did something perfectly absurd. He turned over on his back like a beetle and played dead. He made himself as small as possible and pretended he wasn't there.

The Old Man of Wandering Mountain went on telling and writing the story of how Bastian had stolen the book, how he had fled to the schoolhouse attic and begun to read. And then Atreyu's Quest began all over again, he spoke with Morla the Aged One, and found Falkor in Ygramul's net beside the Deep Chasm, and heard Bastian's cry of fear. Once again he was cured by old Urgl and lectured by Engywook. He passed through the three magic gates, entered into Bastian's image, and spoke with Uyulala. And then came the Wind Giants and Spook City and Gmork, followed by Atreyu's rescue and the flight to the Ivory Tower. And in between, everything that Bastian had done, how he had lit the candles, how he had seen the Childlike Empress, and how she had waited for him in vain. Once again she started on her way to find the Old Man of Wandering Mountain, once again she climbed the ladder of letters and entered the egg, once again the conversation between her and the Old Man was related word for word, and once again the Old Man of Wandering Mountain began to write and tell the Neverending Story.

At that point the story began all over again – unchanged and unchangeable – and ended once again with the meeting between the Childlike Empress and the Old Man of Wandering Mountain, who began once again to write and tell the Neverending Story ...

... and so it would go on for ever and ever, for any change in the sequence of events was unthinkable. Only he, Bastian, could do anything about it. And he would have to do something, or else he too would be included in the circle. It seemed to him that this story had been repeated a thousand times, as though there were no before and after and everything had happened at once. Now he realized why the Old Man's hand trembled. The Circle of Eternal Return was an end without an end.

Bastian was unaware of the tears that were running down his cheeks. Close to fainting, he suddenly cried out: 'Moon Child, I'm coming!'
In that moment several things happened at once.

The shell of the great egg was dashed to pieces by some over-whelming power. A rumbling of thunder was heard. And then the storm wind came roaring from afar.

It blew from the pages of the book that Bastian was holding on his knees, and the pages began to flutter wildly. Bastian felt the wind in his hair and face. He could scarcely breathe. The candle flames in the seven-armed candel-abrum danced, wavered, and lay flat. Then another, still more violent wind blew into the book, and the candles went out.
The clock in the belfry struck twelve.

XIII

Perilin,
the Night Forest

OON CHILD, I'm coming!' Bastian repeated in the darkness. He felt something indescribably sweet and comforting flow into him from the name and fill his whole being. So he said it again and again: 'Moon Child! Moon Child! I'm coming! Moon Child, here I am.'

But where was he?

He couldn't see the slightest ray of light, but this was no longer the freezing darkness of the attic. This was a warm, velvety darkness in which he felt safe and happy.

All fear and dread had left him, ceased to be anything more than a distant memory. He felt so light and gay that he even laughed softly.

'Moon Child, where am I?' he asked.

He no longer felt the weight of his body. He groped about and realized that he was hovering in mid-air. The mats were gone, and there was no ground under his feet.

It was a wonderful feeling, a sense of release and boundless freedom that he had never known before. He was beyond the reach of all the things that had weighed him down and hemmed him in.

Could he be hovering somewhere in the cosmos? But in the cosmos there were stars and here there was nothing of the kind. There was only this velvety darkness and a wonderful, happy feeling he hadn't known in all his life. Could it be that he was dead?

'Moon Child, where are you?'

And then he heard a delicate, birdlike voice that answered him and that may have answered him several times without his hearing it. It seemed very near, and yet he could not have said from what direction it came.

'Here I am, my Bastian.'

'Is it you, Moon Child?'

She laughed in a strangely lilting way.

'Who else would I be? Why, you've just given me my lovely name. Thank you for it. Welcome, my savior and my hero.'

'Where are we, Moon Child?'

'I am with you, and you are with me.'

Dream words. Yet Bastian knew for sure that he was awake and not dreaming.

'Moon Child,' he whispered. 'Is this the end?'

'No,' she replied, 'it's the beginning.'

'Where is Fantastica, Moon Child? Where are all the others? Where are Atreyu and Falkor? And what about the Old Man of Wandering Mountain and his book? Don't they exist any-more?'

'Fantastica will be born again from your wishes, my Bastian. Through me they will become reality.'

'From my wishes?' Bastian repeated in amazement.

He heard the sweet voice reply: 'You know they call me the Com-mander of Wishes. What will you wish?'

Bastian thought a moment. Then he inquired cautiously: 'How many wishes have I got?'

'As many as you want – the more, the better, my Bastian. Fantastica will be all the more rich and varied.'

Bastian was overjoyed. But just because so infinitely many possi-bilities had suddenly been held out to him, he couldn't think of a single wish.

'I can't think of anything,' he said finally.

For a time there was silence. And then he heard the birdlike voice: 'That's bad.'

'Why?'

'Because then there won't be any more Fantastica.'

Bastian made no answer. He felt confused. His sense of unlimited freedom was somewhat marred by the thought that everything depended on him.

'Why is it so dark, Moon Child?' he asked.

'The beginning is always dark, my Bastian.'

'I'd awfully like to see you again, Moon Child. The way you were when you looked at me.'

Again he heard the soft lilting laugh.

'Why are you laughing?'

'Because I'm happy.'

'Happy? Why?'

'You've just made your first wish.'

'Will you make it come true?'

He held out his hand and felt she was putting something into it.

Something very small but strangely heavy. It was very cold and felt hard and dead.

'What is it, Moon Child?'

'A grain of sand,' she replied. 'All that's left of my boundless realm. I make you a present of it.'

'Thank you,' said Bastian, bewildered. What on earth could he do with such a gift? If at least it had been something living.

As he was mulling it over, he felt something wriggling in his hand. He raised his hand to see what it was.

'Look, Moon Child,' he whispered. 'It's glowing and glittering. And there – look! a little flame is coming out of it. No, it's not a grain of sand, it's a seed. It's a luminous seed and it's starting to sprout!'

'Well done, my Bastian!' he heard her say. 'You see how easy it is for you.'

Barely perceptible at first, the glow of the speck in Bastian's palm grew quickly, making the two child faces, so very different from each other, gleam in the velvety darkness.

Slowly Bastian withdrew his hand, and the glittering speck hovered between them like a little star.

The seed sprouted so quickly that one could see it grow. It put forth leaves and a stem and buds that burst into many-colored, phosphorescent flowers. Little fruits formed, ripened, and exploded like miniature rockets, spraying new seeds all around them.

From the new seeds grew other plants, but these had different shapes. Some were like ferns or small palms, others like cacti, bullrushes, or gnarled trees. Each glowed a different color.

Soon the velvety darkness all around Bastian and Moon Child, over and under them and on every side, was filled with rapidly growing luminous plants. A globe of radiant colors, a new, luminous world hovered in the Nowhere, and grew and grew. And in its innermost center Bastian and Moon Child sat hand in hand, looking around them with eyes of wonder.

Unceasingly new shapes and colors appeared. Larger and larger blossoms opened, richer and richer clusters formed. And all this in total silence.

Soon some of the plants were as big as fruit trees. There were fans of long emerald-green leaves, flowers resembling peacock tails with rainbow-colored eyes, pagodas consisting of superimposed umbrellas of violet silk. Thick stems were interwoven like braids. Since they were transparent, they looked like pink glass lit up from within. Some of the blooms looked like clusters of blue and yellow Japanese lanterns. And little by little, as the luminous night growth grew denser, they intertwined to form a tissue of soft light.

'You must give all this a name,' Moon Child whispered.

Bastian nodded.

'Perilin, the Night Forest,' he said.

He looked into the Childlike Empress's eyes. And once again, as at their first exchange of glances, he sat spellbound, unable to take his eyes off her. The first time she had been deathly ill. Now she was much, much more beautiful. Her torn gown was whole again, the soft-colored light played over the pure whiteness of the silk and of her long hair. His wish had come true.

Bastian's eyes swam. 'Moon Child,' he stammered. 'Are you well again?'

She smiled. 'Can't you see that I am?'

'I wish everything would stay like this forever,' he said.

'The moment is forever,' she replied.

Bastian was silent. He didn't understand what she had said, but he was in no mood to puzzle it out. He wanted only to sit there looking at her.

Little by little the thicket of luminous plants had formed a thick hedge around them. As though imprisoned in a tent of magic carpets, Bastian paid no attention to what was happening outside. He didn't realize that Perilin was growing and growing, that each and every plant was getting big or bigger. Seeds no bigger than sparks kept raining down and sprouted as they hit the ground.

Bastian sat gazing at Moon Child. He had eyes for nothing else.

He could not have said how much time had passed when Moon Child put her hand over his eyes.

'Why did you keep me waiting so long?' he heard her ask. 'Why did you make me go to the Old Man of Wandering Mountain? Why didn't you come when I called?'

Bastian gulped.

'It was because,' he stammered, 'I thought – all sorts of reasons – fear – well, to tell you the truth, I was ashamed to let you see me.'

She withdrew her hand and looked at him in amazement.

'Ashamed? Why?'

'B-because,' Bastian stammered, 'you – you must have expected somebody who was right for you.'

'What's wrong with you?' she asked. 'Aren't you right for me?'

Bastian felt that he was blushing. 'I mean,' he said, 'somebody strong and brave and handsome – maybe a prince – anyway, not someone like me.'

He couldn't see her, for he had lowered his eyes, but again he heard her soft lilting laugh.

'You see,' he said. 'Now you're laughing at me.'

There was a long silence, and when Bastian finally brought himself to look up, he saw that she was bending very close to him. Her face was grave.

'Let me show you something, my Bastian,' she said. 'Look into my eyes.'

Bastian obeyed, though his heart was pounding and he felt dizzy.

In the golden mirror of her eyes, he saw, small at first as though far in the distance, a reflection which little by little grew larger and more distinct. It was a boy of about his own age; but this boy was slender and wonderfully handsome. His bearing was proud and erect, his face was noble, manly – and lean. He looked like a young prince from the Orient. His turban was of blue silk and so was the silver-embroidered tunic which reached down to his knees. His high boots, made of the softest red leather, were turned up at the toes. And he was wearing a silver-glittering mantle which hung down to the ground. But most beautiful of all were the boy's hands, which, though delicately shaped, gave an impression of unusual strength.

Bastian gazed at the image with wonder and admiration. He couldn't get enough of it. He was just going to ask who this handsome young prince might be when it came to him in a flash that this was his very own self – his reflection in Moon Child's golden eyes.

In that moment he was transported, carried out of himself, and when he returned, he found he had become the handsome boy whose image he had seen.

He looked down, and saw exactly what he had seen in Moon Child's eyes: the soft, red-leather boots, the blue tunic embroidered with silver, the resplendent long mantle. He touched his turban and felt his face. His face was the same too.

And then he turned toward Moon Child.

She was gone!

He was alone in the round room which the glowing thicket had formed.

'Moon Child!' he shouted. 'Moon Child!'

There was no answer.

Feeling utterly lost, he sat down. What was he to do now? Why had she left him alone? Where should he go – that is, if he was free to go anywhere, if he wasn't caught in a trap?

While he was wondering why Moon Child should have vanished without a word of explanation, without so much as bidding him goodbye, his fingers started playing with a golden medallion that was hanging from his neck.

He looked at it and let out a cry of surprise.

It was A U R Y N, the Gem, the Childlike Empress's amulet, which made its bearer her representative. Moon Child had given him power over every creature and thing in Fantastica. And as long as he wore that emblem, it would be as though she were with him.

For a long while Bastian looked at the two snakes, the one light, the other dark, which were biting each other's tail, and formed an oval. Then he turned the amulet over and to his surprise found an inscription on the reverse side. It consisted of four words in strangely intricate letters:

Do

What You

Wish

There had been no mention of such an inscription in the Neverending Story. Could it be that Atreyu hadn't noticed it?

But that didn't matter now. What mattered was that the words gave him permission, ordered him in fact, to do whatever he pleased.

Bastian approached the wall of luminous plants to see if he could slip through somewhere. To his delight he found that the wall could easily be thrust aside like a curtain. Out he stepped.

In the meantime, the night plants had kept on growing, gently but irresistibly, and Perilin had become a forest such as no human eye had ever beheld.

The great trunks were now as high and thick as church towers, and still growing. In places these shimmering, milky-white pillars were so close together that it was impossible to pass between them. And seeds were still falling like a shower of sparks.

On his way through the luminous forest, Bastian tried hard not to step on the glittering seeds that lay on the ground, but this soon proved impossible. There simply wasn't a foot's breadth of ground from which nothing was sprouting. So he stopped worrying and went wherever the giant trees left a path open for him.

Bastian was delighted at being handsome. It didn't bother him that there was no one to admire him. On the contrary, he was glad to have the pleasure all to himself. He didn't care a fig for being admired by the lugs who had always made fun of him. If he thought of them at all, it was almost with pity.

In this forest, where there were no seasons and no alternation of day and night, the feeling of time was entirely different from anything Bastian had ever known. He had no idea how long he had been on his way. But little by little his pleasure in being handsome underwent a change. He began to take it for granted. Not that he was any less happy about it; but now he had the feeling that he had never been any different.

For this there was a reason which Bastian was not to discover until much later. The beauty that had been bestowed on him made him forget, little by little, that he had ever been fat and bowlegged.

Even if he had known what was happening, he would hardly have regretted the loss of this particular memory. As it happened, he didn't even realize that he had forgotten anything. And when the memory had vanished completely, it seemed to him that he had always been as handsome as he was now.

At that point a new wish cropped up. Just being handsome wasn't as wonderful as he had thought. He also wanted to be strong, stronger than anybody! The strongest in the world!

While going deeper and deeper into the Night Forest, he began to feel hungry. He picked off a few of the strangely shaped luminous fruits and nibbled gingerly to see if they were edible. Edible was no word for it; some were tart, some sweet, some slightly bitter, but all were delicious. He ate as he walked, and felt a miraculous strength flowing into his limbs.

In the meantime the glowing underbrush around him had become so dense that it cut off his view on all sides. To make matters worse, lianas and aerial roots were becoming inextricably tangled with the thicket below. Slashing with the side of his hand as if it had been a machete, Bastian opened up a passage. And the breach closed directly behind him as if it had never been.

On he went, but the wall of giant tree trunks blocked his path.

Bastian grabbed hold of two great tree trunks and bent them apart. When he had passed through, the wall closed soundlessly behind him.

Bastian shouted for joy.

He was the Lord of the Jungle!

For a while he amused himself opening paths for himself, like an elephant that has heard the Great Call. His strength did not abate, he had no need to stop for breath. He felt no stitch in his side, and his heart didn't thump or race.

But after a while he wearied of his new sport. The next thing he wanted was to look down on his domain from above, to see how big it was.

He spat on his hands, took hold of a liana, and pulled himself up hand over hand, without using his legs, as he had seen acrobats do in the circus. For a moment a vision – a pale memory of the past – came to him of himself in gym class, dangling like a sack of flour from the bottommost end of the rope, while the rest of the class cackled with glee. He couldn't help smiling. How they would gape if they saw him now! They'd be proud to know him. But he wouldn't even look at them.

Without stopping once he finally reached the branch from which the liana was hanging, climbed up and straddled it. The branch gave off a red glow. He stood up and, balancing himself like a tightrope walker, made his way to the trunk. Here again a dense tangle of creepers barred his way, but he had no difficulty in opening up a passage through it.

At that height the trunk was still so thick that five men clasping hands could not have encircled it. Another, somewhat higher branch, jutting from the trunk in a different direction, was beyond his reach. So he leapt through the air, caught hold of an aerial root, swung himself into place, made another perilous leap, and grabbed the higher branch. From there he was able to pull himself up to a still higher one. By then he was high above the ground, at least three hundred feet, but the glowing branches and foliage still obstructed his view.

Not until he had climbed to twice that height were there occasional spaces through which he could look around. But then the going became difficult, because there were fewer and fewer branches. And at last, when he had almost reached the top, he had to stop, for there was nothing to hold on to but the smooth, bare trunk, which was still as thick as a telegraph pole.

Bastian looked up and saw that the trunk or stalk ended some fifty feet higher up in an enormous, glowing, dark-red blossom. He didn't see how he could ever reach it, but he had to keep going, for he couldn't very well stay where he was. He threw his arms around the trunk and climbed the last fifty feet like an acrobat. The trunk swayed and bent like a blade of grass in the wind.

At length he was directly below the blossom, which was open at the top like a tulip. He managed to slip one hand between two of the petals and take hold. Then, pushing the petals wide apart, he pulled himself up.

For a moment he lay there, for by then he was somewhat out of breath. But then he stood up and looked over the edge of the great, glowing blossom, as from the crow's nest of a ship.

The tree he had climbed was one of the tallest in the whole jungle and he was able to see far into the distance. Above him he still saw the velvety darkness of a starless night sky, but below him, as far as he could see, the treetops of Perilin presented a play of colors that took his breath away.

For a long time Bastian stood there, drinking in the sight. This was his domain! He had created it! He was the lord of Perilin.

And once again he shouted for joy!

XIV

The Desert of Colors

EVER had Bastian slept so soundly as in that glowing red blossom. When at last he opened his eyes, the sky overhead was still a velvety black. He stretched and was happy to feel miraculous strength in his limbs.

Once again, there had been a change in him. His wish to be strong had come true.

When he stood up and looked out over the edge of the great blossom, Perilin seemed to have stopped growing. The Night Forest looked pretty much the same as when he had last seen it. He didn't know that this too was connected with the fulfillment of his wish, and that his memory of his weakness and clumsiness had been blotted out at the same time. He was handsome and strong, but somehow that wasn't enough for him. He also felt the need to be tough and inured to hardship like Atreyu. But how was he to come by that quality in this luminous garden, where all manner of fruit was to be had for the picking?

The first pearly streaks of dawn appeared over the eastern horizon. And with the rising of the light the phosphorescence of the night plants paled.

'High time!' said Bastian aloud. 'I thought the day would never come.'

He sat down on the floor of the blossom and wondered what he should do. Climb down again and keep going? Of course, since he was lord of Perilin, no one could stop him from wandering around in it for days, if not for months or years. This jungle was so enormous he would never find his way out of it. But beautiful as he found the night plants, he didn't think this prospect would suit him in the long run. Exploring a desert – that would be something else again. The biggest desert in Fantastica. Yes, that would be something to be proud of.

In that same moment, a violent tremor shook the giant tree. The trunk bent, and a crackling, groaning sound could be heard. Bastian had to hold tight to keep from rolling out of his blossom, the stem of which tilted more and more, until at last it lay flat.

The sun, which had risen in the meantime, disclosed a vision of devastation. Hardly anything was left of all the enormous night plants. More quickly than they had sprung up they crumbled under the glaring sunlight into dust and fine, colored sand. Gigantic tree trunks collapsed as sand castles do when they dry out. Bastian's tree seemed to be the last still standing. But when he tried to steady himself by grasping at the petals of his flower, they crumbled in his hands and blew away like a cloud of dust. Now that there was nothing to obstruct the view, he saw how terrifyingly high up he was. He knew he would have to climb down as fast as possible, for the tree was likely to collapse at any moment.

Cautiously, he climbed out of the blossom and straddled the stem, which was now bent like a fishing pole. No sooner had he left the blossom than it broke off behind him and crumbled into dust in falling.

Ever so gingerly Bastian proceeded downward. Many a man would have panicked on seeing the ground so very far below, but Bastian was free from dizziness and his nerves were steel. Knowing that any abrupt movement might reduce the whole tree to dust, he crept along the bough and finally reached the place where the trunk became vertical. Hugging it, he let himself slide, inch by inch. Several times, great clouds of colored dust fell on him from above. There were no branches left, and what towering stumps remained crumbled when Bastian tried to use them for support. As he continued downward, the trunk became too big for him to hold. And he was still far above the ground. He stopped to think: How was he ever going to get down?

But then another tremor passed through the giant stump and relieved him of the need for further thought. What was left of the tree disintegrated and settled into a great mound of sand; Bastian rolled down the side of it in a wild whirl, turning a number of somersaults on the way, and finally came to rest at the bottom. He came close to being buried under an avalanche of colored dust, but he fought his way clear, spat the sand out of his mouth, and shook it out of his ears and clothes.

Wherever he looked, the sand was moving in slow streams and eddies. It collected into hills and dunes of every shape and size, each with a color of its own. Light-blue sand gathered to form a light-blue hill, and the same with green and violet and so on. Perilin, the Night Forest, was gone and a desert was taking its place; and what a desert!

Bastian had climbed a dune of purplish-red sand and all around him he saw nothing but hill after hill of every imaginable color. Each hill revealed a shade or tint that recurred in no other. The nearest was cobalt blue, another was saffron yellow, then came crimson red, then indigo, apple green, sky blue, orange, peach, mauve, turquoise blue, lilac, moss green, ruby red, burnt umber, Indian yellow, vermilion, lapis lazuli. And so on from horizon to horizon. And between the hills, separating color from color, flowed streams of gold and silver sand.

'This,' said Bastian aloud, 'is Goab, the Desert of Colors.'

The sun rose higher and higher and the heat became murderous. The air over the colored sand dunes shimmered, and Bastian realized that he was in a tight spot. He could not stay in this desert, that was certain. If he didn't get out of it soon, he would die of hunger and thirst.

He took hold of the Childlike Empress's emblem in the hope that it would guide him. And then staunchly he started on his way.

He climbed dune after dune; hour after hour he plodded on, never seeing anything but hill after hill. Only the colors kept changing. His fabulous strength was no longer of any use to him, for desert distances cannot be vanquished with strength. The air was a searing blast from hell. His tongue clung to the roof of his mouth and his face streamed with sweat.

The sun was a whorl of fire in the middle of the sky. It had been in the same place for a long time and didn't seem to move. That day in the desert was as long as the night in Perilin.

Bastian's eyes burned and his tongue felt like a piece of leather. But he didn't give up. His body had dried out, and the blood in his veins was so thick it could hardly flow. But on he went, slowly, with even steps, neither hurrying nor stopping to rest, as if he had had years of experience at crossing deserts on foot. He ignored the torments of thirst. His will had become as hard as steel, neither fatigue nor hardship could bend it.

He recalled how easily he had been discouraged in the past. He had begun all sorts of projects and given up at the first sign of difficulty. He had always been afraid of not getting enough to eat, or of falling ill, or having to endure pain. All that was far behind him.

No one before him had dared to cross Goab, the Desert of Colors, on foot, nor would anyone undertake to do so in the future. And most likely no one would ever hear of his exploit.

This last thought saddened Bastian. Goab seemed to be so inconceivably large he felt sure he would never come to the end of it. Despite his phenomenal endurance he was bound to perish sooner or later. That didn't frighten him. He would die with calm dignity like the hunters in Atreyu's country. But since no one ever ventured into this desert, the news of his death would never be divulged. Either in Fantastica or at home. He would simply be reported missing, and no one would ever know he had been in Fantastica or in the desert of Goab. All Fantastica, he said to himself, was contained in the book that the Old Man of Wandering Mountain had written. This book was the Neverending Story, which he himself had read in the attic. Maybe his present adventures and sufferings were in the book even now. And maybe someone else would read the book someday – maybe someone was reading it at that very moment. In that case, it must be possible to give that someone a sign.

The sand hill where Bastian was standing just then was ultramarine blue. And separated from it by a narrow cleft there was a fiery-red dune. Bastian crossed over to it, gathered up sand in both hands and carried it to the blue hill. Then he strewed a long line of red sand on the hillside. He went back, brought more red sand, and repeated the operation. Soon he had fashioned three enormous red letters against the blue ground:

B   B   B

He viewed his work with satisfaction. No reader of the Neverending Story could fail to see his message. So whatever happened to him now, someone would know where he had been.

He sat down to rest on the red hilltop. The three letters glittered bright in the desert sun.

Another piece of his memory of the old Bastian had been wiped out. He forgot that he had once been a namby-pamby, something of a crybaby, in fact. And he was ever so proud of his toughness. But already a new wish was taking form.

'It's true that I fear nothing,' he said aloud, 'but what I still lack is true courage. Being able to endure hardships is a great thing. But courage and daring are something else again. I wish I could run into a real adventure, something calling for great courage. How grand it would be to meet some dangerous creature – maybe not as hideous as Ygramul, but much more dangerous. A beautiful, but very, very dangerous creature. The most dangerous creature in all Fantastica. I'd step right up to it and ...'

Bastian said no more, for in that same moment he heard a roaring and rumbling so deep that the ground trembled beneath his feet.

Bastian turned around. Far in the distance he saw something that looked like a ball of fire. Moving with incredible speed, it described a wide arc around the spot where Bastian was sitting, then came straight toward him. In the shimmering desert air, which made the outline of things waver like flames, the creature looked like a dancing fire-demon.

Bastian was stricken with terror. Before he knew it, he had run down into the cleft between the red dune and the blue dune. But no sooner had he got there than he felt ashamed and overcame his fear.

He took hold of A U R Y N and felt all the courage he had wished for streaming into his heart.

Then again he heard the deep roar that made the ground tremble, but this time it was near him. He looked up.

A huge lion was standing on the fiery-red dune. The sun was directly behind him, and made his great mane look like a wreath of fire. This lion was not a tawny color like other lions, but as fiery red as the dune on which he was standing.

The beast did not seem to have noticed the boy, so much smaller than himself, who was standing in the cleft between the two dunes, but seemed to be looking at the red letters on the opposite hill. The great rumbling voice said: 'Who did this?'

'I did,' said Bastian.

'What is it?'

'It's my initials,' said Bastian. 'My name is Bastian Balthazar Bux.'

Then for the first time the lion turned toward Bastian, who for a moment expected to be burned to a crisp by the flames that seemed to surround the lion. But his fear soon passed and he returned the lion's gaze.

'I,' said the huge beast, 'am Grograman, Lord of the Desert of Colors. I am also known as the Many-Colored Death.'

Bastian felt the deadly power that flowed from the lion's eyes. But he did not avert his own.

When they had measured their strength for some time, the lion looked down. With slow, majestic movements he descended from the dune. When he stepped onto the ultramarine sand, he too changed color, his coat and mane became blue. For a moment the huge beast stood facing Bastian, who had to look up at him as a mouse might look up at a cat. Then suddenly Grograman lay down and touched his head to the ground.

'Master,' he said. 'I am your servant, I await your commands.'

'I'd like to get out of this desert,' said Bastian. 'Can you manage that?'

Grograman shook his mane.

'No, master, that I cannot do.'

'Why not?'

'Because I carry the desert with me.'

Not knowing what to make of this, Bastian asked: 'Isn't there somebody who can get me out of here?'

'How could that be, master?' said Grograman. 'Where I am no other living creature can exist. My presence alone would suffice to reduce everybody – even the most powerful of creatures – into ashes for thousands of miles around. That's why I'm called the Many-Colored Death and Lord of the Desert of Colors.'

'That's not so,' said Bastian. 'Everybody doesn't get burned up in your desert. Look at me.'

'Because you are bearing the Gem, master. AURYN protects you – even from me, the deadliest creature in Fantastica.'

'You mean that if I didn't have the Gem, I'd be reduced to ashes?'

'That's how it is, master. That's what would happen, though personally I'd regret it. Because you're the first and only being who has ever spoken to me.'

Bastian touched the amulet. 'Thank you, Moon Child,' he said under his breath.

Grograman stood up to his full height and looked down at Bastian.

'I believe, master, that we have things to discuss. Perhaps I can acquaint you with certain secrets. And perhaps you can clear up the riddle of my existence for me.'

Bastian nodded. 'But first,' he said. 'Could you possibly get me something to drink? I'm very thirsty.'

'Your servant hears and obeys,' said Grograman. 'Will you deign to sit on my back? I shall carry you to my palace, where you will find everything you need.'

Bastian climbed up on the lion's back and clutched the flaming mane in both hands. Grograman looked back at his passenger.

'Hold on tight, master, I'm a swift runner. And one more thing: as long as you are in my domain and especially when you are with me – promise me that you will never for any reason lay down the amulet that protects you.'

'I promise,' said Bastian.

The lion started off, at first at a slow, dignified gait, then faster and faster. To Bastian's amazement, the lion's coat and mane changed color with every new sand hill. But soon Grograman was making great leaps from hilltop to hilltop, and his coat changed color faster and faster. Bastian's eyes swam, and he saw all the colors at once as in a rainbow. The hot wind whistled around Bastian's ears and tugged at his mantle, which fluttered behind him. He felt the movements of the lion's muscles and breathed the wild, heady smell of the shaggy mane. The triumphant shout that escaped him resembled the cry of a bird of prey, and Grograman answered with a roar that made the desert tremble. For the moment these two different creatures were one. Bastian's heart and mind were in the clouds. He didn't come to himself until he heard Grograman saying: 'We have arrived, master! Will you deign to alight?'

Bastian jumped down from the lion's back and landed on the sandy ground. Before him he saw a cleft mountain of black rock.

Or was it a ruined building? He didn't know, for the stones which made up the doorframes, walls, columns, and terraces of the building, as well as those that were lying about half buried in colored sand, were deeply creviced and smooth, as though the sandstorms of time had smoothed away all sharp edges and roughness.

'This, master, is my palace – and my tomb,' Bastian heard the lion's voice saying. 'You are Grograman's first and only guest. Enter and make yourself at home.'

The sun hung low over the horizon, a great pale-yellow disk, shorn of its searing heat. Apparently the ride had taken much longer than it had seemed to Bastian. The truncated columns or spurs of rock, whichever they might be, cast long shadows. It would soon be night.

As Bastian followed the lion through a dark doorway leading into the palace, he had the impression that Grograman's steps sounded tired and heavy.

After passing a dark corridor and up and down a number of stairways, they came at last to a large double door which seemed to be made of black rock. As Grograman approached, it opened of its own accord, and when they had both gone through, it closed behind them.

Now they were in a large hall, or rather a cave, lit by hundreds of lamps whose flames resembled the play of colors on Grograman's coat. The floor was of colored tiles. At the center was a circular platform surrounded by steps, and on the platform lay an enormous black rock. Grograman seemed spent as he turned to Bastian.

'My time is close at hand, master,' he said, hardly above a whisper. 'There won't be time for our talk. But don't worry, and wait for the day. What has always happened will happen once again. And perhaps you will be able to tell me why.'

Then he pointed his head in the direction of a little gate at the other end of the cave.

'Go in there, master. You will find everything in readiness. That room has been waiting for you since the beginning of time.'

Bastian went to the gate, but before opening it, he glanced back. Grograman had sat down on the black rock. He was as black as the stone. In a faint, far-off voice, he said: 'Quite possibly, master, you will hear sounds that will frighten you. Don't be afraid. As long as you carry the emblem, nothing can happen to you.'

Bastian nodded and passed through the gate.

The room he entered was magnificent. The floor was laid with soft, richly colored carpets. The graceful columns supporting the vaulted ceiling were covered with gold mosaic, which fragmented the varicolored light of the lamps. In one corner Bastian saw a broad divan covered with soft rugs and cushions of all kinds, surmounted by a canopy of azure-blue silk. In the opposite corner the stone floor had been hollowed to form a pool filled with golden liquid. On a low table stood bowls and dishes of food, a carafe full of some ruby-red drink, and a golden cup.

Bastian squatted down at the table and fell to. The drink had a tart, wild taste and was wonderfully thirst-quenching. The dishes were unknown to Bastian. Some looked like cakes or nuts, others like squash or melons, but the taste was entirely different. Sharp and spicy. Everything was delicious, and Bastian ate his fill.

Then he took his clothes off – but not the amulet – and stepped into the pool. For a while he splashed about, washed himself, dived under, and came up puffing like a walrus. Then he discovered some strange-looking bottles at the edge of the pool. Thinking they must be bath oils, he poured a little of each into the water. Green, red, and yellow flames darted hissing over the surface, and a little smoke went up. It smelled of resin and bitter herbs. And then the flames died.

After a while Bastian got out of the water, dried himself with the soft towels that lay ready, and put his clothes on. Suddenly he noticed that the lamps were not burning as brightly as before. And then he heard a sound that sent the cold shivers down his spine: a cracking and grinding, as though a rock were bursting under the pressure of expanding ice.

Bastian's heart pounded. He remembered that Grograman had told him not to be afraid.

The sound softened to a moan and soon stopped. It was not repeated, but the stillness was almost more terrible.

Determined to find out what had happened, Bastian opened the door of the bedchamber. At first he saw no change in the great hall, except that the lamplight now seemed somber and was pulsating like a faltering heartbeat. The lion was still sitting in the same attitude on the black rock. He seemed to be looking at Bastian.

'Grograman!' Bastian cried. 'What's going on? What was that sound? Was it you?'

The lion made no answer and didn't move, but when Bastian approached him, the lion followed him with his eyes.

Hesitantly Bastian stretched out his hand to stroke the lion's mane, but the moment he touched it he recoiled in horror. It was hard and ice-cold like the black rock. And Grograman's face and paws felt the same way.

Bastian didn't know what to do. He saw that the black stone doors were slowly opening. He left the hall, but it wasn't until he had passed through the long dark corridor and was on his way up the stairs that he started wondering what he would do when he was outside. In this desert there couldn't be anyone capable of saving Grograman.

But it wasn't a desert anymore!

Whichever way Bastian looked, he saw glittering dots. Millions of tiny plants were sprouting from the grains of sand which had become seeds again. Perilin the Night Forest was growing once more.

Bastian sensed that Grograman's rigidity was somehow connected with this transformation.

He went back to the cave. The light in the lamps was barely flickering. He went over to the lion, threw his arms around the huge neck, and pressed his face to the beast's face.

The lion's eyes were black and as dead as the rock. Grograman had turned to stone. The lights flared for an instant and went out, leaving the cave in total darkness.

Bastian wept bitterly. The stone lion was wet with his tears. In the end, the boy curled up between the great paws and fell asleep!

XV

Grograman, the Many-Colored Death

MASTER,' said the rumbling lion's voice. 'Have you spent the whole night like this?'

Bastian sat up and rubbed his eyes. He had been lying between the lion's paws, and Grograman was watching him with a look of amazement. His fur was still as black as the rock he was sitting on, but his eyes sparkled. The lamps in the cave were burning again.

'Oh!' Bastian cried. 'I thought you had turned to stone.'

'So I had,' the lion replied. 'I die with every nightfall, and every morning I wake up again.'

'I thought it was forever,' said Bastian.

'It always *is* forever,' said Grograman mysteriously.

He stood up, stretched, and trotted about the cave. His fur shone more and more brightly in the colors of the mosaic floor. Suddenly he stopped still and looked at the boy.

'Did you shed tears over me?' he asked.

Bastian nodded.

'Then,' said the lion, 'you are not only the only being who has ever slept between the paws of the Many-Colored Death, but also the only being who has ever mourned his death.'

Bastian looked at the lion, who was trotting about again, and finally asked him in a whisper: 'Are you always alone?'

Again the lion stood still, but this time he did not turn toward Bastian. He kept his face averted and repeated in his rumbling voice: 'Alone!'

The word echoed through the cave.

'My realm is the desert, and it is also my work. Wherever I go, everything around me turns to desert. I carry it with me. Since I am made of deadly fire, must I not be doomed to everlasting solitude?'

Bastian fell into a dismayed silence.

'Master,' said the lion, looking at the boy with glowing eyes. 'You who bear the emblem of the Childlike Empress, can you tell me this: Why must I always die at nightfall?'

'So that Perilin, the Night Forest, can grow in the Desert of Colors,' said Bastian.

'Perilin?' said the lion. 'What's that?'

Then Bastian told him about the miraculous jungle that consisted of living light. While Grograman listened in fascinated amazement, Bastian described the diversity and beauty of the glimmering phosphorescent plants, their silent, irresistible growth, their dream-like beauty and incredible size. His enthusiasm grew as he spoke and Grograman's eyes glowed more and more brightly.

'All that,' Bastian concluded, 'can happen only when you are turned to stone. But Perilin would swallow up everything else and stifle itself if it didn't have to die and crumble into dust when you wake up. You and Perilin need each other.'

For a long while Grograman was silent.

'Master,' he said then. 'Now I see that my dying gives life and my living death, and both are good. Now I understand the meaning of my existence. I thank you.'

He strode slowly and solemnly into the darkest corner of the cave. Bastian couldn't see what he did there, but he heard a jangling of metal. When Grograman came back, he was carrying something in his mouth. With a deep bow he laid this something at Bastian's feet.

It was a sword.

It didn't look very impressive. The iron sheath was rusty, and the hilt might have belonged to a child's wooden sword.

'Can you give it a name?' Grograman asked.

Bastian examined it carefully.

'Sikanda,' he said.

In that same moment the sword darted from its sheath and flew into his hand. The blade consisted of pure light and glittered so brightly that he could hardly bear to look at it. It was double-edged and weighed no more than a feather.

'This sword has been destined for you since the beginning of time,' said Grograman. 'For only one who has ridden on my back, who has eaten and drunk of my fire and bathed in it like you, can touch it without danger. But only because you have given it its right name does it belong to you.'

'Sikanda!' said Bastian under his breath as, fascinated by the gleaming light, he swung the sword slowly through the air. 'It's a magic sword, isn't it?'

'Nothing in all Fantastica can resist it,' said Grograman, 'neither rock nor steel. But you must not use force. Whatever may threaten you, you may wield it only if it leaps into your hand of its own accord as it did now. It will guide your hand and by its own power will do what needs to be done. But if your will makes you draw it from its sheath, you will bring great misfortune on yourself and on Fantastica. Never forget that.'

'I will never forget it,' Bastian promised.

The sword flew back into its sheath and again it looked old and worthless. Bastian grasped the leather belt on which the sheath hung and slung it around his waist.

'And now, master,' Grograman suggested, 'let us, if you wish, go racing through the desert together. Climb on my back, for I must go out now.'

Bastian mounted, and the lion trotted out into the open. The Night Forest had long since crumbled into colored sand, and the morning sun rose above the desert horizon. Together they swept over the dunes – like a dancing flame, like a blazing tempest. Bastian felt as though he were riding a flaming comet through light and colors.

Toward midday Grograman stopped.

'This, master, is the place where we met.'

Bastian's head was still reeling from the wild ride. He looked around but could see neither the ultramarine-blue nor the fiery-red hill. Nor was there any sign of the letters he had made. Now the dunes were olive green and pink.

'It's all entirely different,' he said.

'Yes, master,' said the lion. 'That's the way it is – different every day. Up until now I didn't know why. But since you told me that Perilin grows out of the sand, I understand.'

'But how do you know it's the same place as yesterday?'

'I feel it as I feel my own body. The desert is a part of me.'

Bastian climbed down from Grograman's back and seated himself on the olive-green hill. The lion lay beside him and now he too was olive green. Bastian propped his chin on his hand and looked out toward the horizon.

'Grograman,' he said after a long silence. 'May I ask you a question?'

'Your servant is listening.'

'Is it true that you've always been here?'

'Always!'

'And the desert of Goab has always existed?'

'Yes, the desert too. Why do you ask?'

Bastian pondered.

'I don't get it,' he finally confessed. 'I'd have bet it wasn't here before yesterday morning.'

'What makes you think that, master?'

Then Bastian told him everything that had happened since he met Moon Child.

'It's all so strange,' he concluded. 'A wish comes into my head, and then something always happens that makes the wish come true. I haven't made this up, you know. I wouldn't be able to. I could never have invented all the different night plants in Perilin. Or the colors of Goab – or you! It's all much more wonderful and real than anything I could have made up. But all the same, nothing is there until I've wished it.'

'That,' said the lion, 'is because you're carrying AURYN, the Gem.'

'But does all this exist only after I've wished it? Or was it all there before?'

'Both,' said Grograman.

'How can that be?' Bastian cried almost impatiently. 'You've been here in Goab, the Desert of Colors, since heaven knows when. The room in your palace was waiting for me since the beginning of time. So, too, was the sword Sikanda. You told me so yourself.'

'That is true, master.'

'But I – I've only been in Fantastica since last night! So it can't be true that all these things have existed only since I came here.'

'Master,' the lion replied calmly. 'Didn't you know that Fantastica is the land of stories? A story can be new and yet tell about olden times. The past comes into existence with the story.'

'Then Perilin, too, must always have been there,' said the perplexed Bastian.

'Beginning at the moment when you gave it its name,' Grograman replied, 'it has existed forever.'

'You mean that I created it?'

The lion was silent for a while. Then he said: 'Only the Childlike Empress can tell you that. It is she who has given you everything.'

He arose.

'Master, it's time we went back to my palace. The sun is low in the sky and we have a long way to go.'

That night Grograman lay down again on the black rock, and this time Bastian stayed with him. Few words passed between them. Bastian brought food and drink from the bedchamber, where once again the little table had been laid by an unseen hand. He seated himself on the steps leading to the lion's rock, and there he ate his supper.

When the light of the lamps grew dim and began to pulsate like a faltering heartbeat, he stood up and threw his arms around the lion's neck. The mane was hard and looked like congealed lava. Then the gruesome sound was repeated. Bastian was no longer afraid, but again he wept at the thought of Grograman's sufferings, for now he knew they would endure for all time.

Later that night Bastian groped his way into the open and stood for a long while watching the soundless growth of the night plants. Then he went back into the cave and again lay down to sleep between the petrified lion's paws.

He stayed with Grograman for many days and nights, and they became friends. They spent many hours in the desert, playing wild games. Bastian would hide among the sand dunes, but Grograman always found him. They ran races, but the lion was a thousand times swifter than Bastian. They wrestled and there Bastian was the lion's equal. Though of course it was only in fun, Grograman needed all his strength to hold his own. Neither could defeat the other.

Once, after they had been wrestling and tumbling, Bastian sat down, somewhat out of breath, and said: 'Couldn't I stay with you forever?'

The lion shook his mane. 'No, master.'

'Why not?'

'Here there is only life and death, only Perilin and Goab,

but no story. You must live your story. You cannot remain here.'

'But how can I leave?' Bastian asked. 'The desert is much too big, I'd never get to the end of it. And you can't carry me out of it, because you take the desert with you.'

'Only your wishes can guide you over the pathways of Fantastica,' said Grograman. 'You must go from wish to wish. What you don't wish for will always be beyond your reach. That is what the words 'far' and 'near' mean in Fantastica. And wishing to leave a place is not enough. You must wish to go somewhere else and let your wishes guide you.'

'But I can't wish to leave here,' said Bastian.

'You must find your next wish,' said Grograman almost sternly.

'And when I find it,' Bastian asked, 'how will I be able to leave here?'

'I will tell you,' said Grograman gravely. 'There is in Fantastica a certain place from which one can go anywhere and which can be reached from anywhere. We call it the Temple of a Thousand Doors. No one has ever seen it from outside. The inside is a maze of doors. Anyone wishing to know it must dare to enter it.'

'But how is that possible if it can't be approached from outside?'

'Every door in Fantastica,' said the lion, 'even the most ordinary stable, kitchen, or cupboard door, can become the entrance to the Temple of a Thousand Doors at the right moment. And none of these thousand doors leads back to where one came from. There is no return.'

'And once someone is inside,' Bastian asked, 'can he get out and go somewhere?'

'Yes,' said the lion. 'But it's not as simple as in other buildings. Only a genuine wish can lead you through the maze of the thousand doors. Without a genuine wish, you just have to wander around until you know what you really want. And that can take a long time.'

'How will I find the entrance?'

'You've got to wish it.'

Bastian pondered a long while. Then he said: 'It seems strange that we can't just wish what we please. Where do our wishes come from? What is a wish anyway?'

Grograman gave the boy a long, earnest look, but made no answer.

Some days later they had another serious talk.

Bastian had shown the lion the inscription on the reverse side of the Gem. 'What do you suppose it means?' he asked. ' "DO WHAT YOU WISH." That must mean I can do anything I feel like. Don't you think so?'

All at once Grograman's face looked alarmingly grave, and his eyes glowed.

'No,' he said in his deep, rumbling voice. 'It means that you must do what you really and truly want. And nothing is more difficult.'

'What I really and truly want? What do you mean by that?'

'It's your own deepest secret and you yourself don't know it.'

'How can I find out?'

'By going the way of your wishes, from one to another, from first to last. It will take you to what you really and truly want.'

'That doesn't sound so hard,' said Bastian.

'It is the most dangerous of all journeys.'

'Why?' Bastian asked. 'I'm not afraid.'

'That isn't it,' Grograman rumbled. 'It requires the greatest honesty and vigilance, because there's no other journey on which it's so easy to lose yourself forever.'

'Do you mean because our wishes aren't always good?' Bastian asked.

The lion lashed the sand he was lying on with his tail. His ears lay flat, he screwed up his nose, and his eyes flashed fire. Involuntarily Bastian ducked when Grograman's voice once again made the earth tremble: 'What do you know about wishes? How would you know what's good and what isn't?'

In the days that followed Bastian thought a good deal about what the Many-Colored Death had said. There are some things, however, that we cannot fathom by thinking about them, but only by experience. So it was not until much later, after all manner of adventures, that he thought back on Grograman's words and began to understand them.

At this time another change took place in Bastian. Since his meeting with Moon Child he had received many gifts. Now he was favored with a new one: courage. And again something was taken away from him, namely, the memory of his past timidity.

Since he was no longer afraid of anything, a new wish began, imperceptibly at first, then more distinctly, to take shape within him: the wish to be alone no longer. Even in the company of the Many-Colored Death he was alone in a way. He wanted to exhibit his talents to others, to be admired and to become famous.

And one night as he was watching Perilin grow, it suddenly came to him that he was doing so for the last time, that he would have to bid the grandiose Night Forest goodbye. An inner voice was calling him away.

He cast a last glance at the magnificently glowing colors. Then he descended to the darkness of Grograman's palace and tomb, and sat down on the steps. He couldn't have said what he was waiting for, but he knew that he could not sleep that night.

He must have dozed a little, for suddenly he started as if someone had called his name.

The door leading to the bedchamber had opened. Through the cleft a long strip of reddish light shone into the dark cave.

Bastian stood up. Had the door been transformed for this moment into the entrance of the Temple of a Thousand Doors? Hesitantly he approached the cleft and tried to peer through. He couldn't see a thing. Then slowly the cleft began to close. In a moment his only chance would pass.

He turned back to Grograman, who lay motionless, with eyes of dead stone, on his pedestal. The strip of light from the door fell full on him.

'Goodbye, Grograman, and thanks for everything,' he said softly. 'I'll come again, I promise, I'll come again.'

Then he slipped through the cleft, and instantly the door closed behind him.

Bastian didn't know that he would not keep his promise. Much much later someone would come in his name and keep it for him.

But that's another story and shall be told another time.

XVI

The Silver City of Amarganth

URPLE light passed in slow waves across the floor and the walls of the room. It was a hexagonal room, rather like the enlarged cell of a honeycomb. Every second wall had a door in it, and on the intervening walls were painted strange pictures representing landscapes and creatures who seemed to be half plant and half animal. Bastian had entered through one of the doors; the other two, to the right and left of it, were exactly the same shape, but the left-hand door was black, while the right-hand one was white. Bastian chose the white door.

In the next room the light was yellowish. Here again the walls formed a hexagon. The pictures represented all manner of contrivances that meant nothing to Bastian. Were they tools or weapons? The two doors leading onward to the right and left were the same color, yellow, but the left-hand one was tall and narrow, while the one on the right was low and wide. Bastian chose the left-hand one.

The next room was hexagonal like the others, but the light was bluish. The pictures on the walls were of intricate ornaments or characters in a strange alphabet. Here the two doors were the same color, but of different material, one of wood, the other of metal. Bastian chose the wooden door.

It is not possible to describe all the doors and rooms through which Bastian passed during his stay in the Temple of a Thousand Doors. There were doors that looked like large keyholes, and others that resembled the entrances to caves, there were golden doors and rusty iron doors, some were padded and some were studded with nails, some were paper-thin and others as thick as the doors of treasure houses; there was one that looked like a giant's mouth and another that had to be opened like a drawbridge, one that suggested a big ear and one that was made of gingerbread, one that was shaped like an oven door, and one that had to be unbuttoned. The two doors leading out of a room always had something in common – the shape, the material, the size, the color – but there was always some essential difference between them.

Bastian had passed many times from one hexagonal room to another. Every decision he made led to another decision that led to yet another decision. But after all these decisions he was still in

the Temple of a Thousand Doors. As he went on and on, he began
to wonder why this should be. His wish had sufficed to lead him
into the maze, but apparently it was not definite enough to enable
him to find the way out. He had wished for company. But now
he realized that by company he had meant no one in particular.
This vague wish hadn't helped him at all. Thus far his decisions
had been based on mere whim and involved very little thought.
In every case he might just as well have taken the other door. At
this rate he would never find his way out.

Just then he was in a room with a greenish light. Three of the
six walls had variously shaped clouds painted on them. The door
to the left was of white mother-of-pearl, the one on the right of
ebony. And suddenly he knew whom he wished for: Atreyu!

The mother-of-pearl door reminded Bastian of Falkor the luckdragon, whose scales glistened like mother-of-pearl. So he decided
on that one.

In the next room one of the two doors was made of plaited grass,
the other was an iron grating. Just then Bastian was thinking of
the Grassy Ocean where Atreyu was at home, so he picked the grass
door.

In the next room he found two doors which differed only in that
one was made of leather and the other of felt. Bastian chose the
leather one.

Then he was faced with two more doors, and again he had time
to think. One was purple, the other olive green. Atreyu was a Greenskin and his cloak was made from the hide of a purple buffalo. A
symbol such as Atreyu had had on his forehead and cheeks when
Cairon came to him was painted in white on the olive-green door.
But the purple door had the same symbol on it, and Bastian didn't
know that Atreyu's cloak had been ornamented with just such
symbols. That door, he thought, must lead to someone else, not
to Atreyu.

He opened the olive-green door – and then he was outside.

To his surprise he found himself not in the Grassy Ocean but
in a bright springtime forest. Sunbeams shone through the young
foliage and played their games of light and shade on the mossy

ground. The place smelled of earth and mushrooms and the balmy air was filled with the twittering of birds.

Bastian turned around and saw that he had just stepped out of a little forest chapel. For that moment its door had been the way out of the Temple of a Thousand Doors. Bastian opened it again, but all he saw was the inside of a small chapel. The roof consisted only of a few rotten beams, and the walls were covered with moss.

Bastian started walking. He had no idea where he was going, but he felt certain that sooner or later he would find Atreyu. The thought made him so happy that he whistled to the birds, who answered him and sang every merry tune that entered his head.

A while later he caught sight of a group of figures in a clearing. As he came closer, they proved to be four men in magnificent armor and a beautiful lady, who was sitting on the grass, strumming a lute. Five richly caparisoned horses and a pack mule were standing in the background. A white cloth laid with all manner of viands and drink was spread out on the grass before the company.

Before joining the group, Bastian hid the Childlike Empress's amulet under his shirt. He thought it best to see what these people were up to before allowing himself to be recognized.

The men stood up and bowed low at his approach, evidently taking him for an Oriental prince or something of the kind. The fair lady nodded, smiled at him, and went on strumming her lute. One of the men was taller than the rest and more magnificently clad. He had fair hair that hung down over his shoulders.

'I am Hero Hynreck,' he announced, 'and this lady is Princess Oglamar, daughter of the king of Luna. These men are my friends Hykrion, Hysbald, and Hydorn. And what may your name be, young friend?'

'I may not say my name – not yet,' Bastian replied.

'A vow?' Princess Oglamar asked on a note of mockery. 'So young, and you've already made a vow?'

'Have you come a long way?' Hero Hynreck inquired.

'A very long way,' Bastian replied.

'Are you a prince?' asked the princess with a gracious smile.

'That I may not reveal,' said Bastian.

'Well, welcome in any case to our gathering!' cried Hero Hynreck. 'Will you honor us by partaking of our repast?'

Bastian accepted with thanks, sat down, and began to eat.

From the conversation between the lady and the four knights Bastian learned that a tournament was to be held in the large and magnificent Silver City of Amarganth, which was not far distant. From far and near the boldest heroes, the most skillful hunters, the bravest warriors, and all manner of adventurers as well, had come to take part. Only the three bravest and best, who defeated all the others, were to have the honor of joining in a long and perilous expedition, the aim of which was to find a certain person, the so-called Savior, who was known to be somewhere in one of the numerous regions of Fantastica. Thus far no one knew his name. It appeared that at some time in the past Fantastica had been struck by disaster, but that this Savior had appeared on the scene and saved it in the nick of time by giving the Childlike Empress the name of Moon Child, by which she was now known to everyone in Fantastica. Since then he had been wandering about the country unknown, and the purpose of the expedition was to find him and keep him safe by serving him as a kind of bodyguard. Only the bravest and ablest men would be chosen for the mission, since it seemed more than likely that formidable adventures awaited them.

The tournament at which the three were to be chosen had been organized by Querquobad, the Silver Sage – the city of Amarganth was always ruled by its oldest man or woman, and Querquobad was a hundred and seven years old. The winners, however, would not be selected by him, but by one Atreyu, a young Greenskin, who was then visiting Sage Querquobad. This Atreyu was to lead the expedition. For he alone was capable of recognizing the Savior, since he had seen him once in his magic mirror.

Bastian listened in silence. It wasn't easy for him, for he soon realized that this Savior was his very own self. And when Atreyu's name came up, his heart laughed within him, and he found it very hard not to give himself away. But he was determined to keep his identity a secret for the present.

Hero Hynreck, as it turned out, was not so much concerned with the expedition as with the heart of Princess Oglamar. Bastian had seen at a glance that he was head over heels in love with the young lady. For no apparent reason he kept sighing and casting mournful glances at her. And she would pretend not to notice. As Bastian learned later on, she had vowed to marry no one but the greatest of all heroes, who proved himself able to defeat all others. She wouldn't be satisfied with less. But how could Hero Hynreck prove that he was the greatest? After all, he couldn't just go out and kill someone who had done him no harm. And as for wars, there hadn't been any for ages. He would gladly have fought monsters or demons, he would gladly have brought her a fresh dragon's tail for breakfast every morning, but far and wide there were no monsters, demons, or dragons to be found. So naturally, when the messenger from Querquobad, the Silver Sage, had invited him to the tournament, he had accepted forthwith. But Princess Oglamar had insisted on coming along, for she wanted to see his performance with her own eyes.

'Everybody knows,' she said with a smile, 'that heroes are not to be believed. They all tend to exaggerate their achievements.'

'Exaggeration or not,' said Hero Hynreck, 'I can assure you that I'm a better man than this legendary Savior.'

'How can you know that?' Bastian asked.

'Well,' said Hero Hynreck, 'if the fellow was half as strong and brave as I am, he wouldn't need a bodyguard to take care of him. He sounds kind of pathetic to me.'

'How can you say such a thing!' cried Oglamar with indignation. 'Didn't he save Fantastica from destruction?'

'What of it!' said Hero Hynreck with a sneer. 'That didn't take much of a hero.'

Bastian decided to teach him a little lesson at the first opportunity.

The three other knights had merely fallen in with the couple en route. Hykrion, who had a bristling black moustache, claimed to be the most powerful swordsman in all Fantastica. Hysbald, who had red hair and seemed frail in comparison with the others, claimed that no one was quicker and more nimble with a sword than he. And Hydorn was convinced that he had no equal for endurance in combat. His exterior seemed to support his contention, for he was tall and lean, all bone and sinew.

After the meal they prepared to resume their journey. The crockery and provisions were packed into the saddlebags. Princess Oglamar mounted her white palfrey and trotted off without so much as a backward look at the others. Hero Hynreck leapt on his coal-black stallion and galloped after her. The three other knights offered Bastian a ride on their pack mule, which he accepted. Whereupon they started through the forest on their splendidly caparisoned steeds, while Bastian brought up the rear. Bastian's mount, an aged she-mule, dropped farther and farther behind. Bastian tried to goad her on, but instead of quickening her pace, the mule stopped still, twisted her neck to look back at him, and said: 'Don't urge me on, sire, I've lagged behind on purpose.'

'Why!' Bastian asked.

'Because I know who you are.'

'How can that be?'

'When a person is only half an ass like me, and not a complete one, she senses certain things. Even the horses had an inkling. You needn't say anything, sire. I'd have been so glad to tell my children and grandchildren that I carried the Savior on my back and was first to welcome him. Unfortunately mules don't get children.'

'What's your name?' Bastian asked.

'Yikka, sire.'

'Look here, Yikka. Don't spoil my fun. Could you keep what you know to yourself for the time being?'

'Gladly, sire.'

And the mule trotted off to catch up with the others.

The group were waiting on a knoll at the edge of the forest, looking down with wonderment at the city of Amarganth, which lay gleaming in the sunlight before them. From the height where they stood, the travelers had a broad view over a large, violet blue lake, surrounded on all sides by similar wooded hills. In the middle of this lake lay the Silver City of Amarganth. The houses were all supported by boats, and the larger palaces by great barges. Every house and every ship was made of finely chiseled, delicately ornamented silver. The windows and doors of the palaces great and small, the towers and balconies, were all of finely wrought silver filigree, unequaled in all Fantastica. The lake was studded with boats of all sizes, carrying visitors to the city from the mainland. Hero Hynreck and his companions hastened down to the shore, where a silver ferry with a magnificently curved prow was waiting. There was room in it for the whole company, horses, pack mule, and all.

On the way over, Bastian learned from the ferryman, whose clothes were of woven silver, that the violet-blue water of the lake was so salty and bitter that only silver, and a special kind of silver at that, could withstand its corrosive action for any length of time. The name of this lake was Moru, or Lake of Tears. In times long past the people of Amarganth had ferried their city to the middle of the lake to protect it from invasion, since ships of wood or iron were quick to disintegrate in the acrid water. And at present there was yet another reason for leaving Amarganth in the middle of the lake, for the inhabitants had got into the habit of regrouping their houses and moving their streets and squares about when the fancy struck them. Suppose, for instance, that two families, living at opposite ends of town, made friends or intermarried. Why, then they would simply move their silver ships close together and become neighbors.

Bastian would gladly have heard more, but the ferry had reached the city, and he had to get out with his traveling companions.

Their first concern was to find lodgings for themselves and their mounts – no easy matter, since Amarganth was literally overrun by visitors who had come from far and near for the tournament. At length they found lodgings in an inn.

After taking the she-mule to the stable, Bastian whispered in her ear: 'Don't forget your promise, Yikka. I'll be seeing you soon again.'

Yikka nodded.

Then Bastian told his traveling companions that he didn't wish to be a burden to them any longer and would look about the town on his own. After thanking them for their kindness, he took his leave. Actually he was intent on finding Atreyu.

The large and small boats were connected by gangplanks, some so narrow that only one person could cross them at a time, others as wide as good-sized streets. There were also arched bridges with roofs over them, and in the canals between the palace-ships hundreds of small boats were moving back and forth. But wherever you went or stood, you felt a gentle rise and fall underfoot, just enough to remind you that the whole city was afloat.

The visitors, who had literally flooded the city, were so varied and colorful that it would take a whole book to describe them. The Amarganthians were easy to recognize, for they all wore clothes of a silver fabric that was almost as fine as Bastian's mantle. Their hair too was silver; they were tall and well-built, and their eyes were as violet-blue as Moru, the Lake of Tears. Most of the visitors were not quite so attractive. There were muscle-bound giants with heads that seemed no larger than apples between their huge shoulders. There were sinister-looking night-rowdies, bold, solitary individuals whom, as one could see at a glance, it was best not to tangle with. There were flimflams with shifty eyes and nimble fingers, and berserkers with smoke coming out of their mouths and noses. There were topsy-turvies who spun like living tops and wood-goblins who trotted about on gnarled, crooked legs, carrying stout clubs over their shoulders. Once Bastian even saw a rock chewer, with teeth like steel chisels jutting out of his mouth. The silver gang-plank bent under his weight as he came stomping along. But before Bastian could ask him if by any chance he was Pyornkrachzark, he had vanished in the crowd.

At length Bastian reached the center of the city, where the tournament was already in full swing. In a circular open space that looked like a giant arena, hundreds of contestants were measuring their strength, showing their mettle. Around the edges a crowd of onlookers egged the participants on, and the windows and balconies of the surrounding palace-ships were packed with enthusiasts. Some had even managed to climb up on the filigree-ornamented roofs.

At first Bastian paid little attention to the tournament. He was looking for Atreyu, feeling sure that he must be somewhere in the crowd. Then he noticed that the onlookers kept turning expectantly toward one of the palaces – especially when a contestant had performed some particularly impressive feat. But before he could get a good look at the palace, Bastian had to thrust his way across one of the bridges and climb a sort of lamppost.

Two silver chairs had been set up on a wide balcony. In one

sat an aged man whose silver beard and hair hung down to his
waist. That must be Querquobad, the Silver Sage. Beside him sat
a boy of about Bastian's age. He was wearing long trousers made
of soft leather, but he was bare from the waist up, and Bastian saw
that his skin was olive green. The expression of his lean face was
grave, almost stern. His long, blue-black hair was gathered together
and held back by leather thongs. Over his shoulders he wore a purple
cloak. He was looking calmly and yet somehow eagerly down at
the arena. Nothing seemed to escape his dark eyes. Who could it
be but Atreyu!

At that moment an enormous face appeared in the open balcony
door behind Atreyu. It looked rather like a lion's, except that it
had white mother-of-pearl scales instead of fur, and long white fangs
jutted out of the mouth. The eyeballs sparkled ruby red, and when
the head rose high above Atreyu, Bastian saw that it rested on a
long, supple neck, from which hung a mane that looked like white
fire. Of course, it was Falkor the luckdragon, and he seemed to
be whispering something in Atreyu's ear, for Atreyu nodded.

Bastian slid down the lamppost. He had seen enough. Now he
could watch the tournament.

'Tournament' was hardly the right word. The contests that were
in progress added up to something more like a big circus. There
was a wrestling match between two giants, who twined their bodies
into one huge knot that kept rolling this way and that; individuals
of like or divergent species vied with one another in swordsmanship
or in skill at handling the club or the lance, but none had any serious
intention of killing his adversary. The rules called for fair fighting
and the strictest self-control. Any contestant so misled by anger or
ambition as to injure an opponent seriously would have been
automatically disqualified.

Many defeated combatants had left the arena when Bastian saw
Hykrion the Strong, Hysbald the Swift, and Hydorn the Enduring
make their appearance. Hero Hynreck and Princess Oglamar were
not with them.

By then there were scarcely more than a hundred contestants
left. Since these were a selection from among the best and strongest,
Hykrion, Hysbald, and Hydorn had a much harder time of it than

they may have expected. It took all afternoon for Hykrion to prove himself the strongest among the strong, Hysbald the swiftest among the swift, and Hydorn the most enduring among the enduring. The onlookers applauded with a will and all three bowed in the direction of the balcony, where Silver Sage Querquobad and Atreyu were sitting. Atreyu was getting up to say something when yet another contestant appeared – Hynreck. An expectant silence fell and Atreyu sat down. Since only three men were to accompany him on his expedition, there was one too many in the field. One would have to withdraw.

'Sires,' said Hynreck in a loud voice, 'I would not suggest that your strength can have been impaired by the little display you have just made of your abilities. Under the circumstances, however, it would be unworthy of me to challenge you singly. Since I have thus far seen no adversary up to my standards, I have not participated in the contests. Consequently, I am still fresh. If any of you should feel too exhausted, he is free to stand aside. Otherwise, I am prepared to face all three of you at once. Any objections?'

'No!' replied all three in unison.

A furious battle followed. Hykrion's blows had lost none of their force, but Hero Hynreck was stronger. Hysbald assailed him from all sides like streaks of lightning, but Hynreck was quicker. Hydorn tried to wear him down, but Hero Hynreck had greater endurance. After barely ten minutes all three were disarmed and all three bent their knees to Hero Hynreck. He looked proudly about him, evidently hoping for an admiring glance from his lady, who must have been somewhere in the crowd. The cheers of the onlookers swept over the arena like a hurricane and could no doubt be heard on the farthermost shore of Lake Moru.

When the applause died down, Querquobad, the Silver Sage, stood up and asked in a loud voice: 'Does anyone wish to oppose Hero Hynreck?'

A hush fell on the crowd. Then a boy's voice was heard: 'Yes! I do!'

All eyes turned toward Bastian. The crowd opened a path for him and he strode into the arena. Cries of amazement and pity were heard. 'How handsome he is!' 'What a shame!' 'This must be stopped!'

'Who are you?' asked Silver Sage Querquobad.

'I will reveal my name afterward,' said Bastian.

He saw that Atreyu had narrowed his eyes and was studying him closely, but had not yet made up his mind.

'Young friend,' said Hero Hynreck. 'We have eaten and drunk together. Why do you want me to put you to shame? I pray you, withdraw your challenge and go away.'

'No,' said Bastian. 'I meant what I said.'

Hero Hynreck hesitated a moment. Then he said: 'It would be wrong of me to measure myself in combat with you. Let us first see who can shoot an arrow higher.'

'Very well!' said Bastian.

A stout bow and an arrow were brought for each of them. Hynreck drew the bowstring and shot the arrow so high that the eye could not follow. At almost the same moment Bastian pulled his bowstring and shot his arrow after it.

It was some time before the arrows came down and fell to the ground between the two archers. Then it became evident that Bastian's red-feathered arrow had struck Hero Hynreck's blue-feathered arrow at its apogee with such force as to split it open and wedge itself into it.

Hero Hynreck stared at the telescoped arrows. He had turned rather pale, but his cheeks had broken out in red spots.

'That can only be an accident,' he muttered. 'Let's see who does better with the foils.'

He asked for two foils and two decks of cards. Both were brought. He shuffled both decks of cards carefully.

Then he threw one deck high into the air, drew his blade with the speed of lightning, and thrust. When all the other cards had fallen to the ground, it could be seen that he had struck the ace of hearts in the center of its one heart. And holding up his foil with the card spitted on it, he again looked about for his lady.

Then Bastian tossed the other deck into the air and his blade flashed. Not a single card fell to the ground. He had pierced all fifty-two cards of the deck exactly in the middle and moreover in the right order – though Hero Hynreck had shuffled them ever so carefully.

Hero Hynreck looked at the cards. He said nothing, but his lips trembled.

'But you won't outdo me in strength,' he stammered finally.

A number of weights were still lying about from the previous contests. He seized the heaviest and slowly, straining every muscle, lifted it. But before he could set it down, Bastian had grabbed hold of him and lifted him along with the weight. Hero Hynreck's face took on a look of such misery that some of the onlookers could not repress a smile.

'Thus far,' said Bastian, 'you have chosen the nature of our contests. Will you allow me to suggest something?'

Hero Hynreck nodded in silence. 'Nothing can daunt my courage.'

'In that case,' said Bastian, 'I propose a swimming race. Across the Lake of Tears.'

A breathless silence fell on the assemblage.

Hero Hynreck turned red and pale by turns.

'That's no test of courage,' he expostulated. 'It's madness.'

'I'm ready,' said Bastian.

At that Hero Hynreck lost his self-control.

'No!' he shouted, stamping his foot. 'You know as well as I do that the water of Moru dissolves everything. It would be certain death.'

'I'm not afraid,' said Bastian calmly. 'I've crossed the Desert of Colors. I've eaten and drunk the fire of the Many-Colored Death and bathed in it. I'm not afraid of any water.'

'You're lying!' roared Hero Hynreck, purple with rage. 'No one in all Fantastica can survive the Many-Colored Death. Any child knows that.'

'Hero Hynreck,' said Bastian slowly. 'Instead of calling me a liar, why not admit that you're just plain scared?'

That was too much for Hero Hynreck. Beside himself with rage, he drew his big sword from its sheath and flung himself on Bastian. Bastian stepped back. He was about to say a word of warning, but

Hero Hynreck didn't leave him time. He struck out in earnest, and in that same moment the sword Sikanda leapt from its rusty sheath into Bastian's hand, and began to dance.

What happened next was so amazing that not one of the onlookers would forget it as long as he lived. Luckily Bastian couldn't let go of the hilt and was obliged to follow all Sikanda's lightninglike movements. First it sliced Hero Hynreck's lovely armor into little pieces. They flew in all directions, but his skin was not even scratched. Hero Hynreck swung his sword like a madman in a desperate effort to defend himself, but he was blinded by Sikanda's whirling light, and none of his blows struck home. At length he was stripped to his underclothes, but still he went on fighting. And then Sikanda cut his weapon into little bits so quickly that what had been a whole sword only a moment before fell tinkling to the ground like a pile of coins. Hero Hynreck stared aghast at the useless hilt, dropped it, and hung his head. Sikanda left Bastian's hand and flew back into its rusty sheath.

A cry of admiration rose from a thousand throats. The onlookers stormed the arena, seized Bastian, lifted him onto their shoulders, and carried him around in triumph. From his lofty perch Bastian looked for Hero Hynreck. He felt sorry for the poor fellow and wanted to give him a kind word; he hadn't intended to make such a fool out of him. But Hero Hynreck was nowhere to be seen.

Then silence fell. The crowd moved aside. There stood Atreyu, smiling up at Bastian. Bastian smiled back. His bearers let him down from their shoulders. For a long while the two boys looked at each other in silence. Then Atreyu spoke:

'If I still needed someone to accompany me on the search for the Savior of Fantastica, I would content myself with just this one, for he is worth more than a hundred others. But I need no companion, because there will be no expedition.'

A murmur of surprise and disappointment was heard.

'The Savior of Fantastica has no need of our protection,' Atreyu went on, raising his voice, 'for he can defend himself better than all of us together could defend him. And we have no need to look for him, because he has already found us. I didn't recognize him at first, for when I saw him in the Magic Mirror Gate of the Southern

Oracle, he was different from now – entirely different. But I didn't forget the look in his eyes. It's the same look that I see now. I couldn't be mistaken.'

Bastian shook his head and said with a smile: 'You're not mistaken, Atreyu. It was you who brought me to the Childlike Empress to give her a new name. And for that I thank you.'

An awed whisper passed over the crowd like a gust of wind.

'You promised,' Atreyu replied, 'to tell me your name, which is known to no one in Fantastica except the Golden-eyed Commander of Wishes. Will you tell us now?'

'My name is Bastian Balthazar Bux.'

At that the onlookers could contain themselves no longer. Their rejoicing exploded in a thousand cheers. Many of them started dancing. Bridges and gangplanks, the whole square for that matter, began to sway.

Laughing, Atreyu held out his hand to Bastian. Bastian took it, and so – hand in hand – they went to the palace. Silver Sage Querquobad and Falkor the luckdragon were waiting on the palace steps.

That night the city of Amarganth staged the finest celebration in all its history. All who had legs, long or short, straight or crooked, danced, and all who had voices, sweet or sour, high or low, sang and laughed.

When night fell, the Amaranthians lit thousands of colored lamps on their silver ships and palaces. And at midnight there were fireworks such as had never been seen in Fantastica. Bastian stood on the balcony with Atreyu. To the left and right of them stood Falkor and Silver Sage Querquobad, watching as sheaves of many-colored light and the Silver City's thousands of lamps were reflected in the dark waters of Moru, the Lake of Tears.

XVII

A Dragon for Hero Hynreck

UERQUOBAD, the Silver Sage, had slumped down in his chair asleep, for already the hour was late. Consequently, he missed an experience more beautiful and more extraordinary than any he had known in the hundred and seven years of his life. And so did many others in Amarganth, citizens as well as visitors, who, exhausted by the festivities, had gone to bed. Only a few were still awake, and those few were uniquely privileged:

Falkor, the white luckdragon, was singing.

High in the night sky, he flew in circles over the Lake of Tears, and let his bell-like voice ring out in a song without words, a simple, grandiose song of pure joy. The hearts of all those who heard it opened wide.

And so it was with Bastian and Atreyu, who were sitting side by side on the broad balcony of Querquobad's palace. Neither had ever heard the song of a luckdragon before. Hand in hand, they listened in silent delight. Each knew that the other shared his feeling, a feeling of joy at having found a friend. And they took care not to spoil it with idle words.

The great hour passed. Falkor's song grew faint and gradually died away.

When all was still, Querquobad woke up and excused himself: 'I'm afraid,' he said, 'that old men like me need their sleep. I'm sure you youngsters will forgive me, I must really be off to bed.'

They wished him a good night and Querquobad left them.

Again the two friends sat for a long while in silence, looking up at the night sky, where the luckdragon was still flying in great slow circles. From time to time he passed across the full moon like a drifting cloud.

'Doesn't Falkor ever sleep?' Bastian asked finally.

'He's asleep now,' Atreyu replied.

'In the air?'

'Oh yes. He doesn't like to stay in houses, even when they're as big as Querquobad's palace. He feels cramped. He's just too big and he's afraid of knocking things over. So he usually sleeps way up in the air.'

'Do you think he'd let me ride him sometime?'

'Of course he would,' said Atreyu. 'Thought it's not so easy. You've got to get used to it.'

'I've already ridden Grograman,' said Bastian.

Atreyu nodded and looked at him with admiration.

'So you said during your contest with Hero Hynreck. How did you tame the Many-Colored Death?'

'I have A U R Y N,' said Bastian.

'Oh!' said Atreyu. He seemed surprised, but he said nothing more.

Bastian took the Childlike Empress's emblem from under his shirt and showed it to Atreyu. Atreyu looked at it for a while. Then he muttered: 'So now *you* are wearing the Gem.'

Thinking he detected a note of displeasure, Bastian hastened to ask: 'Would you like to have it back?'

He started undoing the chain.

'No!'

Atreyu's voice sounded almost harsh, and Bastian wondered what was wrong. Atreyu smiled apologetically and repeated gently: 'No, Bastian, I haven't worn it in a long while.'

'As you like,' said Bastian. Then he turned the amulet over. 'Look,' he said. 'Have you seen the inscription?'

'Yes,' said Atreyu. 'I've seen it, but I don't know what it says.'

'How come?'

'Greenskins can read tracks in the forest, but not letters.'

This time it was Bastian who said: 'Oh!'

'What does it say?' Atreyu asked.

'"DO WHAT YOU WISH,"' Bastian read.

Atreyu stared at the amulet.

'So that's what it says.' His face revealed nothing, and Bastian couldn't guess what he was thinking.

'If you had known,' he asked, 'would it have changed anything for you?'

'No,' said Atreyu. 'I did what I wanted to do.'

'That's true,' said Bastian, and nodded.

Again they were both silent for a time.

'There's something I have to ask you,' said Bastian finally. 'You said I looked different from when you saw me in the Magic Mirror Gate.'

'Yes, entirely different.'

'In what way?'

'You were fat and pale and you were wearing different clothes.'

Bastian smiled. 'Fat and pale?' he asked incredulously. 'Are you sure it was me?'

'Wasn't it?'

Bastian thought it over.

'You saw me. I know that. But I've always been the way I am now.'

'Really and truly?'

'I should know. Shouldn't I?' Bastian cried.

'Yes,' said Atreyu, looking at him thoughtfully. 'YOU should know.'

'Maybe it was a deforming mirror.'

Atreyu shook his head.

'I don't think so.'

'Then how do you explain your seeing me that way?'

'I don't know,' Atreyu admitted. 'I only know that I wasn't mistaken.'

After that they were silent for a long while, and at length they went to sleep.

As Bastian lay in his bed, the head and foot of which were made of the finest silver filigree, his conversation with Atreyu ran through his head. Somehow it seemed to him that Atreyu was less impressed by his victory over Hero Hynreck and even by his stay with Grograman since he heard that he, Bastian, was wearing the Gem. And true enough, he thought, maybe his feats didn't amount to much, considering that he had the amulet to protect him. But he wanted to win Atreyu's wholehearted admiration.

He thought and thought. There had to be something that no one in Fantastica could do, even with the amulet. Something of which only he, Bastian, was capable.

At last it came to him: making up stories.

Time and time again he had heard it said that no one in Fantastica could create anything new. Even the voice of Uyulala had said something of the kind. And just that was his special gift. He would show Atreyu that he, Bastian, was a great storyteller.

He resolved to prove himself to his friend at the first opportunity. Maybe the very next day. For instance, there might be a storytelling contest, and he would put all others in the shade with his inventions!

Or better still: suppose all the stories he told should come true! Hadn't Grograman said that Fantastica was the land of stories and that even something long past could be born again if it occurred in a story.

Atreyu would be amazed!

And while picturing Atreyu's amazement, Bastian fell asleep.

The next morning, as they were enjoying a copious breakfast in the banquet hall of the palace, Silver Sage Querquobad said: 'We have decided to hold a very special sort of festival for the benefit of our guest, the Savior of Fantastica, and his friend, who brought him to us. Perhaps, Bastian Balthazar Bux, it is unknown to you that in keeping with an age-old tradition we Amarganthians have always been the ballad singers and storytellers of Fantastica. From an early age our children are instructed in these skills. When they grow to adulthood they journey from country to country for several years, practising their art for the benefit of all. Everywhere they are welcomed with joy and respect. But we have one regret: Quite frankly, our stock of stories is small. And many of us must share this little. But word has gone round – whether true or not, I don't know – that you, in your world, are famous for your stories. Is that the truth?'

'Yes,' said Bastian. 'They even made fun of me for it.'

Silver Sage Querquobad raised his eyebrows in disbelief.

'Made fun of you for telling stories that no one had ever heard? How is that possible? None of us can make up new stories, and we, my fellow citizens and I, would all be infinitely grateful if you would give us a few. Will you help us with your genius?'

'With pleasure,' said Bastian.

After breakfast Bastian, Atreyu, and the Silver Sage went out to the steps of Querquobad's palace, where Falkor was already waiting for them.

A large crowd had gathered, but on this occasion it included few of the outsiders who had come for the tournament and consisted largely of Amarganthians, men, women, and children, all comely and blue-eyed, and all clad in silver. Most were carrying stringed instruments, harps, lyres, guitars, or lutes, all of silver. For almost everyone there hoped to display his art in the presence of Bastian and Atreyu.

Again chairs had been put in place. Bastian sat in the middle between Querquobad and Atreyu, and Falkor stood behind them.

Querquobad clapped his hands. When the crowd fell silent, he announced: 'The great storyteller is going to grant our wish and make us a present of some new stories. Therefore, friends, give us your best, to put him in the right mood.'

The Amarganthians all bowed low. Then the first stepped forward and began to recite. After him came another and still others. All had fine, resonant voices and told their stories well.

Some of their tales were exciting, others merry or sad, but it would take us too long to tell them here. In all, there were no more than a hundred different stories. Then they began to repeat themselves. Those who came last could only tell what their predecessors had told before them.

Bastian grew more and more agitated while waiting for his turn. His last night's wish had been fulfilled to the letter, and he could hardly bear the excitement of waiting to see whether everything else would come true as well. He kept casting glances at Atreyu, but Atreyu's face was impassive, showing no sign of what he might be thinking.

At length Querquobad bade his compatriots desist and turned to Bastian with a sigh: 'I told you, Bastian Balthazar Bux, that our stock of tales was small. It's not our fault. Won't you give us a few of yours?'

'I will give you all the stories I've ever told,' said Bastian, 'for I can always think up new ones. I told many of them to a little girl named Kris Ta, but most I thought up only for myself. No one else has heard them. But it would take weeks and months to tell them all, and we can't stay with you that long. So I've decided to tell you a story that contains all the others in it. It's called "The Story of the Library of Amarganth," and it's very short.' Then after a moment's thought he plunged in:

'In the gray dawn of time, the city of Amarganth was ruled by

a Silver Sagess named Quana. In those long-past days Moru, the
Lake of Tears, hadn't been made yet, nor was Amarganth built
of the special silver that withstands the water of Moru. It was still
like other cities with houses of stone and wood. And it lay in a
valley among wooded hills.

'Quana had a son named Quin, who was a great hunter. One
day in the forest Quin caught sight of a unicorn, which had a
glittering stone at the end of its horn. He killed the beast and took
the stone home with him. His crime (for it is a crime to kill unicorns)
brought misfortune on the city. From then on fewer and fewer
children were born to the inhabitants. If no remedy were found,
the city would die out. But the unicorn couldn't be brought back
to life, and no one knew what to do.

'Quana, the Silver Sagess, sent a messenger to consult Uyulala
in the Southern Oracle. But the Southern Oracle was far away.
The messenger was young when he started out, but old by the time
he got back. Quana had long been dead and her son Quin had
taken her place. He too, of course, was very old, as were all the
other inhabitants. There were only two children left, a boy and
a girl. His name was Aquil, hers was Muqua.

'The messenger reported what Uyulala's voice had revealed. The
only way of preserving Amarganth was to make it the most beautiful
city in all Fantastica. That alone would make amends for Quin's
crime. But to do so the Amarganthians would need the help of the
Acharis, who are the ugliest beings in Fantastica. Because they are
so ugly they weep uninterruptedly, and for that reason they are
also known as the Weepers. Their stream of tears wash the special
silver deep down in the earth, and from it they make the most
wonderful filigree.

'All the Amarganthians went looking for the Acharis, but were
unable to find them, for they live deep down in the earth. At length
only Aquil and Muqua were left. They had grown up and all the
others had died. Together they managed to find the Acharis and
persuade them to make Amarganth the most beautiful city in
Fantastica.

'First the Acharis built a small filigree palace, set it on a silver
barge, and moved it to the marketplace of the dead city. Then they

made their streams of underground tears well up in the valley among the wooded hills. The bitter water filled the valley and became Moru, the Lake of Tears. On it the first silver palace floated, and in the palace dwelt Aquil and Muqua.

'But the Acharis had granted the plea of Aquil and Muqua on one condition, namely, that they and all their descendants should devote their lives to ballad singing and storytelling. As long as they did so, the Acharis would help them, because then their ugliness would help to create beauty.

'So Aquil and Muqua founded a library – the famous library of Amarganth – in which they stored up all my stories. They began with the one you have just heard, but little by little they added all those I have ever told, and in the end there were so many stories that their numerous descendants, who now inhabit the Silver City, will never come to the end of them.

'If Amarganth, the most beautiful city in Fantastica, is still in existence today, it is because the Acharis and the Amarganthians kept their promise to each other – though today the Amarganthians have quite forgotten the Acharis and the Acharis have quite forgotten the Amarganthians. Only the name of Moru, the Lake of Tears, recalls that episode from the gray dawn of history.'

When Bastian had finished, Silver Sage Querquobad rose slowly from his chair.

'Bastian Balthazar Bux,' he said, smiling blissfully. 'You have given us more than a story and more than all the stories in the world. You have given us our own history. Now we know where Moru and the silver ships and palaces on it came from. Now we know why we have always, from the earliest times, been a people of ballad singers and storytellers. And best of all, we know what is in that great round building in the middle of the city, which none of us, since the founding of Amarganth, has ever entered, because it has always been locked. It contains our greatest treasure and we never knew it. It contains the library of Amarganth.'

Bastian himself could hardly believe it. Everything in his story had become reality (or had it always been? Grograman would probably have said: both!). In any event he was eager to see all this with his own eyes.

'Where is this building?' he asked.

'I will show you,' said Querquobad, and turning to the crowd, he cried: 'Come along, all of you! Perhaps we shall be favored with more wonders.'

A long procession, headed by the Silver Sage, Bastian, and Atreyu, moved over the gangplanks connecting the silver ships with one another and finally stopped outside a large building which rested on a circular ship and was shaped like a huge silver box. The outside walls were smooth, without ornaments or windows. It had only one large door, and that door was locked.

In the center of the smooth silver door there was a stone set in a kind of ring. It looked like a piece of common glass. Over it the following inscription could be read:

> Removed from the unicorn's horn, I lost my light.
> I shall keep the door locked until my light
> is rekindled by him who calls me by name.
> For him I will shine a hundred years.
> I will guide him in the dark depths
> of Yor's Minroud.
> But if he says my name a second time
> from the end to the beginning,
> I will glow in one moment
> with the light of a hundred years.

'None of us can interpret this inscription,' said Querquobad. 'None of us knows what the words "Yor's Minroud" mean. None of us to this day has ever discovered the stone's name, though we have all tried time and again. For we can only use names that already exist in Fantastica. And since these are all names of other things, none of us has made the stone glow or opened the door. Can you find the name, Bastian Balthazar Bux?'

A deep, expectant silence fell on the Amarganthians and non-Amarganthians alike.

'Al Tsahir!' cried Bastian.

In that moment the stone glowed bright and jumped straight from its setting into Bastian's hand. The door opened.

A gasp of amazement arose from a thousand throats.

Holding the glowing stone in his hand, Bastian entered the

building, followed by Querquobad and Atreyu. The crowd surged in behind them.

It was dark in the large circular room and Bastian held the stone high. Though brighter than a candle, it was not enough to light the whole room but showed only that the walls were lined with tier upon tier of books.

Attendants appeared with lamps. In the bright light it could be seen that the walls of books were divided into sections, bearing signs such as 'Funny Stories,' 'Serious Stories,' 'Exciting Stories,' and so on.

In the center of the circular room, the floor was inlaid with an inscription so large that no one could fail to see it:

LIBRARY
OF THE COLLECTED WORKS
OF BASTIAN BALTHAZAR BUX

Atreyu looked around in amazement. Bastian saw to his delight that his friend was overcome with admiration.

'Is it true,' asked Atreyu, pointing at the silver shelves all around, 'that you made up all those stories?'

'Yes,' said Bastian, slipping Al Tsahir into his pocket.

Atreyu could only stand and gape.

'I just can't understand it,' he said.

The Amarganthians had flung themselves on the books and were leafing through them or reading to one another. Some sat down on the floor and began to learn passages by heart.

News of the great event spread though the whole city like wildfire.

As Bastian and Atreyu were leaving the library, they ran into Hykrion, Hysbald, and Hydorn.

'Sir Bastian,' said the red-haired Hysbald, evidently the deftest of the three not only with the sword but with his tongue as well, 'we have heard about your incomparable gifts, and humbly pray you: Take us into your service and let us accompany you on your further travels. Each one of us longs to acquire a story of his own. And though you surely have no need of our protection, you may derive some advantage from the service of three such able and willing knights. Will you have us?'

'Gladly,' said Bastian. 'Anyone would be proud of such companions.'

The three knights wished to swear fealty by Bastian's sword, but he held them back.

'Sikanda,' he explained, 'is a magic sword. No one can touch it without mortal peril, unless he has eaten, drunk, and bathed in the fire of the Many-Colored Death.'

So they had to content themselves with a friendly handshake.

'What has become of Hero Hynreck?' Bastian asked.

'He's a broken man,' said Hykrion.

'Because of his lady,' Hydorn added.

'Perhaps you can do something to help him,' said Hysbald.

All five of them went to the inn where they had stopped on their arrival in Amarganth and where Bastian had brought Yikka to the stable.

When they entered, one man was sitting there, bent over the table, his hands buried in his fair hair. The man was Hynreck.

Evidently he had had a change of armor in his luggage, for the outfit he was now wearing was rather simpler than the one that had been cut to pieces the day before.

In response to Bastian's greeting, he merely stared. His eyes were rimmed with red.

When Bastian asked leave to sit down with him, he shrugged his shoulders, nodded, and sank back in his chair. Before him on the table was a sheet of paper, which looked as if it had been many times crumpled and smoothed out again.

'Can you forgive me?' said Bastian.

Hero Hynreck shook his head.

'It's all over for me,' he said mournfully. 'Here. Read it.'

He pushed the note across the table, and Bastian read it.

'I want only the best. You have failed me. Farewell.'

'From Princess Oglamar?' Bastian asked.

Hero Hynreck nodded.

'Immediately after our contest, she mounted her palfrey and rode off to the ferry. God knows where she is now. I'll never see her again.'

'Can't we overtake her?'

'What for?'

'Maybe she'll change her mind.'

Hero Hynreck gave a bitter laugh.

'You don't know Princess Oglamar,' he said. 'I trained more than ten years to acquire my different skills. With iron discipline I avoided everything that could have impaired my physique. I fenced with the greatest fencing masters and wrestled with the greatest wrestlers, until I could beat them all. I can run faster than a horse, jump higher than a deer. I am best at everything – or rather, I was until yesterday. At the start she wouldn't honor me with a glance, but little by little my accomplishments aroused her interest. I had every reason to hope – and now I see it was all in vain. How can I live without hope?'

'Maybe,' Bastian suggested, 'you should forget Princess Oglamar. There must be others you could love just as much.'

'No,' said Hero Hynreck. 'I love Princess Oglamar just because she won't be satisfied with any but the greatest.'

'I see,' said Bastian. 'That makes it difficult. What *could* you do? Maybe you could take up a different trade. How about singing? Or poetry?'

Hynreck seemed rather annoyed. 'No,' he said flatly. 'I'm a hero and that's that. I can't change my profession and I don't want to. I am what I am.'

'I see,' said Bastian.

All were silent for a time. The three knights cast sympathetic glances at Hero Hynreck. They understood his plight. Finally Hysbald cleared his throat and turned to Bastian.

'Sir Bastian,' he said. 'I think you could help him.'

Bastian looked at Atreyu, but Atreyu had put on his impenetrable face.

'A hero like Hynreck,' said Hydorn, 'is really to be pitied in a world without monsters. See what I mean?'

No, Bastian didn't see. Not yet at any rate.

'Monsters,' said Hykrion, winking at Bastian and stroking his huge moustache, 'monsters are indispensable if a hero is to be a hero.'

At last Bastian understood.

'Listen to me, Hero Hynreck,' he said. 'When I suggested giving your heart to another lady, I was only putting your love to the test. The truth is that Princess Oglamar needs your help right now, and that no one else can save her.'

Hero Hynreck pricked up his ears.

'Is that true, Sir Bastian?'

'It's true, as you will soon see. Only a few minutes ago Princess Oglamar was seized and kidnapped.'

'By whom?'

'By one of the most terrible monsters that have ever existed in Fantastica. The dragon Smerg. She was riding across a clearing in the woods when the monster saw her from the air, swooped down, lifted her off her palfrey's back, and carried her away.'

Hynreck jumped up. His eyes flashed, his cheeks were aglow. He clapped his hands for joy. But then the light went out of his eyes and he sat down.

'That's not possible,' he said. 'There are no more dragons anywhere.'

'You forget, Hero Hynreck, that I come from far away. From much farther than you have ever been.'

'That's true,' said Atreyu, joining in for the first time.

'And this monster really carried her away?' Hero Hynreck cried. Then he pressed both hands to his heart and sighed: 'Oh, my adored Oglamar! How you must be suffering! But never fear, your knight is coming, he is on his way. Tell me, what must I do? Where must I go?'

'Far, far from here,' Bastian began, 'there's a country called Morgul, or the Land of the Cold Fire, because flames there are colder than ice. How you are to reach that country, I can't tell you, you must find out for yourself. In the center of Morgul there is a petrified forest called Wodgabay. And in the center of that petrified forest stands the leaden castle of Ragar. It is surrounded by three moats. The first is full of arsenic, the second of steaming nitric acid, and the third is swarming with scorpions as big as your feet. There are no bridges across them, for the lord of the leaden castle is Smerg, the winged monster. His wings are made of slimy skin and their spread is a hundred feet. When he isn't flying, he stands on his hind legs like a gigantic kangaroo. He has the body of a mangy rat and the tail of a scorpion, with a sting at the end of it. The merest touch of that sting is fatal. He has the hind legs of a giant grasshopper. His forelegs, however, which look small and shriveled, resemble the hands of a small child. But don't let them fool you, there's a deadly power in those hands. He can pull in his long neck as a snail does its feelers. There are three heads on it. One is large and looks like the head of a crocodile. From its mouth he can spit icy fire. But where a crocodile has its eyes, it has two protuberances. These are extra heads. One resembles the head of an old man. With it he can see and hear. But he talks with the second head, which has the wrinkled face of an old woman.'

While listening to this description, Hero Hynreck went pale.

'What was this monster's name?' he asked.

'Smerg,' Bastian repeated. 'He has been wreaking his mischief for a thousand years. Because that's how old he is. It's always a beautiful maiden that he kidnaps, and she has to keep house for him until the end of her days. When she dies, he kidnaps another.'

'Why haven't I ever heard of this dragon?'

'Smerg flies incredibly far and fast. Up to now he has always chosen other parts of Fantastica for his raids. Besides, they only happen once in every fifty years or so.'

'Hasn't any of these maidens ever been rescued?'

'No, that would take a very special sort of hero.'

These words brought the color back to Hero Hynreck's cheeks. And remembering what he had learned about dragons, he asked: 'Has this Smerg a vulnerable spot?'

'Oh,' said Bastian, 'I almost forgot. In the bottommost cellar of Ragar Castle there's a lead ax. It's the only weapon Smerg can be killed with, so naturally he guards it well. You have to cut off the two smaller heads with it.'

'How do you know all this?' asked Hero Hynreck.

Bastian didn't have to answer, for at that moment cries of terror were heard in the street.

'A dragon!' – 'A monster!' – 'Up there in the sky!' – 'Horrible!' – 'He's coming this way!' – 'Run for your lives!' – 'No, he's already got somebody!'

Hero Hynreck rushed out into the street, and all the others followed.

Up in the sky something that looked like a giant bat was flapping its enormous wings. For a moment, as it came closer, he looked exactly as Bastian had just made him up. And in his two shriveled, but oh so dangerous little arms, he was clutching a young lady, who was screaming and struggling with all her might.

'Hynreck!' she screamed. 'Hynreck! Hynreck, my hero! Help!'

And then they were gone.

Hynreck had already brought his black stallion from the stable and boarded one of the silver ferries that crossed to the mainland.

'Faster! Faster!' he could be heard shouting at the ferryman. 'I'll give you anything you ask! But hurry!'

Bastian looked after him and muttered: 'I only hope I haven't made it too hard for him.'

Atreyu cast a sidelong glance at Bastian. Then he said softly: 'Maybe we should get going too.'

'Going where?'

'I brought you to Fantastica,' said Atreyu. 'I think I ought to help you find the way back to your own world. You mean to go back sooner or later, don't you?'

'Oh,' said Bastian. 'I hadn't thought about it. But you're right, Atreyu. Yes, of course you are.'

'You saved Fantastica,' Atreyu went on. 'And it seems to me you've received quite a lot in return. I have a hunch that you're aching to go home and make your own world well again. Or is there something that keeps you here?'

Bastian, who had forgotten that he hadn't always been strong, handsome, and brave, replied: 'No, I can't think of anything.'

Atreyu gave his friend a thoughtful look, and said: 'It may be a long, hard journey. Who knows?'

'Yes,' Bastian agreed. 'Who knows? We can start right now if you like.'

Then the three knights had a short friendly argument, because each claimed the privilege of giving Bastian his horse. Bastian soon settled the matter by asking them for Yikka, their pack mule. Of course, they thought her unworthy of Bastian, but he insisted, and in the end they gave in.

While the knights were making ready for the journey, Bastian and Atreyu went to Querquobad's palace to thank the Silver Sage for his hospitality and bid him goodbye. Falkor the luckdragon, who was waiting for Atreyu outside the palace, was delighted to hear they were leaving. Cities just didn't appeal to him – even if they were as beautiful as Amarganth.

Silver Sage Querquobad was deep in a book he had borrowed from the Bastian Balthazar Bux Library.

'I'm sorry you can't stay longer,' he said rather absently. 'It's not every day that a great author like you comes to see us. But at least we have your works to console us.'

Whereupon they took their leave.

After seating himself on Falkor's back Atreyu asked Bastian: 'Didn't you want to ride Falkor?'

'Later,' said Bastian. 'Now Yikka is waiting for me. And I've given her my promise.'

'Then we'll wait for you on the mainland,' cried Atreyu. The luckdragon rose into the air and was soon out of sight.

When Bastian returned to the inn, the three knights were ready. They had taken the pack saddle off Yikka and replaced it with a richly ornamented riding saddle. Yikka didn't learn why until Bastian came over and whispered in her ear: 'You belong to me now, Yikka.'

As the ferry carried them away from the silver city, the old pack mule's cries of joy resounded over the bitter waters of Moru, the Lake of Tears.

As for Hero Hynreck he actually succeeded in reaching Morgul, the Land of the Cold Fire. He ventured into the petrified forest of Wodgabay, crossed the three moats of Ragar Castle, found the lead ax, and slew the dragon Smerg. Then he brought Oglamar back to her father. At that point she would gladly have married him. But by then he didn't want her anymore. That, however, is another story and shall be told another time.

XVIII

The Acharis

AIN was coming down in buckets. The black, wet clouds hung so low they seemed almost to graze the heads of the riders. Then big, sticky snowflakes began to fall, and in the end it was snowing and raining in one. The wind was so strong that even the horses had to brace themselves against it. The riders' cloaks were soaked through and flapped heavily against the backs of the beasts.

For the last three days they had been riding over a desolate high plateau. The weather had been getting steadily worse, and the ground was a mixture of mud and sharp stones that made for hard going. Here and there the monotony of the landscape was broken by clumps of bushes or of stunted wind-bowed trees.

Bastian, who rode in the lead on his mule Yikka, was fairly well off with his glittering silver mantle, which, though light and thin, proved to be remarkably warm and shed water like a duck. The low-slung body of Hykrion the Strong almost vanished in his thick blue woolen coat. The delicately built Hysbald had pulled his great loden hood over his red hair. And Hydorn's gray canvas cloak clung to his gaunt frame.

Yet in their rather crude way the three knights were of good cheer. They hadn't expected their adventure with Sir Bastian to be a Sunday stroll. Now and then, with more spirit than art, they sang into the storm, sometimes singly and sometimes in chorus. Their favourite song seemed to be one that began with the words:

> 'When that I was a little tiny boy,
> With hey, ho, the wind and the rain . . .'

As they explained, this had been sung by a human who had visited Fantastica long years before, name of Shexper, or something of the sort.

The only one in the group who didn't seem to mind the cold and the rain was Atreyu. On Falkor's back he rode high above the clouds, flying far ahead to reconnoiter and rejoining the company from time to time to report on what he had seen.

They all, even the luckdragon, believed they were looking for the road that would take Bastian back to his world. Bastian thought so too. He himself didn't realize that he had agreed to Atreyu's suggestion only to oblige his friend and that wasn't what he really wanted. But the geography of Fantastica is determined by wishes, which may or may not be conscious. And since it was Bastian who led the way, they were actually going deeper and deeper into Fantastica, heading for the Ivory Tower at its very center. What the consequences for him would be, he wouldn't learn until much later. For the present, neither he nor his companions had any idea where they were going.

Bastian's thoughts were busy with a different problem.

On the second day of their journey, in the forests surrounding the Lake of Tears, he had seen unmistakable traces of the dragon Smerg. Some of the trees had been turned to stone, no doubt by contact with the monster's ice-cold fire. And the prints of the giant grasshopper feet were clearly discernible. Atreyu, who was skilled in woodcraft, had seen other tracks as well, those of Hero Hynreck's horse. Which meant that Hynreck was close on the dragon's heels.

'That doesn't really thrill me,' said Falkor, rolling his ruby-red eyes. 'Monster or not, this Smerg is a relative of mine – a distant one, to be sure, but a relative all the same.' He was only half in jest.

They had not followed Hero Hynreck's track but had taken a different direction, since their supposed aim was to find Bastian's way home.

And now Bastian was asking himself: Had it really been such a good idea to invent a dragon for Hero Hynreck? True, Hynreck had needed a chance to show his mettle. But was it certain that he would win? What if Smerg killed him? And what about Princess Oglamar? Yes, of course, she had been haughty, but was that a reason for getting her into such a fix? And on top of all that, how was he to know what further damage Smerg might do in Fantastica? Without stopping to think, Bastian had created an unpredictable menace. It would be there long after he was gone and quite possibly kill or maim any number of innocents. As he knew, Moon Child drew no distinction between good and evil, beautiful and ugly. To her mind, all the creatures in Fantastica were equally important and worthy of consideration. But had he, Bastian, the right to take the same attitude? And above all, did he wish to?

No, Bastian said to himself, he had no wish to go down in the history of Fantastica as a creator of monsters and horrors. How much finer it would be to become famous for his unselfish goodness, to be a shining model for all, to be revered as the 'good human' or the 'great benefactor.' Yes, that was what he wanted.

The country became mountainous, and Atreyu, returning from a reconnaissance flight, reported that a few miles ahead he had sighted a glen which seemed to offer shelter from the wind. In fact, if his eyes had not deceived him, there were several caves round about where they could take refuge from the rain and snow.

It was already late afternoon, high time to find suitable quarters for the night. So all the others were delighted at Atreyu's news and spurred their mounts on. They were making their way through a valley, possibly a dried-out riverbed, enclosed in mountains which grew higher as the travelers advanced. Some two hours later they reached the glen, and true enough, there were several caves in the surrounding cliffs. They chose the largest and made themselves as comfortable as they could. The three knights gathered brushwood and branches that had been blown down by the storm, and soon they had a splendid fire going in the cave. The wet cloaks were spread out to dry, the beasts were brought in and unsaddled, and even Falkor, who ordinarily preferred to spend the night in the open, curled up at the back of the cave. All in all, it wasn't such a bad place to be in.

While Hydorn the Enduring tried to roast a big chunk of meat over the fire and the others watched him eagerly, Atreyu turned to Bastian and said: 'Tell us some more about Kris Ta.'

'About what?' Bastian asked.

'You friend Kris Ta, the little girl you told your stories to.'

'I don't know any little girl by that name,' said Bastian. 'And what makes you think I told her stories?'

Once again Atreyu had that thoughtful look.

'Back in your world,' he said slowly, 'you used to tell lots of stories, some to her and some to yourself.'

'How do you know that, Atreyu?'

'You said so yourself. In Amarganth. And you also said that people made fun of you for it.'

Bastian stared into the fire.

'That's true,' he muttered. 'I did say that. But I don't know why.
I can't remember.'

It all seemed very strange.

Atreyu exchanged glances with Falkor and nodded gravely as
though something one of them had said had now been proved true.
But he said nothing more. Evidently he didn't wish to discuss such
matters in front of the three knights.

'The meat's done,' Hydorn announced.

He cut off a chunk for each one and they all began to eat. 'Done'
was a gross exaggeration. The meat was charred on the outside
and raw on the inside, but under the circumstances there was no
point in being picky and choosy.

For a while they were all busy chewing. Then Atreyu said to
Bastian: 'Tell us how you came to Fantastica.'

'You know all about that,' said Bastian. 'It was you who brought
me to the Childlike Empress.'

'I mean before that,' said Atreyu. 'In your world. Where did
you live and how did it all happen?'

Then Bastian told how he had stolen the book from Mr
Coreander, how he had carried it off to the schoolhouse attic and
begun to read. When he came to Atreyu's Great Quest, Atreyu
motioned him to stop. He didn't seem interested in what the book
said about him. What interested him in the extreme was the how
and why of Bastian's visit to Mr Coreander and of his flight to the
attic of the schoolhouse.

Bastian racked his brains, but about those things he could
remember nothing more. He had forgotten everything connected
with the fact that he had once been fat and weak and cowardly.
His memory had been broken into bits, and the bits seemed as vague
and far away as if they had concerned an entirely different person.

Atreyu asked for other memories, and Bastian spoke about the
days when his mother was still alive, about his father and his home,
about school and the town he lived in – as much as he remembered.

The three knights had fallen asleep, and Bastian was still talking.
It surprised him that Atreyu should take such an interest in the
most everyday happenings. Maybe it was because of the way Atreyu
listened that these everyday things took on a new interest for Bastian,

as though they contained a secret magic that he had never noticed before.

At last he ran out of memories. It was late in the night, the fire had died down. The three knights were snoring softly. Atreyu sat there with his inscrutable look, as though deep in thought.

Bastian stretched out, wrapped himself in his silver mantle, and had almost fallen asleep when Atreyu said softly: 'It's because of AURYN.'

Bastian propped his head on his hand and looked sleepily at his friend.

'What do you mean by that?'

'The Gem,' said Atreyu, as though talking to himself, 'doesn't work the same with humans as with us.'

'What makes you think that?'

'The amulet gives you great power, it makes all your wishes come true, but at the same time it takes something away: your memory of your world.'

Bastian thought it over. He didn't feel as if anything had been taken away from him.

'Grograman told me to find out what I really wanted. And the inscription on AURYN says the same thing. But for that I have to go from one wish to the next without ever skipping any. That's why I need the Gem.'

'Yes,' said Atreyu. 'It gives you the means, but it takes away your purpose.'

'Oh well,' said Bastian, undismayed. 'Moon Child must have known what she was doing when she gave me the amulet. You worry too much, Atreyu. I'm sure AURYN isn't a trap.'

'No,' said Atreyu. 'I don't think so either.'

And after a while he added: 'Anyway, it's good we're looking for the way back to your world. We are, aren't we?'

'Oh yes,' said Bastian, already half asleep.

In the middle of the night he was awakened by a strange sound. He had no idea what it was. The fire had gone out and he was lying in total darkness. Then he felt Atreyu's hand on his shoulder and heard him whisper: 'What's that?'

'I don't know,' Bastian whispered back.

They crept to the mouth of the cave and listened.

A great many creatures seemed to be trying to fight back their sobs. There was nothing human about it, and it didn't sound like animals in pain. Starting as a whisper, it swelled to a sigh, then ebbed and rose, ebbed and rose. Never had Bastian heard anything so mournful.

'If at least we could see something,' Atreyu whispered.

'Wait,' said Bastian. 'I've got Al Tsahir.'

He took the glittering stone from his pocket and held it high. It gave hardly more light than a candle, but in its faint glow, the friends saw enough to make their skin crawl with horror.

The whole glen was alive with hideous, foot-long worms, who looked as if they had been wrapped in soiled rags. Slimy little limbs protruded from the folds in their skin. At one end, two lidless eyes peered out from under the rags, and from every eye flowed tears. Thousands of tears. The whole glen was wet with them.

The moment the light from Al Tsahir hit them, the creatures froze, and the friends were able to see what they had been doing. At the center of the glen stood a tower of the finest silver filigree – more beautiful and more valuable than any building Bastian had seen in Amarganth. Some of the wormlike creatures had evidently been climbing about on the tower, joining its innumerable parts. But at present they all stood motionless, staring at the light of Al Tsahir.

A ghoulish whisper passed over the glen: 'Alas! Alas! What light has fallen on our ugliness? Whose eye has seen us? Cruel intruder, whoever you may be, have mercy, take that light away.'

Bastian stood up.

'I am Bastian Balthazar Bux. Who are you?'

'We are the Acharis. We are the unhappiest beings in all Fantastica.'

Bastian said nothing and looked in dismay at Atreyu.

'Then,' he said, 'it's you who created Amarganth, the most beautiful city in Fantastica?'

'Yes!' the creatures cried. 'But take that light away! And don't look at us! Have mercy!'

'And with your weeping you made Moru, the Lake of Tears?'

'Master,' they groaned, 'it's true. But we'll die of shame and horror if you make us stand in this light. Why must you add to our torment? We've never done anything to you.'

Bastian put Al Tsahir back in his pocket and again the night was as black as pitch.

'Thank you!' cried the mournful voices. 'Thank you for your merciful kindness.'

'I want to talk with you,' said Bastian. 'I want to help you.'

He was almost sick with disgust, but he felt very sorry for the poor things. It was clear to him that they were the creatures he had mentioned in his story about the origin of Amarganth, but here again he couldn't be sure whether they had always been there or whether they owed their existence to him. In the latter case, he was responsible for their misery. But either way he was determined to help them.

'Oh, oh!' the plaintive voices whimpered. 'No one can help us.'

'I can,' said Bastian. 'I have A U R Y N.'

At that, they all seemed to stop weeping at once.

'Where have you come from?' Bastian asked.

A chorus of many voices whispered: 'We live in the lightless depths of the earth to hide our ugliness from the sun, and there we weep all day and all night. Our tears wash the indestructible silver out of the bedrock, and from it we spin the filigree you have seen. On the darkest nights we mount to the surface, and these caves are our coming-out places. Up here we join together the sections we've made down below. We've come tonight because it was dark enough for us to work without seeing one another. We work to make amends to the world for our ugliness, and that comforts us a little.'

'But you're not to blame for your ugliness,' said Bastian.

'Oh, there are different ways of being to blame,' the Acharis replied. 'In what you do. In what you think ... We're to blame for just living.'

'How can I help you?' Bastian asked. He felt so sorry for them that he could hardly hold back his own tears.

'Ah, great benefactor!' the Acharis cried. 'You've got A U R Y N. With A U R Y N you can save us – we have only one thing to ask of you. Give us different bodies!'

'Don't worry,' said Bastian. 'I will. Here's my wish: That you shall fall asleep. That when you wake up, you shall crawl out of your skins and turn into bright-colored butterflies. That you shall be lighthearted and happy. And that, beginning tomorrow, you shall no longer be the Acharis, the Everlasting Weepers, but the Shlamoofs, the Everlasting Laughers.'

Bastian awaited their answer, but no sound came from the darkness.

'They've fallen asleep,' Atreyu whispered.

The two friends went back into their cave. Hysbald, Hydorn, and Hykrion were still snoring gently. They had slept through the whole incident.

Bastian lay down. He was extremely pleased with himself.

Soon all Fantastica would learn of the good deed he had done. It had really been unselfish, since no one could claim that he had wished anything for himself. There would be nothing to mar the glory of his goodness.

'What do you think, Atreyu?' he whispered.

Atreyu was silent for a while. Then he replied: 'I only wonder what it may have cost you.'

Not until somewhat later, after Atreyu had fallen asleep, did it dawn on Bastian that his friend had been referring, not to his self-abnegation, but to his loss of memory. But he gave the matter no further thought and fell asleep in joyful anticipation of the morrow.

The next morning the three knights woke him up with their cries of amazement.

'Would you look at that! My word, even my old mare is giggling.'

They were standing in the mouth of the cave, and Atreyu was with them. But Atreyu wasn't laughing.

Bastian got up and went out.

The whole glen was crawling and flitting and tumbling with the most comical little creatures he had ever seen. They all had bright-colored butterfly wings on their backs and were wearing the weirdest outfits – some checkered, some striped, some ringed, some dotted. All their clothes looked either too loose or too tight, too big or too small, and they were pieced together every which way. Nothing was right and there were patches all over, even on the wings. No two of these creatures were alike. They had faces like clowns, splotched with every imaginable color, little round red noses or absurdly long ones, and enormous rubbery mouths. Some wore top hats, others peaked caps. Some had only three brick-red tufts of hair, and some had shiny bald heads. Most were sitting or hopping about on the delicate filigree tower, or dangling from it, doing gymnastics, and in general doing their best to wreck it.

Bastian ran out to them.

'Hey, you guys!' he shouted. 'Cut that out! You can't do that!'

The creatures stopped and looked down at him.

One at the very top of the tower asked: 'What did he say?'

And one from further down replied: 'The whatchamaycallim says we can't do this.'

'Why does he say we can't do it?' asked a third.

'Because you just can't!' Bastian screamed. 'You can't just smash everything up!'

'The whatchamaycallim says we can't smash everything up,' the first butterfly-clown informed the others.

'We can too!' said another, tearing a big chunk out of the tower.

Hopping about like a lunatic, the first called down to Bastian: 'We can too!'

The tower swayed and creaked alarmingly.

'Hey, what are you doing?' Bastian shouted. He was angry and he was frightened, but at the same time he had all he could do to keep from laughing.

The first butterfly-clown turned to his companions. 'The what-chamaycallim wants to know what we're doing.'

'What *are* we doing?' asked another.

'We're having fun,' said a third.

'But the tower will collapse if you don't stop!' Bastian screamed.

'The whatchamaycallim,' the first clown informed the others, 'says the tower will collapse if we don't stop.'

'So what?' said another.

And the first called down: 'So what?'

Bastian was speechless, and before he could find a suitable answer, all the butterfly-clowns on the tower began to do a sort of aerial round dance. But instead of holding hands they grabbed one another by the legs or collars, while some simply whirled head over heels through the air. And all bellowed and laughed.

The act that the winged creatures were putting on was so light-hearted and comical that Bastian gave up trying to hold back his laughter.

'But you can't do that,' he called to them. 'The Acharis made it and it's beautiful.'

The first butterfly-clown turned back to the others. 'The whatchamaycallim says we can't do it.'

'We can do anything that's not forbidden!' cried another, turning somersaults in the air. 'And who's going to forbid us? We're the Shlamoofs!'

'Who's going to forbid us anything?' all cried in chorus. 'We're the Shlamoofs!'

'I am!' cried Bastian.

'The whatchamaycallim,' the first clown explained to the others, 'says "I." '

'You?' said the others. 'How can you forbid us anything?'

'No,' said the first. 'Not I. The whatchamaycallim says "he." '

'Why does the whatchamaycallim say "he"?' the others wanted to know. 'And who is he saying "he" to in the first place?'

'Who are you saying "he" to?' the first butterfly-clown called down to Bastian.

'I didn't say "he," ' Bastian screamed, half fuming, half laughing. 'I said I forbid you to wreck this tower.'

'He forbids us,' said the first clown to the others, 'to wreck this tower.'

'Who does?' inquired one who had just turned up from the far end of the glen.

'The whatchamaycallim,' the others replied.

'I don't know any whatchamaycallim,' said the newcomer. 'Who is he anyway?'

The first sang out: 'Hey, whatchamaycallim, who are you any-way?'

'I'm not a whatchamaycallim,' said Bastian, who by then was moderately angry. 'I'm Bastian Balthazar Bux, and I turned you into Shlamoofs so you wouldn't have to cry and moan the whole time. Last night you were still miserable Acharis. It wouldn't hurt to show your benefactor some respect.'

The Shlamoofs all stopped hopping and dancing at once and stood gaping at Bastian. A breathless silence fell.

'What did the whatchamaycallim say?' whispered a butterfly-clown at the edge of the crowd, but his next-door neighbor cracked him on the head so hard that his hat slid down over his eyes and ears, and all the others went: 'Psst!'

'Would you be so kind as to repeat all that very slowly and distinctly,' the first butterfly-clown requested.

'I am your benefactor!' cried Bastian.

This threw the Shlamoofs into an incredible state of agitation. One passed the word on to the next and in the end the innumerable creatures, who up until then had been scattered all over the glen, gathered into a knot around Bastian, shouting in one another's ears.

'Did you hear that? He's our bemmafixer! His name is Nastiban Baltebux! No, it's Buxian Banninector. Rubbish, it's Saratit Buxibem! No, it's Baldrian Hix! Shlux! Babeltran Billy-scooter! Nix! Flax! Trix!'

Beside themselves with enthusiasm, they shook hands all around, tipped their hats to one another, and raised great clouds of dust by slapping one another on the back or belly.

'We're so lucky!' they cried. 'Three cheers for Buxifactor Zanzibar Bastelben!'

Screaming and laughing, the whole great swarm shot upward and whirled away. The hubbub died down in the distance.

Bastian stood there hardly knowing what his right name was.

By that time he wasn't so sure he had really done a good deed.

XIX

The Traveling Companions

UNBEAMS were fighting their way through the cloud cover as the travelers started out that morning. At last the rain and wind had let up. In the course of the morning the travelers ran into two or three sudden showers, but then there was a marked improvement in the weather, and it seemed to grow warmer by the minute.

The three knights were in a merry mood; they laughed and joked and played all sorts of tricks on one another. But Bastian seemed quiet and out of sorts as he rode ahead on his mule. And the knights had far too much respect for him to break in on his thoughts.

The rocky high plateau over which they were riding seemed endless. But little by little the trees became larger and more frequent.

Atreyu had noticed Bastian's bad humor. When he and Falkor started on their usual reconnaissance flight, he asked the luckdragon what he could do to cheer his friend up. Falkor rolled his ruby-red eyeballs and answered: 'That's easy – didn't he want to ride on me?'

When some time later the little band rounded a jutting cliff, they found Atreyu and the luckdragon lying comfortably in the sun.

Bastian looked at them in amazement.

'Are you tired?' he asked.

'Not at all,' said Atreyu. 'I just wanted to ask if you'd let me ride Yikka for a while. I've never ridden a mule. It must be wonderful, because you never seem to get sick of it. I'll lend you my old Falkor in return.'

Bastian flushed with pleasure.

'Is that true, Falkor?' he asked. 'You wouldn't mind carrying me?'

'Of course not, all-powerful sultan,' said the dragon with a wink. 'Hop on and hold tight.'

Without touching the ground, Bastian vaulted directly from mule to dragon back and clutched the silvery-white mane as Falkor took off.

Bastian hadn't forgotten how Grograman had carried him through the Desert of Colors. But riding a white luckdragon was something else again. If sweeping over the ground on the back of the fiery lion had been like a cry of ecstasy, this gentle rising and falling as the dragon adjusted his movements to the air currents was like a song, now soft and sweet, now triumphant with power. Especially when Falkor was looping the loop, when his mane, his fangs, and the long fringes on his limbs flashed through the air like white flames, it seemed to Bastian that the winds were singing in chorus.

Toward noon they sighted the others and landed. The ground party had pitched camp beside a brook in a sunlit meadow. There was a flatbread to eat and a kettle of soup was cooking over a wood fire. The horses and the mule were grazing nearby.

When the meal was over, the three knights decided to go hunting, for supplies, especially of meat, were running low. They had heard the cry of pheasants in the thicket, and there seemed to be hares as well. Knowing the Greenskins to be great hunters, they asked Atreyu to join them, but he declined. Thereupon the knights took their long bows, buckled on their quivers full of arrows, and went off to the woods.

Atreyu, Falkor, and Bastian stayed behind.

After a short silence, Atreyu suggested: 'How about telling us a little more about your world, Bastian?'

'What would interest you?' Bastian asked.

Atreyu turned to the luckdragon: 'What do you say, Falkor?'

'I'd like to hear something about the children in your school,' said the dragon.

Bastian seemed bewildered. 'What children?' he asked.

'The ones who made fun of you,' said Falkor.

'Children who made fun of me?' Bastian repeated. 'I don't know of any children – and I'm sure no child would have dared to make fun of me.'

Atreyu broke in: 'But you must remember that you went to school.'

'Yes,' said Bastian thoughtfully. 'I remember school. Yes, that's right.'

Atreyu and Falkor exchanged glances.

'I was afraid of that,' Atreyu muttered.

'Afraid of what?'

'You've lost some more of your memory,' said Atreyu gravely.

'This time it came of changing the Acharis into Shlamoofs. You shouldn't have done that.'

'Bastian Balthazar Bux,' said the luckdragon – and his tone seemed almost stern – 'if my advice means anything to you, stop using the power that AURYN gives you. If you don't, you're likely to lose your last memories, and without memory how will you ever find your way back to where you came from?'

'To tell the truth,' said Bastian, 'I don't want to go back anymore.'

Atreyu was horrified. 'But you have to go back. You have to go back and straighten out your world so humans will start coming to Fantastica again. Otherwise Fantastica will disappear sooner or later, and all our trouble will have been wasted.'

At that point Bastian felt rather offended. 'But I'm still here,' he protested. 'It's been only a little while since I gave Moon Child her new name.'

Atreyu could think of nothing to say. But then Falkor spoke up. 'Now,' he said, 'I see why we haven't made the slightest progress in finding Bastian's way back. If he himself doesn't want to . . .'

'Bastian,' said Atreyu almost pleadingly. 'Isn't there anything that draws you? Something you love? Don't you ever think of your father, who must be waiting for you and worrying about you?'

Bastian shook his head.

'I don't think so. Maybe he's even glad to be rid of me.'

Atreyu looked at his friend in horror.

'The way you two carry on!' said Bastian bitterly. 'You almost sound as if you wanted to get rid of me too.'

'What do you mean by that?' asked Atreyu with a catch in his voice.

'Well,' said Bastian. 'You seem to have only one thing on your minds: getting me out of Fantastica as quickly as possible.'

Atreyu looked at Bastian and slowly shook his head. For a long while none of them said a word. Already Bastian was beginning to regret his angry words. He himself knew they were unjust.

Then Atreyu said softly: 'I thought we were friends.'

'You were right!' Bastian cried. 'We are and always will be. Forgive me. I've been talking nonsense.'

Atreyu smiled. 'You'll have to forgive us, too, for hurting your feelings. We didn't mean it.'

'Anyway,' said Bastian. 'I'm going to take your advice.'

After a while the three knights returned with several partridges, a pheasant, and a hare. When the party started out again, Bastian was riding Yikka.

In the afternoon, they came to a forest consisting entirely of tall, straight evergreens, which formed, high overhead, a green roof so dense that a ray of sunlight seldom reached the ground. That may have been why there was no underbrush.

The soft, smooth forest floor was pleasant to ride on. Falkor had resigned himself to trotting along with the company, because if he had flown above the treetops with Atreyu, he would undoubtedly have lost sight of the others.

All afternoon they rode through the dark-green twilight. Toward nightfall they spied a ruined castle on a hilltop. They climbed up to it and in the midst of all the crumbling walls and turrets, halls and passageways, they found a vaulted chamber that was in fairly good condition. There they settled down for the night. It was red-headed Hysbald's turn to cook, and he proved to be much better at it than his predecessor. The pheasant he roasted over the fire was as tasty as you please.

The next morning they resumed their journey. All day they rode through the forest, which looked the same on all sides. It was late in the day when they noticed that they must have been riding in a great circle, for ahead of them they saw the ruins of the castle they had left in the morning, but this time they were approaching it from a different direction.

'This has never happened to me before!' said Hykrion, twirling his black moustache.

'I can't believe my eyes!' grumbled Hysbald, stalking through the ruins on his long, thin legs.

But so it was. The remains of yesterday's dinner left no room for doubt.

Atreyu and Falkor said nothing, but their thoughts were hard at work. How could they have made such a mistake?

At the evening meal – this time it was roast hare, prepared more or less competently by Hykrion – the three knights asked Bastian if he would care to impart some of his memories of the world he came from. Bastian excused himself by saying he had a sore throat, and since he had been very quiet all that day, the knights believed him. After suggesting a few effective remedies, they lay down to sleep.

Only Atreyu and Falkor suspected what Bastian was thinking.

Early in the morning they started off again. All day they rode through the forest, trying their best to keep going in a straight line. But at nightfall they were back at the same ruined castle.

'Well, I'll be!' Hykrion blustered.

'I'm going mad!' groaned Hysbald.

'Friends,' said Hydorn disgustedly, 'we might as well throw our licenses in the trash bin. Some knights errant we turned out to be!'

On their first night at the castle, Bastian, knowing that Yikka liked to be alone with her thoughts now and then, had found her a special little niche. The company of the horses, who could think of nothing to talk about but their distinguished ancestry, upset her. That night, after Bastian had taken her back to her place, she said to him: 'Master, I know why we're not getting ahead.'

'How can you know that, Yikka?'

'Because I carry you, master. And because I'm only half an ass, I feel certain things.'

'So, according to you, why is it?'

'You don't want to get ahead, master. You've stopped wishing for anything.'

Bastian looked at her in amazement.

'You are really a wise animal, Yikka.'

The mule flapped her long ears in embarrassment.

'Do you know which way we've been going?'

'No,' said Bastian. 'Do you?'

Yikka nodded.

'We've been heading for the center of Fantastica.'

'For the Ivory Tower?'

'Yes, master. And we made good headway as long as we kept going in that direction.'

'That's not possible,' said Bastian. 'Atreyu would have noticed it, and certainly Falkor would have. But they didn't.'

'We mules,' said Yikka, 'are simple creatures, not in a class with luckdragons. But we do have certain gifts. And one of them is a sense of direction. We never go wrong. That's how I knew for sure that you wanted to visit the Childlike Empress.'

'Moon Child . . .' Bastian murmured. 'Yes, I would like to see her again. She'll tell me what to do.'

Then he stroked the mule's white nose and whispered: 'Thanks, Yikka. Thanks.'

Next morning Atreyu took Bastian aside.

'Listen, Bastian. Falkor and I want to apologize. The advice we gave you was meant well – but it was stupid. We just haven't been getting ahead. Falkor and I talked it over last night. You'll be stuck here and so will we, until you wish for something. It's bound to make you lose some more of your memory, but that can't be helped, there's nothing else you can do. We can only hope that you find the way back before it's too late. It won't do you any good to stay here. You'll just have to think of your next wish and use AURYN's power.'

'Right,' said Bastian. 'Yikka said the same thing. And I already know what my next wish will be. Let's go, I want you all to here it.

They rejoined the others.

'Friends,' said Bastian in a loud voice. 'So far we have been looking in vain for the way back to my world. Now I've decided to go and see the one person who can help me find it. That one person is the Childlike Empress. Our destination is now the Ivory Tower.'

'Hurrah!' cried the three knights in unison.

But then Falkor's bronze voice rang out: 'Don't do it, Bastian Balthazar Bux. What you wish is impossible. Don't you know that no one can meet the Golden-eyed Commander of Wishes more than once? You will never see her again.'

Bastian clenched his fists.

'Moon Child owes me a lot,' he said angrily. 'I'm sure she won't keep me away.'

'You'll see,' Falkor replied, 'that her decisions are sometimes hard to understand.'

Bastian felt the color rising to his cheeks. 'You and Atreyu,' he said, 'are always giving me advice. You can see where your advice has got us. From now on I'll do the deciding. I've made up my mind, and that's that.'

He took a deep breath and went on a little more calmly: 'Besides, you always speak from your point of view. You two are Fantasticans and I'm a human. How can you be sure that the same rules apply to me as to you? It was different when Atreyu had A U R Y N. And who else but me is going to give the Gem back to Moon Child? No one can meet her twice, you say. But I've already met her twice. The first time we saw each other for only a moment, when Atreyu went into her chamber, and the second time when the big egg exploded. With me everything is different. I *will* see her a third time.'

All were silent. The knights because they didn't know what it was all about, Atreyu and Falkor because they were beginning to have doubts.

'Well,' said Atreyu finally, 'maybe you're right. We have no way of knowing how the Childlike Empress will deal with you.'

After that they started out, and before noon they reached the edge of the forest.

Before them lay sloping meadows as far as the eye could see. Soon they came to a winding river and followed its course.

Again Atreyu and Falkor explored the country, describing wide circles around their slow-moving companions. But both were troubled and their flight was not as light and carefree as usual. Looking ahead, they saw that the country changed abruptly at a certain point in the distance. A steep slope led from the plateau to a low-lying, densely wooded plain and the river descended the slope in a mighty waterfall. Knowing that the riders couldn't hope to get that far before the next day, the two scouts turned back.

'Falkor,' Atreyu asked, 'do you suppose the Childlike Empress cares what becomes of Bastian?'

'Maybe not,' said Falkor. 'She draws no distinctions.'

'Then,' said Atreyu, 'she is really a . . .'

'Don't say it,' Falkor broke in. 'I know what you mean, but don't say it.'

For a while Atreyu was silent. Then he said: 'But he's my friend, Falkor. We've got to help him. Even against the Childlike Empress's will, if we have to. But how?'

'With luck,' the dragon replied, and for the first time the bronze bell of his voice seemed to have sprung a crack.

That evening the company chose a deserted log cabin on the riverbank as their night lodging. For Falkor, of course, it was too small, and he preferred to sleep on the air. The horses and Yikka also had to stay outside.

During the evening meal Atreyu told the others about the water-fall and the abrupt change in the country. Then he added casually: 'By the way, we're being followed.'

The three knights exchanged glances.

'Oho!' cried Hykrion, giving his black moustache a martial twirl. 'How many are they?'

'I counted seven behind us,' said Atreyu. 'But even if they ride all night they can't be here before morning.'

'Are they armed?' asked Hysbald.

'I couldn't tell,' said Atreyu, 'but there are more coming from other directions. I saw six in the west, nine in the east, and twelve or thirteen are coming from up ahead.'

'We'll wait and see what they want,' said Hydorn. 'Thirty-five or thirty-six men would hardly frighten the three of us – much less Sir Bastian and Atreyu.'

Ordinarily Bastian ungirt the sword Sikanda before lying down to sleep. But that night he kept it on and slept with his hand on the hilt. In his dreams he saw Moon Child smiling at him and her smile seemed full of promise. If there was any more to the dream, he forgot it by the time he woke up, but his vision encouraged him in his hope of seeing her again.

Glancing out of the door of the cabin, he saw seven blurred shapes through the mist that had risen from the river. Two were on foot, the others mounted on different sorts of steeds. Bastian quietly awakened his companions.

The knights unsheathed their swords, and together they stepped out of the cabin. When the figures waiting outside caught sight of Bastian, the riders dismounted and all seven went down on their left knees, bowed their heads and cried out: 'Hail and welcome to Bastian Balthazar Bux, the Savior of Fantastica!'

The newcomers were a weird-looking lot. One of the two who had come on foot had an uncommonly long neck and a head with four faces, one pointed in each of the four directions. The first was merry, the second angry, the third sad, and the fourth sleepy. All were rigid and unchanging, but he was able at any time to face forward with the one expressing his momentary mood. This individual was a four-quarter troll, sometimes known as a moody-woody.

The second pedestrian was what is known in Fantastica as a headfooter. His head was connected directly with his long, thin legs, there being neither neck nor trunk. Headfooters are always on the go and have no fixed residence. As a rule, they roam about in swarms of many hundreds, but from time to time one runs across a loner. They feed on herbs and grasses. The one that was kneeling to Bastian looked young and red-cheeked.

The three creatures riding on horses no larger than goats were a gnome, a shadowscamp, and a blondycat. The gnome had a golden circlet around his head and was obviously a prince. The shadowscamp was hard to recognize, because to all intents and purposes he consisted only of a shadow cast by no one. The blondycat had a catlike face and long golden-blond curls that clothed her like a coat. Her whole body was covered with equally blond shaggy fur. She was no bigger than a five-year-old child.

Another, who was riding on an ox, came from the land of the Sassafranians, who are born old and die when they have grown (that is, dwindled) to infancy. This one had a long white beard, a bald head, and a heavily wrinkled face. By Sassafranian standards, he was a youngster, about Bastian's age.

A blue djinn had come on a camel. He was tall and thin and was wearing an enormous turban. His shape was human, but his bare torso with its bulging muscles seemed to be made of some glossy blue metal. Instead of a nose and mouth, he had a huge, hooked eagle's beak.

'Who are you and what do you want?' Hykrion asked rather brusquely. Despite the ceremonious greeting, he wasn't quite convinced of the visitors' friendly intentions. He still had his hand on his sword hilt.

The four-quarter troll, who up until then had been keeping his sleepy face foremost, now switched to the merry one. Ignoring Hykrion, he addressed himself to Bastian:

'Your Lordship,' he declared, 'we are princes from many different parts of Fantastica, and we have all come to welcome you and ask for your help. The news of your presence has flown from country to country, the wind and the clouds speak your name, the waves of the sea proclaim your glory, and every last brooklet is celebrating your power.'

Bastian cast a glance at Atreyu, but Atreyu looked at the troll unsmilingly and almost severely.

'We know,' the blue djinn broke in, and his voice sounded like the rasping cry of an eagle, 'we know that you created Perilin, the Night Forest, and Goab, the Desert of Colors. We know you have eaten and drunk the fire of the Many-Colored Death and bathed in it, something that no one else in Fantastica could have done and still lived. We know that you passed through the Temple of a Thousand Doors, and we know what happened in the Silver City of Amarganth. We know, my lord, that there is nothing you cannot do. When you make a wish, your wishes come to pass. And so we invite you to come and stay with us and favor us with a story of our own. For none of our nations has a story.'

Bastian thought it over, then shook his head. 'I can't do what you ask of me just yet. I'll help you later on. But first I must go to the Childlike Empress. I hope you will join us and help me to find the Ivory Tower.'

The creatures didn't seem at all disappointed. After brief deliberation they agreed to accompany Bastian on his journey. Whereupon the procession, which by now had the look of a small caravan, started out again.

Throughout the day they were joined by new adherents, not only those Atreyu had sighted the day before, but many more. There were goat-legged fauns and gigantic night-hobs, there were elves and kobolds, beetle riders and three-legses, a man-sized rooster in jackboots, a stag with golden antlers who walked erect and wore a Prince Albert. Many of the new arrivals bore no resemblance whatsoever to human beings. There were helmeted copper ants, strangely shaped wandering rocks, flute birds, who made music with their long beaks, and there were three so-called puddlers, who moved by dissolving into a puddle at every step and resuming their usual form a little farther on. But perhaps the most startling of all was a twee, whose fore- and hindquarters had a way of running about independently of one another. Except for its red and white stripes it looked rather like a hippopotamus.

Soon the procession numbered at least a hundred. And all had come to welcome Bastian, the Savior of Fantastica, and beg him for a story of their own. But the original seven told the others that they would first have to go to the Ivory Tower, and all were agreed.

Hykrion, Hysbald, and Hydorn rode with Bastian in the lead of the now rather impressive procession.

Toward evening they came to a waterfall. Leaving the plateau, they made their way down a winding mountain trail, at the end of which they found themselves in a forest of tree-sized orchids with enormous spotted blossoms. These blossoms looked so frightening that when the travelers stopped for the night, they decided to post sentries.

Bastian and Atreyu gathered some of the deep, soft moss that lay all about and made themselves a comfortable bed. Falkor protected the two friends by lying down in a circle around them. The air was warm and heavy with the strange and none too pleasant scent of the orchids. That scent seemed fraught with evil.

XX

The Seeing Hand

HE dewdrops on the orchids glistened in the morning sun as the caravan started out again. The night had been uneventful except that more and more emissaries kept trailing in. The procession now numbered close to three hundred.

The farther they went into the orchid forest, the stranger grew the shapes and colors of the flowers. And soon Hykrion, Hysbald, and Hydorn discovered that the fears which had led them to post sentries had not been entirely groundless. For many of the orchids were carnivorous and big enough to swallow a whole calf. True, they could not move of their own volition – it hadn't been really necessary to post sentries – but if something or someone touched them, they snapped shut like traps. And several times when a blossom seized the hand, foot, or mount of a fellow traveler the knights were obliged to draw their swords and hack the blossom to pieces.

Throughout the ride Bastian was besieged by all sorts of fantastic creatures who tried to attract his attention or at least get a look at him. But Bastian rode on in withdrawn silence. A new wish had come to him, and for the first time it was one that made him seem standoffish and almost sullen.

He felt that despite their reconciliation Atreyu and Falkor were treating him like a child, that they felt responsible for him and thought he had to be led by the nose. But come to think of it, hadn't they been that way from the start? Oh yes, they were friendly enough, but they seemed to feel superior to him for some reason, to regard him as a harmless innocent who needed protecting. And that didn't suit him at all. He wasn't innocent, he wasn't harmless, and he'd soon show them. He wanted to be dangerous, dangerous and feared. Feared by all – including Atreyu and Falkor.

The blue djinn – his name, incidentally, was Ilwan – elbowed his way through the crush around Bastian, crossed his arms over his chest, and bowed.

Bastian stopped.

'What is it, Ilwan? Speak!'

'My lord,' said the djinn in his eagle's voice. 'I've been listening in on the conversations of our new traveling companions. Some of them claim to know this part of the country and their teeth are chattering with fear.'

'What are they afraid of?'

'This forest of carnivorous orchids, my lord, belongs to Xayide, the wickedest and most powerful sorceress in all Fantastica. She lives in Horok Castle, also known as the Seeing Hand.'

'Tell the scaredy-cats not to worry,' said Bastian, 'I'm here to protect them.'

Ilwan bowed and left him.

A little later Falkor and Atreyu, who had flown far ahead, returned to Bastian. The procession had stopped for the noon-day meal.

'I don't know what to make of it,' said Atreyu. 'Three or four hours' journey from here, in the middle of the orchid forest, we saw a building that looks like a big hand jutting out of the ground. There's something sinister about it, and it's directly in our line of march.'

Bastian told them what he had heard from Ilwan.

'If that's the case,' said Atreyu, 'wouldn't it be more sensible to change our direction?'

'No,' said Bastian.

'But there's no reason why we should tangle with this Xayide. I think we should steer clear of her.'

'There is a reason,' said Bastian.

'What reason?'

'Because I feel like it,' said Bastian.

Atreyu looked at him openmouthed. The conversation stopped there because Fantasticans were crowding in from all sides to get a look at Bastian. But when the meal was over, Atreyu rejoined Bastian. Trying to make it sound casual, he suggested: 'How about taking a ride with Falkor and me?'

Bastian realized that Atreyu wanted a private talk with him. They hoisted themselves up on Falkor's back, Atreyu in front, Bastian behind him, and the dragon took off. It was the first time the two friends had flown together.

Once they were airborne, Atreyu said: 'It's been hard seeing you alone these days. But we have to talk things over, Bastian.'

'Just as I thought,' said Bastian with a smile. 'What's on your mind?'

Atreyu began hesitantly. 'Have we come to this place and are we heading where we are because of some new wish of yours?'

'I imagine so,' said Bastian rather coldly.

'That's what Falkor and I have been thinking,' said Atreyu. 'What kind of wish is it?'

Bastian made no answer.

'Don't get me wrong,' said Atreyu. 'It's not that we're afraid of anything or anyone. But we're your friends, and we worry about you.'

'No need to,' said Bastian still more coldly.

Falkor twisted his neck and looked back at them.

'Atreyu,' he said, 'has a sensible suggestion. I advise you to listen to him, Bastian Balthazar Bux.'

'Some more of your good advice?' said Bastian with a sardonic smile.

'No, Bastian,' said Atreyu. 'No advice. A suggestion. You may not like it at first. But think it over before you turn it down. We want to help you, and we've been wondering how. The whole trouble is the way the Childlike Empress's amulet affects you. Without AURYN's power you can't wish yourself ahead, but with AURYN's power you're losing yourself and forgetting where you want to go. Pretty soon, unless we do something about it, you won't have any idea where you're going.'

'We've already been through that,' said Bastian. 'So what?'

'When I was wearing the Gem,' said Atreyu, 'it was entirely different. It guided me and it didn't take anything away from me. Maybe because I'm not a human and I have no memory of the human world to lose. In other words, it helped me and did me no harm. So here's what I suggest: Let me have AURYN and trust me to guide you. What do you say?'

Bastian replied instantly: 'I say no!'

Again Falkor looked back.

'Couldn't you at least think it over for a moment?'

'No!' said Bastian.

For the first time Atreyu grew angry.

'Bastian,' he said, 'think sensibly! You can't go on like this! Haven't you noticed that you've changed completely? You're not yourself anymore.'

'Thanks,' said Bastian. 'Thank you very much for minding my business all the time. But frankly, I can get along without your advice. In case you've forgotten, *I* saved Fantastica, and Moon Child entrusted her power to *me*. She must have had some reason for it, because she could have let you keep AURYN. But she took it away from you and gave it to me. I've changed, you say. Yes, my dear Atreyu, you may be right. I'm no longer the harmless innocent you take me for. Shall I tell you the real reason why you want me to give up AURYN? Because you're just plain jealous. You don't know me yet, but if you go on like this – you'll get to know me.'

Atreyu did not reply. Falkor's flight had suddenly lost all its buoyancy, he seemed to be dragging himself through the air, sinking lower and lower like a wounded bird.

At length Atreyu spoke with difficulty.

'Bastian,' he said. 'You can't seriously believe what you've said. Let's forget about it. As far as I'm concerned, you never said it.'

'All right,' said Bastian, 'let's forget it. Anyway, I didn't start the argument.'

For a time they rode on in silence.

In the distance Horok Castle rose up from the orchid forest. It really did look like a giant hand with five outstretched fingers.

'But there's something I want to make clear once and for all,' said Bastian suddenly. 'I've made up my mind. I'm not going back at all. I'm going to stay in Fantastica for good. I like it here. So I can manage without my memories. And if it's the future of Fantastica you're worried about, I can give Moon Child thousands of new names. We don't need the human world anymore.'

Falkor banked for a U-turn.

'Hey!' Bastian shouted. 'What are you doing? Fly ahead! I want to see Horok close up!'

'I can't,' Falkor gasped. 'I honestly can't go on!'

On their return to the caravan they found their traveling

companions in a frenzy of agitation. They had been attacked by a band of some fifty giants, covered with black armor that made them look like enormous two-legged beetles. Many of the traveling companions had fled and were just beginning to return singly or in groups; others had done their best to defend themselves, but had been no match for the armored giants. The three knights, Hykrion, Hysbald, and Hydorn, had fought heroically, but without making a dent in any of their assailants. In the end they had been disarmed and dragged away in chains. One of the armored giants had shouted in a strangely metallic voice:

'Xayide, the mistress of Horok Castle, sends greetings to Bastian Balthazar Bux, the Savior of Fantastica, and makes the following demands: "Submit to me unconditionally and swear to serve me with body and soul as my faithful slave. Should you refuse, or should you attempt to circumvent my will by guile or stratagem, your three friends Hykrion, Hysbald, and Hydorn will die a slow, shameful, and cruel death by torture. You have until sunrise tomorrow to make up your mind." That is the message of Xayide, the mistress of Horok Castle. It has been duly delivered.'

Bastian bit his lips. Atreyu and Falkor had wiped all expression off their faces, but Bastian knew exactly what they were thinking. What he minded most was their mask of secrecy. But this was hardly the time to have it out with them. That could wait. Instead, he addressed the company in a loud voice: 'I will never give in to Xayide's blackmail! We must set the prisoners free, and without delay.'

'It won't be easy,' said Ilwan, the blue djinn with the eagle beak. 'All of us together are no match for those black devils. And even if you, my lord, and Atreyu and his luckdragon were to lead us into battle, it would take us too long to capture Horok Castle. The lives of the three knights are in Xayide's hands. She will kill them the moment she finds out that we are attacking.'

'Then we mustn't let her find out,' said Bastian. 'We must take her by surprise.'

'How can we do that?' asked the four-quarter troll, putting forward his angry face, which was rather terrifying. 'Xayide is crafty. I'm sure she has an answer for anything we can think up.'

'I agree,' said the prince of the gnomes. 'There are too many of us. If we move on Horok Castle, she's sure to know it. Even at night so large a troop movement can't be kept secret. She has her spies.'

'Good,' said Bastian. 'We'll fool her with the help of her spies.'

'How can we do that, my lord?'

'The rest of you will start off in a different direction, to make her think we've given up trying to free the prisoners and we're running away.'

'And what will become of the prisoners?'

'I'll attend to that with Atreyu and Falkor.'

'Just the three of you?'

'Yes,' said Bastian. 'That is, if Atreyu and Falkor agree to come with me. If not, I'll go alone.'

The traveling companions looked at him with admiration. Those closest to him passed his words on to those further back in the crowd.

'My lord,' the blue djinn cried out, 'regardless of whether you conquer or die, this will go down in the history of Fantastica.'

Bastian turned to Atreyu and Falkor. 'Are you coming, or have you got some more of your suggestions?'

'We're coming,' said Atreyu.

'In that case,' Bastian decreed, 'the caravan must start moving while it's still light. You must hurry – make it look as if you were in flight. We'll wait here until dark. We'll join you tomorrow morning – with the three knights or not at all. Go now.'

After taking a respectful leave of Bastian, the traveling companions started out. Bastian, Atreyu, and Falkor hid in a clump of orchid trees and waited for nightfall.

In the late afternoon a faint jangling was heard and five of the black giants approached the abandoned camp. They seemed to be all of black metal, even their faces were like iron masks, and their movements were strangely mechanical. All stopped at once, all looked in the direction where the caravan had gone. Then without a word, all marched off in step.

'My plan seems to be working,' Bastian whispered.

'There were only five,' said Atreyu. 'Where are the others?'

'The five are sure to communicate with the rest,' said Bastian.

At length, when it was quite dark, Bastian, Atreyu, and Falkor crept from their hiding place, and Falkor rose soundlessly into the air with his two riders. Flying as low as possible over the orchid forest to avoid being seen, he headed in the direction they had taken that afternoon. The darkness was impenetrable, and they wondered how they would ever find the castle. But a few minutes later Horok appeared before them in a blaze of light. There seemed to be a lamp in every one of its thousand windows. Evidently Xayide wanted her castle to be seen. But that was only reasonable, for she was expecting Bastian's visit – a different sort of visit, to be sure.

To be on the safe side, Falkor glided to the ground among the orchids, for his pearly-white scales would have reflected the glow of the castle.

Under cover of the trees they approached. Outside the gate, ten of the armored guards were on watch. And at each of the brightly lit windows stood one of them, black, motionless, and menacing.

Horok Castle was situated on a rise from which the orchid trees had been cleared. True enough, it was shaped like an enormous hand. Each finger was a tower, and the thumb was an oriel surmounted by yet another tower. The whole building was many stories high, and the windows were like glittering eyes looking out over the countryside. It was known with good reason as the Seeing Hand.

'The first thing we have to do,' Bastian whispered into Atreyu's ear, 'is locate the prisoners.'

Atreyu nodded and told Bastian to stay there with Falkor. Then he crawled soundlessly away. He was gone a long time.

When he returned, he reported: 'I've been all around the castle. There's only this one entrance, and it's too well guarded. But I've discovered a skylight high up at the tip of the middle finger that seems to be unguarded. Falkor could easily take us up there, but we'd be seen. The prisoners are probably in the cellar. At any rate, I heard a long scream of pain that seemed to come from deep down.'

Bastian thought hard. Then he whispered: 'I'll try to reach that skylight. Meanwhile you and Falkor must keep the guards busy.

Make them think we're trying to get in by the gate. But don't do any more. Don't get into a fight. Keep them here as long as you can. Give me a few minutes' time before you do anything.'

Atreyu pressed his friend's hand in silence. Then Bastian took off his silver mantle and slipped away through the darkness. He had almost circled the castle when he heard Atreyu shouting:

'Attention! Bastian Balthazar Bux, the Savior of Fantastica, is here. He has come not to beg Xayide for mercy, but to give her a last chance to release the prisoners. If she sets them free, her miserable life will be spared!'

Looking around the corner of the castle, Bastian caught a glimpse of Atreyu, who had put on the silver mantle and coiled his blue-black hair into a kind of turban. To anyone who didn't know the two boys very well there was a certain resemblance between them.

For a moment the armored giants seemed undecided. Then Bastian could hear in the distance the metallic stamping of their feet as they rushed at Atreyu. The shadows in the windows also began to move as the guards left their posts to see what was going on. And many more of the armored giants poured out through the gate. When the first had almost reached Atreyu, he slipped nimbly away and a moment later appeared over their heads, riding Falkor. The armored giants brandished their swords and leapt high in the air, but they couldn't reach him.

Bastian started climbing the wall. Here and there he was helped by outcroppings and window ledges, but more often he had to hold fast with his fingertips. Higher and higher he climbed; once the jutting stone he had set his foot on crumbled away and left him hanging by one hand, but he pulled himself up, found a hold for his other hand, and kept climbing. When at last he reached the towers he made better progress, for they were so close together that he could push himself up by bracing himself between them.

At length he reached the skylight and slipped through. True enough, there was no guard in the tower room, heaven knows why. Opening a door, he came to a narrow winding staircase and started down. When he reached the floor below, he saw two black guards standing at a window watching the excitement outside. He managed to pass behind them without attracting their notice.

On he crept, down more stairways, through passages and corridors. One thing was certain. Those armored giants might have been great fighters, but they didn't amount to much as guards.

At last the cold and the musty smell told him he was in the cellar. Luckily all the guards seemed to have raced upstairs in pursuit of the supposed Bastian Balthazar Bux. Torches along the walls lit the way for him. Lower and lower he went. He had the impression that there were as many floors below the ground as above. Finally he came to the bottommost cellar and soon found the dungeon where Hykrion, Hysbald, and Hydorn were languishing. It was a pitiful sight.

They were hanging by their wrists over what seemed to be a bottomless pit. The long iron chains that held them were connected by way of overhead rollers with a winch, but the winch was fastened with a great padlock and couldn't be budged. Bastian stood perplexed.

The three prisoners' eyes were closed. They seemed to be asleep or unconscious. Then Hydorn the Enduring opened his left eye and sang out: 'Hey, friends. Look who's here!'

The others managed to open their eyes and a smile crossed their lips.

'We knew you wouldn't leave us in the lurch!' cried Hydorn.

'How can I get you down?' Bastian asked. 'The winch is locked.'

'Just take your sword and cut the chains,' said Hysbald.

'And drop us into the pit?' said Hykrion. 'That's not such a good idea.'

'Anyway,' said Bastian, 'I can't draw my sword. I can't use Sikanda unless it jumps into my hand.'

'That's the trouble with magic swords,' said Hydorn. 'When you need them, they go on strike.'

'Hey!' Hysbald whispered. 'The guards had the key to that winch. Where could they have put it?'

'I remember a loose stone,' said Hykrion. 'But I couldn't see very well while they were hoisting me up here.'

Bastian looked and looked. The light was dim and flickering, but after a while he discovered a stone flag that was not quite even with the rest. He lifted it cautiously, and there indeed was the key.

He opened the big padlock and removed it from the winch. Then slowly he began to turn. It creaked and groaned so loud that the armored giants must have heard it by then if they weren't totally deaf. Even so, there was nothing to be gained by stopping. Bastian went on turning until the three knights were level with the floor, though still over the pit. Then, after swinging them to and fro until their feet touched the ground, he let them down. They stretched out exhausted and showed no inclination to move. Besides, they still had the heavy chains on their wrists.

Bastian had little time to think, for metallic steps came clanking down the stone stairs. The guards! Their armor glittered in the torchlight like the carapaces of giant insects. All with the same movement, they drew their swords and rushed at Bastian.

Then at last Sikanda leapt from the rusty sheath and into his hand. With the speed of lightning the blade attacked the first of the armored giants and hacked him to pieces before Bastian himself knew what was happening. It was then that he saw what the giants were made of. They were hollow shells of armor. There was nothing inside! He had no time to wonder what made them move.

Bastian was in a good position, for only one giant at a time could squeeze through the narrow doorway of the dungeon, and one at a time Sikanda chopped them to bits. Soon their remains lay piled up on the floor like enormous black eggshells. After some twenty of them had been disposed of, the rest withdrew, evidently in the hope of waylaying Bastian in a position more favorable to themselves.

Taking advantage of the breathing spell, Bastian let Sikanda cut the shackles from the knights' wrists. Hykrion and Hydorn dragged themselves to their feet and tried to draw their swords, which strangely enough had not been taken away from them, but their hands were numb from the long hanging and refused to obey them. Hysbald, the most delicate of the three, wasn't even able to stand by himself. His two friends had to hold him up.

'Never mind,' said Bastian. 'Sikanda needs no help. Just stay behind me and don't get in my way.'

They left the dungeon, slowly climbed the stairs, and came to a large hall. Suddenly all the torches went out. But Sikanda shone bright.

Again they heard the heavy metallic tread of many armored giants.

'Quick!' cried Bastian. 'Back to the stairs! This is where I'm going to fight.'

He couldn't see whether the three knights obeyed his order and there was no time to find out, because Sikanda was already dancing in his hand. The entire hall was ablaze with its sharp white light. The assailants managed to push Bastian back from the top of the stairs and to attack him from all sides, yet not one of their mighty blows touched him. Sikanda whirled around him so fast that it looked like hundreds of swords. And a few moments later he was surrounded by a heap of shattered black armor in which nothing stirred.

'Come on up!' Bastian cried to his companions.

The three knights stood gaping on the stairs. Hykrion's moustache was trembling. 'I've never seen anything like it!' he cried.

'Something to tell my grandchildren!' Hysbald stammered.

'The only trouble,' said Hydorn mournfully, 'is that they won't believe you.'

Bastian stood there with sword in hand, wondering what to do next. Suddenly it sprang back into its sheath.

'The danger seems to be over,' he said.

'At least the part that calls for a sword,' said Hydorn. 'What do we do now?'

'Now,' said Bastian, 'I want to make this Xayide's acquaintance. I've got a bone to pick with her.'

After climbing several more flights of stairs, Bastian and the knights reached the ground floor, where Atreyu and Falkor were waiting for them in a kind of lobby.

'Well done, you two!' cried Bastian, slapping Atreyu on the back.

'What's become of the armored giants?' asked Atreyu.

'Hollow shells!' said Bastian contemptuously. 'Where's Xayide?'

'Up in her magic throne room,' answered Atreyu.

'Come along,' said Bastian, taking the silver mantle which Atreyu held out to him. And all together, including Falkor, they climbed the broad stairway leading to the upper floors.

When Bastian, followed by his companions, entered the magic throne room, Xayide arose from her red-coral throne. She was wearing a long gown of violet silk, and her flaming red hair was coiled and braided into a fantastic edifice. Her face and her long, thin hands were as pale as marble. There was something strangely disturbing about her eyes. It took Bastian a few moments to figure out what it was – they were of different colors, one green, one red. She was trembling, evidently in fear of Bastian. He looked her straight in the face and she lowered her long lashes.

The room was full of weird objects whose purpose it was hard to determine. There were large globes covered with designs, sidereal clocks, and pendulums hanging from the ceiling. There were costly censers from which rose heavy clouds of different-colored smoke, which crept over the floor like fog.

Thus far Bastian hadn't said a word. That seemed to shatter Xayide's composure, for suddenly she threw herself on the floor in front of him, took one of his feet and set it on her neck.

'My lord and master!' she said in a deep voice that sounded somehow mysterious. 'No one in Fantastica can withstand you. You are mightier than the mighty and more dangerous than all the demons together. If you wish to take revenge on me for being too stupid to recognize your greatness, trample me underfoot. I have earned your anger. But if you wish once again to demonstrate your far-famed magnanimity, suffer me to become your obedient slave, who swears to obey you body and soul. Teach me to do what you deem desirable and I will be your humble pupil, obedient to your every hint. I repent of the harm I tried to do you and beg your mercy!'

'Arise, Xayide!' said Bastian. He had been very angry, but her speech pleased him. If she had really acted out of ignorance and really regretted it so bitterly, then it was beneath his dignity to punish her. And since she even wished to learn what he deemed desirable, he could see no reason to reject her plea.

Xayide arose and stood before him with bowed head. 'Will you obey me unconditionally,' he asked, 'however hard you may find it to do my bidding? Will you obey me without argument and without grumbling?'

'I will, my lord and master,' said Xayide. 'You will see there is nothing we cannot accomplish if we combine my artifices and your power.'

'Very well,' said Bastian. 'Then I will take you into my service. You will leave this castle and go with me to the Ivory Tower, where I am expecting to meet Moon Child.'

For a fraction of a second Xayide's eyes glowed red and green, but then, veiling them with her long lashes, she said: 'I am yours to command, my lord and master.'

Thereupon all descended the stairs. Once outside the castle, Bastian observed: 'The first thing to do is find our traveling companions. Goodness knows where they are.'

'Not very far from here,' said Xayide. 'I've led them slightly astray.'

'For the last time,' said Bastian.

'For the last time,' she agreed. 'But how will we get there? Do you expect me to walk? Through the woods and at night?'

'Falkor will carry us,' said Bastian. 'He's strong enough to carry us all.'

Falkor raised his head and looked at Bastian. His ruby-red eyes glittered.

'I'm strong enough, Bastian Balthazar Bux,' boomed the bronze bell-like voice. 'But I will not carry that woman.'

'Oh yes, you will,' said Bastian. 'Because I command it.'

The luckdragon looked at Atreyu, who nodded almost imperceptibly. But Bastian had seen that nod.

All took their places on Falkor's back, and he rose into the air.

'Which way?' he asked.

'Straight ahead,' said Xayide.

'Which way?' Falkor asked again, as if he hadn't heard.

'Straight ahead!' Bastian shouted. 'You heard her.'

'Do as she says,' said Atreyu under his breath. And Falkor complied.

Half an hour later – already the dawn was graying – they saw innumerable campfires down below and the luckdragon landed. In the meantime many more Fantasticans had turned up and a lot of them had brought tents. The camp, spread out on a wide, flower-strewn meadow at the edge of the orchid forest, looked like a tent city.

'How many are you now?' Bastian asked.

Ilwan, the blue djinn, who had taken charge of the caravan in Bastian's absence, replied that he had not yet been able to make an exact count, but that he guessed there were close to a thousand. 'And there's something else to report,' he added. 'Something rather strange. Soon after we pitched camp, shortly before midnight, five of those armored giants appeared. But they were peaceful and they've kept to themselves. Of course, no one dared to go near them. They brought a big litter made of red coral. But it was empty.'

'Those are my carriers,' said Xayide in a pleading tone to Bastian. 'I sent them ahead last night. That's the pleasantest way to travel. If it does not displease you, my lord.'

'I don't like the look of this,' Atreyu interrupted.

'Why not?' said Bastian. 'What's your objection?'

'She can travel any way she likes,' said Atreyu drily. 'But she wouldn't have sent her litter here last night if she hadn't known in advance that she'd be coming here. She had planned the whole thing. Your victory was really a defeat. She purposely let you win. That was her way of winning you over.'

'Enough of this!' cried Bastian, purple with anger. 'I didn't ask for your opinion. You make me sick with your lecturing. And now you question my victory and ridicule my magnanimity.'

Atreyu was going to say something, but Bastian screamed at him: 'Shut up and leave me be! If the two of you aren't satisfied with what I do and the way I am, go away. I'm not keeping you. Go where you please! I'm sick of you!'

Bastian folded his arms over his chest and turned his back on Atreyu. The Fantasticans who had gathered around were dumb-founded. For a time Atreyu stood silent. Up until then Bastian had never reprimanded him in the presence of others. He was so stunned he could hardly breathe. He waited a while, then, when Bastian did not turn back to him, he slowly walked away. Falkor followed him.

Xayide smiled. It wasn't a pleasant smile.

In that moment Bastian's memory of having been a child in his world was effaced.

XXI

The Star Cloister

NINTERRUPTEDLY new emissaries from all parts of Fantastica poured in to swell the army of those accompanying Bastian on his march to the Ivory Tower. It proved impossible to take a count, because new ones kept arriving while the counting was in progress. Each morning an army several thousand strong got under way. And each night it set up the strangest tent city imaginable. Since Bastian's traveling companions varied enormously in shape and size, some of their night lodgings might have been mistaken for circus tents, while others, at the opposite end of the scale, were no bigger than a thimble. Their vehicles also showed astonishing variety, ranging from common covered wagons and diligences to the most extraordinary rolling barrels, bouncing balls, and crawling containers with automotive legs.

Of all the tents the most magnificent was the one that had been procured for Bastian. The shape and size of a small house, it was made of lustrous, many-colored silk, embroidered with gold and silver. A flag affixed to the roof was decorated with Bastian's coat of arms, a seven-armed candelabrum. The inside was furnished with soft blankets and cushions. Bastian's tent was always set up at the center of the camp. And the blue djinn, who had become his factotum, stood guard at the entrance.

Atreyu and Falkor were still among the host of Bastian's companions, but since the public reprimand he hadn't exchanged a word with them. Secretly, he was waiting for Atreyu to give in and apologize. But Atreyu did nothing of the kind. Nor did Falkor show any inclination to humble himself before Bastian. And that, said Bastian to himself, was just what they must learn to do. If they expected him to back down they had another think coming; his will was of steel. But if they gave in, he'd welcome them with open arms. If Atreyu knelt down to him, he would lift him up and say: Don't kneel to me, Atreyu, you are and remain my friend . . .

But for the time being Atreyu and Falkor brought up the rear of the procession. Falkor seemed to have forgotten how to fly; he trudged along on foot and Atreyu walked beside him, most of the time with bowed head. A sad comedown for the proud reconnaissance flyers. Bastian wasn't happy about it, but there was nothing he could do.

He began to be bored riding the mule Yikka in the lead of the caravan, and took to visiting Xayide in her litter instead. She received him with a great show of respect, gave him the most comfortable seat, and squatted down at his feet. She could always think of something interesting to talk about, and when she noticed that he disliked speaking of his past in the human world, she stopped questioning him about it. Most of the time she smoked her Oriental water pipe. The stem looked like an emerald-green viper, and the mouthpiece, which she held between her marble-white fingers, suggested a snake's head. She seemed to be kissing it as she smoked. The clouds of smoke which poured indolently from her mouth and nose changed color with every puff, from blue to yellow, to pink, to green, and so on.

'Xayide,' said Bastian on one of his visits, looking thoughtfully at the armored giants who were carrying the litter. 'There's something I've been wanting to ask you.'

'Your slave is listening,' said Xayide.

'When I fought your guards,' said Bastian, 'I discovered that there was nothing inside their shell of armor. So what makes them move?'

'My will,' said Xayide with a smile. 'It's because they're empty that they do my will. My will can control anything that's empty.'

She turned her red and green gaze on Bastian. For a moment it gave him a strangely eerie feeling, but quickly she lowered her lashes.

'Could I control them with my will?' he asked.

'Of course you could, my lord and master,' she replied. 'You could do it a hundred times better than I. I am as nothing beside you. Would you care to try?'

'Not now,' said Bastian, who was rather frightened at the idea. 'Maybe some other time.'

'Tell me,' said Xayide. 'Do you really enjoy riding an old mule? Wouldn't you rather be carried by beings you can move with your will?'

'But Yikka likes to carry me,' said Bastian almost peevishly. 'It gives her pleasure.'

'Then you do it to please her?'

'Why not?' said Bastian. 'What's wrong with that?'

Xayide let some green smoke rise from her mouth.

'Oh, nothing at all, my lord. How can anything you do be wrong?'

'What are you driving at, Xayide?'

She bowed her head of flaming red hair.

'You think of others too much, my lord and master,' she whispered. 'No one is worthy to divert your attention from your own all-important development. If you promise not to be angry, I will venture a piece of advice: Think more of your own perfection.'

'What has that got to do with Yikka?'

'Not much, my lord. Hardly anything. Just this: she's not a worthy mount for someone as important as you. It grieves me to see you riding such an undistinguished animal. All your traveling companions are surprised. You alone, my lord and master, seem unaware of what you owe to yourself.'

Bastian said nothing, but Xayide's words had made an impression.

Next day, as the procession with Bastian and Yikka in the lead was passing through lush rolling meadows, interspersed here and there by small copses of fragrant lilac, he decided to take Xayide's advice.

At noon, when the caravan stopped to rest, he patted the old mule on the neck and said: 'Yikka, the time has come for us to part.'

Yikka let out a cry of dismay. 'Why, master?' she asked. 'Have I done my job so badly?' And tears flowed from the corners of her dark eyes.

'Not at all,' Bastian hastened to reassure her. 'You've been carrying me so gently all this time, you've been so patient and willing that I've decided to reward you.'

'I don't want any other reward,' said Yikka. 'I just want to go on carrying you. How could I wish for anything better?'

'Didn't you once tell me it made you sad that mules can't have children?'

'Yes,' said Yikka, 'because when I'm very old I'd like to tell my children about these happy days.'

'Very well,' said Bastian. 'Then I'll tell you a story that will come true. And I'll tell it only to you, to you and no one else, because it's your story.'

Then he took hold of one of Yikka's long ears and whispered into it: 'Not far from here, in a little lilac copse, the father of your son is waiting for you. He's a white stallion with the white wings of a swan. His mane and his tail are so long they touch the ground. He has been following you secretly for days, because he's immortally in love with you.'

'With me?' cried Yikka, almost frightened. 'But I'm only a mule, and I'm not as young as I used to be.'

'In his eyes,' said Bastian in an undertone, 'you're the most beautiful creature in all Fantastica just as you are. And also perhaps because you've carried me. But he's very bashful, he doesn't dare approach you with all these creatures about. You must go to him or he'll die of longing for you.'

'Myohmy!' Yikka sighed. 'Is it as bad as all that?'

'Yes,' Bastian whispered in her ear. 'And now, goodbye, Yikka. Just run along, you'll find him.'

Yikka took a few steps, but then she looked back again.

'Frankly,' she said. 'I'm kind of scared.'

'There's nothing to worry about,' said Bastian with a smile. 'And don't forget to tell your children and grandchildren about me.'

'Thank you, master,' said Yikka, and off she went.

For a long while Bastian looked after her as she hobbled off. He wasn't really happy about sending her away. He went to his luxurious tent, lay down on the soft cushions, and gazed at the ceiling. He kept telling himself that he had made Yikka's dearest wish come true. But that didn't make him feel any better. A person's reason for doing someone a good turn matters as much as the good turn itself.

But that made no difference to Yikka, for she really did find the white, winged stallion. They married and she had a son who was a white, winged mule. His name was Pataplan and he made quite a name for himself in Fantastica, but that's another story and shall be told another time.

From then on Bastian traveled in Xayide's litter. She even offered to get out and walk alongside so as to give him every possible comfort, but that was more than Bastian would accept. So they sat together in the comfortable red-coral litter, which from then on led the procession.

Bastian was still rather gloomy and felt a certain resentment toward Xayide for persuading him to part with his mule. He kept answering her in monosyllables, so that no real conversation was possible. Xayide soon realized what the trouble was.

To guide his thoughts into different channels, she said brightly: 'I would like to make you a present, my lord and master, if you deign to accept one from me.'

She rummaged under her cushions and found a richly ornamented casket. As Bastian tingled with eagerness, she opened it and took out a belt with chain links. Each link as well as the clasp was made of clear glass.

'What is it?' Bastian asked.

'It's a belt that makes its wearer invisible. But if you want it to belong to you, my lord, you must give it its name.'

Bastian examined it. 'The belt Ghemmal,' he said then.

Xayide nodded. 'Now it is yours,' she said with a smile. Bastian took the belt and held it irresolutely in his hand.

'Would you like to try it now?' she asked. 'Just to see how it works?'

To Bastian's surprise, the belt was a perfect fit. But it gave him a most unpleasant feeling not to see his own body. He wanted to take the belt off, but that wasn't so easy since he could see neither the buckle nor his own hands.

'Help!' he cried in a panic, suddenly afraid that he would never find the buckle and would remain invisible forever.

'You have to learn to handle it,' said Xayide. 'I had the same trouble at first. Permit me to help you, my lord and master.'

She reached into the empty air. A moment later she had unfastened the belt and Bastian was relieved to see himself again. He laughed, while Xayide drew smoke from her water pipe and smiled.

If nothing else, she had cheered him up.

'Now you are safe from harm,' she said gently, 'and that means more to me than you can imagine.'

'Harm?' asked Bastian, still slightly befuddled. 'What sort of harm?'

'Oh, no one can contend with you,' Xayide whispered. 'Not if you are wise. The danger is inside you, and that's why it's hard to protect you against it.'

'Inside me? What does that mean?'

'A wise person stands above things, he neither loves nor hates. But you, my lord, set store by friendship. Your heart should be as cold and indifferent as a snow-covered mountain peak, and it isn't. That's why someone can harm you.'

'Someone? What someone?'

'Someone you still care for in spite of all his insolence.'

'Speak more plainly.'

'That rude, arrogant little savage from the Greenskin country, my lord.'

'Atreyu?'

'Yes, and that outrageous, impertinent Falkor!'

'You think they'd want to harm me?' Bastian could hardly keep from laughing.

Xayide bowed her head and said nothing.

'I'll never believe that,' said Bastian. 'I won't listen to another word.'

Xayide still said nothing. She bowed her head still lower.

After a long silence Bastian asked: 'What do you suppose Atreyu is plotting?'

'My lord,' Xayide whispered. 'I wish I hadn't spoken.'

'Well, now that you've started,' Bastian cried, 'tell me everything. Stop beating about the bush. What do you know?'

'I tremble at your anger, my lord,' Xayide stammered, and true enough, she was all atremble. 'But even if it costs me my life, I will tell you. Atreyu is plotting to take the Childlike Empress's amulet away from you, by stealth or by force.'

For a moment Bastian could hardly breathe.

'Can you prove it?' he asked.

Xayide shook her head.

'My knowledge,' she murmured, 'is not of the kind that can be proved.'

'Then keep it to yourself,' said Bastian, the blood rising to his face. 'And don't malign the truest, bravest boy in all Fantastica.'

With that he jumped out of the litter and left her.

Xayide's fingers played with the snake's head and her green-and-red eyes glowed. After a while she smiled again. Violet smoke rose from her mouth and she whispered: 'You will see, my lord and master. The belt Ghemmal will show you.'

When the camp was set up that night, Bastian went to his tent. He ordered Ilwan, the blue djinn, not to admit anyone, and especially not Xayide. He wanted to be alone and to think.

What the sorceress had told him about Atreyu hardly seemed worth troubling his head about. He had something else on his mind: those few words she dropped about wisdom.

He had been through so much; he had known joy and fear, discouragement and triumph; he had rushed from wish fulfillment to wish fulfillment, never stopping to rest. And nothing had brought him calm and contentment. To be wise was to be above joy and sorrow, fear and pity, ambition and humiliation. It was to hate nothing and to love nothing, and above all to be utterly indifferent to the love and hate of others. A truly wise man attached no importance to anything. Nothing could upset him and nothing could harm him. Yes, to be like that would be his final wish, the wish that would bring him to what he really wanted. Now he thought he understood what Grograman had meant by those words. And so he wished to become wise, the wisest being in Fantastica.

A little later he stepped out of his tent.

The moon cast its light on a landscape that he had scarcely noticed up until then. The tent city lay in a hollow ringed about by strangely shaped mountains. The silence was complete. The hollow was fairly well wooded, while on the mountain slopes the vegetation became more sparse and farther up there was none at all. The peaks formed all manner of figures, almost as though a giant sculptor had shaped them. No breeze was blowing and there wasn't a cloud in the sky. The stars glittered and seemed nearer than usual.

At the top of one of the highest peaks Bastian made out a sort of cupola. It seemed to be inhabited, for it gave off a faint light.

'I've noticed it too, my lord,' said Ilwan in his rasping voice. He was standing at his post by the entrance to the tent. 'What can it be?'

He had no sooner spoken than Bastian heard a strange cry in the distance. It suggested the long-drawn-out hooting of an owl, but it was deeper and louder. It sounded a second and then a third time, but now there were several voices.

Owls they were indeed, six in number, as Bastian was soon to find out. Coming from the direction of the cupola, they glided at an incredible speed on almost motionless wings. Soon they were close enough for Bastian to see how amazingly large they were. Their eyes glittered, and their erect ears were capped with bundles of down. The flight was soundless, but as they landed, a faint whirring of their wings could be heard.

Then they were sitting on the ground in front of Bastian's tent, swiveling their heads with their great round eyes in all directions. Bastian went up to them.

'Who are you?' he asked, 'and who are you looking for?'

'We were sent by Ushtu, the Mother of Intuition,' said one of the six owls. 'We are messengers from Ghigam, the Star Cloister.'

'What sort of cloister is that?' Bastian asked.

'It is the home of wisdom,' said another of the owls, 'where the Monks of Knowledge live.'

'And who is Ushtu?' Bastian asked.

'One of the Three Deep Thinkers who direct the cloister and instruct the monks,' said a third owl. 'We are the night messengers, which puts us in her department.'

'If it were daytime,' said the fourth owl, 'Shirkry, the Father of Vision, would have sent his messengers, who are eagles. And in the twilight hours between day and night, Yisipu, the Son of Reason, sends his messengers, who are foxes.'

'Who are Shirkry and Yisipu?'

'They are the other Deep Thinkers, our Superiors.'

'And what are you doing here?'

'We are looking for the Great Knower,' said the sixth owl. 'The Three Deep Thinkers know he is in this tent city and have sent us to beg him for illumination.'

'The Great Knower?' asked Bastian. 'Who's that?'

'His name,' replied all six owls at once, 'is Bastian Balthazar Bux.'

'You've found him,' said Bastian. 'It's me.'

They bowed low, which because of their jerky movements looked almost comical in spite of their great size.

'The Three Deep Thinkers,' said the first owl, 'beg you humbly and respectfully to visit them. They hope you will solve a problem they have been trying in vain to solve all their long lives.'

Bastian stroked his chin thoughtfully.

'Very well,' he answered after a while. 'But I must take my two disciples with me.'

'There are six of us,' said the owl. 'Two of us will carry each one of you.'

Bastian turned to the blue djinn.

'Ilwan,' he said. 'Bring me Atreyu and Xayide.'

The djinn bowed and went his way.

'What is this problem they want me to solve?' Bastian asked.

'O Great Knower,' said one of the owls, 'we are only poor ignorant messengers. We don't even belong to the lowest rank of the Monks of Knowledge. How could we possibly have cognizance of the problem which the Deep Thinkers in all their long lives have been unable to solve?'

A few minutes later Ilwan came back with Atreyu and Xayide. On the way he had told them what it was all about.

As he stood before Bastian, Atreyu asked in an undertone: 'Why me?'

'Indeed,' said Xayide. 'Why him?'

'You will find out,' said Bastian.

With admirable foresight, the owls had brought trapezes, one for every two owls. Bastian, Atreyu, and Xayide sat on the bars, and the great night birds, each holding a trapeze rope in its claws, rose into the air.

When the travelers reached the Star Cloister of Ghigam, they found that the great cupola was only the uppermost part of a large building composed of many cubical compartments. It had innumerable little windows and its outer wall might have been taken for the continuation of a sheer cliff. An unbidden visitor could hardly have gained admittance to the place.

The cubical compartments contained the cells of the Monks of Knowledge, the libraries, the refectories, and the lodgings of the messengers. The meeting hall, where the Three Deep Thinkers delivered their lectures, was situated under the cupola.

The Monks of Knowledge were Fantasticans of all kinds, from every part of the realm. But anyone wishing to enter the cloister had to break off all contact with family and country. The lives of these monks were hard and frugal, devoted exclusively to knowledge. The community was far from accepting all applicants. The examinations were difficult and the Three Deep Thinkers set the highest standards. Thus there were seldom more than three hundred monks in the cloister at one time, but these were by far the most intelligent persons in all Fantastica. Occasionally the community dwindled to seven members, but even then there was no thought of relaxing the entrance requirements. At the moment the monks and monkesses numbered roughly two hundred.

When Bastian, followed by Atreyu and Xayide, was led into the large lecture hall, he saw a motley assortment of Fantasticans, who differed from his own retinue only in that they all were dressed in rough dark-brown monk's robes. A wandering cliff or a tiny must have looked very strange in such an outfit.

The Superiors of the order, the Three Deep Thinkers, were built like humans except for their heads. Ushtu, the Mother of Intuition, had the head of an owl; Shirkry, the Father of Vision, the head of an eagle; and Yisipu, the Son of Reason, the head of a fox. They sat in raised stone chairs and looked enormous. The sight of them seemed to intimidate Atreyu and even Xayide. But Bastian stepped right up to them.

With a motion of his head, Shirkry, who was evidently the oldest of the three and was sitting in the middle, indicated an empty chair facing the Deep Thinkers. Bastian sat down in it.

After a prolonged silence, Shirkry spoke. He spoke softly, but his voice sounded surprisingly deep and full.

'Since time immemorial we have been pondering the enigma of our world. Yisipu's reasonings in the matter are different from

Ushtu's intuitions, and Ushtu's intuitions differ from my vision, which in turn is different from Yisipu's reasonings. This is intolerable and must not be allowed to go on. That is why we have asked the Great Knower to come here and instruct us. Are you willing?'

'I am,' said Bastian.

'Then, O Great Knower, hear our question: What is Fantastica?'

After a short silence Bastian replied: 'Fantastica is the Neverending Story.'

'Give us time to understand your answer,' said Shirkry. 'Let us meet again here tomorrow at the same hour.'

Silently the Three Deep Thinkers and the Monks of Knowledge arose, and all left the hall.

Bastian, Atreyu, and Xayide were led to guest cells, where a simple meal awaited them. Their beds were wooden planks covered with rough woolen blankets. Though this didn't matter to Bastian and Atreyu, Xayide would have liked to conjure up a more comfortable bed. But she soon found to her dismay that her magic powers were without effect in this cloister.

Late the following night the monks and the Three Deep Thinkers met again in the great meeting hall. Once again Bastian occupied the high seat. Xayide and Atreyu sat to the left and right of him.

This time it was Ushtu, the Mother of Intuition, who scrutinized Bastian with her great owl's eyes and said: 'We have meditated on your answer, O Great Knower. But a new question has occurred to us. If, as you say, Fantastica is the Neverending Story, where is the Neverending Story to be found?'

After a short silence Bastian replied: 'In a book bound with copper-colored silk.'

'Give us time to understand your words,' said Ushtu. 'Let us meet again tomorrow at the same hour.'

When they had gathered in the meeting hall the following night, Yisipu, the Son of Reason, took the floor.

'Again we have meditated on your answer, O Great Knower,' he said. 'And again a new question comes to perplex us. If our world, Fantastica, is a Neverending Story and if this Neverending Story is in a book bound in copper-colored silk – where then is this book?'

After a short silence Bastian replied: 'In the attic of a schoolhouse.'

'O Great Knower,' said the fox-headed Yisipu, 'we do not doubt the truth of what you say. But now we would like to ask you to let us see this truth. Can you do that?'

Bastian thought it over. Then he said: 'I believe I can.'

Atreyu looked at Bastian with surprise. Xayide too had a questioning look in her red-and-green eyes.

'Let us meet again tomorrow night at the same hour,' said Bastian. 'But not here. Let us meet on the roof of the Star Cloister. And then you must keep your eyes fixed on the heavens.'

The following night was as clear as the three before it. At the appointed hour the Three Deep Thinkers and all the Monks of Knowledge were gathered on the roof of the Star Cloister. Atreyu and Xayide, who had no idea what Bastian was up to, were there too.

Bastian climbed to the top of the great cupola and looked around. For the first time he saw the Ivory Tower far off on the horizon, shimmering in the moonlight.

He took the stone Al Tsahir from his pocket. It sent out a soft glow. He then called to mind the inscription he had seen on the door of the Amarganth Library:

> ... But if he says my name a second time
> from the end to the beginning,
> I will glow in one moment
> with the light of a hundred years.

He held the stone up high and cried out: 'Rihast-la!'

At that moment there came a flash of lightning so bright that the stars paled and the dark cosmic space behind them was illumined. And that space was the schoolhouse attic with its age-blackened beams. In a moment the vision passed and the light of a hundred years was gone. Al Tsahir had vanished without a trace.

It was some time before the eyes of those present, including Bastian's, became accustomed to the feeble light of the moon and the stars.

Shaken by what they had seen, all gathered in the great lecture hall. Bastian was the last to enter. The Monks of Knowledge and the Three Deep Thinkers arose from their seats and bowed low to him.

'I have no words,' said Shirkry, 'with which to thank you for that flash of illumination, O Great Knower. For in that mysterious attic I glimpsed a being of my own kind, an eagle.'

'You are mistaken, Shirkry,' said the owl-faced Ushtu with a gentle smile. 'I saw the creature plainly. It was an owl.'

'You are both mistaken,' cried Yisipu, his eyes aflame. 'That being is a relative of mine, a fox.'

Shirkry raised his hands in horror.

'Here we are back where we started!' he said. 'You alone, O Great Knower, can answer this new question. Which of us is right?'

Smiling serenely, Bastian replied: 'All three.'

'Give us time to understand your answer,' said Ushtu.

'All the time you wish,' Bastian replied, 'for we shall be leaving you now.'

Bitter disappointment could be read on the faces of the Three Deep Thinkers and of the Monks of Knowledge. They implored Bastian to stay longer, or better still, forever, but with a rather disrespectful shrug he declined.

Whereupon the six messengers carried him and his two disciples back to the tent city.

That night the usual harmony of the Three Deep Thinkers was disturbed by a first radical difference of opinion, which years later led to the breakup of the community. Then Ushtu the Mother of Intuition, Shirkry the Father of Vision, and Yisipu the Son of Reason each founded a cloister of his own. But that is another story and shall be told another time.

That night Bastian lost all memory of having gone to school. The attic and the stolen book bound in copper-colored silk vanished from his mind. And he even stopped asking himself how he had come to Fantastica.

XXII

The Battle for the Ivory Tower

IGILANT scouts returned to camp, reporting that the Ivory Tower was not far off and could be reached in two or at the most three days' marches.

But Bastian seemed irresolute. He kept ordering rest stops, but before the troops were half settled he would make them start out again. No one knew why he was behaving so strangely, and no one dared ask him. Since his great feat at the Star Cloister he had been unapproachable, even for Xayide. All sorts of conjectures were rife, but most of the traveling companions were quite willing to obey his contradictory orders. Great wise men, they thought, often strike the common run of people as unpredictable. Atreyu and Falkor were equally at a loss. The incident at the Star Cloister had baffled them completely.

Within Bastian two feelings were at war, and he was unable to silence either one. He longed to meet Moon Child. Now that he was famous and admired throughout Fantastica, he could approach her as an equal. But at the same time he was afraid she would ask him to return AURYN to her. And what then? Would she try to send him back to the world he had almost forgotten? He didn't want to go back. And he wanted to keep the Gem. But then he had another idea. Was it so certain that she wanted it back? Maybe she would let him have it as long as he wished. Maybe she had made him a present of it and it was his for good. At such moments he could hardly wait to see her again. He rushed the caravan on. But then, assailed by doubts, he would order a stop and think it all over again.

After alternating forced marches and prolonged delays, the procession finally reached the edge of the famous Labyrinth, the immense flower garden with its winding avenues and pathways. On the horizon the Ivory Tower gleamed white against the gold-shimmering evening sky.

Awed by the splendor and beauty of the sight, the army of Fantasticans stood silent. And so did Bastian. Even Xayide's face showed a look of wonderment, which had never been seen before and which soon vanished. Atreyu and Falkor, who were in the rear of the procession, remembered how different the Labyrinth had looked the last time they had seen it: wasted with the ravages of the Nothing. Now it was greener and more flourishing than ever before.

Bastian decided to go no farther that day and the tents were pitched for the night. He sent out messengers to bring greetings to Moon Child and let her know that he would be arriving at the Ivory Tower next day. Then he lay down in his tent and tried to sleep. He tossed and turned on his cushions, his worries left him no peace. But he was far from suspecting that this would be his worst night since coming to Fantastica.

Toward midnight, soon after falling into a restless sleep, he was awakened by excited whisperings outside his tent. He got up and went out.

'What's going on?' he asked sternly.

'This messenger,' replied Ilwan, the blue djinn, 'claims he is bringing you news so important that it can't wait until tomorrow.'

The messenger, whom Ilwan had picked up by the collar, was a nimbly, a creature bearing a certain resemblance to a rabbit, except that its coat was of bright-colored feathers instead of fur. Nimblies are among the swiftest runners in Fantastica, and can cover enormous distances with incredible speed. When running they become almost invisible except for the trail of dust clouds they leave behind them. That is why the nimbly had been chosen as messenger. After running to the Ivory Tower and back in next to no time, he was desperately out of breath when the djinn set him down in front of Bastian.

'Forgive me, sire,' he said, bowing and panting. 'Forgive me if I make so bold as to disturb your rest, but you would have every reason to be displeased with me if I failed to do so. Moon Child is not in the Ivory Tower; she has not been there for a long, long time, and no one knows where she is.'

Suddenly Bastian felt cold and empty inside. 'You must be mistaken. That can't be.'

'The other messengers will tell you the same thing when they get back, sire.'

After a long silence Bastian said tonelessly: 'Thank you. Dismissed.'

He went back into his tent, sat down on his bed, and buried his head in his hands. This seemed impossible. Moon Child must have known he was on his way to her. Could it be that she didn't want to see him again? Or had something happened to her? No, how could anything happen to her in her own realm?

But the fact remained: she was gone, which meant that he didn't have to return AURYN to her. At the same time he felt bitterly disappointed that he wouldn't be seeing her again. Whatever her reasons may have been, he found her behavior unbelievable, no, insulting.

Then he remembered what Falkor and Atreyu had told him: that no one could meet the Childlike Empress more than once.

The thought made him so unhappy that he suddenly longed for Atreyu and Falkor. He needed someone to talk to, to confide in.

Then he had an idea: If he put on the belt Ghemmal and made himself invisible, he could enjoy their comforting presence without mentioning the humiliation he felt.

He opened the ornate casket, took out the belt, and put it on. Then, after waiting until he had got used to the unpleasant sensation of not seeing himself, he went out and wandered about the tent city in search of Atreyu and Falkor. Wherever he went he heard excited whispers, figures darted from tent to tent, here and there several creatures were huddled together, talking and gesticulating. By then the other messengers had returned, and the news that Moon Child was not in the Ivory Tower had spread like wildfire.

Atreyu and Falkor were under a flowering rosemary tree at the very edge of the camp. Atreyu was sitting with his arms folded, looking fixedly in the direction of the Ivory Tower. The luckdragon lay beside him with his great head on the ground.

'That was my last hope,' said Atreyu. 'I thought she might make an exception for him and let him return the amulet. Now all is lost.'

'She must know what she's doing,' said Falkor.

At that moment Bastian located them and sat down invisibly nearby.

'Is it certain?' Atreyu murmured. 'He mustn't be allowed to keep AURYN!'

'What will you do?' Falkor asked. 'He won't give it up of his own free will.'

'Then I'll have to take it from him,' said Atreyu.

At those words Bastian felt the ground sinking from under him.

'That won't be easy,' he heard Falkor saying. 'But if you do take it, I trust that he won't be able to get it back.'

'That's not so sure,' said Atreyu. 'He'll still have his great strength and his magic sword.'

'But the Gem would protect you,' said Falkor. 'Even against him.'

'No,' said Atreyu. 'I don't think so. Not against him.'

'And to think,' said Falkor with a grim laugh, 'that he himself offered it to you on your first night in Amarganth.'

Atreyu nodded. 'I didn't realize then what would happen.'

'How are you going to take it from him?' Falkor asked.

'I'll have to steal it,' said Atreyu.

Falkor's head shot up. With glowing ruby-red eyes he stared at Atreyu, who hung his head and repeated in an undertone: 'I'll have to. There's no other way.'

After a long silence Falkor asked: 'When?'

'It will have to be tonight. Tomorrow may be too late.'

Bastian had heard enough. Slowly he crept away. His only feeling was one of cold emptiness. Everything was indifferent to him now, just as Xayide had said.

He went back to his tent and took off the belt Ghemmal. Then he bade Ilwan bring him the three knights, Hysbald, Hykrion, and Hydorn. As he paced the ground waiting, it came to him that Xayide had foreseen it all. He hadn't wanted to believe her, but now he was obliged to. Xayide, he now realized, was sincerely devoted to him. She was his only true friend. But there was still room for doubt. Perhaps Atreyu wouldn't actually carry out his plan. Maybe he had already repented. In that case Bastian wouldn't ever mention it – though friendship now meant nothing to him. That was over and done with.

When the three knights appeared, he told them he had reason to believe that a thief would come to his tent that night. When they agreed to keep watch and lay hands on the thief whoever he might be, he went to Xayide's coral litter. She lay sound asleep,

attended by her five giants in their black armor, who stood motionless on guard. In the darkness they looked like five boulders.

'I wish you to obey me,' Bastian said softly.

Instantly, all five turned their black iron faces toward him.

'Command us, master of our mistress,' said one in a metallic voice.

'Do you think you can handle Falkor the luckdragon?' Bastian
asked.

'That depends on the will that guides us,' said the metallic voice.

'It is my will,' said Bastian.

'Then there is no one we cannot handle was the answer.

'Good. Then go close to where he is.' He pointed. 'That way.
As soon as Atreyu leaves him, take him prisoner. But keep him there.
I'll have you called when I want you.'

'Master of our mistress,' the metallic voice replied, 'it shall be
done.'

The five black giants marched off in step. Xayide smiled in her
sleep.

Bastian went back to his tent. But once in sight of it, he hesitated.
If Atreyu should really attempt to steal the Gem, he didn't want
to be there when they seized him.

He sat down under a tree nearby and waited, wrapped in his
silver mantle. Slowly the time passed, the sky paled in the east,
it would soon be morning. Bastian was beginning to hope that Atreyu
had abandoned his project when suddenly he heard a tumult in
his tent. And a moment later Hykrion led Atreyu out with his arms
chained behind his back. The two other knights followed. Bastian
dragged himself to his feet and stood leaning against the tree.

'So he's actually done it,' he muttered to himself.

Then he went to his tent. He couldn't bear to look at Atreyu,
and Atreyu too kept his eyes to the ground.

'Ilwan,' said Bastian to the blue djinn. 'Wake the whole camp!
I want everyone here. And tell the black giants to bring Falkor.'

The djinn hurried off with the rasping cry of an eagle. Wherever
he went, the denizens of the tents large and small began to stir.

'He didn't defend himself at all,' said Hykrion, with a movement
of his head toward Atreyu, who was standing there motionless with
eyes downcast. Bastian turned away and sat down on a stone.

By the time the five armored giants appeared with Falkor, a large crowd had gathered. At the approach of the stamping metallic steps, the crowd opened up a passage. Falkor was not chained, and the armed guards were not holding him, but merely marching to the left and right of him with drawn swords.

'He offered no resistance, master of our mistress,' said one of the metallic voices.

Falkor lay down on the ground at Atreyu's feet and closed his eyes.

A long silence followed. Creatures poured in from the camp and craned their necks to see what was going on. Only Xayide was absent. Little by little the whispering died down. All eyes shuttled back and forth between Bastian and Atreyu, who stood motionless, looking like stone statues in the gray morning light.

At length Bastian spoke.

'Atreyu,' he said. 'You tried to steal Moon Child's amulet and take it for yourself. And you, Falkor, were an accomplice to his plan. Not only have you both been untrue to our old friendship, you have also been guilty of disobedience to Moon Child, who gave me the Gem. Do you confess your wrong?'

Atreyu cast a long glance at Bastian; then he nodded.

Bastian's voice failed him. It was some time before he could go on.

'I have not forgotten, Atreyu, that it was you who brought me to Moon Child. I have not forgotten Falkor's singing in Amarganth. So I will spare your lives, the lives of a thief and of a thief's accomplice. Do what you will. Just so you go away, the farther the better, and never let me lay eyes on you again. I banish you forever. I have never known you.'

He bade Hykrion remove Atreyu's chains. Then he turned away.

Atreyu stood motionless for a long while. Then he cast another glance at Bastian. It looked as if he wanted to say something, but changed his mind. He bent down to Falkor and whispered something in his ear. The luckdragon opened his eyes and sat up. Atreyu jumped on his back and Falkor rose into the air. He flew straight into the brightening morning sky, and though his movements were heavy and sluggish, he soon vanished in the distance.

Bastian went to his tent and threw himself down on his bed.

'At last you have achieved true greatness,' said a soft voice. 'Now you've stopped caring for anything; now nothing can move you.'

Bastian sat up. It was Xayide. She was squatting in the darkest corner of the tent.

'You?' said Bastian. 'How did you get in?'

Xayide smiled.

'O my lord and master, no guards can shut me out. Only your command can do that. Do you wish to send me away?'

Bastian lay back and closed his eyes. After a while he muttered: 'It's all the same to me. Go or stay!'

For a long while she watched him from under her half-lowered lids. Then she asked: 'What are you thinking about, my lord and master?'

Bastian turned away and did not reply.

It was plain to Xayide that this was no time to leave him to himself. In such a mood he was capable of slipping away from her. She must comfort him and cheer him up – in her own way. For she was determined to hold him to the course she had planned for him – and for herself. And she knew that in the present juncture no magical belts or tricks would suffice. It would take stronger medicine, the strongest medicine available to her, namely, Bastian's secret wishes. She sat down beside him and whispered in his ear: 'When, O lord and master, will you go to the Ivory Tower?'

'I don't know,' said Bastian. 'What can I do there if Moon Child is gone?'

'You could go and wait for her.'

Bastian turned to face Xayide.

'Do you think she'll be back?'

He had to repeat his question more insistently before Xayide replied: 'No, I don't believe so. I believe she has had to leave Fantastica forever, and that you, my lord and master, are her successor.'

Slowly Bastian sat up and looked into Xayide's red-and-green eyes. It was some time before he grasped the full meaning of her words.

'I!?' he gasped. And his cheeks broke out in red spots.

'Do you find the idea so frightening?' Xayide whispered. 'She gave you the emblem of her power. Now she has left you her empire. Now, my lord and master, you will be the Childlike Emperor. It is only your right. You not only saved Fantastica by your coming, you also created it! All of us – I too! – are your creatures. Why should you, the Great Knower, fear to take the power that is rightfully yours?'

Bastian's eyes glowed with a cold fever. And then Xayide spoke to him of a new Fantastica, a world molded in every detail to Bastian's taste, where he could create and destroy just as he pleased, where every creature, good or bad, beautiful or ugly, wise or foolish, would be the product of his will alone, and he would reign supreme and inscrutable, playing an everlasting game with the destinies of his subjects.

'Then alone,' she concluded, 'will you be truly free, free from all obstacles, free to do as you please. Weren't you trying to find out what you really and truly want? Well, now you know.'

That same morning they broke camp, and led by Bastian and Xayide in the coral litter, the great procession set out for the Ivory Tower. A well-nigh endless column moved along the twining paths of the Labyrinth. In the late afternoon, when the head of the column reached the Ivory Tower, the last stragglers had barely entered the great flowering maze.

Bastian could not have wished for a more festive reception. On every roof and battlement stood elves with gleaming trumpets, blaring away at the top of their lungs. The jugglers juggled, the astrologers proclaimed Bastian's greatness and good fortune, the bakers baked cakes as big as mountains, the ministers and councilors escorted the coral litter through the teeming crowd on the High Street, which wound in an ever-narrowing spiral up the conical tower to the great gate leading into the palace. Followed by Xayide and the dignitaries, Bastian climbed the snow-white steps of the broad stairway, traversed halls and corridors, passed through a second gate, through a garden full of ivory animals, trees, and flowers, mounted higher and higher, crossed a bridge, and passed through the last gate. He was heading for the Magnolia Pavilion at the very top of the tower. But the blossom was closed and the last stretch of the way was so steep and smooth that no one could climb it.

Bastian remembered that the wounded Atreyu had not been able to climb that slope, not by his own strength at least, because no one who has ever reached the Magnolia Pavilion can say how he got there. For this victory must come as a gift.

But Bastian was not Atreyu. If anyone was now entitled to bestow the gift of this victory, it was he. And he had no intention of letting anything stop him.

'Bring workmen,' he commanded. 'I want them to cut steps in this smooth surface. I wish to make my residence up there.'

'Sire,' one of the oldest councilors ventured to object, 'that is where our Golden-eyed Commander of Wishes lives when she is here.'

'Do as you're told!' Bastian roared at him.

The dignitaries turned pale and shrank back from him. But they obeyed. Workmen arrived with mallets and chisels. But try as they might, they couldn't so much as chip the smooth surface of the dome. The chisels leapt from their hands without leaving the slightest dent.

'Think of something else,' said Bastian angrily. 'My patience is wearing thin.'

Then he turned away, and while waiting for the Magnolia Pavilion to be made accessible, he and his retinue, consisting chiefly of Xayide, the three knights, Hysbald, Hykrion, and Hydorn, and Ilwan, the blue djinn, took possession of the remaining rooms of the palace.

That same night he summoned all the ministers and councilors who had served Moon Child to a meeting in the large, circular hall where the congress of physicians had once met. There he informed them that the Golden-eyed Commander of Wishes had left him, Bastian Balthazar Bux, power over the endless Fantastican Empire, and that he was now taking her place. In conclusion he demanded perfect obedience.

'Even, or I might say especially,' he added, 'when my decisions are beyond your understanding. For I am not of your kind.'

He then announced that in exactly seventy-seven days he would crown himself Childlike Emperor of Fantastica and that the event

would be celebrated with such splendor that it would outshine anything ever done in Fantastica. And he ordered the councilors to
send messengers forthwith to every part of the realm, for he wished
every nation of the Fantastican Empire to be represented at his
coronation.

Thereupon Bastian withdrew, leaving the councilors and other
dignitaries alone with their bewilderment.

They didn't know what to do. What they had heard sounded
so monstrous that for a long while they could only stand there
silently, hanging their heads. Then they began to deliberate. And
after many hours, they came to the conclusion that they would have
to obey Bastian's commands, for he bore the emblem of the Childlike
Empress, and that that entitled him to obedience regardless of
whether Moon Child had really abdicated in his favor or whether
this was just another of her unfathomable decisions. And so the
messengers were sent and all Bastian's orders were carried out.

He himself took no further interest in the coronation, but left
all the details to Xayide, who kept the whole court so busy that
hardly anyone had time to think.

During the next days and weeks Bastian spent most of his time
in the room he had chosen, staring into space and doing nothing.
He would have liked to wish for something or make up a story to
amuse himself, but nothing occurred to him. He felt hollow and
empty.

At length he hit on the idea of wishing for Moon Child to come
to him. If he was really all-powerful, if all his wishes came true,
she would have to obey him. For whole nights he sat there whispering: 'Moon Child, come! You must come! I command you to come!'
He thought of her glance, which had lain in his heart like a glittering treasure. But she did not come. And the more he tried to make
her come, the fainter became his memory of that glitter in his heart,
until in the end all was darkness within him.

He convinced himself that everything would come right again
if only he could be in the Magnolia Pavilion. Time and again, he
went up to the workmen and tried to spur them with promises or
threats, but all to no avail. Ladders broke, nails bent, chisels split.

Hykrion, Hysbald, and Hydorn, with whom Bastian would gladly have chatted or played games, were as good as useless. In the deepest cellar of the Ivory Tower they had discovered wine. There they sat day and night, drinking, playing dice, bellowing silly songs, or quarreling, and as often as not attacking one another with their swords. Sometimes they staggered up and down the High Street, molesting the fairies, elves, and other female denizens of the Tower.

'What do you expect, sire?' they said when Bastian found fault with them. 'You must give us something to do.'

But Bastian couldn't think of anything and bade them wait until his coronation, though he himself couldn't have said what difference that would make.

Little by little the weather changed for the worse. Sunsets of liquid gold became more infrequent. Almost always the sky was gray and overcast, not a breeze stirred, the air grew sultry and lifeless.

The day appointed for the coronation was near. The messengers returned. Some brought delegates from remote corners of Fantastica. But others arrived empty-handed, for many of the nations refused out of hand to be represented at the ceremony. And in some countries there had been veiled or open rebellion.

Bastian stared into space.

'Once you are emperor,' said Xayide, 'you will put the house in order.'

'I want them to want what I want,' said Bastian.

But already Xayide had hurried off to make new arrangements.

And then came the day of the coronation that did not take place. It went down in the history of Fantastica as the day of the bloody battle for the Ivory Tower.

There was no dawn that morning; the sky was too covered with thick, leaden-gray clouds. The air was almost too heavy to breathe.

Working hand in hand with the Ivory Tower's fourteen masters of ceremony, Xayide had drawn up an elaborate program for the celebration.

Beginning early in the morning, bands on all the streets and squares played music such as had never been heard in the Ivory Tower – strident yet monotonous. None who heard it could help jiggling his feet and dancing. The musicians wore black masks. No one knew who they were or where Xayide had found them.

Every roof and housefront was decorated with bright-colored flags and pennants, but they hung sadly limp, for there was no wind. Along the High Street and on the wall around the palace hundreds of pictures had been set up, ranging in size from small to enormous, and all showed the same face – Bastian's.

Since the Magnolia Pavilion was still inaccessible, Xayide had prepared another site for the coronation. The throne was to be installed at the foot of the ivory steps near the palace gate where the winding High Street ended. Thousands of golden censers were smoldering, and the smoke, with its lulling yet exciting fragrance, drifted slowly up the steps and down the High Street, finding its way into every last nook and cranny. The armored giants were everywhere. Only Xayide knew how she had managed to multiply the five she had left into such an army. And as if that were not enough, fifty of them were mounted on gigantic horses, which were also made of black metal and moved in perfect unison.

The armored horsemen escorted a throne up the High Street in a triumphal procession. It was as big as a church door and consisted entirely of mirrors of every size and shape. Only the cushion on the seat was covered with copper-colored silk. Strangely, this enormous glittering object glided up the spiral street unaided, without being pushed or pulled; it seemed to have a life of its own.

When it stopped at the great ivory gate, Bastian stepped out of the palace and sat down on it. In the midst of all that glitter and splendor he looked like a tiny doll. The crowd of onlookers, who were held back by a cordon of armored giants, burst into cheers, but for some inexplicable reason their cheers sounded thin and shrill.

Then began the most tedious and wearisome part of the ceremony. The messengers and delegates from all over the Fantastican Empire had to form a line, which extended from the mirror throne down the entire spiraling High Street and deep into the labyrinthine garden. Every single delegate, when his turn came, had to bow down before the throne, touch the ground three times with his forehead, kiss Bastian's right foot, and say: 'In the name of my nation and my species I beseech you, to whom we all owe our existence, to crown yourself Childlike Emperor of Fantastica.'

This had been going on for two or three hours when a sudden

tremor passed through the crowd. A young faun came dashing up the High Street, reeled with exhaustion, pulled himself together, ran till he reached Bastian, and threw himself on the ground, gasping for breath. Bastian bent down to him.

'How dare you interrupt this august ceremony!'

'War, sire!' cried the faun. 'Atreyu has gathered a host of rebels and is on his way here with three armies. They demand that you give up AURYN. If you will not, they mean to take it by force.'

The rousing music and the shrill cries of jubilation gave way to a deathly silence. Bastian turned pale.

Then the three knights, Hysbald, Hykrion, and Hydorn, appeared on the run. They seemed to be in a remarkably good humor.

'At last there's something for us to do, sire,' all three cried at once. 'Leave it to us. Just get on with your celebration. We'll round up a few good men and get after those rebels. We'll teach them a lesson they won't forget so soon.'

Among the thousands of creatures present quite a few were utterly useless for military purposes. But most were able to handle some weapon or to fight with their teeth or claws. All these gathered around the three knights, who led their army away. Bastian remained behind with the not-so-martial multitude, to complete the ceremony. But his heart was no longer in it. Time and again his eyes veered toward the horizon, which he could see from his throne. Great clouds of dust showed him that Atreyu's army was no joke.

'Don't worry,' said Xayide, who had stepped up to Bastian. 'My armored giants haven't begun to fight yet. They'll defend your Ivory Tower. No one can stand up to them, except for you and your sword.'

A few hours later the first battle reports came in. Atreyu had enlisted almost all the Greenskins, at least two hundred centaurs, eight hundred and fifty rock chewers, five luckdragons led by Falkor, who kept attacking from the air, a squadron of giant eagles, who had flown from the Mountains of Destiny, and innumerable other creatures, even a sprinkling of unicorns.

Though far inferior in numbers to the troops led by the knights Hykrion, Hysbald, and Hydorn, Atreyu's army fought so vigorously that they were soon approaching the Ivory Tower.

Bastian wanted to go out and lead his army in person, but Xayide advised against it.

'O lord and master,' she said, 'it is unseemly for the Emperor of Fantastica to take up arms. Leave that to your faithful subjects.'

All day the battle raged. The entire Labyrinth became a trampled, blood-soaked battlefield. By late afternoon, despite the stubborn resistance of Bastian's army, the rebels had reached the foot of the Ivory Tower.

Then Xayide sent in her armored giants, both mounted and on foot, and they wrought havoc among Atreyu's followers.

A detailed account of the battle for the Ivory Tower would take us too far. To this day Fantasticans sing countless songs and tell innumerable stories about that day and night, for everyone who took part saw it in his own way. Certain of the stories have it that Atreyu's army included several white magicians, who had the power to oppose Xayide's black magic. Of this we have no certain knowledge, but that would explain how, in spite of the armored giants, Atreyu and his followers were able to take the Ivory Tower. But there is another, more likely explanation: Atreyu was fighting not for himself, but for his friend, whom he was trying to save by defeating him.

The night of the battle was starless, full of smoke and flames. Fallen torches, overturned censers, and shattered lamps had set the Tower on fire in many places. The fighters cast eerie shadows. Weapons clashed and battle shouts resounded. Everywhere, through the flames and the darkness, Bastian searched for Atreyu.

'Atreyu!' he shouted. 'Atreyu, show yourself! Stand up and fight! Where are you?'

But the sword Sikanda didn't budge from its sheath.

Bastian ran from room to room of the palace, then out on the great wall, which at that point was as wide as a street. He was heading for the outer gate where the mirror throne stood – now shattered into a thousand pieces – when he saw Atreyu, sword in hand, coming toward him.

They stood face to face, and still Sikanda did not budge.

Atreyu put the tip of his sword on Bastian's chest.

'Give me the amulet,' he said. 'For your own sake.'

'Traitor!' cried Bastian. 'You are my creature! I created the whole lot of you! Including you! So how can you rebel against me? Kneel down and beg forgiveness.'

'You're mad!' cried Atreyu. 'You didn't create anything! You owe everything to Moon Child! Give me AURYN!'

'Take it if you can.'

Atreyu hesitated.

'Bastian,' he said. 'Why do you force me to defeat you in order to save you?'

Bastian tugged at the hilt of his sword. He tugged with all his might and finally managed to draw Sikanda from its sheath. But it did not leap into his hand of its own accord, and at the same moment a sound was heard, a sound so terrible that even the warriors on the High Street outside the gate stood as though frozen to the spot, looking up at the two adversaries. Bastian recognized that sound. It was the hideous cracking and grinding he had heard when Grograman turned to stone. Sikanda's light went out. And then Bastian remembered how the lion had predicted what would happen if someone were to draw the sword of his own will. But by then it was too late to turn back.

Atreyu tried to defend himself with his own sword. But wielded by Bastian, Sikanda cut it in two and struck Atreyu in the chest. Blood spurted from a gaping wound. Atreyu staggered back and toppled from the wall. But at that moment a white flame shot through the swirling smoke, caught Atreyu in his fall, and carried him away. The white flame was Falkor, the luckdragon.

Bastian wiped the sweat from his brow with his mantle and saw that its silver had turned black, as black as the night. Still with the sword Sikanda in hand, he left the wall and went down to the palace courtyard.

With Bastian's victory over Atreyu, the fortunes of war shifted. The rebel army, which had seemed sure of victory a moment before, took flight. Bastian felt as if he were caught in a terrible dream and could not wake up. His victory left him with a bitter taste in his mouth, but at the same time he felt wildly triumphant.

Wrapped in his black mantle, clutching the bloody sword, he passed slowly down the High Street. The Ivory Tower was blazing like an enormous torch. Hardly aware of the roaring flames, Bastian went on till he reached the foot of the Tower. There he found the remnants of his army waiting for him in the devastated Labyrinth – now a far-flung battefield strewn with the corpses of Fantasticans. Hykrion, Hysbald, and Hydorn were there too, the last two seriously wounded. Ilwan, the blue djinn, was dead. Xayide, holding the belt Ghemmal, was standing beside his corpse.

'He saved this for you, O lord and master,' she said.

Bastian took the belt, folded it up, and put it in his pocket.

Slowly he passed his eyes over his companions. Only a few hundred were left. More dead than alive, they looked like a conclave of ghosts in the flickering light of the fires.

All had their faces turned toward the Ivory Tower, which was collapsing piece by piece. The Magnolia Pavilion at the top flared, its petals opened wide, and one could see that it was empty. Then it too was engulfed by the flames.

Bastian pointed his sword at the heap of flaming ruins and his voice cracked as he declared: 'This is Atreyu's doing! For this I will pursue him to the ends of the world!'

Hoisting himself up on one of the gigantic metal horses, he cried: 'Follow me!'

The horse reared, but he bent it to his will and galloped off into the night.

XXIII

The City of the Old Emperors

HILE Bastian was racing through the pitch-black night miles ahead, his companions were still making preparations for departure. Most were exhausted and none had anything approaching Bastian's strength and endurance. Even the armored giants on their metallic horses had a hard time getting started, and the foot sloggers couldn't manage to fall into their mechanical tramp-tramp-tramp. Xayide's will, which moved them, seemed to have reached the limits of its power. Her coral litter had been devoured by flames. A new conveyance had been built out of shattered weapons and charred planks from the Ivory Tower, but it looked more like a gypsy wagon than a litter. The rest of the army hobbled and shuffled along as best they could. Even Hykrion, Hysbald, and Hydorn, who had lost their horses, had to hold one another up. No one spoke, but they all knew they would never be able to overtake Bastian.

On he galloped through the darkness, his black mantle flapping wildly in the wind, the metallic limbs of his gigantic horse creaking and grinding at every movement as the great hooves pounded the earth.

'Gee up!' cried Bastian. 'Gee up! Gee up!'

The horse wasn't running fast enough for him. He was determined to overtake Atreyu and Falkor at all costs, even if it meant riding this metallic monster to its death.

He wanted vengeance! He would have attained the goal of all his wishes if Atreyu hadn't interfered. Bastian had not become Emperor of Fantastica. And for that he would make Atreyu repent.

The joints of Bastian's metallic steed ground and creaked louder and louder, but still it obeyed its rider's will.

Bastian rode for hours and hours through the endless night. In his mind's eye he saw the flaming Ivory Tower. Over and over he lived the moment when Atreyu had set the point of his sword to his chest. And then for the first time he asked himself why Atreyu had hesitated. Why, after all that had happened, couldn't he bring himself to strike Bastian and take AURYN by force? And suddenly Bastian thought of the wound he had inflicted on Atreyu and the look in Atreyu's eyes as he staggered and fell.

Bastian put Sikanda, which up until then he had been clutching in his fist, back into its rusty sheath.

In the first light of dawn he saw he was on a heath. Dark clumps of juniper suggested motionless groups of gigantic hooded monks or magicians with pointed hats.

And then suddenly, in the midst of a frantic gallop, Bastian's metal steed burst into pieces.

Bastian lay stunned by the violence of his fall. When he finally picked himself up and rubbed his bruised limbs, he found himself in the middle of a juniper bush. He crawled out into the open. The fragments of the horse lay scattered all about, as though an equestrian monument had exploded.

Bastian stood up, threw his black mantle over his shoulders, and with no idea where he was going, started walking in the direction of the rising sun.

But a glittering object was left behind in the juniper bush: the belt Ghemmal. Bastian was unaware of his loss and never thought of the belt again. Ilwan had saved it from the flames for nothing.

A few days later Ghemmal was found by a blackbird, who had no suspicion of what this glittering object might be. She carried it to her nest, but that's the beginning of another story that shall be told another time.

At midday Bastian came to a high earthen wall that cut across the heath. He climbed to the top of it. Behind it, in a craterlike hollow, lay a city. At least the quantity of buildings made Bastian think of a city, but it was certainly the weirdest one he had ever seen.

The buildings seemed to be jumbled every which way without rhyme or reason, as though they had been emptied at random out of a giant sack. There were neither streets nor squares nor was there any recognizable order.

And the buildings themselves were crazy; they had 'front doors' in their roofs, stairways which were quite inaccessible and ended in the middle of nowhere; towers slanted, balconies dangled vertically, there were doors where one would have expected windows, and floors in the place of walls. Bridges stopped halfway, as though the builders had suddenly forgotten what they were doing. There were towers bent like bananas and pyramids standing on their tips. In short, the whole city seemed to have gone mad.

Then Bastian saw the inhabitants – men, women, and children. They were built like ordinary human beings, but dressed as if they had lost the power to distinguish between clothing and objects intended for other purposes. On their heads they wore lampshades, sand pails, soup bowls, wastepaper baskets, or shoe boxes. Their bodies were swathed in towels, carpets, big sheets of wrapping paper, or barrels.

Many were pushing or pulling handcarts with all sorts of junk piled up on them, broken lamps, mattresses, dishes, rags, and knick-knacks. Others were carrying enormous bales slung over their shoulders.

The farther Bastian went into the city, the thicker became the crowd. But none of the people seemed to know where they were going. Several times Bastian saw someone dragging a heavily laden cart in one direction, then after a short time doubling back, and a few minutes later changing direction again. Everybody was feverishly active.

Bastian decided to speak to one of these people.

'What's the name of this place?'

The person let go his cart, straightened up, and scratched his head for a while as though thinking it over. Then he went away, abandoning his cart, which he seemed to have forgotten. But a few minutes later, a woman took hold of the cart and started off with it. Bastian asked her if the junk was hers. The woman stood for a while, deep in thought. Then she too went away.

Bastian tried a few more times but received no answer.

Suddenly he heard someone giggling. 'No point in asking them,' said the giggler. 'They can't tell you anything. One might, in a manner of speaking, call them the Know-Nothings.'

Bastian turned toward the voice and saw a little gray monkey sitting on a window ledge, or rather on what would have been a window ledge if the window hadn't been upside down. The animal was wearing a mortarboard with a dangling tassel and seemed to be busy counting something on his fingers and toes. When he had finished, he grinned and said: 'Sorry to keep you waiting, sir, but there was something I had to figure out.'

'Who are you?' Bastian asked.

'My name is Argax,' said the little monkey, lifting his mortar-board. 'Pleased to meet you. And with whom have I the pleasure?'

'My name is Bastian Balthazar Bux.'

'Just as I thought,' said the monkey, visibly pleased.

'And what is the name of this city?' Bastian inquired.

'It hasn't actually got a name,' said Argax. 'But one might, in a manner of speaking, call it the City of the Old Emperors.'

'Old Emperors?' Bastian repeated with consternation. 'Why, I don't see anybody who looks like an Old Emperor.'

'You don't?' said the monkey with a giggle. 'Well, believe it or not, all the people you've seen were Emperors of Fantastica in their time – or wanted to be.'

Bastian was aghast.

'How do you know that, Argax?'

The monkey lifted his mortarboard and grinned.

'I, in a manner of speaking, am the superintendent here.'

Bastian looked around. Not far away an old man had dug a pit. He put a lighted candle into it, then shoveled earth over the candle.

The monkey giggled. 'What would you say to a little tour of the town, sir? To get acquainted, in a manner of speaking, with your future residence.'

'No,' said Bastian. 'What are you talking about?'

The monkey jumped up on his shoulder. 'Let's go,' he whispered. 'It's free of charge. You've already paid the admission fee.'

Bastian obeyed the monkey's orders, though he would rather have run away. He grew more miserable with every step. He watched the people and was struck by the fact that they didn't talk. They were all so busy with their own concerns that they didn't even seem to see one another.

'What's wrong with them?' Bastian asked. 'Why are they so odd?'

'Nothing odd about them!' said Argax. 'They're just like you, in a manner of speaking, or rather, they were in their time.'

Bastian stopped in his tracks. 'What do you mean by that? Do you mean that they're humans?'

Argax jumped up and down on Bastian's shoulder. 'Exactly!' he said gleefully.

Bastian saw a woman in the middle of the street trying to spear peas with a darning needle.

'How did they get here? What are they doing here?'

'Oh, there have always been humans who couldn't find their way back to their world,' Argax explained. 'First they didn't want to, and now, in a manner of speaking, they can't.'

Bastian looked at a little girl who was struggling to push a doll's carriage with square wheels.

'Why can't they?' he asked.

'They'd have to wish it. And they've stopped wishing. They used up their last wish for something else.'

'Their last wish?' said Bastian, going deathly pale. 'Can't a person go on wishing as long as he pleases?'

Argax giggled again. Then he tried to take off Bastian's turban and pick lice out of his hair.

'Stop that!' Bastian cried. He tried to shake the little monkey off, but Argax held on tight and squealed with pleasure.

'No! No!' he chattered. 'You can only wish as long as you remember your world. These people here used up all their memories. Without a past you can't have a future. That's why they don't get older. Just look at them. Would you believe that some of them have been here a thousand years and more? But they stay just as they are. Nothing can change for them, because they themselves can't change anymore.'

Bastian watched a man who had lathered a mirror and was starting to shave it. Once that might have struck him as funny; now it made him break out in gooseflesh.

He hurried on and soon realized that he was going deeper into the city. He wanted to turn back, but something drew him onward like a magnet. He began to run and tried to get rid of the bothersome gray monkey, but Argax clung fast and even spurred him on: 'Faster! Faster!'

Bastian stopped running. He realized that he couldn't escape.

'You mean,' he asked, gasping for breath, 'that all these people here were once Emperors of Fantastica, or wanted to be?'

'That's it,' said Argax. 'All the ones who can't find their way back try sooner or later to become Emperor. They didn't all make it, but they all tried. That's why there are two kinds of fools here. Though the result, in a manner of speaking, is the same.'

'What two kinds? Tell me, Argax! I have to know!'

'Easy does it,' said the monkey, giggling as he tightened his grip on Bastian's neck. 'The one kind gradually used up their memories. And when they had lost the last one, AURYN couldn't fulfill their wishes anymore. After that, they came here, in a manner of speaking, automatically. The others, the ones who crowned themselves emperor, lost all their memories at one stroke. So the same thing happened: AURYN couldn't fulfill their wishes anymore, because they had none left. As you see, it comes to the same thing. Here they are, and they can't get away.'

'Do you mean that they all had AURYN at one time?'

'Naturally!' said Argax. 'But they forgot it long ago. And it wouldn't help them anymore, the poor fools!'

'Was it . . .' Bastian hesitated. 'Was it taken away from them?'

'No,' said Argax. 'When someone crowns himself emperor, it simply vanishes. Obviously, because how, in a manner of speaking, can you use Moon Child's power to take her power away from her?'

Bastian felt wretched. He would have liked to sit down somewhere, but the little gray monkey wouldn't let him.

'No, no, our tour isn't done yet. The best is yet to come! Keep moving!'

Bastian saw a boy with a heavy hammer trying to drive nails into a pair of socks. A fat man was trying to paste postage stamps on soap bubbles. They kept bursting, but he went on blowing new ones.

'Look!' Bastian heard the giggling voice of Argax and felt his head being twisted by the monkey's little hands. 'Look over there! It's so amusing!'

Bastian saw a large group of people, men and women, young and old, all in the strangest clothes. They didn't speak, each one was alone with himself. On the ground lay a large number of cubes, and there were letters on all six sides of the cubes. The people kept jumbling the cubes and then staring at them.

'What are they doing?' Bastian whispered. 'What sort of game is that?'

'It's called the jumble game,' answered Argax. He motioned to the players and cried out: 'Good work, children! Keep at it! Don't give up!'

Then, turning back to Bastian, he whispered in his ear: 'They can't talk anymore. They've lost the power of speech. So I thought up this game for them. As you see, it keeps them busy. It's very simple. If you stop to think about it, you'll have to admit that all the stories in the world consist essentially of twenty-six letters. The letters are always the same, only the arrangement varies. From letters words are formed, from words sentences, from sentences chapters, and from chapters stories. Now take a look. What do you see there?'

Bastian read:

```
         H G I K L O P F M W E Y V X Q
       Y X C V B N M A S D F G H J K L O A
         Q W E R T Z U I O P U
         A S D F G H J K L O A
       M N B V C X Y L K J H G F D S A
       U P O I U Z T R E W Q A S
     Q S E R T Z U I O P U A S D A F
       A S D F G H J K L O A Y X C
         U P O I U Z T R E W Q
       A O L K J H G F D S A M N B V
         G K H D S R Z I P
         Q E T U O U S F H K O
         Y C B M W R Z I P
         A R C G U N I K Y O
       Q W E R T Z I O P L U A S D
         M N B V C X Y A S D
       L K J U O N G R E F G H I
```

'Yes, of course,' said Argax with a giggle, 'it usually makes no more sense than that. But if you keep at it for a long time, words turn up now and then. Not very brilliant words, but still words. "Spinachcramp," for instance, or "sugarbrush," or "nosepolish." And if you play for a hundred years, or a thousand or a hundred thousand, the law of chances tells us that a poem will probably come out. And if you play it forever, every possible poem and every possible story will have to come out, in fact every story about a story, and even this story about the two of us chatting here. It's only logical, don't you think?'

'It's horrible,' said Bastian.

'I wouldn't say that,' said Argax. 'It depends on your point of view. It keeps these people, in a manner of speaking, busy. And anyway, what else can we do with them in Fantastica?'

For a long time Bastian watched the players in silence. Then he asked under his breath: 'Argax, you know who I am, don't you?'

'Of course I do. Is there anyone in Fantastica who doesn't?'

'Tell me one thing, Argax. If I had become emperor yesterday, would I already be here now?'

'Today or tomorrow,' said the monkey. 'Or next week. One way or another, you'd have ended up here.'

'Then Atreyu saved me?'

'You've got me there,' the monkey admitted.

'But if he had succeeded in taking the Gem away from me, what would have happened then?'

The monkey giggled again.

'You'd have ended up here, in a manner of speaking, all the same.'

'Why?'

'Because you need AURYN to find the way back. But frankly, I don't believe you'll make it.'

The monkey clapped his little hands, lifted his mortarboard, and grinned.

'Tell me, Argax, what must I do?'

'Find a wish that will take you back to your world.'

After a long silence Bastian asked: 'Argax, can you tell me how many wishes I have left?'

'Not very many. In my opinion three or four at the most. And that will hardly be enough. You're beginning rather late, and the way back isn't easy. You'll have to cross the Sea of Mist. That alone

will cost you a wish. What comes next I don't know. No one in
Fantastica knows what road you people must take to get back to
your world. Maybe you'll find Yor's Minroud, that's the last hope
for people like you. But I'm afraid that for you it's, in a manner
of speaking, too far. Be that as it may, you will, just this once, find
your way out of the City of the Old Emperors.'

'Thanks, Argax,' said Bastian.

The little gray monkey grinned.

'Goodbye, Bastian Balthazar Bux.'

With one leap Argax vanished into one of the crazy houses. He
had taken Bastian's turban with him.

For a while Bastian stood motionless. He was so stunned by what
he had just heard that he couldn't decide what to do. All his plans
had collapsed at one stroke. His thoughts seemed to have been stood
on end – like the pyramid he had seen. What he had hoped was
his ruin and what he had feared his salvation.

At the moment only one thing was clear to him: he must get
out of this insane city. And never come back!

He started through the jumble of crazy buildings. He soon discovered that it was much harder to get out than to get in. Time
and time again he lost his way and found himself back in the center
of the city. It took him all afternoon to reach the earthworks. Then
he ran out into the heath and kept going until black night – as
black as the night before – forced him to stop. Exhausted, he
collapsed under a juniper tree and fell into a deep sleep. And while
he slept, the memory that he could once make up stories left him.

All night he had the same unchanging vision before his eyes:
Atreyu, with the gaping wound in his chest, stood there looking
at him in silence.

Awakened by a thunderclap, Bastian started up. Deep darkness
lay all around him, but the massive clouds that had been gathering
for days had been thrown into wild disorder. Lightning flashed,
thunder shook the earth, the storm wind howled over the heath
and the juniper trees were bowed to the ground. Rain fell in dense
sheets.

Bastian arose and stood there wrapped in his black mantle; the
water ran down his face.

Lightning struck a tree directly in front of him and split the gnarled trunk. The branches went up in flames, the wind blew a shower of sparks over the heath. In a moment they were doused by the rain.

The crash had thrown Bastian to his knees. He dug into the earth with both hands. When the hole was big enough, he unslung the sword Sikanda and put it in.

'Sikanda,' he said. 'I am taking leave of you forever. Never again shall anyone draw you against a friend. No one shall find you here, until what you and I have done is forgotten.'

He filled in the hole and covered it over with moss and branches, lest anyone should discover it.

And there Sikanda lies to this day. For not until far in the future will one come who can wield it without danger – but that is another story and shall be told another time.

Bastian went his way through the darkness.

Toward morning the storm abated, the wind died down, and there was no other sound than the rain dripping from the trees.

That night was the beginning of a long, lonely journey for Bastian. He no longer wished to return to his traveling companions or Xayide. Now he wanted to find the way back to the human world – but he didn't know how or where to look for it. Was there somewhere a gate, a bridge, a mountain pass that would take him back?

He had to wish for it, that he knew. But he had no power over his wishes. He felt like a diver who is searching the bottom of the sea for a sunken ship, but keeps being driven to the surface before he can find anything.

He also knew that he had few wishes left, so he was careful not to use AURYN. He was determined to sacrifice his last few remaining memories only if he felt sure that this would help him get back to his world.

But wishes cannot be summoned up or kept away at will. They come from deeper within us than good or bad intentions. And they spring up unannounced.

And so, before he knew it, a new wish arose within him and little by little took form.

For days and nights he had been wandering all alone. And because of being alone, he yearned to belong to some sort of community, to be taken into a group, not as a master or victor or as any special sort of person, but merely as one among many, perhaps as the smallest or least important, provided his membership in the community was unquestioned.

And then one day he came to a seacoast. Or so he thought at first. He was standing on the edge of a sheer cliff, and before him lay a sea of congealed white waves. It was some time before he realized that these waves were not really motionless, but were moving very slowly, that there were currents and eddies that moved as imperceptibly as the hands of a clock.

He had come to the Sea of Mist!

Bastian walked along the cliff. The air was warm and slightly damp. There was not the slightest breeze. It was early morning and the sun shone on the snow-white surface of the fog, which extended to the horizon.

He walked for several hours. Toward noon he espied a small town some distance from the shore. Supported by piles, it formed a sort of island in the Sea of Mist. The long, arching bridge connecting the town with the rocky coast swayed gently as Bastian crossed it.

The houses were relatively small. The doors, windows, and stairways all seemed to have been made for children. And indeed, the people moving about the streets were no bigger than children, though they all seemed to be grown men with beards or women with pinned-up hair. As Bastian soon noticed, these people looked so much alike that he could hardly tell them apart. Their faces were dark brown like moist earth and they looked calm and gentle. When they saw Bastian, they nodded to him, but none spoke. Altogether they seemed a silent lot; the place was humming with activity, yet he seldom heard a cry or a spoken word. And never did he see any of these people alone; they always went about in groups if not in crowds, locking arms or holding one another by the hand.

When Bastian examined the houses more closely, he saw that they were all made of a sort of wicker, some crude and some of a finer weave, and that the streets were paved with the same kind of material. Even the people's clothing, he noticed, their trousers, skirts, jackets, and hats were of wickerwork, though these were artfully woven. Everything in the town seemed to be made of the same material.

Here and there Bastian was able to cast a glance into the artisans' workshops. They were all busy weaving, making shoes, pitchers, lamps, cups, and umbrellas of wickerwork. But never did he see anyone working alone, for these things could be made only by several persons working together. It was a pleasure to see how cleverly they coordinated their movements. And as they worked, they usually sang some simple melody without words.

The town was not very large, and Bastian had soon come to the edge of it. There he saw hundreds of ships of every size and shape. The town was a seaport, but of a most unusual kind, for all these ships were hanging from gigantic fishing poles and hovered, swaying gently, over a chasm full of swirling white mist. These ships, made of wickerwork like everything else, had neither sails nor masts nor oars nor rudders.

Bastian leaned over the railing and looked down into the Sea of Mist. He was able to gauge the length of the stakes supporting the town by the shadows they cast on the white surface below.

'At night,' he heard a voice beside him say, 'the mists rise to the level of the town. Then we can put out to sea. In the daytime the sun reduces the mist and the level falls. That's what you wanted to know, isn't it, stranger?'

Three men were leaning against the railing beside Bastian. They seemed gentle and friendly. They got to talking and in the course of his conversation with them Bastian learned that the town was called Yskal or Basketville. Its inhabitants were known as Yskalnari. The word meant roughly 'the partners.' The three were mist sailors. Not wishing to give his name for fear of being recognized, Bastian introduced himself as 'Someone.' The three sailors told him the Yskalnari had no names for individuals and didn't find it necessary. They were all Yskalnari and that was enough for them.

Since it was lunchtime, they invited Bastian to join them, and he gratefully accepted. They went to a nearby inn, and during the meal Bastian learned all about Basketville and its inhabitants.

The Sea of Mist, which they called the Skaidan, was an enormous ocean of white vapor, which divided the two parts of Fantastica from each other. No one had ever found out how deep the Skaidan was or where all this mist came from. It was quite possible to breathe below the surface of the mist, and to walk some distance on the bottom of the sea near the coast, where the mist was relatively shallow, but only if one was tied to a rope and could be pulled back. For the mist had one strange property: it fuddled one's sense of direction. Any number of fools and daredevils had died in the attempt to cross the Skaidan alone and on foot. Only a few had been rescued. The only way to reach the other side was in the ships of the Yskalnari.

The wickerwork, from which the houses, implements, clothing, and ships of Yskal were made, was woven from a variety of rushes that grew under the surface of the sea not far from the shore. These rushes – as can easily be gathered from the foregoing – could be cut only at the risk of one's life. Though unusually pliable and even limp in ordinary air, they stood upright in the sea, because they were lighter than the mist. That was what made the wickerwork ships mistworthy. And if any of the Yskalnari chanced to fall into the mist, his regular clothing served the purpose of a life jacket.

But the strangest thing about the Yskalnari, so it struck Bastian, was that the word 'I' seemed unknown to them. In any case, they never used it, but in speaking of what they thought or did always said 'we.'

When he gathered from the conversation that the three sailors would be putting out to sea that night, he asked if he could ship with them as a cabin boy. They informed him that a voyage on the Skaidan was very different from any other ocean voyage, because no one knew how long it would take or exactly where it would end up. When Bastian said that didn't worry him, they agreed to take him on.

At nightfall the mists began to rise and by midnight they had reached the level of Basketville. The ships that had been dangling in midair were now floating on the white surface. The moorings of the one on which Bastian found himself – a flat barge about a hundred feet long – were cast off, and it drifted slowly out into the Sea of Mist.

The moment he laid his eyes on it, Bastian wondered what propelled this sort of ship, since it had neither sails nor oars nor propeller. He soon found out that sails would have been useless, for there was seldom any wind on the Skaidan, and that oars and propellers do not function in mist. These ships were moved by an entirely different sort of power.

In the middle of the deck there was a round, slightly raised platform. Bastian had noticed it from the start and taken it for a sort of captain's bridge. Indeed, it was occupied throughout the voyage by two or more sailors. (The entire crew numbered fourteen.) The men on the platform held one another clasped by the shoulders and looked fixedly forward. At first sight, they seemed to be standing motionless. Actually they were swaying very slowly, in perfect unison – in a sort of dance, which they accompanied by chanting over and over again a simple and strangely beautiful tune.

At first Bastian regarded this song and dance as some sort of ceremony, the meaning of which escaped him. Then, on the third day of voyage, he asked one of his three friends about it. Evidently surprised at Bastian's ignorance, the sailor explained that those men were propelling the ship by thought-power.

More puzzled than ever, Bastian asked if some sort of hidden wheels were set in motion.

'No,' one of the sailors replied. 'When you want to move your legs, you have only to think about it. You don't need wheels, do you?'

The only difference between a person's body and a ship was that to move a ship at least two Yskalnari had to merge their thought-powers into one. It was this fusion of thought-powers that propelled the ship. If greater speed was desired, more men had to join in. Normally, thinkers worked in shifts of three; the others rested, for easy and pleasant as it looked, thought-propulsion was hard work, demanding intense and unbroken concentration. But there was no other way of sailing the Skaidan.

Bastian became the student of the mist navigators and learned the secret of their cooperation: dance and song without words.

Little by little, in the course of the long voyage, he became one of them. During the dance he felt his thought-power merging with those of his companions to form a whole, and this gave him a strange and indescribable sense of harmony and self-forgetfulness. He felt accepted by a community, at one with his companions – and at the same time he totally forgot that the inhabitants of the world from which he came, and to which he was seeking the way back, were human beings, each with his own thoughts and opinions. Dimly he remembered his home and parents, but nothing more.

His wish to be no longer alone had come true. But now, deep in his heart, a new wish arose and began to make itself felt.

One day it struck him that the Yskalnari lived together so harmoniously, not because they blended different ways of thinking, but because they were so much alike that it cost them no effort to form a community. Indeed, they were incapable of quarreling or even disagreeing, because they did not regard themselves as individuals. Thus there were no conflicts or differences to overcome, and it was just this sameness, this absence of stress that gradually came to pall on Bastian. Their gentleness bored him and the unchanging melody of their songs got on his nerves. He felt that something was lacking, something he hungered for, but he could not yet have said what it was.

This became clear to him sometime later when a giant mist crow was sighted. Stricken with terror, the sailors vanished below deck as fast as they could. But one was not quick enough; the monstrous bird swooped down with a cry, seized the poor fellow, and carried him away in its beak.

When the danger was past, the sailors emerged and resumed their song and dance, as though nothing had happened. Their harmony was undisturbed, and far from grieving, they didn't waste so much as a word on the incident.

'Why should we grieve?' said one of them when Bastian inquired. 'None of us is missing.'

With them the individual counted for nothing. No one was irreplaceable, because they drew no distinction between one man and another.

Bastian, however, wanted to be an individual, a someone, not just one among others. He wanted to be loved for being just what he was. In this community of Yskalnari there was harmony, but no love.

He no longer wanted to be the greatest, strongest, or cleverest. He had left all that far behind. He longed to be loved just as he was, good or bad, handsome or ugly, clever or stupid, with all his faults – or possibly because of them.

But what was he actually like?

He no longer knew. So much had been given to him in Fantastica, and now, among all these gifts and powers, he could no longer find himself.

He stopped dancing with the mist sailors. All day long and sometimes all night as well, he sat in the prow, looking out over the Skaidan.

At last the crossing was completed and the mist ship docked. Bastian thanked the Yskalnari and went ashore.

This was a land full of roses, there were whole forests of roses of every imaginable color. A winding path led through the endless rose garden, and Bastian followed it.

XXIV

Dame Eyola

AYIDE's end is soon told, but hard to understand and full of con-
tradictions like many things in Fantastica. To this day many scholars
and historians are racking their brains for an explanation of what
happened, while some deny the whole incident or try to interpret
it out of existence. Here we shall simply state the facts, leaving others
to explain them as best they can.

Just as Bastian was arriving at the town of Yskal, Xayide and
her black giants reached the spot were his metallic horse had
collapsed under him. In that moment she suspected that she would
never find him, and her suspicions became a certainty when she
came to the earthen wall and saw Bastian's footprints on it. If he
had reached the City of the Old Emperors, he was lost to her plans,
regardless of whether he stayed there or whether he managed to
escape. In the first case, he would become powerless like everyone
there, no longer able to wish for anything – and in the second,
all wishes for power and greatness would die within him. For her,
Xayide, the game was over in either case.

She commanded her armored giants to halt. Strangely, they did
not obey but marched on. She flew into a rage, jumped out of her
litter, and ran after them with outstretched arms. The armored
giants, foot soldiers and riders alike, ignored her commands, turned
about, and trampled her with their feet and hooves. At length, when
Xayide had breathed her last, the whole column stopped like run-
down clockwork.

When Hysbald, Hydorn, and Hykrion arrived with what was
left of the army, they saw what had happened. They were puzzled,
because they knew it was Xayide's will alone that had moved the
hollow giants. So, they thought, it must have been her will that they
should trample her to death. But knotty problems were not the
knights' forte, so in the end they shrugged their shoulders and let
well enough alone. But what were they to do next? They talked
it over and, deciding that the campaign was at an end, discharged
the army and advised everyone to go home. They themselves, however, felt bound by the oath of fealty they had sworn to Bastian
and resolved to search all Fantastica for him. That was all well
and good, but which way were they to go? They couldn't agree,
so deciding that each would search separately, they parted and

hobbled off each in a different direction. All three had countless adventures, and Fantastica knows numerous accounts of their futile quest. But these are other stories and shall be told another time.

For years the hollow, black-metal giants stood motionless on the heath not far from the City of the Old Emperors. Rain and snow fell on them, they rusted and little by little sank into the ground, some vertically, some at a slant. But to this day a few of them can be seen. The place is thought to be cursed, and travelers make a wide circle around it. But let's get back to Bastian.

While following the winding path through the rose garden, he saw something that amazed him, because in all his wanderings in Fantastica he had never seen anything like it. It was a pointing hand, carved from wood. Beside it was written: 'To the House of Change.'

Without haste Bastian took the direction indicated. He breathed the fragrance of the innumerable roses and felt more and more cheerful, as though looking forward to a pleasant surprise.

At length he came to a straight avenue, bordered by round trees laden with red-cheeked apples. At the end of the avenue a house appeared. As he approached it, Bastian decided it was the funniest house he had ever seen. Under a tall, pointed roof that looked rather like a stocking cap, the house itself suggested a giant pumpkin. The walls were covered with large protuberances, one might almost have said bellies, that gave the house a comfortably inviting look. There were a few windows and a front door, but they seemed crooked, as though a clumsy child had cut them out.

On his way to the house, Bastian saw that it was slowly but steadily changing. A small bump appeared on the right side and gradually took the shape of a dormer window. At the same time a window on the left side closed and little by little disappeared. A chimney grew out of the roof and a small balcony with a balustrade appeared over the front door.

Bastian stopped still and watched the changes with surprise and amusement. Now he understood why the place was called the House of Change.

As he stood there, he heard a warm, pleasant voice – a woman's – singing inside.

'A hundred summers to a day
We have waited here for you.
Seeing that you've found the way,
It must certainly be you.
Your hunger and your thirst to still,
All is here in readiness.
You shall eat and drink your fill,
Sheltered in our tenderness.
Regardless whether good or bad,
You've suffered much and traveled far.
Take comfort for the trials you've had.
We'll have you just the way you are.'

Ah! thought Bastian. What a lovely voice! If only that song were meant for me!

The voice began again to sing:

'Great lord, I pray, be small again,
Be a child and come right in.
Don't keep standing at the door,
You are welcome here, and more.
Everything for many a year
Has been ready for you here.'

Bastian felt irresistibly drawn by that voice. He felt sure the singer must be a very friendly person. He knocked at the door and the voice called out:

'Come in, come in, dear boy!'

He opened the door and saw a small but comfortable room. The sun was streaming in through the windows. In the middle of the room there was a round table covered with bowls and baskets full of all sorts of fruits unknown to Bastian. At the table sat a woman as round and red-cheeked and healthy-looking as an apple.

Bastian was almost overpowered by a desire to run to her with outstretched arms and cry: 'Mama, Mama!' But he controlled himself. His mama was dead and was certainly not here in Fantastica.

This woman, it was true, had the same sweet smile and the same trustworthy look, but between her and his mother there was little resemblance. His mother had been small and this woman was large and imposing. She was wearing a broad hat covered with fruits and flowers, and her dress was of some sort of bright, flowered material. It was some time before Bastian realized that it consisted of leaves, flowers, and fruits.

As he stood looking at her, he was overcome by a feeling that he had not known for a long time. He could not remember when and where; he knew only that he had sometimes felt that way when he was little.

'Sit down, dear boy,' said the woman, motioning him to a chair. 'You must be hungry. Do have a bite to eat.'

'I beg your pardon,' said Bastian. 'You're expecting a guest. I've only come here by accident.'

'Really?' said the woman with a smile. 'Oh well, it doesn't matter. You can have a bite to eat all the same. Meanwhile I'll tell you a little story. Go on, don't stand on ceremony.'

Bastian took off his black mantle, laid it on a chair, and hesitantly reached for a fruit. Before biting into it, he asked: 'What about you? Aren't you eating? Or don't you care for fruit?'

The woman laughed heartily, Bastian didn't know why.

'Very well,' she said after composing herself. 'If you insist, I'll have something to keep you company, but in my own way. Don't be frightened.'

With that she picked up a watering can that was on the floor beside her, held it over her head, and sprinkled herself.

'Oh!' she said. 'That *is* refreshing!'

Now it was Bastian's turn to laugh. Then he bit into the fruit and instantly realized that he had never eaten anything so good. He took a second fruit and that was even better.

'You like it?' asked the woman, watching him closely.

Bastian couldn't answer because his mouth was full. He chewed and nodded.

'I'm glad,' the woman said. 'I've taken a lot of pains with that fruit. Eat as much as you please.'

Bastian took a third fruit, and that was a sheer delight. He sighed with well-being.

'And now I'll tell you the story,' said the woman. 'But don't let it stop you from eating.'

Bastian found it hard to listen, for each new fruit gave him a more rapturous sensation than the last.

'A long, long time ago,' the flowery woman began, 'our Childlike Empress was deathly ill, for she needed a new name, and only a human could give her one. But humans had stopped coming to Fantastica, no one knew why. And if she had died, that would have been the end of Fantastica. Then one day – or rather one night – a human came after all. It was a little boy, and he gave the Childlike Empress the name of Moon Child. She recovered, and in token of her gratitude she promised the boy that all his wishes in her empire would come true – until he found out what he really and truly wanted. Then the little boy made a long journey from one wish to the next, and each one came true. And each fulfillment led to a new wish. There were not only good wishes but bad ones as well, but the Childlike Empress drew no distinction; in her eyes all things in her empire are equally good and important. In the end the Ivory Tower was destroyed, and she did nothing to prevent it. But with every wish fulfillment the little boy lost a part of his memory of the world he had come from. He didn't really mind, for he had given up wanting to go back. So he kept on wishing, but by then he had spent all his memories, and without memories it's not possible to wish. So he had almost ceased to be a human and had almost become a Fantastican. He still didn't know what he really and truly wanted. It seemed possible that his very last memories would be used up before he found out. And if that happened, he would never be able to return to his own world. Then at last he came to the House of Change, and there he would stay until he found out what he really and truly wanted. You see, it's called the House of Change not only because it changes itself but also because it changes anyone who lives in it. And that was very important to the little boy, because up until then he had always wanted to be someone other than he was, but he didn't want to change.'

At this point she broke off, because her visitor had stopped chewing and was staring openmouthed.

'If that one doesn't taste good,' she said with concern, 'just put it down and take another.'

'W-what?' Bastian stammered. 'Oh no, it's delicious.'

'Then everything's fine,' said the woman. 'But I forgot to tell you the name of the little boy, who had been expected so long at the House of Change. Many in Fantastica called him simply "the Savior," others "the Knight of the Seven-armed Candelabrum," or "the Great Knower," or "Lord and Master." But his real name was Bastian Balthazar Bux.'

The woman turned to Bastian with a smile. He swallowed once or twice and said very softly: 'That's my name.'

'Well then!' said the woman, who didn't seem the least surprised. Suddenly the buds on her hat and dress burst into bloom.

'But,' said Bastian hesitantly. 'I haven't been in Fantastica a hundred years.'

'Oh, we've been waiting for you much longer than that,' said the woman. 'My grandmother and my grandmother's grandmother waited for you. You see, now someone is telling *you* a story that is new, even though it's about the remotest past.'

Bastian remembered Grograman's words. That had been at the beginning of his journey. And now suddenly it seemed to him that a hundred years had indeed elapsed since then.

'But by the way, I haven't introduced myself. I'm Dame Eyola.'

Bastian repeated the name several times before he was able to pronounce it properly. Then he took another fruit. He bit into it, and as usual thought the one he was eating was the most delicious of all. But then he noticed with some alarm that there was only one left.

'Do you want more?' asked Dame Eyola, who had caught his glance. When Bastian nodded, she plucked fruit from her hat and dress until the bowl was full again.

'Does the fruit grow on your hat?' Bastian asked in amazement.

'Hat? What *are* you talking about?' cried Dame Eyola. But then she understood and broke into a loud, hearty laugh. 'So you think it's a hat I've got on my head? Not at all, dear boy. It all grows out of me. Just as your hair grows out of you. That should show you how glad I am that you've finally come. That's why I'm flowering and bearing fruit. If I were sad, I'd wither. But come now, don't forget to eat.'

Bastian was embarrassed. 'I don't know,' he said. 'Is it all right to eat something that comes out of somebody?'

'Why not?' asked Dame Eyola. 'Babies drink milk that comes out of their mothers. There's nothing better.'

'That's true,' said Bastian with a slight blush. 'But only when they're very little.'

'In that case,' said Dame Eyola, beaming, 'you'll just have to get to be very little again, my dear boy.'

Bastian took another fruit and bit into it. Dame Eyola was delighted and bloomed more than ever.

After a short silence she said: 'I think it would like us to move into the next room. I believe it may have arranged something for you.'

'Who?' Bastian asked, looking around.

'The House of Change,' said Dame Eyola, as if that were the most natural thing in the world.

And indeed a strange thing had happened. The living room had changed without Bastian noticing that anything was going on. The ceiling had moved upward, while three of the walls had come close to the table. There was still room on the fourth side, where there was a door, which now stood open.

Dame Eyola rose, and then he saw how big she was.

'We'd better go,' she suggested. 'It's very stubborn. Opposition is useless if it has thought up a surprise. We may as well let it have its way. It usually means well.'

Bastian followed her through the door, but took the fruit bowl with him as a precaution.

He found himself in a large dining room that looked somehow familiar. Only the furniture seemed strange – the table and especially the chairs were so large that he couldn't possibly have sat in them.

'Fancy that!' said Dame Eyola with a chuckle. 'The House of Change is always thinking up something new. Now for your benefit it has provided a room as it must look to a small child.'

'You mean,' said Bastian, 'that this room wasn't here before?'

'Of course not. The House of Change is very wide-awake, you see. This is its way of taking part in our conversation. I think it's trying to tell you something.'

Then she sat down in one of the chairs at the table, while Bastian tried in vain to climb up on the other. Dame Eyola had to pick him up and put him on it, but even then his nose was barely level with the tabletop. He was glad he had taken the bowl of fruit, and kept it on his lap. If it had been on the table, it would have been beyond his reach.

'Do you often have to change rooms this way?' he asked.

'Not often,' said Dame Eyola. 'Never more than three or four times a day. Sometimes the House of Change *will* have its little jokes, and then the rooms are suddenly reversed, the floor on top and the ceiling at the bottom, that sort of thing. But it's only being bumptious and it stops when I give it a piece of my mind. All in all, it's a well-behaved house and I feel very comfortable in it. We have good laughs together.'

'But isn't it dangerous?' Bastian asked. 'For instance, if you're asleep at night and the room gets smaller and smaller?'

'What nonsense, dear boy!' cried Dame Eyola, pretending to be angry. 'It's very fond of me, and it's fond of you too. It's glad to have you here.'

'What if it takes a dislike to somebody?'

'No idea,' she replied. 'What questions you ask! There's never been anyone here but you and me.'

'Oh!' said Bastion. 'Then I'm your first guest?'

'Of course!'

Bastian looked around the enormous room.

'This room doesn't seem to go with the house. It didn't look so big from outside.'

'The House of Change,' said Dame Eyola, 'is bigger inside than out.'

Meanwhile night was falling, and it was growing darker and

darker in the room. Bastian leaned back in his big chair and propped his head on his hands. He felt deliciously sleepy.

'Why,' he asked, 'did you wait so long for me, Dame Eyola?'

'I always wanted a child,' she said, 'a child I could spoil, who needed my tenderness, a child I could care for – someone like you, my darling boy.'

Bastian yawned. He felt irresistibly lulled by her sweet voice.

'But,' he objected, 'you said your mother and grandmother waited for me.'

Dame Eyola's face was now in the darkness.

'Yes,' he heard her say. 'My mother and my grandmother also wanted a child. They never had one but I have one now.'

Bastian's eyes closed. He barely managed to ask: 'How can that be? Your mother had you when you were little. And your grandmother had your mother.'

'No, my darling boy,' said the voice hardly above a whisper. 'With us it's different. We don't die and we're not born. We're always the same Dame Eyola, and then again we're not. When my mother grew old, she withered. All her leaves fell, as the leaves fall from a tree in the winter. She withdrew into herself. And so she remained for a long time. But then one day she put forth young leaves, buds, blossoms, and finally fruit. And that's how I came into being, for I was the new Dame Eyola. And it was just the same with my grandmother when she brought my mother into the world. We Dames Eyola can only have a child if we wither first. And then we're our own child and we can't be a mother anymore. That's why I'm so glad you're here, my darling boy ...'

Bastian spoke no more. He had slipped into a sweet half-sleep in which he heard her words as a kind of chant. He heard her stand up and cross the room and bend over him. She stroked his hair and kissed him on the forehead. Then he felt her pick him up and carry him out in her arms. He buried his head in her bosom like a baby. Deeper and deeper he sank into the warm sleepy darkness. He felt that he was being undressed and put into a soft, sweet-smelling bed. And then he heard her lovely voice singing far in the distance:

'Sleep, my darling, good night.
Your sufferings are past.
Great lord, be a little child at last.
Sleep, my darling, sleep tight.'

When he woke up the next morning, he felt better and happier than ever before. He looked around and saw that he was in a cozy little room – lying in a crib. Actually, it was a very large crib, or rather it was as large as a crib must look to a baby. For a moment this struck him as ridiculous, because he certainly wasn't a baby anymore, and he was still in possession of all the powers and gifts that Fantastica had given him. The Childlike Empress's amulet was still hanging from his neck. But in the very next moment he stopped caring whether it was ridiculous or not. No one but him and Dame Eyola would ever find out, and they both knew that everything was just as it should be.

He got up, washed, dressed, and left the room. A flight of wooden steps took him to the big dining room, which had turned into a kitchen overnight. Dame Eyola had breakfast all ready for him. She too was in high spirits, her flowers were in full bloom. She sang and laughed and even danced around the kitchen table with him. After breakfast she sent him outside to get some fresh air.

In the great rose garden around the House of Change it was summer, a summer that seemed eternal. Bastian sauntered about, watched the bees feasting on the flowers, listened to the birds that were singing in every rosebush, played with the lizards, which were so tame that they crawled up on his hand, and with the hares, which let him stroke them. From time to time he crept under a bush, smelled the sweet scent of the roses, blinked up at the sun, and thinking of nothing in particular, let the time glide by like a brook.

Days became weeks. He paid no attention. Dame Eyola was merry, and Bastian surrendered himself to her motherly care and tenderness. It seemed to him that without knowing it he had long hungered for something which was now being given him in abundance. And he just couldn't get enough of it.

He spent whole days rummaging through the House of Change from attic to cellar. He never got bored, because the rooms were always changing and there was always something new to discover. Clearly the house was at pains to entertain its guest. It produced playrooms, railway trains, puppet theaters, jungle gyms. There was even a big merry-go-round.

Or else he would explore the surrounding country. But he never went too far from the House of Change, for suddenly he would be overcome by a craving for Dame Eyola's fruit, and when that happened, he could hardly wait to get back to her and eat his fill.

In the evening they had long talks. He told her about all his adventures in Fantastica, about Perilin and Grograman, about Xayide and Atreyu, whom he had wounded so cruelly and perhaps even killed.

'I did everything wrong,' he said. 'I misunderstood everything. Moon Child gave me so much, and all I did with it was harm, harm to myself and harm to Fantastica.'

Dame Eyola gave him a long look.

'No,' she said. 'I don't believe so. You went the way of wishes, and that is never straight. You went the long way around, but that was *your* way. And do you know why? Because you are one of those who can't go back until they have found the fountain from which springs the Water of Life. And that's the most secret place in Fantastica. There's no simple way of getting there.'

After a short silence she added: 'But every way that leads there is the right one.'

Suddenly Bastian began to cry. He didn't know why. He felt as if a knot in his heart had come open and dissolved into tears. He sobbed and he sobbed and couldn't stop. Dame Eyola took him on her lap and stroked him. He buried his face in the flowers on her bosom and wept until he was too tired to weep anymore.

That evening they talked no more.

But next day Bastian brought up the subject again.

'Do you know where I can find the Water of Life?'

'On the borders of Fantastica.'

'I thought Fantastica had no borders.'

'It has, though. Only they're not outside but inside. In the place where the Childlike Empress gets all her power from, but where she herself cannot go.'

'How am I to find the way there?' asked Bastian. 'Isn't it too late?'

'There's only one wish that can take you there: your last.'

Bastian was terrified. 'Dame Eyola – all the wishes that have come true thanks to AURYN have made me forget something. Will it be the same with this one?'

She nodded slowly.

'But if I don't notice it!'

'Did you notice it other times? Once you've forgotten something you don't know you ever had it.'

'What am I forgetting now?'

'I'll tell you at the proper time. If I told you now, you'd hold on to it.'

'Must I lose everything?'

'Nothing is lost,' she said. 'Everything is transformed.'

'But then,' said Bastian in alarm, 'I ought to hurry. I shouldn't be staying here.'

She stroked his hair.

'Don't worry. It will take time, but when your last wish is awakened, you'll know it – and so will I.'

From that day on something began indeed to change, though Bastian himself noticed nothing at first. The transforming power of the House of Change was taking effect. But like all true transformations, it was as slow and gentle as the growth of a plant.

The days in the House of Change passed, and it was still summer. Bastian still enjoyed letting Dame Eyola spoil him like a child. Her fruit still tasted as delicious to him as at the start, but little by little his craving had been stilled. He ate less than before. Dame Eyola noticed, though she never mentioned it. He also felt that he had had his fill of her care and tenderness. And as his need for them dwindled, a longing of a very different kind made itself felt, a desire that he had never felt before and that was different in every way from all his previous wishes: the longing to be capable of loving. With surprise and dismay he recognized that he could not love. And the wish became stronger and stronger.

One evening as they were sitting together, he spoke of it to Dame Eyola.

After listening to him, she said nothing for a long while. She looked at Bastian with an expression that puzzled him.

'Now you have found your last wish,' she said finally. 'What you really and truly want is to love.'

'But why can't I, Dame Eyola?'

'You won't be able to until you have drunk of the Water of Life,' she said. 'And you can't go back to your own world unless you take some of it back for others.'

Bastian was bewildered. 'But what about you?' he asked. 'Haven't you drunk of it?'

'No,' said Dame Eyola. 'It's different for me. I only needed someone to whom I could give my excess.'

'But isn't that love?'

Dame Eyola pondered a while, then she said: 'It was the effect of *your* wish.'

'Can't Fantasticans love? Are they like me?' he asked anxiously.

She answered: 'There are some few creatures in Fantastica, so I'm told, who get to drink of the Water of Life. But no one knows who they are. And there is a prophecy, which we seldom speak of, that sometime in the distant future humans will bring love to Fantastica. Then the two worlds will be one. But what that means I don't know.'

'Dame Eyola,' Bastian asked, 'you promised that when the right moment came you'd tell me what I had to forget to find my last wish. Has the time come?'

She nodded.

'You had to forget your father and mother. Now you have nothing left but your name.'

Bastian pondered.

'Father and mother?' he said slowly. But the words had lost all meaning for him. He had forgotten.

'What must I do now?' he asked.

'You must leave me. Your time in the House of Change is over.'

'Where must I go?'

'Your last wish will guide you. Don't lose it.'

'Should I go now?'

'No, it's late. Tomorrow at daybreak. You have one more night in the House of Change. Now we must go to bed.'

Bastian stood up, and went over to her. Only then, only when he was close to her, did he notice that all her flowers had faded.

'Don't let it worry you,' she said. 'And don't worry about tomorrow morning. Go your way. Everything is just as it should be. Good night, my darling boy.'

'Good night, Dame Eyola,' Bastian murmured.

Then he went up to his room.

When he came down the next day, he saw that Dame Eyola was still in the same place. All her leaves, flowers, and fruits had fallen from her. Her eyes were closed and she looked like a black, dead tree. For a long time he stood there gazing at her. Then suddenly a door opened.

Before going out, he turned around once again and said, without knowing whether he was speaking to Dame Eyola or to the house or both: 'Thank you. Thank you for everything.'

Then he went out through the door. Winter had come overnight. The snow lay knee-deep and nothing remained of the flowering rose garden but bare, black thornbushes. Not a breeze stirred. It was bitter cold and very still.

Bastian wanted to go back into the house for his mantle, but the doors and windows had vanished. It had closed itself up all around. Shivering, he started on his way.

XXV

The
Picture Mine

OR, the blind miner, was standing beside his hut, listening for sounds on the snow-covered plain around him. The silence was so complete that his sensitive hearing picked up the crunching of footsteps in the snow far in the distance. And he knew that the steps were coming his way.

Yor was an old man, but his face was beardless and without a wrinkle. Everything about him, his dress, his face, his hair, was stone gray. As he stood there motionless, he seemed carved from congealed lava. Only his blind eyes were dark, and deep within them there was a glow, as of a small, bright flame.

The steps were Bastian's. When he reached the hut, he said: 'Good day. I've lost my way. I'm looking for the fountain the Water of Life springs from. Can you help me?'

The miner replied in a whisper: 'You haven't lost your way. But speak softly, or my pictures will crumble.'

He motioned to Bastian, who followed him into the hut.

It consisted of a single small, bare room. A wooden table, two chairs, a cot, and two or three wooden shelves piled with food and dishes were the only furnishings. A fire was burning on an open hearth, and over it hung a kettle of soup.

Yor ladled out soup for himself and Bastian, put the bowls on the table, and with a motion of his hand invited his guest to eat. They ate in silence.

Then the miner leaned back. His eyes looked through Bastian and far into the distance as he asked in a whisper: 'Who are you?'

'My name is Bastian Balthazar Bux.'

'Ah, so you still know your name.'

'Yes. And who are you?'

'I am Yor; people call me the blind miner. But I am blind only in the daylight. In the darkness of my mine, I can see.'

'What sort of mine is it?'

'The Minroud Mine, they call it. It's a picture mine.'

'A picture mine?' said Bastian in amazement. 'I never heard of such a thing.'

Yor seemed to be listening for something.

'And yet,' he said. 'It's here for just such as you. For humans who can't find the way to the Water of Life.'

'What kind of pictures are they?' Bastian asked.

Yor shut his eyes and was silent for a while. Bastian didn't know whether to repeat his question. Then he heard the miner whisper: 'Nothing gets lost in the world. Have you ever dreamed something and when you woke up not known what it was?'

'Yes,' said Bastian. 'Often.'

Yor nodded. Then he stood up and beckoned Bastian to follow him. Before they left the hut, he dug his fingers into Bastian's shoulders and whispered: 'But not a word, not a sound, understand? What you are going to see is my work of many years. The least sound can destroy it. So tread softly and don't talk.'

Bastian nodded and they left the hut. Behind it there was a wooden headframe, below which a shaft descended vertically into the earth. Passing these by, the miner led Bastian out into the snow-covered plain. And there in the snow lay the pictures, like jewels bedded in white silk.

They were paper-thin sheets of colored, transparent isinglass, of every size and shape, some round, some square, some damaged, some intact, some as large as church windows, others as small as snuffbox miniatures. They lay, arranged more or less according to size and shape, in rows extending to the snowy horizon.

What these pictures represented it was hard to say. There were figures in weird disguise that seemed to be flying through the air in an enormous bird's nest, donkeys in judge's robes, clocks as limp as soft butter, dressmaker's dummies standing in deserted, glaringly lighted squares. There were faces and heads pieced together from animals and others that made up a landscape. But there were also perfectly normal pictures, men mowing a wheat field, women sitting on a balcony, mountain villages and seascapes, battle scenes and circus scenes, streets and rooms and many, many faces, old and young, wise and simple, fools and kings, cheerful and gloomy. There were gruesome pictures, executions and death dances, and there were comical ones, such as a group of young ladies riding a walrus or a nose walking about and being greeted by passersby.

The longer Bastian looked at the pictures, the less he could make of them. He and Yor spent the whole day walking past row after row of them, and then dusk descended on the great snowfield.

Bastian followed the miner back to the hut. After closing the door
behind them Yor asked in a soft voice: 'Did you recognize any of
them?'

'No,' said Bastian.

The miner shook his head thoughtfully.

'Why?' Bastian asked. 'What are they?'

'They are forgotten dreams from the human world,' Yor explained. 'Once someone dreams a dream, it can't just drop out of
existence. But if the dreamer can't remember it, what becomes of
it? It lives on in Fantastica, deep under our earth. There the forgotten
dreams are stored in many layers. The deeper one digs, the closer
together they are. All Fantastica rests on a foundation of forgotten
dreams.'

Bastian was wide-eyed with wonderment. 'Are mine there too?'
he asked.

Yor nodded.

'And you think I have to find them?'

'At least one,' said Yor. 'One will be enough.'

'But what for?' Bastian wanted to know.

Now the miner's face was lit only by the faint glow of the hearth
fire. Again his blind eyes looked through Bastian and far into the
distance.

'Listen to me, Bastian Balthazar Bux,' he said. 'I'm no great
talker. I prefer silence. But I will answer this one question. You
are looking for the Water of Life. You want to be able to love,
that's your only hope of getting back to your world. To love – that's
easily said. But the Water of Life will ask you: Love whom? Because
you can't just love in general. You've forgotten everything but your
name. And if you can't answer, it won't let you drink. So you'll
just have to find a forgotten dream, a picture that will guide you
to the fountain. And to find that picture you will have to forget
the one thing you have left: yourself. And that takes hard, patient
work. Remember what I've said, for I shall never say it again.'

After that he lay down on his wooden cot and fell asleep.
Bastian had to content himself with the hard, cold floor. But he
didn't mind.

When he woke up the next morning feeling stiff in all his joints,

Yor was gone – to the mine, no doubt, Bastian decided. He took a dish of the hot soup, which warmed him but didn't taste very good. Too salty. It made him think of sweat and tears.

Then he went out into the snow-covered plain and walked past the pictures. He examined one after another attentively, for now he knew how important it was, but he found none that meant anything in particular to him.

Toward evening Yor came up from the mine. Bastian saw him step out of the pit cage. In a frame on his back he was carrying different-sized sheets of paper-thin isinglass. Bastian followed him in silence as he went far out into the plain and carefully bedded his new finds in the soft snow at the end of a row. One of the pictures represented a man whose chest was a birdcage with two pigeons in it, another a woman of stone riding on a large turtle. One very small picture showed a butterfly with letters on its wings. And many more, but none meant anything to Bastian.

Back in the hut with the miner, he asked: 'What will become of the pictures when the snow melts?'

'It's always winter here,' said Yor.

They had no other conversation that evening.

In the following days Bastian kept searching among the pictures for one with some special meaning for him – but in vain. In the evening he sat in the hut with the miner. Since the miner kept silent, Bastian got into the habit of saying nothing, and little by little he adopted Yor's careful way of moving for fear of making the pictures crumble.

'Now I've seen all the pictures,' Bastian said one night. 'None of them is for me.'

'That's bad,' said Yor.

'What should I do?' Bastian asked. 'Should I wait for you to bring up new ones?'

Yor thought it over, then he shook his head.

'If I were you,' he whispered, 'I'd go down into the mine and dig for myself.'

'But I haven't got your eyes,' said Bastian. 'I can't see in the dark.'

'Weren't you given a light for your long journey?' Yor asked, looking through Bastian. 'A sparkling stone or something that might help you now?'

'Yes,' said Bastian sadly. 'But I used Al Tsahir for something else.'

'That's bad,' Yor said again.

'Then what do you advise?' Bastian asked.

After a long silence the miner replied: 'Then you'll just have to work in the dark.'

Bastian shuddered. He still had all the strength and fearlessness AURYN had given him, but the thought of crawling on his belly in the black underground darkness sent the shivers down his spine. He said nothing more and they both lay down to sleep.

The next morning the miner shook him by the shoulders.

Bastian sat up.

'Eat your soup and come with me,' said Yor.

Bastian obeyed.

He followed the miner to the shaft and got into the pit cage with him. Together they rode down into the mine. At first a faint beam of light followed them down the shaft, but it vanished as the cage went deeper. Then a jolt signaled that they had reached the bottom.

Here below it was much warmer than on the wintry plain. The miner walked very fast, and trying to keep up for fear of losing him in the darkness, Bastian was soon covered with sweat. They twined their way over endless passages and galleries, which sometimes opened out into spacious vaults, as Bastian could tell by the echo of their footfalls. Several times Bastian bruised himself against jutting stones or wooden props, but Yor took no notice.

On this first day and for several that followed, the miner, by wordlessly guiding Bastian's hand, instructed him in the art of separating the paper-thin leaves of isinglass from one another and picking them up. There were tools for the purpose, they felt like wooden or horn spatulas, but Bastian never saw them, for when the day's work was done they stayed down in the mine.

Little by little he learned to find his way in the darkness. A new sense that he could not have accounted for taught him to distinguish one gallery from another. One day Yor told him silently, with the mere touch of his hands, to work alone in a low gallery, which

he could enter only by crawling. Bastian obeyed. It was very close
and cramped, and above him lay a mountain of stone.

Curled up like an unborn child in its mother's womb, he lay
in the dark depths of Fantastica's foundations, patiently digging
for a forgotten dream, a picture that might lead him to the Water
of Life.

Since he could see nothing in the eternal night of the mine, he
could not choose or come to any decision. He could only hope that
chance or a merciful fate would eventually lead him to a lucky
find. Evening after evening he brought what he had managed to
gather from the Minroud Mine into the failing daylight. And
evening after evening his work had been in vain. But Bastian did
not complain or rebel. He had lost all self-pity. Though his strength
was inexhaustible, he often felt tired.

How long this painful work went on it is hard to say, for such
labor cannot be measured in days and months. Be that as it may,
one evening he brought to the surface a picture. It moved him so
deeply the moment he looked at it that he needed all his self-control
to keep from letting out a cry of surprise that would have crumbled
the picture to dust.

On the fragile sheet of isinglass – it was not very large, about
the size of a usual book page – he saw a man wearing a white smock
and holding a plaster cast in one hand. His posture and the troubled
look on his face touched Bastian to the heart. But what stirred him
the most was that the man was shut up in a transparent but impenetrable block of ice.

While Bastian looked at the picture that lay before him in the
snow, a longing grew in him for this man whom he did not know,
a surge of feeling that seemed to come from far away. Like a tidal
wave, almost imperceptible at first, it gradually built up strength
till it submerged everything in its path. Bastian struggled for air.
His heart pounded, it was not big enough for so great a longing.
That surge of feeling submerged everything that he still remembered
of himself. And he forgot the last thing he still possessed: his own
name.

Later on, when he joined Yor in the hut, he was silent. The miner
was silent too, but for a long while he faced Bastian, his eyes once

again seeming to look through him and far into the distance. And for the first time since Bastian had come, a smile passed briefly over the miner's stone-gray features.

That night, tired as he was, the boy who no longer had a name could not sleep. He kept seeing the picture before his eyes. It was as though this man wanted to say something to him but could not, because of the block of ice he was imprisoned in. The boy without a name wanted to help him, wanted to make the ice melt. As in a waking dream he saw himself hugging the block of ice, trying in vain to melt it with the heat of his body.

But then all at once he heard what the man was trying to say to him; he heard it not with his ears but deep in his heart.

'Please help me! Don't leave me! I can't get out of this ice alone. Help me! Only you can help me!'

When they awoke next morning at daybreak, the boy without a name said to Yor: 'I won't be going down into the mine with you anymore.'

'Are you going to leave me?'

The boy nodded. 'I'm going to look for the Water of Life.'

'Have you found the picture that will guide you?'

'Yes.'

'Will you show it to me?'

Again the boy nodded. They went out into the snow where the picture lay. The boy looked at it, but Yor directed his blind eyes at the boy's face, as though looking through it into the distance. For a long while he seemed to be listening for some sound. At length he nodded.

'Take it with you,' he whispered, 'and don't lose it. If you lose it, or if it is destroyed, you will have nothing left in Fantastica. You know what that means.'

The boy who no longer had a name stood with bowed head and was silent for a while. Then he said just as softly: 'Thank you, Yor, for what you have taught me.'

They pressed each other's hands.

'You've been a good miner,' Yor whispered. 'You've worked well.'

Then he turned away and went to the mine shaft. Without turning around he got into the pit cage and descended into the depths.

The boy without a name picked the picture out of the snow and plodded out into the snow-covered plain.

He had been walking for many hours. Yor's hut had long since disappeared below the horizon. On all sides there was nothing to be seen but the endless snow-covered plain. But he felt that the picture, which he was holding carefully in both hands, was pulling him in a certain direction.

Regardless of how far it might be, he was determined to follow this pull, for he was convinced that it would take him to the right place. Nothing must hold him back. He felt sure of finding the Water of Life.

Suddenly he heard a clamor in the air, as though innumerable creatures were screaming and twittering. Looking up into the sky, he saw a dark cloud like a great flock of birds. But when the flock came closer, he saw what it really was and terror stopped him in his tracks.

It was the butterfly-clowns, the Shlamoofs.

Merciful heavens! thought the boy without a name. If only they haven't seen me! They'll shatter the picture with their screams!

But they had seen him.

Laughing and rollicking, they shot down and landed all around him in the snow.

'Hurrah!' they croaked, opening wide their motley-colored mouths. 'At last we've found him! Our great benefactor!'

They tumbled in the snow, threw snowballs at one another, turned somersaults, and stood on their heads.

'Be still! Please be still!' the boy without a name whispered in desperation.

The whole chorus screamed with enthusiasm: 'What did he say?' – 'He said we were too still!' – 'Nobody ever told us that before!'

'What do you want of me?' asked the boy. 'Why won't you leave me alone?'

All whirled around him, cackling: 'Great benefactor! Great benefactor! Do you remember how you saved us, when we were the Acharis? Then we were the unhappiest creatures in all Fantastica, but now we're fed up with ourselves. At first what you did to us was a lot of fun, but now we're bored to death. We flit and we flutter and we don't know where we're at. We can't even plan any decent games, because we haven't any rules. You've turned us into preposterous clowns, that's what you've done. You've cheated us!'

'I meant well,' said the horrified boy.

'Sure, you meant well by yourself,' the Shlamoofs shouted in chorus. 'Your kindness made you feel great, didn't it? But we paid the bill for your kindness, you great benefactor!'

'What should I do?' the boy asked. 'What do you want of me?'

'We've been looking for you,' screamed the Shlamoofs with grimacing clown faces. 'We wanted to catch you before you could make yourself scarce. Now we've caught you, and we won't leave you in peace until you become our chief. We want you to be our Head Shlamoof, our Master Shlamoof, our General Shlamoof! You name it.'

'But why?' the boy asked imploringly.

The chorus of clowns screamed back: 'We want you to give us orders. We want you to order us around, to make us do something, to forbid us to do something. We want you to give us an aim in life!'

'I can't do that. Why don't you elect one of your number?'

'No, we want you. You made us what we are.'

'No,' the boy panted. 'I have to go! I have to go back!'

'Not so fast, great benefactor!' cried the butterfly-clowns. 'You can't get away from us. You think you can sneak away from Fantastica, don't you? You'd like that, wouldn't you?'

'But I'm at the end of my rope,' the boy protested.

'What about us?' the chorus replied.

'Go away!' cried the boy. 'I can't bother with you anymore.'

'Then you must turn us back!' cried the shrill voices. 'Then we'd rather be Acharis. The Lake of Tears has dried up, Amarganth is on dry land now. And no one spins fine silver filigree anymore. We want to be Acharis again.'

'I can't!' the boy replied. 'I no longer have any power in Fantastica.'

'In that case,' the whole swarm bellowed, whirling and swirling about, 'we'll kidnap you!'

Hundreds of little hands seized him and tried to lift him off the ground. The boy struggled with might and main and the butterflies were tossed in all directions. But like angry wasps they kept coming back.

Suddenly in the midst of this hubbub a low yet powerful sound was heard – something like the booming of a bronze bell.

In a twinkling the Shlamoofs took flight and their cloud soon vanished in the sky.

The boy who had no name knelt in the snow. Before him, crumbled into dust, lay the picture. Now all was lost. Now nothing could lead him to the Water of Life.

When he looked up, he saw, blurred by his tears, two forms in the snow. One was large, the other small. He wiped his eyes and took another look.

The two forms were Falkor, the white luckdragon, and Atreyu.

XXVI

The Water of Life

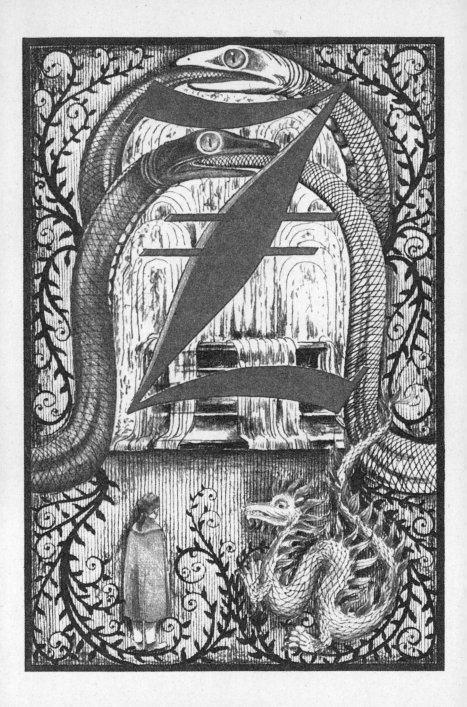

IGZAGGING unsteadily, scarcely able to control his feet, the boy who had no name took a few steps toward Atreyu. Then he stopped. Atreyu did nothing, but watched him closely. The wound in his chest was no longer bleeding.

For a long while they faced each other. Neither said a word. It was so still they could hear each other's breathing.

Slowly the boy without a name reached for the gold chain around his neck and divested himself of AURYN. He bent down and carefully laid the Gem in the snow before Atreyu. As he did so, he took another look at the two snakes, the one light, the other dark, which were biting each other's tail and formed an oval. Then he let the amulet go.

In that moment AURYN, the golden Gem, became so bright, so radiant that he had to close his eyes as though dazzled by the sun. When he opened them again, he saw that he was in a vaulted building, as large as the vault of the sky. It was built from blocks of golden light. And in the middle of this immeasurable space lay, as big as the ramparts of a town, the two snakes.

Atreyu, Falkor, and the boy without a name stood side by side, near the head of the black snake, which held the white snake's tail in its jaws. The rigid eye with its vertical pupil was directed at the three of them. Compared to that eye, they were tiny; even the luckdragon seemed no larger than a white caterpillar.

The motionless bodies of the snakes glistened like some unknown metal, the one black as night, the other silvery white. The havoc they could wreak was checked only because they held each other prisoner. If they let each other go, the world would end. That was certain.

But while holding each other fast, they guarded the Water of Life. For in the center of the edifice they encircled there was a great fountain. Its beam danced up and down and in falling created and dispersed thousands of forms far more quickly than the eye could follow. The foaming water burst into a fine mist, in which the golden light was refracted with all the colors of the rainbow. The fountain roared and laughed and rejoiced with a thousand voices.

As though parched with thirst, the boy without a name looked at the water – but how was he to reach it? The snake's head did not move.

Then Falkor raised his head. His ruby-red eyeballs glittered.

'Do you understand what the Water is saying?' he asked.

'No,' said Atreyu. 'I don't.'

'I don't know why,' said Falkor. 'But I understand perfectly. Maybe because I'm a luckdragon. All the languages of joy are related.'

'What does the Water say?' Atreyu asked.

Falkor listened closely, and slowly repeated what he heard:

> 'I am the Water of Life,
> Out of myself I grow.
> The more you drink of me,
> The fuller I will flow.'

Again he listened awhile. Then he said: 'It keeps saying: "Drink! Drink! Do what you wish!" '

'How can we get to it?' Atreyu asked.

'It's asking us our names,' Falkor reported.

'I'm Atreyu!' Atreyu cried.

'I'm Falkor!' cried Falkor.

The boy without a name was silent.

Atreyu looked at him, then took him by the hand and cried: 'He's Bastian Balthazar Bux!'

'It asks,' Falkor translated, 'why he doesn't speak for himself.'

'He can't,' said Atreyu. 'He has forgotten everything.'

Falkor listened again to the roaring of the fountain.

'Without memory, it says, he cannot come in. The snakes won't let him through.'

Atreyu replied: 'I have stored up everything he told us about himself and his world. I vouch for him.'

Falkor listened.

'It wants to know by what right?'

'I am his friend,' said Atreyu.

Again Falkor listened attentively.

'That may not be acceptable,' he whispered to Atreyu. 'Now it's speaking of your wound. It wants to know how that came about.'

'We were both right,' said Atreyu, 'and we were both wrong. But now Bastian has given up AURYN of his own free will.'

Falkor listened and nodded.

'Yes,' he said. 'It accepts that. This place is AURYN. We are welcome, it says.'

Atreyu looked up at the enormous golden dome.

'Each of us,' he whispered, 'has worn it around his neck – you too, Falkor, for a while.'

The luckdragon motioned him to be still and listened again to the sound of the Water. Then he translated:

'AURYN is the door that Bastian has been looking for. He carried it with him from the start. But – it says – the snakes won't let anything belonging to Fantastica cross the threshold. Bastian must therefore give up everything the Childlike Empress gave him. Otherwise he cannot drink of the Water of Life.'

'But we are in her sign!' cried Atreyu. 'Isn't she herself here?'

'It says that Moon Child's power ends here. She is the only one who can never set foot in this place. She cannot penetrate to the center of AURYN, because she cannot cast off her own self.'

Atreyu was too bewildered to speak.

'Now,' said Falkor, 'it's asking whether Bastian is ready.'

At that moment the enormous black snake's head began to move very slowly, though without releasing the white snake's tail. The gigantic bodies arched until they formed a gate, one half of which was black and the other white.

Atreyu took Bastian by the hand and led him through the terrible gate toward the fountain, which now lay before them in all its grandeur. Falkor followed. As they advanced, one after another of Bastian's Fantastican gifts fell away from him. The strong, handsome, fearless hero became again the small, fat, timid boy. Even his clothing, which had been reduced almost to rags in the Minroud Mine, vanished and dissolved into nothingness. In the end he stood naked before the great golden bowl, at the center of which the Water of Life leapt high into the air like a crystal tree.

In this last moment, when he no longer possessed any of the Fantastican gifts but had not yet recovered his memory of his own world and himself, he was in a state of utter uncertainty, not knowing which world he belonged to or whether he really existed.

But then he jumped into the crystal-clear water. He splashed and spluttered and let the sparkling rain fall into his mouth. He drank till his thirst was quenched. And joy filled him from head to foot, the joy of living and the joy of being himself. He was newborn. And the best part of it was that he was now the very person he wanted to be. If he had been free to choose, he would have chosen to be no one else. Because now he knew that there were thousands and thousands of forms of joy in the world, but that all were essentially one and the same, namely, the joy of being able to love.

And much later, long after Bastian had returned to his world, in his maturity and even in his old age, this joy never left him entirely. Even in the hardest moments of his life he preserved a lightheartedness that made him smile and that comforted others.

'Atreyu!' he cried out to his friend, who was standing with Falkor at the edge of the great golden bowl. 'Come on in! Come and drink! It's wonderful!'

Atreyu laughed and shook his head.

'No,' he called back. 'This time we're only here to keep you company.'

'This time?' Bastian asked. 'What do you mean by that?'

Atreyu exchanged a glance with Falkor. Then he said: 'Falkor and I have already been here. We didn't recognize the place at first, because we were asleep when we were brought here and when we were taken away. But now we remember.'

Bastian came out of the water.

'Now I know who I am,' he said, beaming.

'Yes,' said Atreyu, and nodded. 'And now I recognize you. Now you look the way you did when I saw you in the Magic Mirror Gate.'

Bastian looked up at the foaming, sparkling water.

'I'd like to bring my father some,' he shouted. 'But how?'

'I don't think you can do that,' said Atreyu. 'It's not possible to carry anything from Fantastica across the threshold.'

'For Bastian it is!' said Falkor, whose voice had resumed its full bronze resonance. 'He can do it.'

'You really are a luckdragon,' said Bastian.

Falkor motioned him to be still while he listened to the roaring voice of the Water.

Then he said: 'The Water says you must be on your way now and so must we.'

'Which is my way?' Bastian asked.

'Out through the other gate,' Falkor answered. 'Where the white snake's head is lying.'

'All right,' said Bastian. 'But how will I get out? The white head isn't moving.'

Indeed, the white snake's head lay motionless. It held the black snake's tail in its jaws and stared at Bastian out of its great eyes.

'The Water asks you,' Falkor translated, 'whether you completed all the stories you began in Fantastica.'

'No,' said Bastian. 'None of them really.'

Falkor listened awhile. His face took on a worried look.

'In that case, it says, the white snake won't let you through. You must go back to Fantastica and finish them all.'

'All the stories?' Bastian stammered. 'Then I'll never be able to go back. Then it's all been for nothing.'

Falkor listened eagerly.

'What does it say?' Bastian wanted to know.

'Hush!' said Falkor.

After a while he sighed and said: 'It says there's no help for it unless someone promises to do it in your place. But no one can do that.'

'I can! I will!' said Atreyu.

Bastian looked at him in silence. Then he fell on his neck and stammered: 'Atreyu! Atreyu! I'll never forget this!'

Atreyu smiled.

'That's good, Bastian. Then you won't forget Fantastica either.'

He gave him a brotherly pat on the back, then quickly turned around and headed for the black snake's gate, which was still up-raised and open as when they had entered.

'Falkor,' said Bastian. 'How will you and Atreyu finish the stories I have left behind?'

The white dragon winked one of his ruby-red eyes and replied: 'With luck, my boy! with luck!'

Then he followed his friend and master.

Bastian watched as they passed through the gate on their way back to Fantastica. They turned again and waved to him. Then as the black snake's head sank to the ground, Atreyu and Falkor vanished from Bastian's sight.

Now he was alone.

He turned towards the white snake's head. It had risen and the snake's body now formed a gate just as the black snake's body had done.

Quickly Bastian cupped his hands, gathered as much of the Water of Life as he could hold, ran to the gate, and flung himself into the empty darkness beyond.

'Father!' he screamed. 'Father! I – am – Bastian – Balthazar – Bux!'

'Father! Father! I – am – Bastian – Balthazar – Bux!'

Still screaming, he found himself in the schoolhouse attic, which long, long ago he had left for Fantastica. At first he didn't recognize the place, and because of the strange objects around him, the stuffed animals, the skeleton, and the paintings, he thought for a brief moment that this might be a different part of Fantastica. But then, catching sight of his school satchel and the rusty seven-armed candelabrum with the spent candles, he knew where he was.

How long could it have been since he started on his long journey through the Neverending Story? Weeks? Months? Years? He had once read about a man who had spent just an hour in a magic cave. When he returned home, a hundred years had passed, and of all the people he had known as a child he remembered only one, and he was an old old man.

Bastian was aware of the gray daylight, but he could not make out whether it was morning or afternoon. It was bitter cold in the attic, just as on the night of Bastian's departure.

He disentangled himself from the dusty army blankets, put on his shoes and coat, and saw to his surprise that they were wet as they had been the day when it had rained so hard.

He looked for the book he had stolen that day, the book that had started him on his adventure. He was determined to bring it back to that grumpy

Mr Coreander. What did he care if Mr Coreander punished him for stealing it, or reported him to the police? A person who had ridden on the back of the Many-Colored Death didn't scare so easily. But the book wasn't there.

Bastian looked and looked. He rummaged through the blankets and looked in every corner. Without success. The Neverending Story had disappeared.

'Oh well,' Bastian finally said to himself. 'I'll have to tell him it's gone. Of course he won't believe me. There's nothing I can do about that. I'll just have to take the consequences. But maybe he won't even remember the book after all this time. Maybe the bookshop isn't even there anymore.'

He would soon find out how much time had elapsed. If when he passed through the schoolhouse the teachers and pupils he ran into were unknown to him, he would know what to expect.

But when he opened the attic door and went down the stairs, there wasn't a sound to be heard. The building seemed deserted. And then the school clock struck nine. That meant it was morning, so classes must have begun.

Bastian looked into several classrooms. All were empty. When he went to a window and looked down into the street, he saw a few pedestrians and cars. So the world hadn't come to an end.

He ran down the steps and tried to open the big front door, but it was locked. He went to the janitor's office, rang the bell and knocked, but no one stirred.

What was he to do? He couldn't just wait for someone to turn up. Even if he had spilled the Water of Life, he wanted to go home to his father.

Should he open a window and shout until somebody heard him and had the door opened? No, that would make him feel foolish. It occurred to him that he could climb out of a window, since the windows could be opened from the inside. But the ground-floor windows were all barred. Then he remembered that in looking out of the second-floor window he had seen some scaffolding. Evidently the façade was being refurbished.

Bastian went back up to the second floor and opened the window. The scaffolding consisted only of uprights with boards placed horizontally between them at intervals. He stepped out on the top board, which swayed under his weight. For a moment his head reeled and he felt afraid, but he fought his dizziness and fear. To someone who had been lord of Perilin, this was no problem, even if he had lost his fabulous strength and even though the weight of his little fat body was making things rather hard for him. Calmly and deliberately he found holds for his hands and feet and climbed down. Once he got a splinter in his hand, but such trifles meant nothing to him now. Though slightly overheated and out of breath, he reached the street in good shape. No one had seen him.

Bastian ran home. He ran so hard that the books and pens in his satchel jiggled and rattled to the rhythm of his steps. He had a stitch in his side, but in his hurry to see his father he kept on running.

When at last he came to the house where he lived, he stopped for a moment and looked up at the window of his father's laboratory. Then suddenly he was seized with fear. For the first time it occurred to him that his father might not be there anymore.

But his father was there and must have seen him coming, for when Bastian rushed up the stairs, his father came running to meet him. He spread out his arms and Bastian threw himself into them. His father lifted him up and carried him inside.

'Bastian, my boy!' he said over and over again. 'My dear little boy, where have you been? What happened to you?'

A few minutes later they were sitting at the kitchen table and Bastian was drinking hot milk and eating breakfast rolls, which his father had lovingly spread with butter and honey. Then the boy noticed that his father's face was pale and drawn, his eyes red and his chin unshaven. But otherwise he looked the same as he had long ago, when Bastian went away. And Bastian told him so.

'Long ago?' his father asked in amazement. 'What do you mean?'

'How long have I been gone?'

'Since yesterday, Bastian. Since you went to school. But when you didn't come home, I phoned your teachers and they told me you hadn't been there. I looked for you all day and all night, my boy. I feared the worst, I put the police on your trail. Oh God, Bastian! What happened? I've been half crazy with worry. Where have you been?'

Then Bastian began to tell his father about his adventures. He told the whole story in great detail. It took many hours.

His father listened as he had never listened before. He understood Bastian's story.

At about midday he interrupted Bastian for a little while. First he called the police to tell them his son had come home and that everything was all right. Then he made lunch for both of them, and Bastian went on with his story.

Night was falling by the time Bastian came to the Water of Life and told his father how he had wanted to bring him some but had spilled it.

It was almost dark in the kitchen. His father sat motionless. Bastian stood up and switched on the light. And then he saw something he had never seen before.

He saw tears in his father's eyes.

And he knew that he had brought him the Water of Life after all.

Bastian's father sat him down on his lap and hugged him. When they had sat like that for a long while, his father heaved a deep sigh, looked into Bastian's face, and smiled. It was the happiest smile Bastian had ever seen on his face.

'From now on,' said his father, 'everything is going to be different between us. Don't you agree?'

Bastian nodded. He couldn't speak. His heart was too full.

Next morning the winter's first snow lay soft and clean on Bastian's windowsill. The street sounds that came to him were muffled.

'Do you know what, Bastian?' said his father at breakfast. 'I think we two have every reason to celebrate. A day like this happens only once in a lifetime – and some people never have one. So I suggest that we do something really sensational. I'll forget about any work and you needn't go to school. I'll write an excuse for you. How does that sound?'

'School?' said Bastian. 'Is it still operating? When I passed through the building yesterday, there wasn't a soul. Not even the janitor was there.'

'Yesterday?' said his father. 'Yesterday was Sunday.'

Bastian stirred his cocoa thoughtfully. Then he said in an undertone: 'I think it's going to take me a little while to get used to things again.'

'Exactly,' said his father. 'And that's why we're giving ourselves a little holiday. What would you like to do? We could go for a hike in the country or we could go to the zoo. Either way we'll treat ourselves to the finest lunch the world has ever seen. This afternoon we could go shopping and buy anything you like. And tonight – how about the theater?'

Bastian's eyes sparkled. Then he said firmly: 'Wonderful! But there's something I must do first. I have to go and tell Mr Coreander that I stole his book and lost it.'

Bastian's father took his hand.

'If you like,' he said, 'I'll attend to that for you.'

'No,' said Bastian. 'It's my responsibility. I want to do it myself. And I think I should do it right away.'

He stood up and put on his coat. His father said nothing, but the look on his face was one of surprise and respect. Such behavior in Bastian was something new.

'I believe,' he said finally, 'that I too will need a little time to get used to things.'

Bastian was already in the entrance hall. 'I'll be right back,' he called. 'I'm sure it won't take long. Not this time.'

When he came to Mr Coreander's bookshop, his courage failed him after all. He looked through the pane with the ornate lettering on it. Mr Coreander was busy with a customer, and Bastian decided to wait. He walked up and down outside the shop. It was snowing again.

At last the customer left.

'Now!' Bastian commanded himself.

Remembering how he had gone to meet Grograman in Goab, the Desert of Colors, he pressed the door handle resolutely.

Behind the wall of books at the far end of the dimly lit room he heard a cough. He went forward, then, slightly pale but with grave composure, he stepped up to Mr Coreander, who was sitting in his worn leather armchair as he had been at their last meeting.

For a long time Bastian said nothing. He had expected Mr Coreander to go red in the face and scream at him: 'Thief! Monster!' or something of the kind.

Instead, the old man deliberately lit his curved pipe, screwed up his eyes, and studied the boy through his ridiculous little spectacles. When the pipe was finally burning, he puffed awhile, then grumbled: 'What is it this time?'

'I . . .' Bastian began haltingly. 'I stole a book from you. I meant to return it, but I can't, because I lost it, or rather – well, I haven't got it anymore.'

Mr Coreander stopped puffing and took his pipe out of his mouth.

'What sort of book?' he asked.

'The one you were reading the last time I was here. I walked off with it. You were telephoning in the back room, it was lying on the chair, and I just walked off with it.'

'I see,' said Mr Coreander, clearing his throat. 'But none of my books is missing. What was the title of this book?'

'It's called the Neverending Story,' said Bastian. 'It's bound in copper-colored silk that shimmers when you move it around. There are two snakes on the cover, a light one and a dark one, and they're biting each other's tails. Inside it's printed in two different colors — and there are big beautiful capitals at the beginning of the chapters.'

'This is extremely odd,' said Mr Coreander. 'I've never had such a book. You can't have stolen it from me. Maybe you swiped it somewhere else.'

'Oh no!' Bastian assured him. 'You must remember. It's —' He hesitated, but then he blurted it out. 'It's a magic book. While I was reading it, I got into the Neverending Story, and when I came out again, the book was gone.'

Mr Coreander watched Bastian over his spectacles.

'Would you be pulling my leg, by any chance?'

'No,' said Bastian in dismay. 'Of course not. I'm telling you the truth. You must know that.'

Mr Coreander thought for a while, then shook his head.

'Better tell me all about it. Sit down, boy. Make yourself at home.'

He pointed his pipe stem at a second armchair, facing his own, and Bastian sat down.

'And now,' said Mr Coreander, 'tell me the whole story. But slowly, if you please, and one thing at a time.'

And Bastian told his story.

He told it a little more briefly than he had to his father, but since Mr Coreander listened with keen interest and kept asking for details, it was more than two hours before Bastian had done.

Heaven knows why, but in all that long time they were not disturbed by a single customer.

When Bastian had finished, Mr Coreander puffed for a long while, as though deep in thought. At length he cleared his throat, straightened his little spectacles, looked Bastian over, and said: 'One thing is sure: You didn't steal this book from me, because it belongs neither to me nor to you nor to anyone else. If I'm not mistaken, the book itself comes from Fantastica. Maybe at this very moment — who knows? — someone else is reading it.'

'Then you believe me?' Bastian asked.

'Of course I believe you,' said Mr Coreander. 'Any sensible person would.'

'Frankly,' said Bastian, 'I didn't expect you to.'

'There are people who can never go to Fantastica,' said Mr Coreander, 'and others who can, but who stay there forever. And there are just a few who go to Fantastica and come back. Like you. And they make both worlds well again.'

'Oh,' said Bastian, blushing slightly. 'I don't deserve any credit. I almost didn't make it back. If it hadn't been for Atreyu I'd have been stuck in the City of Old Emperors for good.'

Mr Coreander nodded and puffed at his pipe.

'Hmm,' he grumbled. 'You're lucky having a friend in Fantastica. God knows, it's not everybody who can say that.'

'Mr Coreander,' Bastian asked, 'how do you know all that? I mean – have you ever been in Fantastica?'

'Of course I have,' said Mr Coreander.

'But then,' said Bastian, 'you must know Moon Child.'

'Yes, I know the Childlike Empress,' said Mr Coreander, 'though not by that name. I called her something different. But that doesn't matter.'

'Then you must know the book!' Bastian cried. 'Then you have read the Neverending Story.'

Mr Coreander shook his head.

'Every real story is a Neverending Story.' He passed his eye over the many books that covered the walls of his shop from floor to ceiling, pointed the stem of his pipe at them, and went on:

'There are many doors to Fantastica, my boy. There are other such magic books. A lot of people read them without noticing. It all depends on who gets his hands on such books.

'Then the Neverending Story is different for different people?'

'That's right,' said Mr Coreander. 'And besides, it's not just books. There are other ways of getting to Fantastica and back. You'll find out.'

'Do you think so?' Bastian asked hopefully. 'But then I'd have to meet Moon Child again, and no one can meet her more than once.'

Mr Coreander leaned forward and lowered his voice.

'Let an old Fantastica hand tell you something, my boy. This is a secret that no one in Fantastica can know. When you think it over, you'll see why. You can't visit Moon Child a second time, that's true. But if you can give her a new name, you'll see her again. And however often you manage to do that, it will be the first and only time.'

For a moment Mr Coreander's bulldog face took on a soft glow, which made it look young and almost handsome.

'Thank you, Mr Coreander,' said Bastian.

'I have to thank you, my boy,' said Mr Coreander. 'I'd appreciate it if you dropped in to see me now and then. We could exchange experiences. There aren't many people one can discuss these things with.'

He held out his hand to Bastian. 'Will you?'

'Gladly,' said Bastian, taking the proffered hand. 'I have to go now. My father's waiting. But I'll come and see you soon.'

Mr Coreander took him to the door. Through the reversed writing on the glass pane, Bastian saw that his father was waiting for him across the street. His face was one great beam.

Bastian opened the door so vigorously that the little glass bells tinkled wildly, and ran across to his father.

Mr Coreander closed the door gently and looked after father and son.

'Bastian Balthazar Bux,' he grumbled. 'If I'm not mistaken, you will show many others the way to Fantastica, and they will bring us the Water of Life.'

Mr Coreander was not mistaken.

But that's another story and shall be told another time.

FOR THE BEST IN PAPERBACKS, LOOK FOR THE

In every corner of the world, on every subject under the sun, Penguin represents quality and variety—the very best in publishing today.

For complete information about books available from Penguin—including Pelicans, Puffins, Peregrines, and Penguin Classics—and how to order them, write to us at the appropriate address below. Please note that for copyright reasons the selection of books varies from country to country.

In the United Kingdom: For a complete list of books available from Penguin in the U.K., please write to *Dept E.P., Penguin Books Ltd, Harmondsworth, Middlesex, UB7 0DA.*

In the United States: For a complete list of books available from Penguin in the U.S., please write to *Consumer Sales, Penguin USA, P.O. Box 999—Dept. 17109, Bergenfield, New Jersey 07621-0120.* VISA and MasterCard holders call 1-800-253-6476 to order all Penguin titles.

In Canada: For a complete list of books available from Penguin in Canada, please write to *Penguin Books Canada Ltd, 10 Alcorn Avenue, Suite 300, Toronto, Ontario, Canada M4V 3B2.*

In Australia: For a complete list of books available from Penguin in Australia, please write to the *Marketing Department, Penguin Books Ltd, P.O. Box 257, Ringwood, Victoria 3134.*

In New Zealand: For a complete list of books available from Penguin in New Zealand, please write to the *Marketing Department, Penguin Books (NZ) Ltd, Private Bag, Takapuna, Auckland 9.*

In India: For a complete list of books available from Penguin, please write to *Penguin Overseas Ltd, 706 Eros Apartments, 56 Nehru Place, New Delhi, 110019.*

In Holland: For a complete list of books available from Penguin in Holland, please write to *Penguin Books Nederland B.V., Postbus 195, NL-1380AD Weesp, Netherlands.*

In Germany: For a complete list of books available from Penguin, please write to *Penguin Books Ltd, Friedrichstrasse 10-12, D-6000 Frankfurt Main I, Federal Republic of Germany.*

In Spain: For a complete list of books available from Penguin in Spain, please write to *Longman, Penguin España, Calle San Nicolas 15, E-28013 Madrid, Spain.*

In Japan: For a complete list of books available from Penguin in Japan, please write to *Longman Penguin Japan Co Ltd, Yamaguchi Building, 2-12-9 Kanda Jimbocho, Chiyoda-Ku, Tokyo 101, Japan.*

FOR THE BEST LITERATURE, LOOK FOR THE

☐ THE BOOK AND THE BROTHERHOOD
Iris Murdoch

Many years ago Gerard Hernshaw and his friends banded together to finance a political and philosophical book by a monomaniacal Marxist genius. Now opinions have changed, and support for the book comes at the price of moral indignation; the resulting disagreements lead to passion, hatred, a duel, murder, and a suicide pact.   *602 pages   ISBN: 0-14-010470-4*

☐ GRAVITY'S RAINBOW
Thomas Pynchon

Thomas Pynchon's classic antihero is Tyrone Slothrop, an American lieutenant in London whose body anticipates German rocket launchings. Surely one of the most important works of fiction produced in the twentieth century, *Gravity's Rainbow* is a complex and awesome novel in the great tradition of James Joyce's *Ulysses.*   *768 pages   ISBN: 0-14-010661-8*

☐ FIFTH BUSINESS
Robertson Davies

The first novel in the celebrated "Deptford Trilogy," which also includes *The Manticore* and *World of Wonders, Fifth Business* stands alone as the story of a rational man who discovers that the marvelous is only another aspect of the real.   *266 pages   ISBN: 0-14-004387-X*

☐ WHITE NOISE
Don DeLillo

Jack Gladney, a professor of Hitler Studies in Middle America, and his fourth wife, Babette, navigate the usual rocky passages of family life in the television age. Then, their lives are threatened by an "airborne toxic event"—a more urgent and menacing version of the "white noise" of transmissions that typically engulfs them.   *326 pages   ISBN: 0-14-007702-2*

FOR THE BEST LITERATURE, LOOK FOR THE

☐ **A SPORT OF NATURE**
Nadine Gordimer

Hillela, Nadine Gordimer's "sport of nature," is seductive and intuitively gifted at life. Casting herself adrift from her family at seventeen, she lives among political exiles on an East African beach, marries a black revolutionary, and ultimately plays a heroic role in the overthrow of apartheid.

354 pages   ISBN: 0-14-008470-3

☐ **THE COUNTERLIFE**
Philip Roth

By far Philip Roth's most radical work of fiction, *The Counterlife* is a book of conflicting perspectives and points of view about people living out dreams of renewal and escape. Illuminating these lives is the skeptical, enveloping intelligence of the novelist Nathan Zuckerman, who calculates the price and examines the results of his characters' struggles for a change of personal fortune.

372 pages   ISBN: 0-14-009769-4

☐ **THE MONKEY'S WRENCH**
Primo Levi

Through the mesmerizing tales told by two characters—one, a construction worker/philosopher who has built towers and bridges in India and Alaska; the other, a writer/chemist, rigger of words and molecules—Primo Levi celebrates the joys of work and the art of storytelling.

174 pages   ISBN: 0-14-010357-0

☐ **IRONWEED**
William Kennedy

"Riding up the winding road of Saint Agnes Cemetery in the back of the rattling old truck, Francis Phelan became aware that the dead, even more than the living, settled down in neighborhoods." So begins William Kennedy's Pulitzer-Prize winning novel about an ex-ballplayer, part-time gravedigger, and full-time drunk, whose return to the haunts of his youth arouses the ghosts of his past and present. *228 pages   ISBN: 0-14-007020-6*

☐ **THE COMEDIANS**
Graham Greene

Set in Haiti under Duvalier's dictatorship, *The Comedians* is a story about the committed and the uncommitted. Actors with no control over their destiny, they play their parts in the foreground; experience love affairs rather than love; have enthusiasms but not faith; and if they die, they die like Mr. Jones, by accident.

288 pages   ISBN: 0-14-002766-1   **$4.95**

FOR THE BEST LITERATURE, LOOK FOR THE

☐ **HERZOG**
Saul Bellow

Winner of the National Book Award, *Herzog* is the imaginative and critically acclaimed story of Moses Herzog: joker, moaner, cuckhold, charmer, and truly an Everyman for our time.

342 pages   ISBN: 0-14-007270-5

☐ **FOOLS OF FORTUNE**
William Trevor

The deeply affecting story of two cousins—one English, one Irish—brought together and then torn apart by the tide of Anglo-Irish hatred, *Fools of Fortune* presents a profound symbol of the tragic entanglements of England and Ireland in this century.   *240 pages   ISBN: 0-14-006982-8*

☐ **THE SONGLINES**
Bruce Chatwin

Venturing into the desolate land of Outback Australia—along timeless paths, and among fortune hunters, redneck Australians, racist policemen, and mysterious Aboriginal holy men—Bruce Chatwin discovers a wondrous vision of man's place in the world.   *296 pages   ISBN: 0-14-009429-6*

☐ **THE GUIDE: A NOVEL**
R. K. Narayan

Raju was once India's most corrupt tourist guide; now, after a peasant mistakes him for a holy man, he gradually begins to play the part. His succeeds so well that God himself intervenes to put Raju's new holiness to the test.

220 pages   ISBN: 0-14-009657-4

You can find all these books at your local bookstore, or use this handy coupon for ordering:

Penguin Books By Mail
Dept. BA Box 999
Bergenfield, NJ 07621-0999

Please send me the above title(s). I am enclosing _____
(please add sales tax if appropriate and $1.50 to cover postage and handling). Send check or money order—no CODs. Please allow four weeks for shipping. We cannot ship to post office boxes or addresses outside the USA. *Prices subject to change without notice.*

Ms./Mrs./Mr. _____

Address _____

City/State _____ Zip _____

FOR THE BEST LITERATURE, LOOK FOR THE

☐ **THE LAST SONG OF MANUEL SENDERO**
Ariel Dorfman

In an unnamed country, in a time that might be now, the son of Manuel Sendero refuses to be born, beginning a revolution where generations of the future wait for a world without victims or oppressors.

464 pages   *ISBN: 0-14-008896-2*

☐ **THE BOOK OF LAUGHTER AND FORGETTING**
Milan Kundera

In this collection of stories and sketches, Kundera addresses themes including sex and love, poetry and music, sadness and the power of laughter. *"The Book of Laughter and Forgetting* calls itself a novel," writes John Leonard of *The New York Times*, "although it is part fairly tale, part literary criticism, part political tract, part musicology, part autobiography. It can call itself whatever it wants to, because the whole is genius."

240 pages   *ISBN: 0-14-009693-0*

☐ **TIRRA LIRRA BY THE RIVER**
Jessica Anderson

Winner of the Miles Franklin Award, Australia's most prestigious literary prize, *Tirra Lirra by the River* is the story of a woman's seventy-year search for the place where she truly belongs. Nora Porteous's series of escapes takes her from a small Australia town to the suburbs of Sydney to London, where she seems finally to become the woman she always wanted to be.

142 pages   *ISBN: 0-14-006945-3*

☐ **LOVE UNKNOWN**
A. N. Wilson

In their sweetly wild youth, Monica, Belinda, and Richeldis shared a bachelor-girl flat and became friends for life. Now, twenty years later, A. N. Wilson charts the intersecting lives of the three women through the perilous waters of love, marriage, and adultery in this wry and moving modern comedy of manners.

202 pages   *ISBN: 0-14-010190-X*

☐ **THE WELL**
Elizabeth Jolley

Against the stark beauty of the Australian farmlands, Elizabeth Jolley portrays an eccentric, affectionate relationship between the two women—Hester, a lonely spinster, and Katherine, a young orphan. Their pleasant, satisfyingly simple life is nearly perfect until a dark stranger invades their world in a most horrifying way.

176 pages   *ISBN: 0-14-008901-2*